BRAVE SPIRITS L

CREDITS

Thank you to my lifeboat crew-mate, Colin, for his help in self-publishing this book and creating the original covers. More recently to Tim Glasspool for the cover of this 2nd edition. Also thank you to everybody whose feedback, advice, encouragement and reviews so far have kept my enthusiasm for this project alive.

AUTHOR'S NOTE

This book was only written for one reason. I always wanted to write a book. So I have. The idea for this book is based on a few things.

My personal experiences of travel, spiritual healing, the influence of people I've met and events in my life. And a genuine belief that if you can intervene and help, then you should. It's why I've served a voluntary organisation, along with some great people, for over twenty years. Which is all about intervening when somebody is in trouble.

And a belief that there are forces that guide many of us. Illogical, yes. But these aren't miracles or credited to any religion. These are personal and, I believe, guided by conscience. Evil does not have one. You can indiscriminately kill or maim in the name of a religion or pursuit of money or power. You can't kill in the name of good except, I believe, at times to protect it from evil where necessary. You can easily lie to, or hurt somebody, if you are without conscience. You can't if you have one.

And finally. I've always wondered what would happen if a few, truly good, seriously wealthy people, were finally worried enough about today's system of government to try to really make a change. What would happen if we voted for skilled, capable, honest, individual people who could run our country's constituencies and government departments for us. Based on ability to do it. Rather than the current "parties" that clearly can't in the modern world. A cabinet reshuffle just moves a career politician who knows bugger all about health, to another department they know roughly the same about. But these offices and departments are vast, take our money and have huge power over our lives and well-being. I believe they are too big to be run the way they are and far too unaccountable to the people that fund them. Us.

This book is a novel that basically embraces all of that. I haven't written the author's note to impose my views on anyone. There's enough of that going on already! It's just to explain how the book came to be written in the way it is and how the story-line evolved.

This book won't change a thing. But it was enjoyable to write it and I hope, whatever you believe in, you enjoy the story. Because that is all it is.

CONTENTS

Prologue.

The humid atmosphere in the courtroom, stifling and oppressive, was causing those in it to slouch, quiet and listless in their seats; apart from occasional muffled coughs as the portly, elderly judge droned on. Judge Kimbunu was having his moment of glory, trying the white man who looked tired and weak in the dock and summing up interminably before passing sentence.

For the benefit of his own importance, and the fact that a couple of western journalists were present, he raged and ranted about the severity of the crimes committed. Of illegal entry to Rumburu. Attacking a prison, with the sole aim of freeing rebels hostile to the President and having caused the escape of a justly convicted man from that prison. The fact that the prisoner, a fifty five year old western businessman, one Norman Shand, had escaped the country, again, by the use of an unauthorized incursion of a helicopter, was intolerable. The accused was nothing more than a mercenary, working for western big business who thought they could interfere in the running of our country, and evade its justice at will. The accused, Adrian Jones, would be sentenced with the maximum term of imprisonment at the judge's disposal.

Daniel Cade, being tried under the name of Adrian Jones, had other plans. He was slouched in the dock, eyes almost closed, with a guard seated to his right, dirty and unwashed prison overalls and soft sneakers all he was wearing. Unshaven and gaunt, he appeared ill and exhausted - the image he wished to portray. He'd felt better in the past, for sure. He'd been held for three months in a vile prison. Things had gone wrong, just a bit of bad luck on the night. But he was glad Shand had been freed. Jailed on trumped up charges, the poor bastard wouldn't have lived much longer in prison. When the one man Daniel owed his life and freedom to had asked him to intervene and had financed the operation, Daniel hadn't been happy to do it. It was high risk, but do it he had. It had gone wrong but all who had helped him had got away, Daniel had made sure of it, but was captured himself.

But now he was as ready as he would ever be for action. The whole image he portrayed was working. Exhausted, indifferent, non-threatening. The guard seated next to him was wilting in the heat in his uniform. Daniel peered discreetly around the courtroom and everybody seemed listless and slouched in their chairs. Another glance at the doorway ahead of him, behind and to the left of the judge's raised bench, open to let in some air, showed the guard leaning against the wall, just inside the building to escape the fierce sun and tiring humidity .

It was time. Daniel concentrated his highly trained mind on the movements required in the next few seconds, rehearsing them one more time in his head, watching what he was about to do as if on a loop of film. Colours swirled, the guards, the door, the gun. The colours cleared. He saw light. And with the light came clarity. It was time. He channelled the full force of years of meditation, martial arts training and combat situations. This had to go well and quickly. The guard next to him turned his head away as the judge droned on, looking up at the clock on the wall, which showed just before noon.

The steel edge of Daniel's hand slammed into the guard's larynx, the force of the blow knocking him backwards in his chair. Quickly, so quickly that it appeared impossibly so, the unkempt prisoner leapt cleanly over the wooden rail of the dock. Shouts of rage from the fat judge and shouting from the galleries behind him. He covered the forty feet to the door and the armed guard standing at it in seconds. A flying leap ended with a savage kick to the solar plexus of the guard, who had stood and turned to face him. It slammed the guard through the door into the street outside with a massive force.

Daniel wrenched the automatic weapon from the prone guard and ran rapidly through, and out of, the small city centre. Shops and street stalls and groups of local people flashed by as he focused on his path ahead. Excited, noisy clamouring voices. Then on past the ramshackle, tin roofed hovels, on the outskirts of the city. Fewer people giving curious glances, no sounds of any pursuit. And then, finally, out into the open plains and jungle areas. He stopped running. They wouldn't catch him or find him now. He was going to another part of Africa. To the nearest of the two places he had to call home.

At around the same time this took place, a Turkish policeman was shot in the back in the city of Istanbul. The two events were totally unrelated. But the people involved and affected by them would become intertwined in the future. With devastating results.

Chapter 1. No turning back now.

10th February 2016. 0030.

In a five star hotel in Guildford, a very beautiful young Turkish woman sat in her room at one-thirty in the morning. Tired, but unable to sleep, she knew that in the same county, that very night and not that far away, men were going to die. Violently, in the cold and dark. And it was because of her. That same night, in the sea port of Harwich, a huge drug shipment was going to be intercepted by police and customs, also because of her. Both events would badly affect the man she lived with. A man of utter ruthlessness, cruelty and violence. And in the morning, she had to go and face him.

She'd have to thank him for the lovely room he'd paid for while she had met friends for a girls' night out. She had done, her story would hold up, but he would be enraged. She shivered involuntarily, despite the warmth of the room. She was scared. But this was what she had wanted. And what she had started. Her revenge against a drug baron from home who she hated with a passion but who loved her very much.

She thought of Daniel, a very strange young man, shrouded in mystery, but a good man, who had appeared in her family's lives not so very long ago, who she had come to adore. He was out there somewhere, in the cold and dark, putting her revenge into action. That revenge started in about half an hour.

She made another black coffee and walked to the window and looked out at the stars in the clear sky, thinking of what was about to happen under them. She looked at the clock yet again. There was no going back now. She shuddered again, wondered if she should ever have started this at all. She sat back down on the edge of the bed and delicately sipped her coffee and waited for the time to pass. She knew the fear wouldn't.

Chapter 2. Drugs and money.

It was dark and quiet and very cold, but fortunately a clear night. Daniel Cade looked through the night vision equipment towards the high steel gates that accessed the large yard, that had once formed the loading area of the long derelict warehouse below the equally derelict first floor office he was now occupying, illegally, and in the dead of night.

It was ten past one in the morning. If this deal was going to happen, and happen on time, it was going to do so in around twenty minutes. Everything was in place, including Quan, who was in concealment as well, in the long neglected uncut grass near the perimeter fence, directly opposite Daniel's position.

Quan was the same as Daniel, apart from being Vietnamese - ex Foreign Legion where they had met and served together. They had stayed together later, after the Legion, as mercenary soldiers or close personal security to whoever was paying. Thirty-three years old, just a year older than Daniel.

They trusted each other implicitly. They had to, because this was dangerous. They were both happy to take the risk. Quan, because of his loyalty to Daniel. And because, in his simple opinion, the people they were waiting for had it coming and it gave him the lifestyle he enjoyed. Daniel had his own reasons, nothing to do with lifestyle. Daniel just wanted this over and done with and to get out of the UK.

Quan had carried out a private matter a couple of days ago on his behalf before Daniel had flown into the UK on an assumed name. The matter should prove untraceable to himself, or anybody else. But there was always a chance. He wasn't regretting it. It was very personal, and had, in his opinion, needed to be done. But there was an outside chance that it could have repercussions - very slim, but there. There were three people in the world that linked him to what he had felt obliged to have done. Two of them were dead. That's why he had asked Quan to do it. And it was done. It couldn't be undone.

He put it from his mind and glanced at his watch. Just a few minutes now, if their information was correct, and he was sure it would be. He smiled as he thought of Ray. A kind-hearted, then nineteen-year-old, Daniel had met him just over twenty years ago when he was an eleven-year-old, scared little boy in a care home before he had been lucky enough to be fostered by wonderful people. He had never lost touch with Ray.

Ray had suffered with an illness that had finally confined him to a wheelchair but his skills with computers and technology were as good as Daniel's with martial arts and weapons. As good as you could get. He had supplied this intel, and it would be right because, thanks to Ray, it came from the drug baron himself. The equipment Ray supplied to obtain it had been placed in the man's penthouse with the help of the gang leader's girlfriend, Irena, who the drug baron was deeply in love with.

This was a continuation of a scenario that had started some six months ago. Daniel had met Irena after befriending her younger sister, Aisha, about eight months ago, in Turkey. Aisha had been desperate for Daniel to go to the UK and meet Irena there. She had been very concerned about Irena, and rightly so but Irena could not be persuaded to stop what she had started. Daniel had easily understood why. Irena was adamant that she would not cease doing what she had come to the UK to do but she had gladly accepted Daniel's help to achieve her aims, and that had led him here tonight. It had been meant to be and Daniel hadn't questioned it, despite being horrified at what Irena was doing to achieve it and the terrible risks she was taking in the process of doing so. But he understood her motives and was easily able to justify what he would do here tonight.

He smiled as he thought about Aisha and her family in Turkey. He loved it there and it would be nice to get back there soon, around May, after a bit of time in the Gambia. He hated the UK with a passion. Sad when it was the country of his birth, but he'd spent little time in it these last fifteen years. He snapped out of his thoughts. Time to focus on the job in hand. Then he could go home.

Chapter 3. Take-down.

He glanced at his watch and keyed the mike on his radio set. "Final comms check", he murmured.

"Received."

Daniel hefted his trusted, Accuracy International, AWM sniper rifle, onto the window ledge of the first floor office he was in and laid prone on the stable platform of two old heavy desks he'd set up, end to end, against the window. He trained the telescopic sight with the Milsight night vision attached on the area the targets should be in very soon. Not a breath of wind. Perfect conditions, short range.

He shivered, missing the African sunshine. Poxy place. At least it wasn't raining, no mist or fog. Clear vision, no water droplets on sights. It was as good as it got. And it was time.

He saw the headlights before he heard the engines. One of the two parties that were meeting here were early, casing the area no doubt. Well they wouldn't find him or Quan. He just hoped nothing else spooked them. This would put them one step nearer to their goal. Destroying Amir Ferez. It should be over in less than two minutes, which suited him fine. All he wanted to do was go back to where he was happiest – a bit wealthier, although that didn't matter to him, and having been instrumental in one more step towards Irena's cold revenge for the hurt inflicted on her and Aisha's family. Which did matter to him. And to all involved. The money would be just a bonus and paid the expenses to do this. He liked the poetic justice of criminals funding their own downfall. He'd been doing it for some years.

Headlights! He murmured softly again into the mike, "First vehicle inbound."

"Copied."

The first vehicle drew up at the gates and immediately turned off its headlights. Through the night vision scope, Daniel saw the front seat passenger alight and unlock the heavy duty padlock and remove the chain securing the double steel gates together.

They were big high gates. This old depot had probably been a busy heavy haulage yard and warehouse at one time, serving the local farms that had been all there was in rural Surrey, before the creeping purchase of farms and land for wealthy people's residential needs had changed the area. Derelict now, earmarked for yet more houses in time. But, for now, the freehold was owned by Amir

Ferez, through one of his several legitimate front companies. A long term investment of his dirty money with its clandestine uses in the meantime.

The passenger looked around the area. Apparently satisfied, he got back in and the huge, black Cherokee jeep drove into the yard, its headlights still off. It turned in a wide slow circle, then reversed back to a position on the far side of the yard, to a spot against the perimeter fence some seventy metres away from, and facing, the gates. Daniel murmured into the mike, "Your driver."

"Copied."

Daniel checked his watch again, 0125. Five minutes to the scheduled meet time. The fact that the gates were left open told him these guys were in touch with each other and the other vehicle wasn't far away. A minute later he saw the headlights approaching.

"Second car inbound," softly into the microphone.

"Copied," from Quan. This was it.

The second vehicle, a Toyota Land Cruiser, rolled into the yard and immediately stopped, killing its lights. The front passenger alighted and closed the gates, trapping themselves in the yard with no chance of a quick exit. But then, they weren't expecting trouble and they needed privacy more than anything else. That some nosy, late night passer-by could report the gates open would be their biggest concern. The small village of Sharbourne was the closest place to this depot, and that was well over a mile away. It was a perfect meeting place. But then, you could never take chances, not in their world. The Land Cruiser then moved further in, to some twenty-five metres from the Cherokee facing it directly.

Daniel watched intently as the deal started to unfold, calmly looking through the scope. Three men got out of each vehicle, just leaving both drivers in place. A large holdall was removed from the back of the Land Cruiser by one man. The other two were holding weapons, small automatics. Most likely machine pistols, short range gangster weapons of choice in the drug fraternity. Daniel panned across to the Cherokee. A short, stocky man was alighting with a medium size suitcase. Again with two men. One with a similar weapon to the other team, one with a pistol, looked like an automatic. The case was what Daniel and Quan were going to take. A lot of money, in cash.

He watched as the two groups of three men walked slowly towards each other, each centre man in the two groups carrying the holdall and the case respectively. He heard the faint sounds of their voices. They were now around twenty feet apart, the best effective range for the weapons they were carrying. He trained the sight onto the driver's window of the Toyota. And said, "now" into the mike. He pulled the trigger on the rifle as Quan did the same to the Cherokee. The respective windows exploded. Blood splattered across both vehicles from the instantly dead drivers.

Then all hell broke loose. The suppressed rifles used by Quan and Daniel made a sound barely louder than a cough but the weapons used by the gangs were deafening. The machine pistols of the Land Cruiser gang fired first. Noise and flashes lit the night and savagely cut down two of the Cherokee gang. One of them was the man with the case, the other was the carrier of the machine pistol to his left. Daniel swung the rifle and quickly took down the nearest of the two shooters from the Land Cruiser crew. Head shot. Just as the pistol carrier got his act together, and hit the other one, wounding him, which preceded the wounded man, and the man with the holdall, trying to take cover by running back to their car. Daniel heard the cough of Quan's rifle and the wounded man fell unmoving well before he got to the car.

The guy with the holdall panicked and dropped it, and started to run towards the gates. Daniel waited until he got there and was stationery, while fumbling with the latch mechanism. And fired. The man's head literally burst open and he slid down the gates to the ground. Pistol man was the sole survivor and he had nowhere left to go. He stepped out from behind the Cherokee with the gun held high above his head, shouting something in what sounded like an East European accent. The only one to realise, far too late, that there were others on the site beside the two car crews. Quan shot him in the head and he fell. It was done.

Daniel was dismantling the rifle and packing the unused grenades, bar two, which he hooked on his belt, into the purpose-built soft case. He knew Quan would be doing the same. He put the shoulder sling of the case over his head and double-checked all was stowed, then quickly moved the desks away from the window and closed it. He poured the half-gallon of bleach he'd brought up with him across the desks and ran a cloth over the surface of both of them.

Then he ran quickly down the stairs and out into the car park, across to where the case-carrying man lay dead, blood pooling around him. He grabbed the blood-spattered suitcase with his double latex gloved hands. Carefully. Like most suitcases, it had two handles, one centre on the longest side, one at the top of it, next to the handle that pulled out to drag it by the wheels. Daniel only used the top one. The dead man who had been carrying it had used the usual, easier, centre one. He wanted that untouched. It wasn't locked. The drug sellers would have wanted a look in it before the handover if the deal had gone smoothly. He quickly looked inside, at the money. That was what they had come for. The drugs the police could have.

He quickly threw a grenade in through the missing driver's window on each car and then raced towards the fence and dived through the hole Quan had snipped open before the firefight. The old yard and buildings erupted into noise and light again behind them. The vehicles exploded into flame as the fuel in the tanks went up. Quan snapped another photograph with a small digital camera. They gave each other a terse grin, their faces illuminated strangely in the dancing light from the inferno they were leaving behind.

They walked swiftly towards the hi top Transit panel van parked discreetly nearby, slipping on hi vis yellow overalls that bore the same logo as the name on the van, of a contractor to Surrey Highways. Traffic management division. A commonly seen type of vehicle for the many ongoing night road works. Once there, they calmly but quickly stowed everything behind the false compartment across the bulkhead.

They got into the vehicle's two front seats and Daniel drove away. They were through Sharbourne and were nine minutes away and on the main road, heading towards the A3, before they heard the first of the sirens. A police car flew by them, heading towards the carnage they had left behind, without giving the garishly marked and striped van with its yellow lights flashing a second glance. They drove on. They had one more rendezvous in the morning. Then they were done.

Chapter 4. Time to go home.

After sleeping for a couple of hours in a lay-by, they drove to another prearranged lay-by on the A3 and pulled in. Two cars, a white Audi saloon and a black Mercedes convertible, were already there. A big, bearded man, wearing the same overalls as them and a very stunning, smartly-dressed woman in a tight black business dress suit which accentuated her lovely figure. Shapely, black nylon clad legs and long jet black hair framed a beautiful, sharply featured face. Both there on time, despite the early hour. The road was quiet. Perfect for the last part of this dangerous night's work.

Quan and Daniel had removed their overalls and quickly changed into smart casual clothes while inside the back of the van.

The bearded man drove calmly away with the van after just the case had been removed from it. The rather stunning lady, after a long hug with Daniel, took a quick look in the suitcase, turning her nose up a little at the obvious bloodstains on the case. She nodded approval.

Daniel carefully unpacked the money into the aluminium case the woman had brought, with both cases in the trunk of her car, concealing anything from the odd vehicle that sped past. And then, still only carefully holding the end handle, Daniel had placed the empty case in the trunk of the Audi. Quan was in the driving seat, ready to go.

Daniel said, "Are you okay Irena?"

She looked at him and replied, "Yes Daniel. I am okay. I have to go face Amir now. But it will be fine."

"I hope so Irena. He will be very angry, so be careful. The police seized his heroin shipment at Harwich last night. His cocaine is where the police can find it, along with his men. He has taken a huge loss last night. And will find it hard to believe that what has happened is a coincidence."

"Yes. Yes he will. But he cannot prove otherwise. And you will deal with that police officer Amir has control over? Davidson."

"Yes I will. He may well be very useful to us in the future. We must all go. Take care Irena, keep me informed."

She kissed him on the cheek. "As always Daniel I will." She got into her car.

She drove away in her black Mercedes convertible to deliver the money to another contact of Daniel's who would get it where it needed to be, carefully and over time. Then she would go back to Amir Ferez and all the dangers that went with doing that, which would increase dramatically from now on. But it was her choice. Ferez mocked the law and evaded justice. Her goal was to destroy Ferez and she was very lucky to have had Daniel Cade appear in her life to help her achieve it. She adored him. Maybe once this was over? Who knew? She had to survive this first. Then she would think about the future.

Daniel got into the Audi that the bearded man had arrived in and Quan drove them away, heading towards Gatwick airport, where Quan dropped Daniel off with the ticket and passport the woman had given him. Daniel hugged Quan and said goodbye, after stressing again to keep the case safe and not touch it any differently to how he had. He headed to the departure lounge, via the toilets to change his appearance a little. And then the Gambia.

Quan got back in the car, and headed to London and the Vietnamese community where he blended in unnoticed. He lived quietly with his long-time girlfriend, in his smart but modest apartment in Lambeth and ran his martial arts school for young people. Among other things he earned a living at. What he had just done was the latest of many illegal things he had done over time, both alone, or with and for Daniel. And others of a like mind. He would get paid for it. But he would have done it for nothing. For Daniel, and the reasons Daniel did it. And the bond they had formed in the Foreign Legion and kept ever since.

Irena got back to the luxurious penthouse in Sutton where she now lived with Amir Ferez and found him, along with Bogdan Gentian, his Albanian distributor, both in a terrible rage. She went to him and embraced him.

"Hello my darling. Thank you for my room, it was a lovely place. And it was such a...."

He cut across her with venom in his voice.

"I have no time for idle conversation, woman."

"What is wrong darling?"

"Wrong? The latest shipment was intercepted by the police in Harwich after the lorry left the ship. That is what is fucking wrong! The fucking lot. Gone!"

"Oh Amir. What on earth happened?"

"I do not know. Yet. But it now appears that something also went terribly wrong with another deal elsewhere last night. I am awaiting details of that fucking disaster as well."

"I don't understand you Amir. Another deal?"

"I will talk with you later. Bogdan. We must go."

"Well, I am sorry you have such problems Amir. I was looking forward to some time with you darling."

"I am sorry Irena."

His cruel eyes softened as he looked at her. "Please darling. I have to meet my lawyer. The police are demanding my presence. Shooting. Men dead at the warehouse site in Surrey. This is very bad. I will be back later. I have much to sort out."

And he was gone. Bogdan gave her an evil look behind Amir's back as they walked to the door.

She shuddered. There was no love lost between her and Bogdan. She would have to be very careful now. More so than ever before. This dangerous game had moved up to a whole new level.

Chapter 5. Time to stop grieving.

Later that same day, in the same beautiful Surrey countryside, Alan Shand drove up the long tarmac drive, after the electronic gates opened, towards the luxurious mansion house owned by his long-time friend, business colleague and ultimately his boss now, Lee Tremayne. Wondering what he could expect from him or if he would even get to see him. He mused to himself how money couldn't insulate anyone from crime or the heartbreak and pain it caused. Not even an heir to a fortune estimated at over a billion pounds with the combined values of business and family wealth.

A man who had led, by any standards, a charmed and full life with a wonderful childhood, a great education and a fine military career. Then a good marriage to a beautiful girl and two beautiful children, followed by a progression into the family business where he had irritatingly, and quite naturally, proved a natural businessman. Not really surprising as he was very much his father's son.

Two men had been in the process of burgling Lee's parents' home, a beautiful house on what had once been a farm, just under five miles away from here, back in December. They had been disturbed by his parents returning home early from a Christmas function. A struggle with John Tremayne had resulted in the drug-fuelled pair bludgeoning the elderly couple in a frenzied attack.

John Tremayne's wife, Ann, had her skull shattered and was virtually unrecognisable. John Tremayne bled out laying next to her after being stabbed with a large carving knife snatched up and used by one of the burglars during the struggle. Two wonderfully happy people in their early seventies in good health, with potentially a lot of good years of retirement ahead. Cruelly snuffed out for no good reason.

The police had caught the perpetrators quite quickly in a seedy flat where one of them lived. But then the bombshell had hit. A young officer at the crime scene had made what the defence team described as, procedural errors, with physical evidence. Cross contamination and other jargon. And had rendered it inadmissible. Alibis provided by the two serial criminals had also held up despite the best efforts of the police to crack the people who had supplied them in full knowledge they were false. And the case was eventually dropped as it had no chance of success.

Leonard Mason and Tyrone Wesley were freed. They swaggered away from the court steps after giving interviews to the press, complaining of false accusations and police malpractice while standing there with their respective lawyers. Alan recalled how he had watched that on television with revulsion. John and himself had been very close. Alan's father had been a good friend of John's. Long-term family friends as well as business associates. Alan could only begin to imagine how Lee and the family felt watching two killers mock both the law and their victims' memory.

It had been fairly big news because John Tremayne was an enormously wealthy, although rather reclusive businessman. Not a Sugar or Branson, both of whom he had admired greatly. He just disliked publicity and shunned personal headlines. The financial news and his wealth were the testament to his business skills and the only one he wanted. He lived quietly, it was his way. A thoroughly decent man. Very kind, discreetly, incredibly generous. A pleasure to both work with and for and to have known.

Predictably, the Crown Prosecution Service caught some flak and the case was left open though with little chance of any further action. The police stated they were not looking for anybody else in connection with the crime. They knew who had done it and apparently screwed up. Action would be taken and, as always, lessons learned, would be the line pitched to the press. But unless anything dramatic happened, like a confession, or any new witnesses came forward, that was the end of the line.

Newspaper headlines briefly sensationalized the crime and the case, mostly because of the Tremayne fortune, rather than because murder was particularly shocking any more. The police were criticised for being inept but, as with all things, the news died along with the victims and the family were left to pick up the pieces. That was just under a month ago. Lee had been quiet and introverted ever since and sadly neglecting both his family, who he adored, and the vast family business it now fell to him to run without the background guidance of his semi-retired father, John Tremayne.

Alan parked his treasured old SAAB 900 and sat staring at the huge house for a while. It was a magnificent building and looked even more so in the bright, sadly rare, February sunlight. Alan had been Lee's right hand man ever since Lee had left the military twelve years ago and taken over from his chairman father, John, who had then semi-retired. He had carried on the role he had carried out for Lee's father. CEO. Every major deal. All the important meetings. And he was a good CEO, respected in the corporate business world.

Tasked by John, then later, Lee, to keep his experienced hand on the tiller of the corporate trading conglomerate that was Tremayne Holdings, with its myriad, worldwide subsidiaries, he had done just that - alone, since the awful news had broken. The business was solid, with a wide range of investments and a great management team, so it wasn't that hard to do. A damn sight easier than getting Lee back on track was proving so far, that was for sure.

Alan eased his six foot frame out of the warm car, into the chilly temperature despite the bright sunshine, and saw the door open. Lee's rather stunning blonde wife, Angelica, who was only ever called Angel, waved to him. He sighed and walked to the door, wondering how things were. He knew Angel was worried sick and he knew it was only the children keeping her sane, as she watched her husband suffer in virtual silence.

"Hi Angel." He gave her a hug and followed her into the beautiful home. Tasteful and immaculate, he had always enjoyed the good feeling of a happy place here. Until now. "How's he doing now Angel? We've heard nothing from him regarding business. He's got to get back and soon but I don't like to pressure him." He left out the matter which was uppermost on his mind. Today he had to see Lee. And Lee had to listen because it sure as hell wasn't going to go away. It hadn't hit the press yet so Lee wouldn't know about it. He hoped. But he doubted it would be long before it did if it wasn't dealt with and quickly.

Angel gave him the reply he was pretty much expecting. "He's not doing well Alan. Every bloody day he just picks up a shotgun and goes out for hours round the estate. Seems to be killing things out of rage. Drinking at night, he's not sleeping, hardly eats. This can't go on. Even the children seem wary of him." She looked on the verge of tears. Alan really felt for her, but it was pretty much what he had expected to hear.
"Where is he Angel?"
"Out there somewhere, with his bloody gun. If you're going to talk to him you'll find him by following the fucking bangs." Angel looked gaunt, far from the outrageous, funny and positive woman they all adored and Alan knew she was at the end of her tether. "Let me get a gun from the rack and I'll go find him. After you've made me a coffee."

Angel made the coffee in the spacious modern kitchen and brought Alan up to date on everything that had happened since the ghastly day of the joint funeral three weeks ago. How the estate had been settled, with the couple's company shareholdings going in trust to their grandchildren, Lee and Angel's two kids, Ian and Natalie. The house had been emptied a few days ago. The decision on what to do with the place didn't need to be rushed.

The will had been read and was being discharged by the appointed solicitors. Lee had wanted nothing from his parents home so everything in the property had been cleared into secure rented storage and the property secured. Angel had arranged that so Lee could go through his parents personal belongings at a later date, as she believed he one day would want to. Alan listened attentively and asked a few questions but it was pretty much as he had expected. And feared.

He finished his coffee and rose from the chair. "I'll go get some boots and a wax jacket from the gun room and go find him"

"You go find him Alan, and you bring him back. Back to how he was. Because I won't do this for much longer. Because I can't." Then she did start to cry. Really cry. Alan looked at the long blond hair hanging down and her shoulders heaving.

This was fucking wrong. Angelica had been very close to Lee's parents. Coping with the grief was bad enough. Coping with Lee was pushing her too far. He left the room. He was going to bring Lee back. The time was past for pissing around and being careful around him. Lee Tremayne was going to get it as it was. Like it or not, this had to stop. Three weeks is a long time in business. A whole lot longer in grief and misery.

Around the same time Daniel Cade was boarding a plane to the Gambia. Blond hair now. His passport accepted with no problems. He was looking forward to getting home. The pretty flight attendant smiled at him as she checked his boarding pass and assured him the flight was all on time. He settled into his extra legroom front seat after casting a distasteful eye over the rowdy holidaymakers cramming the plane. He knew the Gambians needed them, but he wouldn't be going anywhere near them.

He was going home and that lot would be nowhere near it out there. He closed his eyes and blocked them out as the plane thundered down the runway and soared into the sky. Yet again he had left carnage and questions behind him. And he'd dealt with grief too. In his own way.

Chapter 6. Ultimatum time.

Alan walked out through the French doors and looked across the fields beyond the immaculate garden area, glistening with dew after the early hard frost had thawed, in the rare February bright sun. With its magnificent patio areas, huge brick barbecue, the indoor swimming pool set back in the trees. Complete with an outbuilding incorporating a sauna and steam room and gym. Bigger than a lot of people's bungalows.

He gazed around remembering the summer days. The gatherings of friends and family and close, long-term business associates. Lee's father holding court as he always did with stories from the business world and foreign travel. Lee as master chef at the barbecue, the children playing. He sighed. It seemed a world away.

He hefted the Benelli Super Black Eagle under and over shotgun over his forearm and walked, crunching up the neat gravel path towards the gate that opened out onto the fields and woodlands that formed the nine acres of land surrounding the Surrey property owned by Lee. And went to follow the bangs. At least it was bright and sunny, unlike the gloomy atmosphere that enveloped the house these days and for so many, even the company head offices.

He soon heard a shot and headed towards a small wooded copse about two hundred metres away, across a grassy meadow. As he got closer he could see Lee, peering intently into the tops of the trees. Then another shot roared, and a flurry of feathers puffed into the air as what looked to be a pigeon, tumbled down through the branches.

Alan called out. Lee turned towards him and lowered the gun and broke it. Alan walked towards him. This was it. Lee would see reason or Alan was quitting. He had realised as he walked that there was no way he could carry on like this. No way at all. So there was nothing to lose. Which might be a good thing. That thought crossed his mind as he got close enough to see Lee's face. It wasn't the face of the man he'd been happy to work with for so long, known since he was a boy. Not his face at all. He looked gaunt and haggard and had clearly lost weight. He was tall and good looking. Jet black hair with a tiny hint of grey, normally immaculately groomed, looking unkempt. A hint of stubble. He looked awful.

"Lee. We need to talk my friend and today I won't be taking no for an answer. This has gone on long enough."

"What the hell do you want me to say Alan? I just want to be left alone. It isn't too much to ask."

"Actually Lee, it is too much to ask. You've got a wife and children and a business that need you, you can't carry on neglecting any of them. And you need to bloody realise that. It's selfish and wrong."

"Selfish! What's selfish is you getting in my face. What's wrong is no justice for my parents."

"Well it's no longer a fucking issue Lee. Believe me, if you don't actually already know why I'm saying that, you need listen to me. Because the police want to see you as a matter of urgency. If you send me packing I am out of Tremayne Holdings. I mean it Lee and the police will come here if you don't go to them. You'll talk to them one way or the other."

Alan watched Lee's face intently as he awaited a response. Either Lee knew nothing about the information Alan had, which Alan hoped was the case, or he did. Which Alan knew would alter everything he felt about Lee Tremayne. Lee looked pretty shocked. But then Alan had never once sworn directly at him, or threatened to resign. The silence reigned for about a minute before Lee broke it.

"Walk with me. And tell me what the hell you are talking about. How the hell can my parents' killers getting away with it no longer be a fucking issue?" Lee started walking across the grass towards the beautiful house in view a few hundred metres away.

"Because they're both dead Lee." That caused Lee to stop in his tracks. He turned to Alan with an incredulous expression and just said, "Both dead? I don't understand. I mean how?"

At that moment, a great feeling of relief went through Alan. Lee didn't know anything. and he was glad beyond measure. Because he had no idea how he would have felt if he had.

"According to the police, Leonard Mason and Tyrone Wesley fought in Mason's flat. Mason died of a massive blow to the head from Wesley. Wesley died from a stab wound inflicted, apparently, by Mason."

"When did this happen Alan?"

"Three days ago, according to the police. Between midnight and four in the morning." They started walking again. Lee said nothing until they were in the grounds of his house. They got to a barbecue bench under a pergola, overgrown with honeysuckle, and Lee stopped.

"Would you wait here please Alan, give me your gun. I'll go put them away and have a quick word with Angel and I'll get us some coffee." Alan handed him the gun and sat down as Lee walked towards the house. Lee stopped and turned. "I'm sorry Alan. I've been in a bad place. I'll just go tell Angel the same and I'll be back out." He turned then stopped again. Turned again to face Alan and said, "I won't lie to you my friend, I'm glad they're dead. I just hope you can understand that." Then he walked away. Alan breathed a sigh of relief. That had gone better than he thought it might have. But there were more bridges to cross. There was no telling how Lee was going to react to the position of the police on this.

Chapter 7. Questions.

Alan recalled the police visit as he waited for Lee to return.

A rather arrogant man, young for a DS, named Colin Fleming had shown up yesterday, with another, older, rather scruffy DC, Michael Davidson, at the offices that were Tremayne Holdings corporate headquarters in Canary Wharf. Demanding to speak with Lee. Alan had fielded the visit and explained that Lee was on compassionate leave until further notice.

At which point DS Fleming had said he was going to find him at home. Alan had listened to what he had to say regarding the urgency but had managed to get him to agree to give him twenty four hours to get Lee to come in as he didn't want Angel and the children to suffer any more upset. He had asked for what reason they needed to talk to him and got a shock when told of the two deaths - and a bigger one when Fleming had voiced his suspicions about them. In fact, after the officers had left, Alan had had a surreal feeling that he was in a bad dream and he knew he had to get Lee to cooperate with both himself and the police.

He heard voices from across the lawn from the house and looked up. Lee had put a tray of coffee down on a patio table by the French doors, and was hugging Angel, which was good to see. He watched as Lee picked up the tray and walked towards him. The next bit might not be so good to see. But it had to be dealt with. Like everything else in life and, in this case, death.

Lee returned to the shaded bench table, set the tray down and poured the black coffee they both drank the same way, as it came. Lit a very rare cigarette and said, "Okay talk to me. Give me the business updates first please. Then the details about those two bastards. Because that's the order of importance." Alan let the ghost of a smile appear. This was the Lee he knew slowly creeping back.

Alan gave Lee a brief rundown on the business front. A bit of a share wobble on the news of John's death. A few smart ass financial articles, about whether Lee would have the experience to run the company without John Tremayne's background input. But a timely flotation completion on the stock market, of an Asian electronics company in which Tremayne's had invested heavily with start-up capital, had ended that train of thought. The returns had been huge, the project had been Lee's alone.

Everything else was good. Basically, business as usual and nothing dramatic to report. A lot of uncertainty in the run up to the in or out referendum the UK was having, with regard to remaining in the EU, was the big issue of the financial press and markets. But Tremaynes' worldwide spread of companies and investments would put them in a good place. Certainly a better place than a lot of others with owners and executives who were so fanatical about the EU that they were making dire forecasts and statements should the nation vote to leave and bringing their own share values down. Tremayne's had simply stated when asked that they would trade confidently whatever the decision as they always had. And that was about it.

Lee's only comment to that was that the EU could do with a kick up the arse in the direction of making itself popular, rather than hated by so many. But it was, in many ways, good for European business and Lee knew that. They both did. But a lot of policies outside of trading seemed breathtakingly foolish, designed to alienate and unsettle the European people, rather than please them.

"Right, now give me the details about those two murderers please. And why exactly the police want to see me about it. Because I can't think of one good reason why they should."

"Well it's a bit of a shock to me, Lee. But apparently, the first assumptions of the officers who found them, and the initial forensics, were simple. They'd fought and killed each other. But that was brought into question after a more detailed report from the autopsies carried out later and resulted in a new investigation angle."

"Go on."

Alan pulled a folded sheet of paper from his jacket. "Read this Lee. I typed it out while it was all fresh in my mind." Lee took it and read it attentively. It detailed how the blow to the head and the stab wound to the respective individuals were the only wounds sustained by them both. How there had been no disturbance or noise reported, nor signs of a real struggle. And how, basically, the police had a train of thought. That there was a real chance that, although Mason's fingerprints were on the knife and Wesley's on a cosh, that the two were killed by a third party. And the crime scene was set up to give the impression they'd killed each other. He finished it and looked up with a questioning expression.

"And that Lee, is I assume, why they want to talk to you."

Lee Tremayne looked incredulously at Alan. "Are you seriously telling me they think I killed them?"

"No Lee. I am not. But I do think they're maybe looking at billionaires' parents killed. Justice is not served and maybe some serious money was spent dispensing it ? Doing a bit of joined-up thinking."

"Pity they weren't doing some joined-up thinking when they investigated my parents' murders isn't it? Because if those two bastards had been in prison where they belonged, this conversation wouldn't be taking place. Would it?"

"I know Lee. And the last thing I wanted was to be bringing this shit to your door. But you need to see them and get this put to bed, before those vultures in the press get hold of it and maybe start publishing their great theories. Let me arrange it. You don't want them coming here and making things worse for Angel. And I need you back at the office as well, even if only for a few hours Lee. I can't do my job without being able to consult you any longer. If any of this could wait I wouldn't be here. But it can't."

Lee sat in silence, drinking his coffee, deep in thought.

Then said, "Okay, make the call. I'll see them at the office tomorrow. After ten in the morning, but before two in the afternoon. I will meet you in the office at seven-thirty. And Alan, I'm sorry I left you holding the fort for too long. I've been a fool. The old man wouldn't have wanted me acting this way. Towards my family and you, and the business. I'm going to see you to your car and then go see Angel. We are going out to dinner this evening and we're going to be taking the kids out tomorrow afternoon, it's half term. So tell the police no later than two or it won't be tomorrow please."

Alan breathed an inward sigh of relief. "That's good to hear Lee. I know my way to the car, go see your wife. I need to get my jacket and shoes as well. See you tomorrow." He walked away across the lawn, feeling a lot better than he had when he arrived.

Chapter 8. Carnage and theories.

Detective Inspector Marshall Bland, just Marsh to his team, of the Surrey Regional Serious Crimes squad, had surveyed the scene at the old derelict haulage yard with a sense of combined incredulity and anger.

Months of work by the drugs squad collating evidence against a seriously big Albanian and Turkish drugs operation had been getting nowhere until, apparently, a hot tip from an anonymous source had resulted in a huge seizure of heroin last night, en route to the villains in question. Great result.

But then this bloody fiasco the same night. The same outfit expecting the heroin. Four of its known players dead. Four more dead from what was clearly another criminal gang. In a shoot-out, in the Surrey countryside. And now it had landed in his lap as a multiple homicide.

But maybe fiasco was the wrong word, because this looked like a well-planned, meticulously carried out hit on what was clearly a drugs and money exchange, by a third party. No survivors from the two drug gangs, no material evidence. And no money at the scene. Just a huge amount of cocaine clearly being purchased by Amir Ferez, the short, fat, seemingly untouchable, Turkish drug baron with respectable front companies, one of which owned this site, who offended Marsh by living and running his flashy clubs and casino from his manor. With Bogdan Gentian running the street dealing of large quantities of drugs he could never connect to either of the bastards.

He looked as Nigel Carash, his chief scene of crime analyst and one of the best forensic men in the business, walked towards him after over two hours of painstaking examination of the area, with hours left to do. They exchanged weary nods. "Got any first thoughts Nigel?"

"Yes Marsh, two shooters ambushed these guys." He pointed up to the first floor window to their right.

"One was up there, firing down." He pointed left towards the perimeter fence. "The other was firing from the ground, from over there on the fence line." He started flicking through the notepad he was carrying.

"My first take, and it won't be far wrong, is this." He waved a hand in the general direction of the two burnt out vehicles, now tented over to hide the charred corpses that were almost welded to the wreckage. "They hit the two drivers simultaneously after the rest were out of the vehicles. They knew the gangs would react and they did."

He pointed to the body bags covering the dead gang members one after the other. "Those were killed in the firefight between the gangs. Outright, multiple gunshot wounds. That one," He pointed towards the gate, "tried to leg it. The shooter up there in the office waited until he was at the gate and stationery - and blew his head off. That one took a non-fatal in the gang exchange and was trying to get to that car. And took a head shot from the shooter by the fence. And that one there, was hit by the shooter in the fence line. Straight in the head, still had his pistol in his hand."

He flicked through the book some more. "Two incendiary grenades, flipped into the two cars by window guy as he left the office after bleaching the bloody desks he was laying on to remove any possible DNA. Grabbing the money as he left. Which we have to assume, as there isn't any here. Then he went out through the hole in the fence to join his partner in crime. Then they had it away in a medium-sized commercial van that was parked for at least two hours from the tyre evidence on a dirt track about 100 metres up the road. The whole thing was probably over in less than two minutes from the time the gangs got out of their cars. There'll be a whole lot more detail as we get it all together. But that's the nub of it."

"Bloody hell," growled Marsh. "Want a coffee?" Nigel nodded and they walked out of the gates and over to the gaggle of support vehicles and cars parked outside the yard, ignoring the reporters who hassled for updates as they went. Once they'd got into the welfare trailer and closed the door they were alone. Marsh did the honours with the coffees, and looked at Nigel. "Weapons used?"

"Well the gang lads, as per normal, had machine pistols. Bar one, who had a .45 automatic pistol. Close range burp guns, pretty inaccurate, especially in the wrong hands. These guys are not trained in their use. Mostly for show and threatening with. But at twenty feet apart, when the snipers fired at the drivers, deadly. The two shooters. High grade 7.65 soft tipped sniper ammo, likely fired from high end military sniper rifles. Suppressed with hardly any sound, and, no doubt, night vision sights. The two grenades were incendiary, rather than fragmentation. To burn the cars, which they did."

Marshall pondered this for a moment. "Where the hell does another gang get off on this sort of activity? This is mass murder. They have to be in the drugs game to know where these type of meets are going down. They could have just got the drop on them and taken the money and drugs." Nigel hesitated before answering. Marsh could be a bit up his own arse if you questioned his theories.

"For what it's worth as a humble forensic investigator, I don't think these guys are rival drug gang members."

"You don't? Well who then? Bored local clay pigeon club members? Chuck fucking Norris having a bad day?"

"No Marsh. If you want my input you can have it, but not at the expense of getting my ear bent."

"Okay sorry. I'm shagged out Nigel. Give me your take. Fuck knows but I'm out of ideas. And I know this is gonna be a tough one to get a handle on. The men in the Cherokee are no doubt goons from Amir Ferez. The others are as yet unidentified. But apparently a huge heroin consignment Ferez was expecting was seized at Harwich last night as well after an anonymous informant flagged it up. The first ever success against his supply line. The fat bastard is not having a very good day today I would imagine. But I don't see the link between that and this bloodbath. Do you?"

Nigel collected his thoughts and spoke quietly.

"No Marsh, I don't. And although that's not my line of work, personally I really can't see a connection. If the Harwich informant also knew about this deal, then surely the police could have been tipped off about this meet; and arrested them all ? They weren't, this was an ambush. All the drug gang members here were meant to die, and they did."

"Okay, so what is your take on this bloody mess?"

"Looking at this crime scene, I'm wondering if these guys are from the criminal drug world at all?"

"I've got eight corpses here! They aren't bloody vicars!"

"How about they are ex-military? Marsh, I think you need to take a look at this line of thinking. I know you think I'm a political bore, but I do keep up to date with events. And the UK has been treating its soldiers like shit these last few years. Allowing legal action against them for killings on active service while granting amnesty to terrorists. Making long service soldiers redundant, often when they are close to getting their pensions. Some of these guys are SAS, SBS, marine commandos."

"You think a pissed off Andy McNab clone shot these arseholes to supplement his pension? Bit far out there Nigel, isn't it?"

Nigel shrugged his shoulders and continued. "This is just a theory, Marsh. But what if a few, or even just a couple, of these disgruntled, highly trained guys are pissed off? Sick to the back teeth of seeing drug dealers living the life of luxury. While they feel shat on. Or, what if it's a combination of the two? A drug gang hiring in ex-military to really hit rivals hard? But that doesn't add up for one obvious reason. These guys only took the cash. They leave the drugs for the police? Never in a million years. It's just a theory Marsh. But these shooters were perfectly and strategically positioned. They must have had comms between each other, they dictated and controlled events. Picked off the drivers. Let the gangs blast the hell out of each other, but picked off anyone who might get away. It has all the hallmarks of special ops and hardly any of gang warfare. And apparently only done for the money that was up for grabs. That's my take on it for what it's worth, Marsh. I better get back to the scene."

"Okay Nigel," replied Marshall. Then grudgingly, "Thanks, I think you might just have something here. Fuck knows we need lines of enquiry bad enough. It will be checked out."

Nigel nodded and headed back to the carnage that needed every shred of information gleaned from it before the place could be cleared.

Chapter 9. A life-changing meeting.

Nearly three thousand miles away, an airliner had landed at Banjul airport in the Gambia. Mostly UK tourists and holidaymakers made up the passengers. A slim man of medium height, with a clearly good physique, made his way through the jostling crowd towards the exit. Daniel Cade was pleased to be back in the country he loved. And where he found the peace he needed.

At thirty two years old, he'd seen more of life than most. And an awful lot more of death. As he exited the airport after the bizarre ritual the Gambians had of scanning your luggage into the country, he skilfully avoided the noisy porters jostling to carry his bag as he strode towards the exit. Sighed gratefully, as he felt the warmth of the African sun again, and the Gambian breeze and looked around and found Solomon waiting for him. The twenty-eight-year-old Gambian with the big gappy smile walked over and they had a quick hug.

"Good to see you back, boss man," came the standard greeting, in the usual casual manner.

"It's good to be back my friend. Let's get to the wheels and get the hell out of this bedlam."

"Is it okay to stop at the Palm Trees hotel, boss man? I has to deliver something for a friend."

"Only if you drop the boss man shit and call me Daniel."

"Cool boss man."

Solomon eased the air-conditioned Toyota Land Cruiser into the airport traffic, little knowing that his delivery was about to change Daniel Cade's life forever.

Solomon watched Daniel in the rear view mirror as he removed a blond hairpiece and a false, neat, fair moustache, spitting out two wads of cotton wool that had puffed out his face a little to reveal a jet black short crew cut and clean-shaven sharp features. Solomon smiled widely, "It suited you man, you looked better with it on."

"Just drive, you nosy bastard," was the reply. Solomon grinned broadly and just drove. He never asked questions. No point. You never got an answer.

They pulled up at the Palm Tree Sands hotel resort after driving through the choked streets of Banjul, then out onto the open sunny main road to Kololi. Daniel decided to grab a cold beer at the bar while Solomon conducted whatever on earth business he had to do. Daniel knew Solomon used the Toyota for all manner of deliveries. He took people and parcels to and from the airport, and did private tourist trips, enjoying the status locally that the vehicle gave him. It didn't matter.

Solomon was honest, trustworthy and discreet and looked after Daniel and his home and boats and car along with Rosie, one of Solomon's several aunts, his live-in housekeeper, whether he was there or not. Solomon appreciated his job and wage and the use of the car and the extra he made from it, and the fact he could look after his family who lived in a village nearby. He could provide malaria jabs and medical and dental care for them all.

They did well by Gambian standards. It was how life rolled in the Gambia. In fact it was how life rolled in Africa. You got a break and lived well. Or, as in millions of cases, you didn't. You got malaria, or any one of a myriad of illnesses, or caught up in a war or a famine or a drought. And you died. Africa was beautiful but cruel. Daniel loved it there.

As he walked through the reception area towards the bar, in what was one of the cheapest, and worst, chalet-type resorts in the Gambia, he heard a commotion going on at the reception desk. A very pretty, but obviously very angry, English woman in her late twenties was giving the receptionist a bit of a hard time. The receptionist was a big, buxom, Gambian lady of about forty years of age, and she was clearly having a tough time in placating the very upset young mother of the two young children at her side. A boy and a girl of about ten and eight respectively. Daniel hesitated, he preferred to keep himself to himself. But then he caught the young mother's eye as she turned to scan the room. He felt an almost electrical jolt in the pit of his stomach and knew right then he couldn't not intervene. He not only had to, he wanted to. He walked across to the desk.

"Any problem here Mama?" he addressed the receptionist.
"Ah hi Mr Daniel. This lady she says her bag is gone from the room. With all her money and passports, and that the room am shit. And all she does want is to go home. And I ain't got no clue what the hell she wants me to do about any of that for sure."
The angry young woman said, "The room is shit and my bag is gone. And you have to do bloody something."
Daniel said to her , "How about you calm down a little and tell me your name." She turned and looked at him.

"It's Janet. Jan. Wallace. And I can't calm down with no bloody passports or money. And talking to people who keep telling me they can't help." She looked on the verge of tears. "I've only been here two days. Just trying to give the kids a holiday after a real shit time back home, and now this. And I can't find that smug fat git of a holiday rep anywhere. I keep looking out for him, he's useless."

"Come and sit in the bar for a while with me, bring the children. We'll sort something out."

"How can you sort it out? It's really gone, and I don't have credit cards or anything. You don't need to waste your holiday on it, do you?"

Daniel smiled at her. "I live here, I will help you sort it out. In fact I want to help." Daniel knew as he said it that he meant it. Which wasn't strange to him. He was meant to meet her. The same as he was meant to meet Aisha in Turkey. Jan was meant to be here right now. It was where they were all guided to, the few that could be. It wasn't complicated, unless you tried to explain it, so Daniel rarely tried.

Daniel didn't really like other people much, according to the very few people that even knew him. But then Daniel never questioned anything either. If he was anywhere and something happened he accepted it, and dealt with it. A lifetime starting with an abusive childhood, leading to foster homes, then salvation, that then gave him a purpose and a course through life. Then soldiering and danger and close proximity to death. It made you like that. Along with a deep, inner spirituality, that was part of his martial arts and isolated lifestyle. That was his simple explanation. Other people didn't understand his need to intervene where he had no obvious reason to. Or his utter determination not to interact with others unless there was a good reason to. He didn't care if they did. The way he felt about Janet instantly was just how it was, and was meant to be.

He gently guided her towards the bar area, with the solution already forming in his mind. Janet allowed herself to be guided. Alone in Africa she hadn't got much choice and despite her previous bad experiences with men, there was something about this one. He seemed very kind. But very, in a strange way, dangerous at the same time. She would find out she was right in time. But he was no danger to her, somehow quite the opposite. She knew that instinctively too, but hadn't a clue why.

After they'd sat down, and he'd ordered beer for himself and orange juice for Janet, the children asked if they could go to the beach. Just as Janet was trying to tell them they couldn't, as she had to sort things out, Solomon appeared. "Ready to go when you are boss man."

"We're going nowhere yet. But you, in return for the constant misuse of my wheels, are going to go find Kuombi. Ask her to shut the stall for a while and come here. Like now."

Solomon quickly took off, in the direction of the beach, a short walk away. He knew that tone. Used very rarely but meaning what was said.

"Who's he gone for?" asked Janet.

Daniel took a grateful drink of the cold beer, and replied, "A young girl who works on a stall on the beach. She'll take the children to the beach while we talk this through."

Solomon returned with a cheerful smiling Kuombi. A chubby, happy young girl, in her late teens, who adored Daniel for the help he had given her over time. And she gave him a hug saying, "It's good to see you again Daniel."

"You too Kuombi. I have a few things to sort out with this lady. I want you to take the children down to the beach, and keep an eye on them for me. We'll come down and find you in a while." He pressed a wad of the grubby dalasi currency into her hand. "Take this, to cover your losses on the stall. Buy drinks and ice cream for the children. And stay away from the sea, it's rough today."

He turned to Solomon, who was grinning widely at him, obviously sensing the fact that Daniel was actually with a woman - and wanting to be alone with her "And you are going with them."

"Yes boss man." The two young Gambians left for the beach with the children leaving Daniel and Janet alone. Daniel smiled at her. She was very pretty, with shoulder length, auburn hair and had a shapely, curvaceous, full figure. A pretty face without make-up, and bright green eyes. The simple white dress looked lovely on her. She was, he thought, just beautiful.

They talked about the immediate situation. Daniel explained how the Gambians were, mostly, totally honest. But there were other African nationalities around as well and like most Africans they were poor. And these chalet in the grounds places were not very secure. And if the bag was gone then it wouldn't be recovered. Jan was upset but realised that it had been pretty dumb just to hide it in a wardrobe to save on paying for a safe. And the lock was faulty on the chalet.

Daniel really felt for her, as she'd explained how she'd been through a really bad time she didn't want to talk about but had just scraped the money together to try and give the children a break during half term. The place was driving her mad. The room and the toilet were horrible. The constant hassling by young men on the beach. Daniel smiled. "The bumsters. They're a pain. Solomon was one once. It's how they get by."

"Well I've got nothing for them to scrounge now, have I? I'm wiped out of the little I had. I shouldn't have come here. I want to go home."

"You don't need to worry. It's lovely here if you give it a chance."

"Of course I'm worried. I'm in Africa penniless!"

"I'll replace the money Janet. Just relax now. You'll be fine."

"But you don't even know me."

"I do now."

"Yes. For the last two minutes."

"I still know you."

"But it's a lot of money."

"It's only a couple of hundred pounds."

"That's a lot to me."

"It isn't to me."

"What about our passports?"

"I'll help you sort replacements. There's a British consul in Banjul."

"I can't take the money, I can't pay it back. Even when I get home I can't. I'm broke Daniel. It's nice of you to offer, but I can't accept it. Maybe I can go to the consul place and they'll help? I have got travel insurance."

"Very well, let's go and find your children." Daniel finished his beer and rose from his chair.

Janet felt a sudden sense of panic, strangely mixed with the fact that she didn't want him to just vanish. "Wait. I'm sorry, perhaps you're right. I do need some help don't I?"

"It's been offered."

"I know. And thank you."

"It's your choice to take it."

"Are you always so abrupt?"

"Are you always so indecisive?"

"Well it's difficult, I don't even know you."

"You just got to know me."

"Not well enough to borrow money."

"That's true."

"Well then."

"That's why I'll give you the money."

"Why would you just give money to someone you don't know?"

"You have a problem, you need help. I want to help."

"I know. But it's still difficult."

"It's been offered. What's difficult?"

"Okay, then thank you."

"No need, you're welcome."

Then Daniel added, "And I think you should leave here. And come and spend the rest of your holiday at my place."

Janet looked shocked. "Your place? I don't even know you!"

Daniel realised what she was thinking and rushed out, "I mean I have a big mobile home in the grounds of my place. You and the children can use it. I've got a pool and it's near the beach. It's much better than here. You won't see anything of me, unless you want to. Until it's time for you to go home."

Janet smiled. She realised this rather handsome, good looking, confident man was actually embarrassed at the thought of her thinking he was hitting on her. It had made him use what was obviously a very long sentence, for him, in explanation.

"That is just so very kind of you Daniel. Thank you for offering."

"It's not a problem."

"Can we come with you and look at it? Before we agree anything?"

Daniel visibly relaxed. "Sure. Let's go find the children."

As Janet followed his easy, fluid strides towards the beach, she was thinking that maybe it would be nice to see more of him. Because she actually wanted to. Which was strange. After her experiences with men, she tried to keep away from them these days. But this man. She felt there was something special about him, special to her. But for the life of her she couldn't explain why. She walked close to him towards the beach. She saw the nods and smiles from the Gambians who obviously knew him and liked him and smiled as she realised there would be no hassling from the bumsters while she was with him. If she knew nothing else about him, she knew he was definitely not a man you would hassle.

Chapter 10. A bent copper.

A lot of air miles away, in a Croydon Police Station the next day, Detective Constable Michael Davidson was sitting having a coffee with uniformed sergeant Brett Evans. Mick, or Bad News, as he was now known throughout the station, was bemoaning his luck at ending up working with DS Colin Fleming who was, in his often repeated opinion, a fast-tracked windbag climbing to the top by the easy route.

"I tell you Brett, the man's a basket case. Anybody else in the world would be glad to hear that two serial offending scumbags, who'd literally got away with murder, had killed each other. But oh no. Not Fleming. He has to start poking around and coming up with daft theories that they were killed by somebody else, and it was just made to look like they'd iced each other. And now he wants to go give the third degree to a massively wealthy top businessman who had his parents killed by the bastards. Winds me up!"

He took a loud slurp of his coffee. Brett smiled. Mick was always whinging about something these days, hence the nickname.

"Mick. I ain't trying to crank your handle mate. But if there is any way at all that these guys were killed by someone, well it's still murder. You can't just not investigate because you think the victims are scumbags."

Mick glared at him. "Why not? He's the first to clang on about the force being short of cash and knock my bloody overtime because of it. Then wastes hours on crap like this. I tell you, those two jerks were probably high as kites on drugs, fell out over who was getting the last hobnob, and had a fight. And managed to off each other. First useful thing either of them ever did."

Mick's phone rang. He hauled it from his inside jacket pocket and glared at it. "Fleming. One sec." He took the call and said, "yes," a couple of times. "Gotta go. Shit for brains wants to get going to Canary Wharf to see this poor sod. Later." Brett nodded. Pleased. Mick was bad enough on the ears at any time. But early in the morning. It was just too much.

Mick walked away with a lot on his mind. A phone call, from a person he was providing a discreet service to, was causing him a lot of worry. As was the text message demanding another payment off the loan he'd racked up with a local bookmaker come loan shark. Life was shit these days. He cursed inwardly and tried to put it from his mind as he went to find Fleming.

Chapter 11. The new dawn.

At six a.m. the Gambian beach was deserted. The weather was cloudy and quite cool, as was usual in February until the sun came up and it would be beautiful. The palm trees swayed and shivered in the dawn light. As the Atlantic rolled on to the sandy beach, the waves reached towards a lone figure running quickly along the shoreline.

Daniel Cade's heavy boots splashed water and wet sand, as he ran steadily at a brisk pace right on the waterline. He breathed steadily and, as always, let the exhilaration of physical exertion grip him. The measured six-mile run or swim was undertaken every other day as part of a regime of training that had been part of his life for as long as he could remember.

Stamina training, on this beautiful beach, involved either running or swimming the same distance either in or out of the water every other day when he was here. The days in between were devoted to martial arts, a minimum of two hours every day. He cycled miles, on a top of the range Pinarello road bike, with cyclo cross tyres. He had always lost himself in this world of training wherever he was in the world. He lived his solitary life and had never once considered changing it. He never timed himself, he just always put in maximum effort. As he did to everything. It was what, at times, had kept him alive.

He noticed the light increasing as he reached the turn round point and saw the trees a little more clearly. Later the beach would fill with European tourists, mostly British, who came here to escape the dreary winter weather of home. He stayed away from them. They appalled him mostly. Arrogant, often drunken and rude to the Gambians. Older, middle-aged men and women, often using young Gambians for sex in return for pitifully low amounts of cash.

He had no time for them. No urge to talk to anybody from "home". Because he was born there didn't make it home. Daniel Cade was English by birth, but he despised the place. And life had panned out that he would spend little time there. He doubted that he could.

He ran past the few ramshackle, small fishing boats, of the locals. And then round them, without pause, heading back towards where he had begun. Increased the pace slightly for the return leg, breathing a little harder as he did so. The small boats were soon left behind as he sped back through the surf towards one of the two places he had ever called home. The only places he guessed he ever would.

He finished his run, and quietly went through the gate into his villa grounds, silently walking past the mobile home where he knew that, inside, the very pretty young mum of two was sleeping. He hoped she didn't want to live in the UK very much any more. Because he knew they would be spending the rest of their lives together. In anybody else's world that would seem crazy, after just meeting somebody for the first time.

But in Daniel's world it was just logical. She was meant to come to the Gambia. And she was meant to find him. He wouldn't rush anything. Not because he thought it wouldn't turn out like that. But because she would need a bit longer to see it. He looked forward to seeing her when she got up later. He'd waited a very long time for her to show up. He was nervous too, almost scared. But it would work out. It always did if you just let yourself be guided.

Chapter 12. Theories and clashes.

Mick walked out to the car park, mentally cursing the cold weather, and saw Fleming in his car. He went over and got in with a brief nod and immediately got his newspaper out and started reading it to avoid conversation. Without success, as Fleming started in straight away about the forthcoming interview with Lee Tremayne.

"You let me lead on the questioning okay. This guy is pretty influential, I don't want him wound up."

"Oh right. Accusing him of murder won't wind him up one bit, will it?"

"Mick. I'm not accusing him of anything. But there's a strong possibility that those two men were murdered and a crime scene set to make it look like they killed each other. If that's right then it needs to be investigated. And Tremayne has the motive. They walked free after killing his parents."

"Exactly. So why not just let it be? There's every chance those two scrotes did off each other. So why make it complicated? And you'll piss Tremayne right off."

"Because I'm a copper, and a bloody good one, despite what you think. Murder is still murder. And if they were killed, this is pre-meditated and cold-blooded. And I want to arrest the killer or killers. Understood?"

"Understood." Mick read the paper while Fleming drove into the increasingly heavy traffic.

"And don't take an attitude Michael. You might want to overlook a possible contract killing. I don't."

"Okay I get it. But I still think you're barking up the wrong tree by questioning Tremayne about it."

"Is that a fact, detective? Well let me point out one thing you just might have overlooked."

"Which is?"

"Mason and Wesley died of exactly the same wounds inflicted on Tremayne's parents. One head wound, one fatal knife wound to the heart. Which makes it look to me a bloody sight more suspect. As in revenge. That might not have occurred to you, which is probably why you're still a DC, and always will be, given the time you have left. But it gives me grounds to ask questions. Because I don't like corpses or coincidences. Understood?"

"Understood," Mick said again. And immersed himself in the pearls of wisdom in the Sun newspaper as they headed towards Canary Wharf.

Chapter 13. Difficult questions.

Lee arrived at his office block in Canary Wharf early in the morning, after driving himself in. Dinner with Angel had been good. They'd talked over everything and gone home and made love. Lee knew life was never going to be the same again. Even at thirty-eight he knew he would miss his parents terribly. It was the sheer horror of their deaths and no time to say goodbye. The wisdom and guidance from his father gone. He tried to push it from his mind as he entered the offices.

"Good to see you back sir," from the night security man seated at the main reception. "Morning Bill. Thanks," he replied as he headed towards the lifts.

Alan arrived as planned and they sat in the plush boardroom going through the most important papers and points of discussion. There was little movement the other side of the doors, in the vast suite of open plan office space but there would be from about eight-thirty. By nine, all the staff would be in and the place would be a hive of activity. They retired from the boardroom to Lee's equally plush, immaculately furnished, private office. The conversation turned to the forthcoming interview with the policemen who had called ahead to say they were on their way. It was a conversation that fizzled out quite quickly. As they both agreed, it was nothing they could second guess. They would just have to wait and see what these officers wanted. So they drank coffee. And waited.

Fleming and Davidson duly arrived and were shown up to Lee's office. Tea and coffee were served and Fleming got to the point.

"The fact is Mr Tremayne, these two deaths are not as straightforward as first thought."

"Really?"

"The nature of the wounds themselves being the main factor."

"Well at least they were fatal," replied Lee.

"I understand your anger, sir. But we have had a second forensic visit to the crime scene, after the autopsies. Because these deaths, and the wounds sustained, have indications of a double homicide."

"In what way is this indicated?" asked Lee.

"Well, the fact that each victim sustained just one fatal wound each for a start. If men fight there would generally be signs of a struggle. Other, more minor injuries, furniture disturbed, things knocked flying. There was virtually no sign of anything like that. Which leads us to believe silence was the order of the day, to avoid attention." Fleming looked intently at Lee as he was talking but was getting no real reaction.

He continued. "Contrary to the movies, many chest wounds are survivable, as are head injuries. You might die later from complications, but instantaneous death is not as common as you might think. Neither victim had dragged themselves from where they fell. Both, according to our forensic medical teams, died instantly."

"And you are saying what in the light of this?" asked Alan.

"We are saying nothing at this stage, Mr Shand. We are investigating the possibility that these two men were killed by a person, or persons, unknown. And the crime scene set to make it look as if the victims had killed each other."

"I see."

"The fatal wounds." Fleming looked at his notebook. "Are indicative of military special services training. In infliction of instantaneous death. And that leads to questions that need to be asked Mr Tremayne."

"Well, here's my next question," said Lee. "Why do you want to talk to me about it? I couldn't care less if they are dead. In fact I'm glad they are. I'll grieve for my parents though, not them. If you don't mind?"

Alan shot Lee a warning glance but he knew Lee was furious.

Fleming replied, "Sir, I understand your terrible loss, and the circumstances after it. And your grief. Asking you questions at this time is not a thing I take any pleasure in doing. But. You watched these two men, now dead, walk free from killing your parents."

"So you think I killed them?" asked Lee.

"No, Mr Tremayne. I do not."

"Then what do you think?"

"I don't think anything. Other than, regrettably, you have a very strong motive."

"So you think I maybe arranged their murders?"

"You said that Mr Tremayne, not me. Did you?"

"No I most certainly did not. And never would even think of or contemplate such a thing!" Lee and Fleming locked eyes. Fleming could see Lee was enraged at the suggestion. He continued,

"Then that brings me to my next question. If you don't mind?"

"I mind very much, but that won't stop you asking it. Go ahead."

"Both you and your father were from a military background, as well as business?"

"You no doubt already know the answer to that."

"I do. So my question is. Do you know anybody, close to you or your father, who would contemplate doing such a thing?"

Lee reacted just momentarily to the question. A hesitation just before his reply. A microsecond of it. But Fleming caught it.

"No, I can't say I do." Lee answered.

"You're quite sure Mr Tremayne? You seemed a little hesitant when you replied."

"I was simply trying to think. Dad was a soldier, I was. But no. I don't know of anyone who would murder anyone, whatever the reason."

"Well, we have to ask the question. Because both wounds were precise and deadly. The knife was exactly the right length to serve its purpose. We don't know if it was brought to the scene for sure, but we assume it was. It was driven upwards into the heart with extreme force, between the ribs. A difficult thing to do by chance. The heart stopped instantly. The head wound was precise to an area of the temple that rendered instant, life-ending damage to the brain. These wounds are commensurate with an in-depth knowledge of deadly force. Attack rather than defence. Aggressive martial arts skills or combat training. You do understand?"

Lee replied angrily, "Yes I do understand. But I repeat. My father and myself were armoured division, tanks. We were not SAS, we were never trained in those skills. And what's more we didn't serve with anyone who was. I don't know what else I can tell you."

"Well something else I can tell you is this. That the injuries were exactly identical to the ones that killed your respective parents. So hopefully you can understand why I have to pursue this enquiry. It screams retribution at me. If that's the case then it is murder. And it will be investigated."

"I fully understand that now," replied Lee. "If that's the case as you say. I assume there is a possibility they did kill each other? However strange or lethal their injuries were. Or you think they are?"

"As you say sir, there is still that possibility. If you or anybody else can't shed any further light, or offer any further information, the case will either be left open. Or closed as a mutual homicide."

"Well I can assure you I can't."

"Then that concludes my enquiries with you Mr Tremayne, for now. All I can ask is, that if you do think of anything, that you'll contact me?"

"Of course. But I won't. There's nothing to think of. It's both absurd, and insulting."

"Again Mr Tremayne, my deepest sympathies for your loss. And my profound apologies for the way the original investigation turned out. There was no intention to insult you I assure you. It is a police enquiry into a possible double homicide. All possible avenues have to be explored."

"Thank you. Well hopefully you have explored as much as you need to in regard to me?"

"I can safely say yes to that. At this time."

"Good."

Fleming stood up and said, "The irony is, of course, that if Wesley and Mason had pleaded guilty or the people who provided false alibis had been truthful, they would still be alive, albeit in prison. The case in regard to your parents Mr Tremayne - that case is now obviously closed. They were the perpetrators beyond any reasonable doubt, in fact, any doubt. I hope you and your family can find some closure from that at least now. We'll make our own way out. Thank you for the drinks." Fleming nodded to Mick and they left the office.

Fleming was on the phone on hands-free in the car on the way back as Mick pretended to read his Sun again. Asking the team for data to be collated on ex-military men with criminal records.

But Mick wasn't really concentrating. He had a bit of a bad feeling about this enquiry. If Fleming started to look in the wrong places, it would mean he might end up looking into places Mick would very much rather he didn't. Surely there could be no connection between these two dead scumbags and the dubious activities Mick was involved in? The violent scenes at a drug and cash exchange, that were the talk of the Surrey force right now. Bland at serious regional was looking into a possible military angle. That crime involved somebody Mick had an ongoing financial arrangement with. He hoped not. Fleming ended the call.

"Mick," said Fleming. "When you have digested the tits and lies in that ghastly rag, the forensic report from the autopsy is on the back seat. Have a read Mick, you might find it enlightening." Then Fleming lapsed into silence. Mick reached for the report and started reading. His face gave nothing away but it was interesting. And not in a good way. Not after Amir Ferez' last text message to him.

Lee stood and was looking out of the window, rigid as a statue after they left.

"Are you okay Lee?" asked Alan.

"I'm fine."

"You seemed troubled Lee, the copper noticed it. So did I. Is there anything or anyone? I have to ask."

"And I'll answer you my friend, there might be. I can't say any more but there just might be. We need to catch up on the business front Alan. Don't ask me any more about it please. I need to think about this very carefully." Alan didn't. They set about catching up on the business front but Alan had that bad feeling back again.

Irena smiled as she tapped out an email to Daniel, telling him Amir and Bogdan had been running around like headless chickens trying to get answers to the calamities that had happened to them. But they were getting nowhere. She was safe. Her email had confirmed what had already been sent to Daniel by Ray, who was busy monitoring Amir's communications. Amir was getting no answers; he was spending big money obtaining heroin from wherever he could to supply Bogdan and his network of dealers. Bogdan was pressuring Amir over the shortages since the seizure. Amir was pressuring his suppliers for a new shipment urgently. But they were careful men. It wasn't going to happen until they were confident it would get through. Amir had been warned by them that it better had this time. He was under pressure. Everything was going to plan.

Chapter 14. Early days and mysteries.

Three days later, out in the Gambia, Janet Wallace was, along with her children, having the best time of her life. Daniel Cade was the strangest man. But so kind. He seemed to be adored locally and his home was amazing. A four-bedroomed villa, last in a row of four, right on the beach and very private. High walls and gates, but with an incredible view of the ocean from his balcony. Large well-kept grounds, with a huge swimming pool and a full-size, luxury, two-bedroom mobile home that Janet and the kids were using.

He had a small inflatable boat with a single outboard and a huge rib with twin engines that he'd taken them all out on. He'd taken James fishing and swimming in the sea. She'd never seen her son so motivated and happy since the abuse he'd suffered from his bloody stepfather, Janet's second, soon as possible to be, ex-husband. The beautiful beach near the house was lovely but they also went to the beach at Kololi, near the resort they had been staying at until Daniel had shown up. She was very glad he had. This trip had been wonderful.

Solomon came and went, carrying out work in the grounds and bringing in shopping and supplies. Ferried them, in air-conditioned luxury, to the beach and the townships where they took books and toys Daniel had shipped in for the wonderful, smiling, local children who swarmed like flies over them and were so grateful for the smallest treat or kindness.

And they went to an amazing place called Dentonbridge where the boats moored that went out to sea, or up the river inland. Got up close and personal with crocodiles at a sacred pool. Fed monkeys by hand. Watched the vultures feed at the Senegambia Hotel. She learned of the reason Gambia was encompassed by Senegal on all sides. The British had only wanted the river and claimed both banks of it to use as a slave trading port.

There was a delightful, chubby, middle-aged Gambian lady called Rosie who lived in and cooked and cleaned and fussed over Daniel incessantly, to his light-hearted annoyance. Daniel took Janet out to dinner every evening, while the old lady babysat. The passports were dealt with. Daniel had replaced her missing two hundred pounds in the grubby dalasi currency. But she'd barely touched it. He paid for everything when they went out. Day and night.

And the only time Daniel seemed to get remotely annoyed was when Janet said it was wrong for her to keep accepting his paying for everything after letting them stay there for free. So she stopped saying anything. Bit daft to really anyway. The money she had he'd given to her. And it did seem to piss him off. So as she was never likely to see paradise again, she had decided she wasn't going to let anything spoil it and quit fussing about it.

And now it was nearly time to go home. Her heart sank at the thought of it. Going back to the UK, constantly on the lookout for her horrible, controlling, lying and aggressive second husband, Barry, who had sexually abused her boy. And got away with it. Because after he had blurted it out to a teacher at school, that had been it. Social services had got involved. He wouldn't talk about it again. Got hysterical if you even tried to talk to him. He was bed-wetting and hopelessly unhappy. It was breaking Janet's heart. But he was so much better out here, away from home. That alone had made this trip worth doing.

And Barry was still controlling the situation. Janet had had to move out of her nice council house nearly a year ago, as he refused point blank to leave. She was now living in a two-bedroom flat in a horrible concrete cube with stairwells that stank of piss and were plastered with vile graffiti. Because he said he was innocent and going nowhere over her lying little bastard of a son. Denying everything and getting away with it and continuing to ruin their lives.

Because James was terrified of him and they just couldn't get him to talk about it. Barry kept breaking the hard-won, temporary restraining order against him. Hard-won because his ghastly lawyer had tried to get Barry access to James and Katie! It was only the obvious state of James, when it was suggested he might have to see Barry, that finally penetrated the thick skulls of social services and the family court. A temporary one while they, "reviewed the situation," and, "looked for the way forward."

Gormless university graduates, who hadn't ever been parents, focused earnestly on a cunning, controlling abuser's "rights." The useless, politically correct police officers and social workers failed her and James all the time, seemingly endlessly. Constrained by petty rules and an enthusiastic urge to address Barry's "parental rights" that her ex played on with great skill, aided by his heartless, greedy lawyer, who thought his legal aid income was far more important than the mental health of a young boy. And threw every obstacle in the path of any peace for her son.

Because, as he'd loftily sneered, when she'd broken protocol and gone to see him and begged him to agree to get Barry to back off. "His client was fighting not only for access to his stepchildren, who he loved, that she'd just walked out of his life with. He was refuting the allegations of a disturbed young boy to protect his reputation." He'd filed a complaint about her visit which she had been given a harsh warning over. She had been in and out of court and police stations ever since and come here on a payday loan to just get James somewhere he wasn't looking over his shoulder terrified, if only for a few days.

The endless grind of low paid, part-time cleaning jobs, topped up with complicated benefits. Endless form-filling and arguing with the housing and benefit offices to get them. No help whatsoever from her first husband, who she'd run away from, due to his violence when the kids were little. Having to find a way to pay back the payday loan that had paid for this trip. She felt on the verge of tears but decided to snap out of it and enjoy today and most of tomorrow.

She headed towards the villa from the mobile home, smiling as she saw the kids in the pool with Rosie watching them like a hawk. The little buggers would grow fins. And the trip had at least, after a bumpy start, followed by amazing luck, worked. James was just so relaxed and happy. She was dreading taking him home to more interviews implying he was a liar and a real fear that they might decide he was.

She thought about Daniel as she walked towards the house. He was incredibly fit. Lean, not an ounce of fat. He swam and ran and cycled and worked out. She'd watched him, very early one morning, when she couldn't sleep, down on the beach by the shoreline, doing what she guessed were martial arts exercises, graceful and supple. Then sitting, cross legged, stock still for what seemed like ages, just facing the ocean. He was a total enigma. And getting anything out of him was like pulling teeth! He had got her life story out of her, as she babbled on day and night and somehow, skilfully, managed to tell her bugger all!

He was vague to the point of being infuriating, and logical to the same degree. Like he really couldn't understand her saying he shouldn't pay for things. He never mentioned money, or seemed to worry about it, but seemed to have plenty. But he never seemed to work. There was no office. Nothing going on. It was all rather strange, but he'd made this trip amazing.

He was great with the children and they seemed really at ease with him. He had been the perfect gentleman, walking her to the mobile home when they got in from a night out. Never tried anything on. Never even tried to kiss her goodnight. But he seemed to like her very much. In fact, he rarely took his eyes from her when they were together, and loved being alone with her, which Solomon seemed to find hilarious, grinning broadly at Daniel every time Daniel made him clear off.

Rosie had told her the most about him. She had sat down with her near the pool and struck up a conversation.

"How long has he lived here Rosie?"

"Well for sure that boy don't live nowhere for long honey. But he showed up here and bought this place about three years ago."

"How did you end up working here Rosie?"

"Solomon, he's my sister's boy. He was working the beaches and met Daniel who just asks him right out of the blue if he can drive. Says he needs a driver. And damned if he don't just give him the keys to that damn great thing he showed up in. And a mobile phone, and wages in advance. Gets him to drop him here. And tells him he needs a housekeeper if he knows one. And he'll see him tomorrow. Solomon goes to walk back to Kololi and Daniel tells him he'd forgotten the damn car." She was chuckling away as she recalled it. "Let that boy just drive away in it and keep the damn thing ever since."

"And then you came here?"

"Yeah hunny, the very next day with Solomon. Daniel gives me a job. A room. All he asks is that if I want to go home, ask Solomon to stay here instead. Gives me wages in advance. And then he left two days later, never come back for six weeks. Our wages gets paid into Western Union and Solomon collects it while he's away. I had nothing to do all that time but he never worried me about it."

"And you've been here since?"

"For sure girl. I love working for him. He's quiet and strange and private. That man would go weeks without talking if I didn't get him to talk to me. And he sure don't like other people much. Had a couple come here a couple of times, wealthy, nice folks. And a couple of women once, sisters they were. One of them is the wife of a guy he knows in the UK. All lovely people. But that's all honey. The rest of the time he ain't here or he's here alone."

"No family? Ex-wife? Girlfriends?"

Rosie looked at her with a smile. "Now why would a pretty thing like you want to be knowing that honey?" Which made Janet blush as the bloody woman had intended.

Rosie continued, "Not that the damn boy ever told me about. He's a loner and that is that. But he's kind through and through. Paid all manner of medical bills and malaria jabs for our family and local people. Gives the schools computers and books. He's a good man Janet."

And then, with a loud cackle of laughter, how it was, "About damn time that boy got himself a good woman." Lecherously grinning at Janet as she said it. She'd blushed again. That woman knew she liked Daniel despite her thinking she'd kept her feelings well hidden.

But she couldn't shake the way she was starting to feel about him. But couldn't understand at all why a man like this, with looks and money and an amazing lifestyle, would want a broke, single mum of two, from South London. She knew she was attractive. But so were millions of other women. Without baggage. She wouldn't let her feelings go any further. She couldn't stand to get hurt again. And she wasn't going to make a fool of herself on, what was, after all, a holiday romance. If it was a romance at all. She smiled to herself.

With Daniel Cade it was hard to tell what anything was outside of the moment you were living in, because he never said anything to give you a clue. She hoped he might agree to at least keep in touch after she went home but she just couldn't get a handle on who he was deep down. He was a loner for sure but he was just so focused on her and everything about her. She smiled. Bloody man! But he'd been better to her for three days than any man had in years, after her past experiences. She strolled up the path, deep in thought.

She got to the villa and called out Daniel's name.

"On the balcony."

She went into the building, admiring as always the furnishings, the huge TV, the top of the range sound system and computer set up. The bar, although he seldom drank more than the odd beer. His place had everything. But nothing he didn't use. No ornaments or paintings, he kept no pets. It was Spartan yet efficient in its simplicity. She went up the marble effect spiral stairs, through his bedroom and out on to the balcony.

"Hi."

"Hi Jan," said Daniel. "Coffee?"

"Yes please. Thank you."

He got the coffee from the clearly expensive, high end machine, and brought it to the swing seat she'd sat down on and said, "I'm glad you're here. I wanted to talk to you in private."

"Oh right. Everything okay?"

"No, not really."

"What's wrong? Have the kids or me done something?"

"Not yet." Daniel looked at her intently with his strange, flecked eyes.

"Not yet?"

"I don't want you to go home tomorrow."

"Daniel!"

"I'd like you to stay for longer please."

"But I have to go home Daniel."

"Why?"

"I have airline tickets."

"That wasn't what I asked."

"But even if I could stay, I couldn't afford to change the flights. Or get new ones."

"You are obsessed with money."

"Because I don't have any."

"I have money."

"But it's your money."

"Would you like to stay?"

"Of course I would. It's been the best time of my life. And the children's."

"If I sort out the tickets, can you stay?"

"I can't keep taking your money Daniel."

"If you were my girlfriend it would be our money."

"But I'm not."

"I know."

"Well, then that's a bloody silly thing to say."

"Sorry."

"So why did you say it?"

"Because I wish you were, I want you to be." He'd rushed out the words as if he found them embarrassing.

Janet looked at him intently. He was looking really awkward. "You hardly know me Daniel."

"I know all I need to know."

Janet felt her frustrations with him fraying her nerves. And it burst out of her in a torrent.

"Well I don't know enough about you. You don't tell me anything outside of short vague answers. I've got two kids Daniel. And a shit track record of picking the wrong men. My son was abused. I can't put them through any more. And why would a man like you want a woman like me? Two kids and skint. A part time cleaner with a poxy council flat in a shit area of London? I don't understand you at all Daniel. If you just want a shag….well just bloody say so!"

"A shag?"

"I'm sorry Daniel. That was wrong of me."

"It was."

"I am sorry. It's just all some men want."

"Is that all you want?"

"Of course not!"

"It's not all I want."

"Well what do you want?"

"You."

"But I do have kids."

"I know. Two. I've met them."

She glared at him. "And problems. Big problems."

"I know."

"Money problems. Domestic and personal problems."

"I know."

"I am sorry for talking to you like that Daniel."

"It doesn't matter. Really."

"Thank you."

"I know about James, the abuse."

"How?"

"He told me."

"He never talks to anyone about it."

"He talked to me."

"Really? What did he say?"

"He told me what happened."

"Well tell me."

"You already know."

"He really talked to you?"

"I don't lie. Ever."

"Well he wouldn't talk to a child therapist."

"That was then."

"He does seem much happier in himself."

"He is."

Janet decided to leave that one for now. She'd try talking to her son later. This bloody man! But they had spent some hours together, just the two of them. Fishing. Either from a boat or off the beach.

"Okay we'll come back to that another time maybe?"

"Maybe."

"My kids do seem to like you very much."

"Well they would."

"Really? And why is that Daniel?"

"Because they know I like them."

"I really believe you do."

"Good."

"But what difference does it make? You live here. I live in the UK. I still know nothing about you."

"True."

"Well then."

"Well I suppose I have to start telling you a bit more."

"That would be nice."

"Then I'll make a start." Daniel looked at her and said, "I love you Janet. Very much. Come and walk on the beach with me and I'll tell you anything else you think you might need to know as you are so inquisitive."

He took her hand. She got up and walked with him towards the doors into the villa, then down the stairs and out, down the path to the beach. She was a bit too shocked to do anything else. She heard Rosie chuckling away in the kitchen, as she saw them hand in hand. That bloody woman! She didn't miss anything!

Chapter 15. Time to visit my brother.

Lee and Angel had taken the children out during the late afternoon and evening, and everything seemed a whole lot better. Later in the evening, after the nanny had taken the children off to go to bed, they sat talking. And, of course, Angel asked about the police visit.

"How did it go Lee?"

"Okay. We locked horns a bit but they didn't really push it. Just clanging on about the fact that those two bastards were skilfully killed by an intruder and the crime scene set up to look like they killed each other. And implying the rich guy paid for it, I guess."

"How ridiculous," said Angel.

Lee nodded. But he had never kept anything from her. "There is one person springs to mind Angel."

Angel looked at him. And immediately answered the question for him. "Daniel."

Lee looked at her. "Well, it crossed my mind straight away."

"But he's in Africa isn't he? At home in the Gambia."

"You never quite know where he is. I wondered if you fancied a holiday? We should go and see him after what happened to Mum and Dad. They loved him very much." Angel smiled. She loved Daniel too. She had an affinity and a mutual bond with him through the late John Tremayne. They had never discussed it. There had never been the need to. But she knew he was aware of it, through the strange senses and abilities that they both had that not many were possessed of.

They'd had some lovely times in the Gambia the two times they had been to Daniel's villa and Daniel had a room here at their house where he kept a few belongings for his rare visits to the UK. She knew that Lee liked him a lot, despite their very different lifestyles and opinions. As his only brother. Ann and John, Lee's recently murdered parents, had decided to foster children years ago - older, troubled kids were offered due to their age. After Lee went to the army college at sixteen, they wanted to do something worthwhile. And that was their choice.

And they had been Daniel Cade's foster parents from when he was a terribly troubled eleven-year-old nightmare of a boy right up until he vanished at seventeen. The next time they heard from him, he was in the Foreign Legion! John had always laughed when he told the story. Daniel had always appreciated their kindness, basically keeping him out of care homes and getting him on track.

He'd always kept in touch, visited from time to time, the last time being John's seventieth birthday.

And Angel knew one thing. If anybody in the world had killed Wesley and Mason and if anybody would have avenged John and Ann - that person was Daniel.

"We should go, it will do us good. We won't take the kids, they can go to my sister. And, I haven't said anything while you've been so distant, your Mum and Dad's solicitor has a letter for Daniel. We can take it with us."

They talked for a while longer. Angel could see Lee was troubled about the police visit. "Darling think carefully before you ask him about it. You know what he's like. He might not give you an answer. And you might not like it if he does."

Lee agreed. "I'll play it by ear after we get together. If he's even there."

It would put him in a very awkward situation if Daniel had done such a thing. Having to keep that information to himself would, he knew, make him complicit. His beautiful wife was a wise lady. He'd make his mind up after he met up with Daniel. But strangely enough, Lee not only actually wanted to just get away. With Angel.

He needed to see his strange but strong, closest thing he'd ever had to a brother. He liked him very much and shared his interest in martial arts, cycling and shooting, although to a far lesser degree. Daniel had helped him with his martial arts whenever he'd come home on leave. Despite being just fourteen to Lee's twenty, he was gifted at martial arts after just three years of training. And deadly, as a few local bullying types found out through Daniel's teenage years.

Lee admired, but didn't envy, his free and easy lifestyle as a young man, even if he didn't truly condone it. Daniel was different to anybody else he'd ever known. Totally self-sufficient. He lived by his own rules, even as a teenager. And Lee knew that a lot of what Daniel had done, both in the Foreign Legion and, even more so after he had left it after eight years, was very dangerous. And often illegal. He knew the vague details. Mercenary soldiering. Close personal protection. Daniel travelled the globe doing his own thing.

But Daniel had never tried to tap in to the family fortune. In fact he had turned it down flat, when John had offered him an allowance per month. Lee smiled as he recalled his Dad saying very little, when he'd asked how Daniel could afford homes in the Gambia and Turkey. Working as a bodyguard, mercenary soldiering and armed close protection to anyone who'd pay for it, surely couldn't be that well paid? Some vague answers, but no specifics. Ever. It was all part of the mystery that surrounded Daniel. Which was what set him apart. And made Lee look forward to seeing him.

He sat at his computer and fired off an email. If the bloody man wasn't crossing a desert or hacking through a jungle somewhere he'd get a prompt reply. He was very efficient. Lee thought to himself, "Yes. Very efficient. And not just at replying to emails."

Chapter 16. It ends now. Or else.

Barry Wallace woke up and found he couldn't breathe. And couldn't move. He panicked as consciousness came with a wave of terror. He snorted through his nose to get air as his brain recognised the fact his mouth was taped over, as it started to comprehend the fact his hands were taped as well as his feet. And he was trapped. On his own bed. It was dark. He was making weird sounds he could hear himself making. Trying to talk. Trying to understand what was happening to him. Then a bright light shone into his face from only a couple of feet away. His own desk lamp, moved to beside his bed.

By who? It was blinding him with its intensity. He made louder sounds. He writhed and struggled. Then, as his eyes adjusted to the light, he saw a figure come towards him. He felt the warmth in his crotch as he urinated out of sheer fear and tried to scream. But all he could hear was the muffled sounds of his own terror. A voice said, "Calm down Barry." He tried. And he focused on the figure.

In the murky light behind the lamp, he made out a figure in a balaclava with just slits for the eyes and mouth. The utter terror he felt made him lay dead still. Then the voice spoke again. "Will you calm down and listen? You don't want me here. I don't want to be here in your vile presence. Nod yes if you understand."

Barry found the presence of mind to nod frantically.

"Good. Now we can get on with this." The voice was foreign. Lilting oriental accent. Calm. Assured. Frightening.

"Every question I ask you, can be answered with a yes or no nod. Do you understand?"

Barry nodded yes. "Good. Depending on the answers I get you will be left here alive. Or dead. The choice will be yours. Do you understand that Barry?" Barry nodded, his eyes wide with shock and fear.

"If you lie to me at any time, you will be left here dead. I know the truth. Keep it in mind okay."

Barry nodded.

"I have a few things to say before we conclude our meeting. You are Barry Wallace?"

Nod. "Married to Janet Wallace?"

Nod. "Excellent. Be awful if I had the wrong address. Frightened a decent human being by mistake. And not a piece of shit like you. You do agree that would be awful Barry?" More nodding.

"Now Barry, here's the deal. You are making Janet's life a misery. You won't leave her or her children alone. You sexually abused her son and scared him into silence. You keep breaking restraining orders. You don't seem to want to stop this behaviour. Because you are a perverted control freak. That needs a yes nod by the way." Barry nodded frantically.

"The problem is, in these situations, cowards like you will say anything to survive and live. See Barry, that wouldn't be good enough. Because if I have to come back you won't survive and live. You do understand that?" Barry nodded.

"Excellent. Now here's the facts. Janet does not even know I am here and she possibly never will. Is that clear Barry?" Nod.

"Good. Tomorrow you are going to go to your solicitor. And you will instruct the very unpleasant Mr Parry to give Janet's solicitor your assurance that you will be moving a long way from the area. And you wish to apologise for your appalling behaviour. And you fully admit to the abuse of James. That you wish to confess that abuse to the police in the very unpleasant Mr Parry's presence. And agree that you will never knowingly be within one hundred miles of her and her family, or contact them ever again. You will permit an immediate divorce on the grounds of your disgusting behaviour. Do you understand?" Barry nodded.

The calm voice continued to speak. "And you will leave this area Barry. You have one week. And I will be watching. I will always have someone watching. Do you know how many people I have killed Barry?" Barry frantically nodded no.

"Neither do I Barry. One more scummy nonce will make no difference to me. I'm leaving now Barry. I am going to cut the tape on your hands and walk out of that door. Do as I have said and you will never see me again. If you go near, or try to contact Janet, or those children, ever again, you will. And I will be the last thing you will ever see. Understood?"

A final nod. Then his body went rigid as the figure approached. And a large knife appeared near his throat.

"I guess you're wondering how I know all this Barry?" He nodded, wide eyed, looking at the glinting knife in sheer terror.

"We hacked that charming little group of nonces you belong to. Every email. You told them what you did to James in your emails. We have clear ID on you all. Every email, including yours. Every attachment of an abused child you all sent to each other is with the police. You understand me Barry?"

Barry nodded again.

"Good. And if you get time to fire off another email to your vile friends, maybe warn them not to go ahead with any travel plans you have been discussing.

To Cambodia. For a kiddy-fiddling vacation. If any of them show up there it won't end well for them. Do you understand me Barry?"

He nodded again, sick with fear. This man knew everything. And he continued to talk quietly. "There was one thing you sent to them all, some article by a total prick saying being a child abuser should be classed as an illness and not be a criminal matter. And can be used as a legal defence. Do you recall that Barry? Nod yes. Because I read it you see." Barry nodded yes.

Still watching the knife, he never even saw the other hand as it crashed into his nose shattering it. "That's the first part of the cure you dirty bastard. Don't make me come back to give you a total cure Barry."

The knife sliced through the tape on his wrists, and the figure moved like a ghost to the door. And was gone.

Barry ripped the tape from his mouth and tore at the tape binding his feet with shaking hands. Blood streamed freely from his nose. He put his hands to it gasping with the pain, then tried to stand but couldn't. He collapsed back on the bed, horribly conscious of the wetness around his crotch. Lay there, soaked in blood and piss. In agony. Who the hell had that been? And where the hell had Janet ever gone in her life that anyone like that would even know her?

The rage came, along with the immediate thought of getting her back for this. Then the fear returned like an icy feeling in his heart and gut. And he knew he would do as he'd been told. He lay face down and sobbed into the blood soaked pillow. The shame of what he had done and the humiliation he was going to endure washed over him, along with the fact that he knew he had no choice. And the fact he totally deserved it. He knew he should never have abused James. Young boys stimulated him. His desires had increased over time. Other men with the same interests had built on that desire.

Justifying to each other what they did, in their own, private, dark world. Meeting Janet had given him the opportunity to indulge. He'd known James was vulnerable, easy to control. He'd wanted to do it, and he could. So he had. But he never, ever, again wanted to see that demonic bastard who'd just been here. Who'd known everything about him - all his contacts in a dark world he'd been ever more interested in being part of. Even his bloody solicitor's name. Except in his nightmares. He rang a taxi to take him to hospital. He changed his clothes and went outside, with a towel to his face, peering fearfully into the night, hoping that his terrifying visitor was really gone.

Chapter 17. A slim connection.

Fleming was staring intently at his computer. The data requesting and cross-referencing system, used by the Surrey force, had flagged up a request from County Regional, asking for any crimes that had been committed by suspects with possibly military backgrounds.

Fleming had hesitated, but then decided to submit the Wesley Mason killing. And that had taken him into the combined data pool where the main crime seemed to be a big multiple homicide. He'd heard about it, everyone had. It was a huge crime, involving two lots of drug gang members being wiped out at the scene of what appeared to be an exchange meet. Large cash sum and large amount of cocaine changing hands. Strange MO. A very military style one.

Snipers had apparently ambushed the two parties. Money gone. Drugs still there. Then he saw the date for the homicides. It was just after the Wesley Mason murders. He wrote down the mobile number of a Detective Inspector Marshall Bland. He added the number into his own mobile. He was going to give it a bit of thought.

He knew of the man. Bit of a hard case who didn't suffer fools. He didn't want to make the call and get told he was a tit. But then again these killings and his case had something in common. A military aspect, a ruthless efficiency. No loose ends and no leads to follow. If, and he knew it was a big if, these suspects, or at least one of them, that Bland was chasing down had a reason to off Wesley and Mason, known to circulate in the drugs world - well it just might lead somewhere. The hell with it. He called the number. Answerphone. He left a brief message then went off to look for Mick in the canteen chatting up the women who worked there, because that slob definitely wouldn't be at his desk.

He found Mick in the canteen as expected and asked him if he'd completed the check on any ex-military personnel with criminal records in the area. Amazingly, he actually had, so Fleming, much to Mick's annoyance, grabbed a tea and sat down with Mick.

He was surprised to see there were quite a few. But then he knew quite a few of the poor bastards were suffering post-traumatic stress disorders among other problems. But only two violent assaults were on record locally. One was still in jail. Fleming decided to go see the other one. They left to do just that but it came to nothing. The guy wasn't home. They found out from a neighbour he worked as a long distance lorry driver, and who for. A quick call put him in Poland at the time of the killings. Fleming left it at that as they had major caseloads besides this, and he had a court appearance coming up.

Then his cell phone rang, and it was Bland. Fleming explained the reason for his call and got a pleasant surprise when Bland was very appreciative. They arranged a meeting half way between their stations for the next day. Fleming was pleased. A bit of kudos from a senior inspector never went amiss on the promotion ladder.

And he sure as hell wasn't taking Mick with him. Mick could make you look bad just by being with him. Fleming's own Super didn't like Fleming which was why he'd lumbered him with Mick. Fleming sighed, and looked at his watch. He cursed under his breath. Time to head to court and get asked stupid questions by lawyers. Who he hated just as much as villains. And Mick.

Chapter 18. A new romance.

Daniel and Janet were walking along the beach, hand in hand. Daniel had had to talk more than he'd ever talked in his life. Janet had heard the most amazing story of a life. Of martial arts training in Japan. Of Foreign Legion service. Then working in close protection security. A life lived overseas with lots of travel. She had no idea she'd only heard a fraction of the real story. Daniel hadn't lied to her, he never would. But there would be a time for the rest of it. And that time wasn't now.

And when she'd asked him if there had been other women, and he'd said no, she'd questioned him over it and realised, when he got a little angry, that he meant it. He seemed to only get angry if you questioned him about spending money on you. Or if you hinted he was being untruthful.

"So if there's truly been no other women in your life. Why now? And why not? You're a good looking healthy guy. With needs surely?"

"I just haven't wanted anybody in my life." He looked awkward, stressed. But she believed him. And moved on quickly.

"Then why me? Why now?"

"Because I love you."

"But I've got two kids."

"I know. I've met them."

She tried another tack. "I'm not exactly a supermodel."

"A supermodel wouldn't be you."

"I mean there are far prettier girls out there. Without two kids and emotional baggage."

"You're very beautiful. But it wouldn't matter. I love you. Not anybody else"

"But I live in the UK."

"You're not in the UK now."

"But I have to go home."

"Actually. You don't."

"I can't live here for ever!"

"I know. I don't."

"But I have a flat in the UK."

"I have a place in the UK."

"What? So you don't live here all the time?"

"No. It's all humidity and mosquitoes in the summer."

"So you live in the UK a fair bit?"

"No. I hate it there."

"Well where DO you go when you're not here?"

"I've got a place in Turkey as well."

He'd said it so matter of fact as if it was nothing.

Janet glared at him but then burst out laughing. This bloody man was something else!

They ended up agreeing that she would try to stay longer . But she had to make some calls to the UK . Schools and other things she'd said. Daniel walked her back to the villa and left her at his desk in the lounge to do just that.

He was sitting watching the two children in the pool. James smiled over at him and Katie waved. It felt good. It felt right. He didn't question it. He knew exactly how he felt. About her and the children. Just struggled to make Janet understand. He was glad she'd agreed to stay. He knew she wanted to. Daniel couldn't comprehend why she would argue against doing something she wanted to do. He guessed she was just illogical. He smiled to himself. That was the only logical reason he could think of. But he knew she was the one for him. And he didn't ask questions about his own emotions or choices or how things came into his life. He never had since he was eleven years old. And never felt the need to since.

About half an hour later Janet appeared. She looked a bit confused.

"Are you okay Jan?" he asked her.

"I think so. Yeah, I'm fine. It's just, well, Barry."

"Who?"

"My ex."

"What about him?"

"Can we go for a walk again please?"

"Sure."

They walked away together towards the beach again. Janet said nothing until they were well away from the pool and the children. She was struggling to find the words to say. "You okay?" asked Daniel again.

"Yeah. Sorry yes. The schools are fine. It's still half term but I got hold of a secretary. They'll only miss two days after they go back"

"Good."

"I said I was going to make another week of it as I couldn't book the hotel for less. They were fine with it."

"Good."

"Well is another whole week okay with you?"

"No."

"Oh."

"Make it a month."

"Daniel!"

"Sorry."

"Well then I rang my solicitor. To see if we had a court date regarding extending the temporary restraining order."

"The what?"

"Sorry. A restraining order against my ex. It was up. He was trying to stop it being continued."

"Oh right."

"Well I just don't understand what's happened. She says Barry has admitted abusing James. Confessed to the police. Agreed to move right away from the area. He will be put on the sex offenders register and undergo therapy, in return for a suspended prison sentence. And he has submitted a letter through his solicitor agreeing to never come near us again. And agree to a no contact court order. In fact, he's moving away to Manchester where he has family. He says that he's deeply sorry and ashamed of what he's done. Said he will agree to an immediate divorce, on the grounds of his behaviour. My solicitor is applying through the courts for it immediately."

"Well that's good isn't it?"

"Oh my God! Good? Oh Daniel. It's finally over. It's been a nightmare!"

She started to sob uncontrollably and Daniel put his arms around her. As he held her he made a mental note to email Quan again. He owed him another one.

They talked for a while as Janet composed herself, then walked back to the pool. Daniel jumped in and started throwing a ball around with James and Katie, who were laughing and shrieking. Rosie watched the proceedings. And then looked at Janet with a knowing smile on her face as she saw the expression on the pretty young mum's face as she watched the children with Daniel.

Because Janet knew right then that that bloody man in the pool had something to do with what had happened in the UK, thousands of miles away. She knew right then that she would never ever know exactly what had happened. She knew right then that she would never know everything about Daniel Cade.

But, as she would recall, that was when she finally fell in love with him. And had no fears about it whatsoever. Because she suddenly knew beyond any doubt that she could trust him. And he loved her. Because he'd said so. And Daniel didn't lie. She walked to the pool and took off her sari style wrap round, revealing her now tanned body in the white bikini Daniel had bought her just because she said it was nice. And dived in.

She felt like she'd just dived in to the start of the rest of her life. Because this man, this place and feeling safe and secure and carefree was no more than a daydream when you bought a Lotto ticket on a South London council estate. This man, who had appeared in her life out of nowhere, seemed to think it was all quite normal. And had chosen her, and her children, to share it with, with absolutely no hesitation from the very second they had met. And somehow, from a long way away, removed a horror from all their lives. She swam up to Daniel and kissed him in front of the children. They all looked a bit taken aback. Except Rosie who announced she was going to go cook some lunch. "For de young master and his good lady." And wandered away, shoulders shaking, cackling with laughter.

Chapter 19. Bad to worse.

In the UK, in a room above a small casino in Croydon, three men were sitting around a large table, all holding drinks and all smoking cigars and cigarettes. It wasn't a place the law poked its nose into very often.

One Albanian, one Englishman and one Turk made up the group. Two with gold neck chains and expensive clothes and watches. And the Englishman, who was a rather shabby-looking individual. All involved in a heated debate over a totally unacceptable situation.

The Englishman was Mick Davidson and the other two were giving him a very hard time. Gambling debts, and an expensive drinking habit, had brought him to this sort of company and he was not enjoying the backlash of recent events.

He said, "Look. For the last time. All I have ever done is watch points and keep you posted, right? I agreed to keep an eye on things. And give you the heads up if the police were monitoring anything you were doing. And I've done that, right?"

The Turk snarled out, "I had a huge shipment seized in Harwich, Davidson."

"For fuck's sake Amir. I can keep an eye on the manor locally and a bit around London. I can't tell you what's going on with Harwich docks or bloody customs, can I?"

Amir Ferez looked at him. "Maybe not. But I also lost a lot of money and a lot of cocaine that same night in another deal. And I got hauled in."

"Yeah I know. Bland at SRSC is investigating it. Bloody massacre with eight dead. We got the heads up some of the dead were linked to you. I already called you with that Amir. I knew he would call you in. I warned you up front. Your bloody company does own that site Amir, he was bound to call you in."

"We have eight men dead, Davidson. Four were mine and Bogdan's, four from North London from a supplier who is asking me how the fuck such a thing has happened. Eighty grand's worth of cars burnt with the drivers still sat in them. And over a hundred grand missing. We all want answers as to why this has happened. Right?"

Mick was worried. Amir Ferez was a dangerous animal. Bogdan Gentian was worse. "But for fuck's sake. It wasn't the bloody police, was it? They were never onto your operation locally. And I told you that. Still aren't. They weren't even in the area Amir. That was your bloody warehouse. It's in the middle of nowhere, way off our manor. Bland is Surrey county, not Croydon local. You've been on his radar for over three years. He knows you operate businesses in Surrey. He's had you in over it as you owned the bloody site it happened on. But they were as shocked to find out what had happened there as you were. I swear the first they knew about it was when they got to that freight depot. It must have been a rival gang. And I can't tell you anything about other outfits, can I?"

Amir looked at Davidson with evil eyes. His money gone. His drugs in the hands of the police. The struggle to now supply Bogdan's network of dealers was weakening his Albanian partner's grip on his turf. And it had cost him an awful lot of money and a lot of reputation. He laid into Mick some more. "But you knew about our business Davidson. Maybe you told somebody else, yes? For money? A part of our money that went missing? You seem to need money."

Mick was getting angry now. "For fuck's sake. Who the hell would I know that would do a thing like that? And you never ever told me where or when about any of your meetings. And you know it. Maybe one of your own lot sold you out?"

The Albanian, the street dealer for Amir, Bogdan, smashed his fist onto the table, rocking the glasses. "You think we sell out our own operations you fool?"

"I don't think anything. I'm just pissed off at you people dragging me in here and giving me a hard time when you know damn well you never told me any details about the actual exchanges. You never have. And I never want you to. Okay?"

Mick was sounding braver than he was feeling. These were dangerous people. And now they were very pissed-off dangerous people.

Amir held up a hand. "Bogdan, we need to keep calm. Accusations will get us nowhere. We need information. Davidson, I agree with you. That you indeed did not know the locations and dates and times."

Mick breathed a sigh of relief. Amir continued. "However, we need your further assistance. The police investigation may well provide an answer to our questions. So from now on, you will not only be our eyes and ears within the police, to see we are not being watched or monitored. You will inform us if the police investigation throws up any names of the people who may have killed our men and stolen from us."

He looked around at the other man. "Are we agreed Bogdan. Mr Davidson continues to work on our behalf. And we rely on him to carry out this extra service."

Bogdan nodded. Then the fist-slamming Albanian said, "As long as you let me deal with him if he lets us down."

"Why of course," murmured Amir. "And this, I believe, is yours," he said, reaching into an inside pocket and pulling out a fat envelope. He slid it across the table from where Mick picked it up.

"You may leave us now Davidson. We have business to discuss that does not concern you. But serve us well. Bogdan seems most offended at your implying we betray our own. I would hate to have to let him demonstrate his anger."

Mick rose and headed for the door without a word. He felt a bit sick. And he desperately needed another drink.

He got to his local watering hole, bought a pint of lager and a large scotch and went to sit by himself near the log fire. He was seething inside. Okay, taking envelopes from scum like Amir. Hell yeah, that was wrong. But all he was doing was keeping an eye out. And justifying it by thinking that the bloody stuff got onto the streets anyway. no matter what the force did. It was pissing into the wind in the drugs war. Making millionaires out of arseholes like Amir and Bogdan in the process.

But it had been money for old rope. The heads up to Amir, once every couple of weeks that he and his cohorts weren't being flagged up for attention. And a nice problem-solving envelope as a result. And now this! All this aggravation because of some maniacs killing eight people at a time. And stealing the money from the barons. Well he was damn sure of one thing.

If he could get a handle on these bastards who'd rocked his world, he would pass it to Amir. To safeguard himself. And because they were still murderers who'd left a scene of crime like a war zone for police and paramedics to clear up after them. And they'd ballsed things up for him. So, if the Bravo Two Zero style, money-grabbing lunatics ended up with Amir and co on their ass it would serve them right. And it would be a right result if one of them offed that bastard Bogdan if it all kicked off. He finished his drinks and went to the bar to get the same again.

"Fourteen months to getting my pension and sodding off out of it", he thought to himself. And it couldn't pass quickly enough. In the meantime, he would have to start being a bit nicer to bloody Fleming because, twat that he was, that guy could dig. And Mick very much wanted to be there if he dug something up about these snipers.

Lee Tremayne had concluded a full catch-up on the business front. Alan was pleased to see him back in action and very pleased to hear he was taking a holiday. Lee said he was going to see Daniel in the Gambia to catch up with him after the death of his parents and see how he was. Alan knew a little about Daniel but had never actually met him. Most of what he knew, he had heard from Lee's father, John, who was very proud of how the lad had turned out after fostering him and had followed his Foreign Legion service avidly. He had had a little concern about his rather freelance lifestyle after he left the Legion but no real negatives. And he knew Lee and Daniel had been close in their younger days, and had met up a few times since over the years. He told Lee to have a great time. And they agreed to keep in touch.

Chapter 20. Making connections.

Fleming was sitting with Marshall Bland in a large restaurant which formed part of the Imperial Hotel in Carshalton, where they had arranged to meet. The guy looked exhausted and Fleming sympathised. The matter of the violent shoot-out had been prominently featured in the press and had even been brought up in parliament by the indignant windbag MP for the local area. It was the apparent paramilitary aspect, emphasised by the press to make headlines, that was causing the big fallout. The usual pressure being applied to the police top brass to get it dealt with. And that pressure being forced down onto the officers on the ground.

Fleming had drawn unwanted attention from the press too over Wesley and Mason turning up dead so soon after the court case fiasco, but had managed to keep it pitched as a mutual homicide committed by two known criminals with a history of violence. And thankfully, no smart arse journo had come up with any other bright ideas or theories. So far.

Marsh had explained the situation to Fleming.

"Amir Ferez suffered two incidents. One seizure by the police after a solid tip off at Harwich docks, of a very large consignment of heroin. Street value of well in excess of a million pounds. Can't tie it to the bastard, but the consignment was definitely for him." Fleming nodded. Marsh looked at the thick file and continued.

"Then the very same night, what was also known to be Ferez purchasing a large amount of cocaine from another source that was UK based, turned into a shoot-out. Four men known to have worked for Ferez were among the eight dead at the site. It's a pretty remote, disused commercial property owned by one of Amir's front companies. The other four, assumed to have been delivering the cocaine, were from the north London area. All known players in the drug scene. All armed. We wheeled Ferez in over the property connection. But his slimy lawyer just blew us off saying that it was hardly his client's fault if people were trespassing on a vacant property in a remote area. Implied it was actually more ours, the twat. Ferez, of course, had a cast iron alibi."

He took another mouthful of coffee, then said, "Some of the killings were actually committed by the gangs, on each other. Triggered by the actions of the, as yet, unknown third parties who merely provoked, then controlled the event as it unfolded. And made sure there were no survivors. My forensic guy, he's a good one too, Colin - he came up with the military style angle. And I have to agree it makes sense. It still could be drug gang related of course. There is plenty of money in the drug trade to fund the hire of ex-military personnel. The elephant in the front room, of course, is the failure to take the drugs themselves from the scene. It's a real dead end to investigate. But, the MO. The weapons. They must have had support. The vehicle, everything the two shooters needed, was safely taken away after the event. And where to look? Maybe they are not resident in the UK. Probably no criminal records."

Fleming nodded. And said, "The other big question must be. If they're not involved in the drug-running game, how the hell did they know where this big delivery, and the exchange, was taking place?"

Marsh nodded wearily. "Got it in one. It could, of course, be an informer, who works for one of the gangs. Selling information for a far bigger cut of money than he'd get just being a shitty criminal."

He sipped his coffee again and continued, "Or worse. It would have to be us, one of our own. Well in to major long term investigations. Which leaves muggins the option of pissing off the world interrogating every ex special services soldier who might have the hump. Or pissing off the police force by investigating every officer who's undercover, or intelligence gathering, on a major drug ring. Which would give them the hump. What a bloody disaster that could turn out to be. Even if, and you wouldn't get it, we had the manpower and budget to do it"

Fleming nodded again. "And in reality you could be looking for two men with the required skills, anywhere in the world. They don't even have to be British ex-military."

Marsh looked at him and opened his notebook, scribbling something down. "That is a very good point, and one I've missed. We need to cross-reference this with at least all the European police forces. Ex special forces from European armies with criminal records. And any similar crime scenes. If they're roaming around bloody Europe as well they might have done it before. Thank you."

"Well sometimes it just helps to get a new input from somebody outside the team" said Fleming, inwardly pleased.

"Yeah it often does," agreed Marshall. "Another, more obvious angle of course, is simply that Amir Ferez is being targeted. If the two events are linked. But if they are, why not just give the police both deals? Why the seizure at the docks by the police, legal and proper, and then a violent multiple homicide, illegal and aggravating me?"

"Coincidence?" asked Fleming.

"I don't like those," growled Marshall.

Fleming laughed. "Neither do I. And I have a coincidence with the case that I think has, admittedly vague, similarities to yours. So on that note, maybe you'd take a quick look at this file? I'll use the bog and order us more coffee while you do if you'd like?"

Marsh agreed and took the file. Fleming left the table.

When he returned and sat down, Marsh was still reading. The waitress brought fresh coffee. They both admired her black nylon clad, shapely legs as she walked away. Then Marshall resumed reading the file.

After a couple of minutes he closed it and said ,"I see where you've made the connection, Colin. Too neat. And too efficient. Those men died instantly, from very skilfully inflicted injuries. No forensic, bar the obvious, that the perpetrator wanted us to see. No loose ends. And all it needed was a couple of lazy coppers to take the first impression of the scene as gospel, and it would have buried itself. And yeah, the date, two days before my bloody war zone. The grey area is that those two scumbags were lowlife users. Committed crimes to get a fix. Area wise they may well buy from Amir, or rather, his scummy network of dealers run by that thug Bogdan Gentian. What we need is the angle. Of what interest these guys might have been, to the guys who whacked the drug exchange, if there is one. Any thoughts Colin?"

Colin had one immediate thought. That lazy bastard Mick had wanted to do just that, bury it as a closed case. But he didn't voice it. Instead he said, "Well I interviewed Lee Tremayne yesterday. Obvious huge motive. He was, as expected, very indignant about it. And to be honest, yes, he is ex-military. But both he and his father served in the same armoured regiment. Tank boys, cavalry. So I truly don't think he knows anybody, through his military career, that he could pay to off those two, although he has one hell of a motive after the court case fiasco. And about a billion quid to buy it with. There was one thing he hesitated on. When I asked him if he knew anybody who might avenge his parents death, he dithered a bit. I asked him why point blank. He explained it away saying he was thinking it over. Maybe he was, Marsh. But I think something or someone came into his mind. I never mentioned the crime you're investigating so he doesn't know of any possible connection. The only reason I called you was the date and the MO."

"Yeah I see where you're coming from. But he's a respectable guy. It would be a hell of a leap of faith to think he'd know where to hire a hit man. Or actually do it if he did. He'd have a hell of a lot to lose if it was ever discovered. But the wounds being identical to his parents and the sheer efficiency of the killings leave a lot to answer. I think we're in the same boat Colin. Only I've got six more bodies than you. I suggest we just keep each other posted. If you get a break and it is in any way linked to my case, well, it could be the key to it and vice versa."

Colin agreed and they made a bit of small talk while they finished the coffee. Marsh parted in the car park with, "I'll be in touch and let you know if the European angle throws up anything, Colin."

"I'll keep you posted if we turn up any decent leads, Marsh. Nice to talk to you. Good luck."

They got into their respective vehicles and went off to resume their enquiries.

Chapter 21. Mysterious healing.

As Lee Tremayne and Angel were preparing for their holiday back in the UK, Janet Wallace was walking along the beach with her son James. She had to know how he was feeling now. And why he had apparently talked to Daniel.

She started with, "You like Daniel, don't you?"

He looked up at her, "So do you."

"Great! Don't say he's turning into him already," thought Janet.

"He told me you talked to him about, you know, what Barry did?"

"He sexually abused me Mum. Yes. I talked to Daniel."

"But you wouldn't talk to anyone, even me, at home."

"I couldn't."

"Why?"

"Barry said people he knew would hurt you and Katie if I got him in trouble."

Janet started to feel tears welling up, but she kept her composure.

"You don't think that now then?"

"No Mum."

"Would you be a good boy and tell me why?"

"Well because Daniel said so. He said if I wanted to talk about what happened he would listen. Because the same thing happened to him when he was a boy. So I knew he would understand right?"

"So you'd told him about it already then?"

"No Mum," James said, a little impatiently. "He already knew. He just does you see. He said if I wanted to talk to him I could. But it was up to me. And I really did want to. So I did, right."

"Yes darling. Sorry. Go on."

"Well I told him about it. And he listened. And we talked a lot. Out on the boat. And he did understand. About being scared of Barry. And wetting the bed and stuff like that. He said you do that if you're scared. And how it was important to believe it wasn't my fault it happened. Or yours Mum. Because evil people are very clever at hiding how bad they are from everyone else. And that sometimes bad people do bad things to good people. If they get the chance. And if they can. And that's just how life goes sometimes."

"Right. And you agreed with that?"

"Well of course Mum. It's true. Barry had the chance so he did it. And then Daniel asked me if I wanted him to help me feel better about it?"

"And you said yes?"

"Of course I did."

"So what happened James?"

"Well. First he sat down facing me. And he put a black towel on the seat between us. And held his hands facing up just above it. And he asked me to really concentrate on his hands. And tell me when I could see like light connecting his fingertips from one hand to the other."

"And could you?"

"Not at first. But he said to focus my eyes and really concentrate on them. To just take my time. And then I could. It was really strange. But there was a light between each of his fingertips on one hand, connecting to the opposite one. And as he moved his fingers the lights moved with them."

"How strange. Then what happened darling?" Janet was talking very quietly, as she watched him concentrating on his thoughts.

"Then I sat with my back to him on the seat in the boat. And he sat behind me and put his hands on my head very gently, on each side. Told me to close my eyes and think of nothing. His hands seem to get warm and he sounded like he was like getting further away. His voice seemed far away. But I could hear him. Every word."

"Then what happened next?" Janet was intrigued and, had to admit it, a little worried at what she was hearing. Despite her son being so much happier.

"Well everything that had happened to me rushed by in front of my eyes. Like a film on fast forward. It was horrible. Daniel could see it too. He told me to stay calm and not be frightened. He was with me on my journey and would stay with me."

"And were you frightened?"

"A bit. But he told me we had to get those thoughts where we could see them. And I would be okay."

"What happened next?"

"The thoughts suddenly turned into scary toys. All looking at me."

"Scary toys?"

"Yeah. They were horrible and I knew they hated me. So I hated seeing them. I wanted to run away. But I could hear Daniel saying I had to go towards them."

"Did you do it?"

"Oh yeah. I knew Daniel was with me. They were really nasty, Mum. Evil eyes. Some of them even had dicks."

Janet visibly winced, "Then what?"

"He said I had to keep concentrating. No matter how horrible they were, I had to face them. And there was a big box there. Like a pirate's chest. And I had to pick all those horrible toys up and put them in it. No matter how much I was scared of them. Then shut the lid and lock it with the big key. And throw the key away so they could never ever get out again. So I did."

"And that was it?"

"Oh no Mum. He said I had to finish the job."

"So then what happened?"

"Well there was a muddy path up a steep hill. I could see it in front of me. And it was very windy and spitting with rain. And dark. Then he told me I had get up to the top. Struggle up the path on that hill with the box. I really struggled Mum. Because it was very steep and slippery. And the box was very heavy. And I was so scared. But I had to get to the top. Had to keep going no matter what."

"Did you do it?"

"Yeah. It was so hard to do Mum. And then at the top it was a cliff. And if I looked down I could see the sea. Huge waves pounding against the rocks. The wind howling. I was looking down into the sea. I could hear it. I could see it swirling around. It felt really strange and real Mum. I heard Daniel talking to me. Saying not to be scared. He said to remember that if I made one mistake near the edge I would fall. I had to get it right. Not back away. Face the fear of standing right on the edge if I wanted to get rid of my problems."

"And then what? Janet looked at her boy intently. He believed he'd truly been there.

"He told me to hurl the box in to the sea. Watch it fall. Hear the evil toys scream as they felt themselves falling and then vanish for ever into the waves. With all those horrible thoughts as evil toys destroyed. So I did."

"And you felt better after you did it?"

"Oh yeah Mum. They were gone forever. Then Daniel did something really strange."

Janet visibly stiffened. Really strange? How much more strange could this get? "What was that darling?"

"Well the boats got a radio on it to call other boats right?"

"I guess it would have."

"Well, on that radio there's a big red button to switch it on and off. And Daniel pointed to it and said I had to just imagine one more thing. That button was a special button right?"

Janet murmured, "Yes, special darling. Go on."

"Well he said if I pressed it Barry would never bother me again. Or hurt you and Katie. But it had to be my choice to make it happen. And I had to take control of my life again, now the bad thoughts were gone in the sea. But it was up to me alone. Nobody else could press it. Except me. And I had to believe that if I pressed it that Barry would be gone. But I had to truly believe in that button."

"What did you do?"

"I pressed it. And then Daniel was just there again in the boat with me. And Daniel said that was it. We would never be bothered by Barry again. Then we got on with fishing Mum. I really like fishing now."

Janet looked at him intently. "That all happened the third day we were here at Daniel's, didn't it?"

"I think so. I can't really remember. Did Daniel tell you then? He said he wouldn't tell anyone about the toys and the cliff. Ever."

Janet looked at him again. "No darling he didn't, truly he didn't. He just said you two talked. Nothing else."

"Well how do you know when it was, then?"

Janet hugged him to her and this time she couldn't stop the tears. "Because that night was the first night you never wet the bed, wasn't it? And you don't any more do you?"

"I suppose so. It's nice not to do that Mum. I felt silly. I never meant to do it."

"I know darling," Janet replied. "It's over now. I'm very proud of you for climbing that hill to the cliff and then pressing that button."

"Barry is gone now isn't he?"

"Yes darling. I heard from my solicitor. The police have arrested him and he has moved a long way away. That's why I asked you about what happened. Because you got rid of him for us all."

"Good. I knew he was gone anyway. I just did. Can we go back to the pool now Mum?"

"Of course we can. Thank you for telling me James."

"That's okay."

He darted away towards the villa while Janet strolled slowly getting her thoughts together. So Daniel told James he was abused as a child? Well if he did then he was. Because that bloody man never lies. And he always seemed to know exactly what to do about, well, bloody everything apparently! Janet smiled. The two previous men in her life had one thing in common. They were wicked and fucking useless!

She had a bigger smile on her face as she opened the gate into the villa grounds and headed up towards the villa and the balcony. And Daniel. She had a lot to find out about him. And with little more than a few words at a time it wasn't going to be a short job. But she hoped it took the rest of her life.

Chapter 22. Passing information.

Lee had had a reply from Daniel. Said he was looking forward to seeing them and would be there at the airport to meet them. And that he had visitors right now but it wasn't a problem. He'd arranged the villa next door for them, with the British couple who owned it. Lee recalled that Daniel looked after it for them the long periods they were away, using the staff that looked after his. Visitors? That was a rarity. Daniel lived like a bloody hermit most of the time. He mentioned it to Angel, who light-heartedly said perhaps he'd got himself a lady. Lee laughed and said he doubted that very much. He didn't know he was soon going to be proved very wrong indeed.

And there was a strange request about a property near Hastings in Sussex that apparently Tremayne's managed for him. Daniel wanted it empty. Lee rang Alan and asked him about it. Alan knew about it. Said it was something John had set up for Daniel, years before when he was his legal guardian. Lee told him what was required by Daniel. Alan said leave it to him. More mystery.

They'd made arrangements to leave the children with Angel's sister Carla. They loved going there to the seaside town of Rye, and playing with their three cousins.

The school was still on half term and Carla was happy to have them. She understood the difficult times for the family, since the dreadful loss of parents and grandparents and in-laws. They were good to go. Lee had arranged the use of the private jet he co-leased with two other companies. He emailed Daniel the arrival time, and let him know that the property request was being dealt with, and that was about it. They went to bed. The car would run them to Gatwick at seven in the morning.

Lee was looking forward to it very much. So was Angel. The loss of his parents still hurt so much. But it was getting better all the time. And Daniel had a way of sorting things out. It was strange, but Lee always felt better after being around him. He was a strange man and he'd been very different as a young boy. He had a way of making things simple that was very refreshing, in the complicated, modern world Lee lived and worked in. Although it seemed stupid that was the only way Lee could describe it. Lee put his arms around Angel and fell asleep.

Back at Croydon Police Station, Fleming was in early and very surprised to see

Mick there as well. Although he looked like shit. And equally surprised when Mick asked him if he'd thought any more about Lee Tremayne after his meeting with Marshall Bland. "I thought you were anti the Tremayne line of enquiry," said Fleming.

Mick replied, "Well I was. But to be honest guv I have been a bit of an arse. It's wrong to say Mason and Wesley shouldn't be investigated. And I'm sorry about the attitude."

"Well I appreciate your honesty Mick. I've not been here that long. But a lot of people say you were one hell of a copper not so long ago."

"I was, but I don't know. Divorce I don't want creeping nearer, sheer battle fatigue. Wishing time away now my pension's close. I guess it was getting to me more than I knew."

"Yeah, they're tough times sometimes Mick. I'm divorced. This bloody job wrecks a lot of marriages."

"Well, I don't want to finish my time with a shit reputation guv. And I was there at that interview. I know I sat there like a twat and didn't back you up. But I saw Tremayne's reaction to the question about if he knew anyone who might have done those scrotes. And I have a gut feeling something was bothering him."

Fleming said, "Well Bland saw the possible, very slim, military-style link between his multiple homicide and those two murders. He's checking out Europe for similar cases. But he asked for us to let him know if we get any further with this to keep him posted. And those two were users. The dead are all in the dealing side, so there is a connection of sorts. So maybe you'd like to do a bit more digging? I would appreciate it. I'm snowed under with the court case on the Marden estate rapes. It's bloody never-ending."

Mick said, "Maybe I could try Tremayne again? He didn't like you much. But I could give it the 'sorry to bother you again, but I have my orders' routine. See if he lets anything slip maybe?"

"Mick. Do it with my blessing. It's a shot in the dark. Bit like the ones those snipers took."

Mick actually laughed. A bit shocked that Fleming even had a sense of humour.

"Yes guv. But probably not as accurate. I'll get an interview set up and call you later."

He left the office with a grim smile Fleming couldn't see. He wanted to see Tremayne again anyway. But no matter what the man said he was going to throw his name in to Amir. He needed to show that bastard that he was at least doing something. And he needed the money badly. That thug of a loan shark was getting really heavy. Threatening all sorts.

That silver spoon business magnate Tremayne could look after himself. He'd have to if those vicious shits were after him. But, as Mick thought to himself, "better they were after Tremayne than me." He got to his desk and picked up the phone. Five minutes later he slammed the phone down with a loud, "bollocks' that made other officers look across momentarily then just resume what they were doing. It was just Mick kicking off, they were used to it. Mick went out into the car park and lit a fag, then took a cheap, pay as you go mobile from his inside jacket pocket and called a saved number. It was answered. Mick said, "Tonight. Eight pm. Usual place." And ended the call.

Tremayne had pissed off on holiday. Great! Well he'd throw his name in the hat anyway. He headed for the canteen.

Chapter 23. A new beginning.

Janet and Daniel were out for the evening as usual. Janet really thought a girl could get used to this, out every night with a baby sitter on tap. And with a man she loved being with for once. They were at a lovely restaurant called Scalas, and had enjoyed the steaks they were famous for. And amazingly, Daniel was a bit more talkative. He seemed far more relaxed now, since Janet had told him how she felt about him.

She said, "I talked to James, Daniel. I am so very grateful to you for making him so much better. It's wonderful. But what he told me was very strange. He's my son. I think I should know what you did."

Daniel replied, "Of course you should." And then picked up his wine glass.

Janet looked daggers at him, her green eyes looking intently into his. "At this point," she said quietly, "you now carry on and tell me Daniel Cade. Don't keep making me pry it out of you one sentence at a time, you aggravating sod."

"Sorry." He smiled at her. "I don't mean to annoy you."

"Then don't. Now tell me. You talk, I listen. It's called conversation, Cade."

"I guess. I just haven't done it very much."

"It shows, we'll get there. Now please, tell me."

He looked at her with a serious expression on his face.

"Okay, I will try to explain it but it's difficult. I am very spiritual. Not religious, I detest religion. I am guided by my beliefs and spiritual guides. I can be healed by a spiritual healer because I am receptive to it through my own belief. I can, to a degree, heal others if they are receptive. It's a huge and complicated subject Jan."

"Just tell me in regard to James for now Daniel. I have to know."

"Well he was receptive. He is young. With a wonderful, open and honest mind. He dearly wanted to feel better. So he was easy to work with."

"He said you already knew he'd been abused? Surely you can't read minds Daniel?"

Daniel looked at her and smiled. "Of course not."

"Well I hadn't told you. How did you know?"

"You'd told me about your husband bothering you. So I got his computer hacked. Read his emails. And believe me you are well out of there. He was involved with a paedophile network. He'd told them all about James."

"Oh Daniel. I thought it was maybe just a one-off. A disgusting sudden urge."

"Might have started like that. But his urges were escalating. He was discussing going to Cambodia with others in the group. It's a popular destination. Cheap ten year olds. Little chance of getting caught."

"Oh, that's awful. Have you reported them?"

"Of course. They won't be going. If they do- they won't get back."

He smiled at her again. "Forget him Jan. Or try to. It's over."

"Okay. But thank you Daniel, so much. But you with James. What was the light between the fingers he saw? Was there any? It doesn't seem possible, Daniel."

He smiled. "There was light to him. Not a magic beam. It was basically hypnosis if you like. As he focused hard, so hard, the light appeared in his imagination, his mind was empty of any distractions."

"You put your hands on his head. He said they got warm?"

"Healers hands do get warm. They are channelling a form of energy in a way. It's well documented. Hospitals allow them in now. You can heal minds, as well as bodies. Which was all I did. James did it. I just took him on the journey he needed to make."

"Was it the journey you took Daniel," she asked softly.

He looked rather bleak as he replied, "Yes Janet. But I made the journey alone." She gazed softly at him. "Thank you. That's enough for one evening. I didn't want to upset you."

"You haven't. It was a long time ago Jan. Anyway, as you say, enough for one evening. I need to talk to you about other things."

"Oh wow. You're going to talk to me without being prompted?"

He laughed. "I suppose I had that coming. Yes Jan, I am." He leaned over and kissed her.

"I have visitors coming Janet, I can't say no. Lee and Angelica. Lee is the only son of my foster parents, John and Ann. My brother."

"Oh right. Well it's not a problem, is it?"

"No, not really. I would have liked more time with just you though."

"I hope they like me."

"They will. They are both very nice people."

"What do they do? In the UK?"

"Angel, nothing now. She worked for Lee's father. Met Lee when he joined the firm after the army. They got married, had two kids. She doesn't work any more."

"He's got a good job then?"

"Well yeah, he owns the company. Took over after Dad retired. He's actually a billionaire now, I guess. Or best part of it."

"A billionaire!" Janet said that a little loud and a couple of people looked round. "Sorry," she whispered.

"That's okay." He smiled at her. "John Tremayne, my foster father, owned a huge company. Built from nothing. Offices in Canary Wharf and all over the world. That company has a huge stock market value. And it's Lee's now."

"But don't you get involved in it?"

"Me? No, wouldn't dream of it. John did enough for me as a child. I do my own thing. Lee is his only biological son. Only child. Very like John, a lovely man. And the same head for business. You'll like them. I promise."

"Well it will be good they will be here with you. After I go home."

Daniel said, "Do you really want to go home?"

She answered honestly, "Of course not."

"Then we need to talk."

"No, you do." Janet smiled at him. "I can play that game too."

He held her hands in his. "I want you to stay with me Jan, live here. Then move on to Turkey in May through to October."

"What about the children's schooling?"

"There are English teachers here. And in Turkey."

"Private tuition?"

"Yes."

"But isn't it expensive?"

"A bit probably. We will want the best."

"Daniel. This is a massive commitment you're making."

"So are you."

"I can't argue with that."

"Makes a change."

She laughed. "Can you get the bill please? I want to go back to the villa."

"It's still early."

"I know."

"I thought we were talking about the future?"

"Tomorrow."

He paid the bill and phoned Solomon to come and get them. The young Gambian sauntered through the door with a huge grin across his face after a few minutes. And they left.

They arrived at the villa after a ten minute drive, and said goodnight to Solomon.

Daniel started the walk down the path, towards the mobile home. But Janet stopped him.

"Let's go in to the villa."

"You want a nightcap?"

"No. It's just that I can't go to the mobile home tonight."

"Why?"

"Because Rosie is sleeping in my room there tonight."

"Why?"

"Because I asked her to, Daniel Cade. Tonight, I am going to be the one who knows all the answers. What to do next in the situation. And decide what's going to happen next."

"Oh."

"Yes. Oh. Now be the perfect gentleman you always are. And take me to bed." Her green eyes sparkled under the African moon as she looked up at him and pulled him down to kiss her.

They walked up to the villa door. She smiled as he unlocked the door. Daniel Cade was a man of few words. But right now, he wasn't saying anything at all. Because he wasn't in control of the situation. And the last time that had happened was not long before he was eleven years old. And although he should be feeling good about the situation, he wasn't.

Chapter 24. All there is to tell you.

Back in the dingy room above the pub, Mick Davidson was talking to Amir. The drug baron had just one thuggish minder with him who sat across the other side of the room, his personal bodyguard and driver, Hassan.

"What have you got for me?" asked Amir.

"All there is so far," replied Mick, handing him a bit of paper. Amir read it carefully. It explained the killing of Tremayne's parents and the failure to prosecute. And the deaths of Wesley and Mason. The military style similarities in the two lots of murders. And the very slim link between those two deaths, and the carnage at the freight yard exchange. As in drug dealers and drug users. And the MO. It was slim but all they had to work on.

Amir considered the information in silence, then said, "Those two had dealt with one of Bogdan's street dealers. I checked after you called."

"Well there aren't many others in that area Amir, are there?"

"That is true. But, as you say, a slim connection."

"I guess."

"But this is definitely all there is?"

"Yes."

"Well it is not much to go on."

"I know. But it's all the police have. I was asked to re-interview him today. But Tremayne is going on holiday, his secretary said, to the Gambia. Tomorrow."

"Shit. How long for?"

"I don't know."

"I see. Well perhaps a couple of my men could do with a holiday, yes? May be better. He will have less security out there."

"Bloody hell Amir. That's a bit strong, isn't it?"

"Strong! I have lost a small fortune, Davidson. And men. And most importantly, my supplies. And if this man knows anything I want to know what it is. That Wesley and Mason were customers of Bogdan's. Your superior thinks there is a link. I will find out for sure. One way or the other. Easier than the police can, I assure you."

"Up to you Amir. He probably knows bugger all about your losses. The chances are he didn't even have those two lowlifes whacked. And if he did - well, the chances of them being involved with whoever hit your meet are remote as well. But you asked for all the police get. Well now you've got it."

"I see. Then if that is all there is then we shall have to use what we have, yes?"

"You do what you like Amir. Just tell that Bogdan to back off hassling me. I've kept my part of the deal. Like I always bloody have."

"You worry too much Michael. Bogdan is angry, we are all angry. You have done well."

He passed Mick an envelope and nodded to Hassan. And they left the room.

Mick left five minutes later with a bad feeling about what he had just done. And went off to pay the man who had made it necessary for him do it.

Chapter 25. Seduction and revenge.

Amir made a call. To Irena, his financial adviser and personal assistant, and now his life partner. A beautiful girl who he had met in one of his two night clubs in Croydon one evening. She was simply stunning. Long, jet black hair and sharp features formed a beautiful face. Very slim, but with a busty, very curvaceous figure. She looked like an Arabian princess. She told him she was Turkish, but resident in the UK, working in the city, in high finance and investment. Specialising in deals involving Turkey and Russia, which she was fluent in the languages of, as well as English. He loved switching between Turkish and English with her in conversation.

Amir was both flattered and confused when she had struck up that first conversation with him. Yes, he had money, and was on the ascent in the drug world. Had moved to Britain from Turkey as his power and influence escalated. Became a big importer. Set up a deal with Bogdan to distribute it. The money flowed in. He had acquired two night clubs and a small, discreet casino which gave him a business front and a veneer of respectability. His drug money then flowed through them and appeared cleansed, as it emerged from the other side.

But he was a short, balding, fat, middle-aged man, who was a criminal. And he knew it. And in time she knew it. Because he told her as they seemed to be getting closer by the day. He had to. He was crazy about her. Didn't want it all to go wrong if she couldn't live with the real him. But the girl seemed to like him very much. He was flattered when she wanted to see him again after a first date and seemingly as often as he was free to do so, even after he told her about his criminal activities.

He was even more flattered when she had slept with him. He had never touched such loveliness. Well, unless he'd paid for it. Or threatened some cowed, frightened, trafficked woman of Bogdan's. That was just over six months ago.

She'd quit working in the city of London now. Since they had been in a relationship, she had, after pitching the idea to Amir, who jumped at it, come to work for him. She knew what he did. She had no issues with it. She had said she wanted to be with him and her attitude was simply that if fools were willing to pay for drugs, then it was nothing more than a commodity. And commodities were what she dealt in.

She knew what salary she commanded in the city. She was a natural financial talent, with a top degree in accountancy and she loved him and wanted to use her skills to help him. And they could be together more. Live together. He made her feel safe unlike being alone in London did. Amir had accepted her one and only demand. That he matched that city salary and that she was paid in full, every month, and had her own financial independence.

He didn't mind. Cleaning money cost him big time anyway. Skilled bent accountants weren't cheap. She had family that relied on her back in Turkey as her father had been ill and wheelchair bound, and unable to provide for them, and had subsequently died about a year ago. She had, very bluntly, told him that she wasn't going to be put in a situation where she was dependent on him, or anybody else and, given his line of business, well, he might not be around one day.

He had agreed and their relationship remained unchanged since he had. Once she worked for him, Amir's personal fortune increased. She knew everything about offshore investment accounts and tax havens and how to move and clean and invest his dirty money.

And everything about how to please a man when she wasn't working. She was worth every penny. And Amir loved her. He really did. He never knew the one thing Irena did keep secret from him. She hated him. More than anyone else in the world. And was bent on destroying him. Getting deep into his life was the only way to do it and, as much as it repulsed her, that was what she had done.

He spoke to Irena briefly and asked her to book two flights to the Gambia. For two men. And gave her the names. She agreed she would. And told him she had bought some very nice new underwear, and to get home soon. He was grinning widely, for possibly the first time since he'd suffered his recent losses, as he put his phone back in his pocket.

Irena made the bookings. For three days' time. Text messaged Amir the details, saying that was the earliest she could get as it was school half-term. It wasn't. But he was too stupid and lazy to check. She then sent an email that would have taken the smile off of Amir's face if he'd seen it. But he never would.

Irena knew he would only see the underwear. The fat pig. But she was quite happy to do what she had to do. The money was better than the city and revenge even made her orgasm now and again, despite Amir's fat physique and sweaty bald head. The last time she'd seen the man she sent the email to was in a lay-by on the A3 not so long ago.

When Amir got home to the luxury apartment in Central London he truly did enjoy the underwear and its gorgeous wearer. Afterwards they talked. And he boasted about how he was going to avenge the losses and humiliation he'd suffered from having his meet with his suppliers destroyed, and his money stolen. His shipment seized. She ran her delicate fingers over his chest as he ranted on to impress her. She murmured how bad a thing that was to happen. And how she knew she he would sort it out. "Well it will be sorted out," he'd snarled. "Because if Tremayne knows anything my boys will get it out of him in the Gambia if the fucking police can't do it here. And if he doesn't know anything I'll turn them loose on that bent piece of filth Davidson to make him work harder."

She snuggled up tight against him, inwardly cringing. That corrupt policeman. Davidson. The Gambia? Daniel had a home there. She smiled as she started to drift off to sleep. Pillow talk from an arrogant man was a very useful source of information. She would have to be a bit more careful now, as the long game plan started to come together. She wasn't going to have to sleep next to this fat pig for that much longer. She was going to destroy him, with the help of others, and walk away from this seedy, vile world as a wealthy young woman and make her family secure. After Amir had left them anything but, several years ago.

She drifted off to sleep despite Amir's snoring. In the morning, she got up as Amir snored on, made coffee and orange juice,and fired off another email in pursuit of the one she'd sent last night. To Daniel Cade. A good man who put things right. However, it had to be done.

Chapter 26. The morning after.

Daniel was sleeping as Janet quietly got out of bed. She smiled at him as he lay there. It had been quite a night. She had gone to the bathroom after Daniel came out from it and when she returned he was in bed. It was pitch dark. She got in to bed naked and embraced him but had felt the rigid, fearful tension in his body. And sensed he was not at ease with this at all. She'd kissed him gently and held him. Reached down to him. And realised he wasn't at all aroused.

She'd realised he was something far from aroused. He was actually scared. He'd murmured he was sorry. And it wasn't her and maybe they shouldn't try this. She'd lightly placed a finger on his lips to silence him. Then kissed him again, slowly and for a long time. Gradually feeling him relaxing, as he started to return the kisses and caress her. Then she'd climbed astride him, and placed his hands on her full breasts. Still leaning down and kissing him. Then she'd whispered, "I think you need to put those thoughts back in the box and throw them into the sea darling."

She moved up his body until she could lower herself on to his mouth. He responded with his lips and tongue. And as her first climax hit her and passed she reached behind her. And realised the bad thoughts and the fear were gone. At least for now. She slid sensuously back down his lean body and lowered herself down onto him with a low groan. It was the start of a very long night of passion.

She got an orange juice from the refrigerator on the balcony and sat in the early African sun on the soft couch. She smiled as she recalled Daniel's face, as they lay next to each other after that first time. It had so reminded her of Arnold Schwarzenegger's face after he got laid for the first time ever, in the scene from the Twins movie. He was wonderfully inexperienced. But a bloody quick learner. And oh boy, was he fit. She had never held, or been held, by such a fit man. His body was just so strong. She shivered with the sensations her memory was giving her. It had been a beautiful first night.

She heard the door slide and Daniel appeared. He walked over and kissed her and sat down next to her.

"Are you okay?", asked Janet.

"You know the answer to that. And you're beautiful."

"I'll take that as a yes then."

"You definitely can."

"Maybe we could do it again some time?"

"I think we should."

Daniel got up and got a coffee and sat back down. "You were wonderful Jan. You understood my fears and problems. But then I knew, the first time I saw you, that you would."

"I don't understand you Daniel. It's a lovely thing to say. But I can't see how you'd just know that."

"It's not easy to explain. Not without making you think I'm crazy."

"Well try. I really do love you Daniel. And I so want to know more about you. And I know you're not crazy. Different, yeah. But you aren't crazy."

"Okay. Try this. You know you can meet somebody and really like them. From the first time you meet? People say things like, we hit it off, or, we just clicked?"

Janet nodded. "Sure, it happens a lot."

"Well imagine that in a more spiritual way. A hundred times more intense. And a hundred per cent accurate if you train your mind. Being able to tell if somebody is pure good, or as in most cases, somewhere in between. Or, as in many cases, pure evil."

"That sounds wonderful. But hard to imagine."

"Well if I told you that I knew when I met you, that you were the only woman for me. And that the only reason we met, was because we were meant to. And I know your pure good brought you to me to change your life. And you would change mine. Would that make you think I was crazy?"

"Well, not crazy. But I can't comprehend it Daniel. My pure good? I'm just a single mum from South London. I was pregnant at seventeen with James so I got married. And again at nineteen with Katie. Divorced after two years. He was violent to me, it was awful. I had a very tough childhood. Both my parents are dead. And I went on to pick two bad men to marry. Life's been shit. Sorry but it has. It was only the kids that have made it remotely worthwhile. And then I let them down. By meeting and marrying Barry. Especially James. I was lonely, never got out much. Barry was just desperation. He was all lovely at first. But a total vile pig who abused my little boy. So I swore never again. Well, until now maybe. Well I hope so." She smiled at him as she said it.

"But that's what you don't understand, unless you can embrace the concept. Good attracts evil because evil wants to destroy it. Why did bad men target you? Your child? How many good people have their lives ruined by bad people? Murderers, rapists, traffickers and pimps. Drug dealers and terrorists. Their prey, their victims, are always people who have done no wrong. Just been in the wrong place at the wrong time. You were vulnerable. He knew that."

Janet had never known Daniel talk this much. But he was calm and focused and just seemed to desperately want her to understand him.

"So you embrace that concept? You know good or evil by, like, instinct?"

"Yes, I am one of the few that truly do. Or can. My training at the dojo's, my time with the senseis and the masters, my discipline and meditation, brought out the ability I always had, but to the highest degree. It is not a thing anyone can master or acquire. It's something spiritual you already have, that can be honed and refined. I can meet pure good, and feel like a jolt of electricity between us. Like a bond, a connection. Like I had with you in that reception area. I just know. I can meet pure evil and sense it, and be alert to the danger it poses. I could feel James' pain and address it by a meeting of minds. I could love you knowing you'd love me. It leaves no question unanswered. And no doubts."

Janet smiled at him. "So you knew I would be the one that would feel your hurt and problems, from the abuse you suffered. Understand it and address it?"

"Yes. The same as I know a spiritual healer can help me if I'm ill or hurt. They have. I can do that. It's how I helped James"

"But Daniel, I am not one of the few. I can't sense good or evil like you say you can."

"No Jan, you can't. That's why you got hurt. But you did it, didn't you?"

She looked at him intently. As a very faint glimmer of understanding started to set in for the first time. "Yes, I did."

"Did it even occur to you not to? Even for a second?"

She paused briefly then said, "It felt instinctive. Something was wrong, I had to make it right. Because I so wanted to. It was important. For us both"

"Exactly. You never thought to be hurt or angry. You wanted to put things right. That is what I spend my life doing Jan."

"I never felt like that before. It was very intense. It was, well, a wonderful feeling. Loving and warm."

"Well, put simply, that instinct to put things right, to intervene rather than walk away - that is what separates us from everybody else."

"Well yeah I guess. But I'm not like you Daniel."

"You are. Just not to the extremes I do it. But I bet you have always helped people, rather than not."

"Yes. Actually I have. Just never thought about it before."

"Well it's what makes me love you."

"Then I'm very glad it does."

"Good. Shall we go shower and find the children?"

"Sure." She stood and kissed him.

It was quite a while before they went to find the children, who were already in the pool. Janet didn't blush at all as Rosie's knowing, lecherous, smile was trained on her. Just smiled back. Because for the first time in her adult life she was truly happy to be alive. She was good-hearted. And she bloody well deserved it after all this time. She was never going back to South London, other than to empty that crappy flat and tidy up her affairs. She knew that beyond any doubt.

This was her life now. Here, hearing the ocean, watching the palm trees swaying. With her man. Who had told her that in some strange way it was ordained and meant to happen. That was good enough for her. Because Daniel wouldn't lie to her. And she wasn't going to lose a minute's sleep worrying about it any more. She smiled. Any lost sleep wouldn't be lost in a bad way. That was one thing she did know for sure.

Chapter 27. Focus and plan.

Daniel had excused himself, saying he needed a bit of computer time. Business stuff. And gone back to the villa. He read the emails from Irena again. Carefully. And weighed up the situation. It had to happen sometime was all he thought. But bringing Lee into it. Well that wasn't expected. Or right. Lee wouldn't kill, or even think to kill. He was, as far as Daniel was concerned, his brother. But he was not of Daniel's world.

A bent copper, this Michael Davidson, who had investigated the demise of Wesley and Mason, being in the pay of Amir Ferez - that was just sheer bad luck. Then a smart copper, Davidson's superior, Colin Fleming, had seen a possibility, of a remote connection between the gang deaths and those two thugs. Well that was just more bad luck. Probably, in part, caused by Daniel's insistence they left the drugs for the police at the scene. He smiled wryly. And Quan being so efficient.

None of this would have happened if Wesley and Mason hadn't murdered his foster parents, one of whom was his saviour as a child. Or if the useless UK legal system wasn't weighted towards criminals and they had been jailed. Well, what was done was done. Daniel just needed to make sure it turned into Amir's bad luck. And he would. Everything happened for a reason. He would find it.

Irena had been smart enough to buy him the time to do it. He worried about her. He wanted her out of there but it was her choice, and she who had started this. Alone. As brave as a lioness guarding its cubs. She was pure good and made literally every sacrifice to deal with Amir, who was utterly evil. He knew she would see this through. He just hoped it would be over soon, and before her luck ran out. He would talk to her soon. But first there was work to do. He locked the villa door.

He sat quietly, closed his eyes. His heart rate slowed dramatically. He sank into a deep place in his mind. Factored in all the details of the situation. And thought intensely as the swirling colours came into his mind. Each colour a part of the problem. Davidson. A bent police officer. Useful? A young Syrian, why Ahmet? The real current fear of jihadist terrorism. Why that? Irena. Ray. Amir. This recent apparent bad luck. Was it? Or was it meant to be? The suitcase that had held Amir's money. Why had he thought it important? Why? There was a reason for it. There was a reason for everything. Find it. All of it whirled in his mind shrouded in colours. All of these things were part of a puzzle. All puzzles have a solution. Think. Be guided. The colours slowly began to merge as the parts of the puzzle came together.

Turn Davidson against Amir. He was good. And had been a good officer. Just in a bad place now. Young Ahmet. Wanted dearly to repay him a huge debt of gratitude. Use it.

Call it in. Ahmet was needed in this affair. But where? Think. The suitcase. The handle. It was Amir's suitcase. Amir's cash had been in it. Jihadists in the UK. A hired car. Two of Amir's men. To the airport. A plane to Gambia. Bent on hurting Lee. Fear. Of terrorism. The airport. High alert. Amir. Jihadists. A fearful Amir? Of course.

Then suddenly there were no varied colours. Just light. The way forward. All of this was meant to be. He saw the solution, right there in front of him, like a clearly marked road ahead. They had taken him to it. He had known they would. He never questioned or doubted it. He had only to walk that road to finish this. Finish Amir. It was all there and he knew exactly what he had to do. And in what sequence. And he had to start right now.

He unlocked a desk drawer and took out a mobile phone and called Quan, who answered straight away. Daniel explained the situation and heard Quan curse. Then he told him of Amir planning to send two men to the Gambia to get at Lee. Quan cursed again. Then Daniel told him of the idea he'd had to deal with it and push forward in the quest to destroy Amir Ferez in the process, if Quan could put it together in the time available. A vehicle, had to be a pick-up truck. And why. A single, special round of ammunition. The suitcase from the take-down. A tip-off to the authorities would be Ray's department. Other things to be put in place by Irena. Quan had listened intently. And then he'd actually laughed at the sheer audacity of it. It was doable. And little short of brilliant.

He'd never cease to be amazed at Daniel's mental abilities. He had been very glad of them over the years, since they had met in the Foreign Legion. Daniel had a gift for these things that Quan had never quite understood, even after Daniel had tried to explain it. But he knew Daniel understood it and never questioned it. And that was all they needed at times like this.

After agreeing the plan, Quan listened to Daniel as he explained about Janet and the children, and Lee's visit. He cheerfully accepted Daniel's apology for not coming over to assist. It was foolish to travel to the UK for no good reason, with this investigation on and it was an easy enough thing to do in the forty eight hours Irena had bought them. It only needed one of them. And Daniel was busy in a good way. He was pleased for him.

Quan finished with, "Leave it with me, Daniel. Please. I'm already here. I have enough time. I need to get hold of Irena. Send us both an email to work to. Keep an eye on your email. And I am very pleased about Janet and look forward to meeting her. Long overdue my friend. Later." And he'd hung up.

Daniel emailed Quan, then Irena, with careful attention to detail then returned to the pool area. Lee would be here in two days and he wanted to make the most of the time with Jan before he got here. Then he shut his mind off to the things he'd just dealt with. There was nothing more he could do. And he wouldn't concern himself about it unless it went wrong. But with Quan on the case, it wouldn't.

Back in the UK, Quan was out gathering the required items to carry out Daniel's plan, which involved meeting some very shady people who had some very raised eyebrows at his requests. But he got it all.

Irena had booked a rental car for the two men Amir was sending to the Gambia that could be left at the airport on arrival there. She had arranged things with Ali, one of the two men going, to get to the rental company with his driving licence to collect it. Then she text messaged Ali's address to Quan.

She smiled to herself as things were put in motion. How Daniel could think of such things so quickly was beyond her. But it was good that he could. If this came off that fat pig Amir was going to really blow a fuse. With a bit of luck the shock would kill him. And that bastard bent copper Davidson. He would really be in the shit. Good. He had it coming to him as far as Irena was concerned. She was very wrong about that. But then she wasn't Daniel.

Chapter 28. Fears and regrets.

Fleming only saw Davidson briefly over the next couple of days, tasked him to various enquiries on the many other cases currently under investigation. Davidson went about his work with his mind on other things. He had real doubts now about the sense in passing the Tremayne stuff to Amir. If the heavies put the screws on Lee Tremayne and he reported it, things could really go tits up. But he'd had to give Amir something. And that was literally all there was.

Loan shark breathing down his neck. He needed the money. The problem was that, apart from a couple of admin staff, only he and Fleming really knew about it. He could only hope the heavies believed Tremayne if they got to him. And he really hoped Lee Tremayne wouldn't be harmed and Amir would let it drop so it all died away.

He was feeling awful about it now. The guy had lost his parents in a terrible murder. Now he was responsible for turning the guy's holiday into a nightmare. He wondered how the hell he had got in this deep. His own stupidity was how.

Gambling and drinking out of misery and loneliness. Missing his wife. He cursed his recent past in his mind, as he went through forty-eight hours of nail-biting over it. He even thought about actually warning Lee Tremayne. But dismissed it. If that ever got found out, he was a dead man.

Chapter 29. Family reunion.

In the Gambia, Lee and Angelica had arrived, happily oblivious to the issues their travels were creating elsewhere. Introductions were made and after the initial shock of Daniel being clearly in a relationship had worn off they were all getting along well.

Janet liked Angelica immediately. The bloody woman was gorgeous, with long natural blonde hair that framed a delightful, oval face with large, smoky grey eyes. On top of a body like Jennifer Aniston's. After having two kids! She was earthy and funny with a wicked laugh. Janet sensed that this lady was somebody you could talk to despite, she assumed, being born into a world of wealth and luxury. And made up her mind to do just that and find out more about Daniel. Because there was no point in asking the bloody man himself!

That Lee was a hunk too. Tall and slim, with a handsome square-jawed face. A slight tint of early grey at the tips of his full head of immaculately groomed, black hair. Softly spoken and well-mannered. But she could sense the authority he could command if he needed to. They were a lovely-looking couple, exuding the health that vast wealth bought. And they seemed so really happy together despite the awful news she'd heard about Lee's parents from Angel, who wasn't the least surprised that she didn't know. "Bloody Daniel never tells you anything," were her exact words. Which made her smile, as those words echoed a regularly occurring thought.

Chapter 30. Ambush and execution.

Quan was out early on a road that approached Gatwick airport, tasked to see that two other, far more unpleasant people, didn't get to the Gambia. Driving a taxi he'd borrowed for the day. Inconspicuous. He even had a couple of passengers for effect. He drove around. He watched. And he saw what he was looking for. He was in business. The police had bought the tip off. In these days of high terrorism alerts, especially regarding airports, they'd had to. And this one was confirmed. The suspect vehicle was under surveillance and on its way to the airport. He surveyed the area they were setting up. Good choice, easy to isolate. Far enough away from the airport not to cause attention. No public anywhere near.

Now he needed to find the right place. Near enough to their chosen site, to take just one shot from, and get out of fast. He soon found it. A concrete service road to an old cement works, with a good view of the area he needed to see. He stopped by the pick-up truck he was going to use. One of his passengers took the wheel and drove the taxi away. Quan set off in the truck and drove the short distance to the location he'd chosen, and reverse parked against the road's low perimeter barrier. And waited. It would be a short wait.

He passed the time watching the police anti-terrorist team quickly setting up shop with their vans and equipment, from four hundred and thirty-three metres away, through the space created by dropping the tail gate at the rear of the crew cab pick-up he was laying in. He chambered the special round and double-checked the range. It was the first time in this type of circumstances he'd ever had to fire a shot not intending to kill. He smiled. Just as well. As he was going to shoot a policeman.

He glanced at his watch. Ten minutes, if that. They were twenty minutes from the airport here. He knew the flight times. To get there two hours before, Amir's men would be here any minute. The police were watching the vehicle for sure. If they weren't, these guys wouldn't be here. He settled down and waited.

Chapter 31. Girl talk.

The morning after the first night out they all had together, Lee and Daniel went for a trip on the boat. Daniel explained to James, who wanted to go, that Lee and he had business to discuss but he would come back and pick him up later, saying he would appreciate it if he would stay with Katie. James was fine. He was so relaxed lately, it was good to watch.

While Rosie watched the children, Angel and Janet went for a walk through the local stalls in Kololi after Solomon dropped them off. Jan was pleased to get Angel alone. She had liked her instantly. She was very easy to talk to, for a woman of class and wealth. She smiled as she recalled Daniel and the term "clicked." Girl talk was an international class-free language. And Jan wanted to hear about Daniel. From another girl. However rich and wealthy.

Angel had explained how Daniel was fostered by Lee's parents, John and Ann, from the age of eleven. Ann had told her that the boy was a nightmare and had been through serious abuse by his own step father, after his mother had died. Ann and John were hugely wealthy and had been able to get the boy to the best practitioners of child therapy.

Nothing had seemed to work at first. The nightmares and the bed-wetting and the violent outbursts had continued, until one day, according to Ann, he had changed overnight. And that day had been the one on which John Tremayne had totally, and unusually, lost his temper with him after Daniel had sworn vilely at Ann. John had dragged Daniel outside to the car and shoved him in to it, telling him he was going back to a care home because enough was enough.

John had returned nearly four hours later, but still had Daniel with him. And from that day Daniel had changed. He took up martial arts immediately, and was gifted at it. He read a lot of strange books apparently, on spiritualism and meditation. He spent a lot of time alone. Always out of choice and never seemingly unhappy. He was a very strange, isolated young boy. A few fights at school because of that. But nothing he ever lost!

No real academic interest at all, no team games. His only involvement with others was with his martial arts teachers who trained the gifted boy intensely. John paid for one-to-one teaching for him gladly, as it focused him on something. He ran and cycled alone all the time.

Bonded well with Lee, when Lee came home from the army on leave, despite Lee being older. Left school at sixteen, had some time out. Asked if he could go to Japan for a year, to further his martial arts. And never came back. Wrote to say he was in the French Foreign Legion! John had just laughed about it at the time and ever since, until his recent death, along with his wife. Daniel had always kept in touch with them, but rarely came back to the UK. They had flown out several times to meet up with him in whatever country he was in. And that was about it.

Janet had commiserated with Lee about the terrible loss of his parents. And was going to give Daniel a piece of her mind. For not bothering to mention his foster parents had been recently murdered! But she had changed her mind. Daniel just wouldn't see the logic in telling her, so he wouldn't. She smiled as she thought about him.

"But you never said what happened that day with John to change him?" Jan said.

Angel replied, "No. Because it was never talked about. All John ever said to Ann was to please not ever ask him about it. So she didn't. She just said to me that she knew John well enough, that he would have had his reasons to say nothing. And she just got on with enjoying watching Daniel get better and better."

Janet told Angel everything bar the bedroom stuff about Daniel and how they'd met.

"The thing is, he was committed to a relationship with me from the very first moment we met. It freaked me out and to be honest it still does a bit. I've been badly hurt in the past Angelica. I just hope I've made the right call. He's very different to anyone I ever met. I've got two kids and feel I'm taking one hell of a gamble. But I love him. Truly I do."

Angel replied with a gentle smile, "It's Angel. And you have made the right call Jan. Daniel truly doesn't lie. Ever. And he is so different, and confident and kind. He wouldn't hurt you for the world. I understand that you might struggle to believe all this, but you truly can. I promise you, you can. I know him very well. And for what it's worth you're a lovely girl with two great kids. You two deserve each other." They had a hug and then continued walking.

Then Angel said, "If I had known you had your kids here I would have brought ours with us. Daniel never told us."

Janet started to say, "Daniel never tells you anything," at exactly the same time

Angel started to say it, and they both burst out laughing. As they walked back together, Janet thought to herself how strange it was that just a few days ago she was a worried sick, single mum, in a dingy council flat. And now she was strolling along a path in Africa. With a billionaire's wife. Who really was very nice.

When they got back to the villas, Angel asked Janet to come to theirs for a moment. When they got there, Angel opened the safe in the lounge and took an A4 envelope out from it, heavily sealed, and handed it to Janet.

"Can you give this to Daniel please? It's from John Tremayne. His solicitor gave it to me and asked me to get it to Daniel."

"Sure", Janet replied. "I'll go put it in the bedroom then see you by the pool?"

"See you in a minute. I'll get a bikini on."

Janet left, looking at the large envelope in her hand, stamped highly confidential, and heavily sealed. Another mystery. She guessed she'd better get used to them if she was going to make a life with Daniel. And she was.

Chapter 32. Get the police to do it.

Quan, peering through his binoculars, saw a flurry of activity by the police vehicles as the armed, Kevlar-wearing officers left the vans parked each side of the road and crouched beside them, ready to move. Quan looked to his left. Two hundred yards beyond the officers, on the road towards the airport, was a roundabout. And suddenly, the traffic police appeared, out of nowhere and put up accident and diversion signs, blocking the exit road with two cars, so that nothing could drive towards the armed police.

He looked to his right. There was the car with Amir's men in it, the hire company logo clear to see. Behind it, two plain cars travelling one behind the other, slowed gradually, holding back the traffic, then clamped on flashing blue lights, and they stopped, two abreast blocking the road. They put out signs in the road behind them saying 'accident'. The hire car was now rounding the slight bend, travelling away from them, isolated and continuing towards the vans. The driver and his passenger no doubt chatting, oblivious to the fact that no traffic was coming towards them. And that now none was behind them.

They drew closer. Quan steadied the rifle and trained the powerful telescopic sight on the scene. Saw the stinger mat roll across the road stopping the vehicle in seconds as the driver braked hard on punctured tyres.

The armed police approached the vehicle from both sides. Two lines of three officers, forward of the vehicle, diagonally opposite each other to avoid any chance of hitting each other, all with guns aimed at the, no doubt, shocked, occupants of the car. Yelling instructions that Quan was too far away to hear. He saw both the hire car doors start to open. He aimed the rifle at the centre police officer in the line facing him. And fired.

The suppressed rifle made a sound like a loud cough. The officer fell backwards as if pushed hard. The others immediately opened fire, into the front of the car. Quan saw all the front windows explode in the second before he took his eye from the scope. He covered the rifle with a blanket, slid out, and lifted the tail gate into place. Quickly got into the front, and drove calmly away. As he did so, the waiting medical and forensic teams turned up at the scene.

After confirming the occupants were dead, the car was quickly covered with a tarpaulin and winched on to a recovery vehicle to get it to a place where it could be minutely examined, away from prying eyes. The only piece of evidence picked up and bagged was the bullet that had struck an officer named Colin Bewes, who was a bit shaken, but with only a minor bruise to the breastbone.

And to the relief of the frustrated motorists, the road was quickly re-opened. It would take a few hours to analyse the evidence, then cross-reference it and piece it all together. They didn't know right then that it would throw up more questions than answers.

Chapter 33. Brotherly love.

Back in the Gambia, Daniel and Lee were afloat, a hundred metres off the shore, in the unusually calm Atlantic. There was just a tiny breeze. It was hot. They were saying nothing, both enjoying the moment and the gentle motion of the small inflatable boat, as it drifted where it would. And the silence. Daniel had killed the engine. Lee broke the silence.

"You obviously know all the details about Mum and Dad? And what happened in the courts?"

"Of course. I'm truly sorry Lee. I loved them very much."

"I know. And what's more, they knew."

"I can only imagine how you feel. You were their son. And you were there."

"It was hell Daniel."

"I was never there much."

"That never mattered to them. They understood you Daniel."

"More than you know Lee. Especially John."

Lee pondered that. Thought it a bit of a strange thing to say. Then said, "You also know the killers walked free?"

"Yes."

"Do you know they are both dead?"

"Yes."

They were both silent. Lee was thinking of what Angel had said. Should he ask the question? Or not?

Daniel broke the silence, "I didn't kill them Lee. That's the truth"

Lee looked at him. He knew Daniel wasn't lying to him. But he then said, "But I did arrange it."

"I see." Another long silence. This time Lee broke it, "The police asked me about it Daniel. Thought I'd paid for it or some such bullshit."

"I thought they just might."

"That didn't bother you?"

"No, because you hadn't. You wouldn't do that."

"But you did?"

"We're different Lee. I don't care if you approve."

"I do approve though. They deserved it."

"Good. They did. If they'd owned up, they'd be alive."

Lee looked at him. "You'd have settled for a jail sentence?"

"Yes Lee. That's all there is in the UK. It's all we can expect. But they chose to lie. They took some clever dick, shiny-arsed lawyer's slick manoeuvring as a way to get away with it. That was their choice."

Lee nodded. "And you were the consequences of that choice. I'm glad you arranged it. And if I had the faintest idea how to do it, I would have. That's also the truth."

"Then we're not so different."

"I guess not." Lee paused before asking, "Any reason why you didn't do it?"

"Only one. Too personal. You have to be apart from it. Indifferent. Or you make mistakes."

"Did you pay for it?"

"No."

"You're seriously telling me somebody would do that? And risk their liberty. For nothing?"

"No. The Legion sticks together. And he owed me one."

"Well, I owe you one as well."

"No you don't. I owed John one."

"For what?"

"Saving my life."

"Want to tell me about it?"

"No."

"I thought not." Lee smiled at Daniel and his serious expression and said, "You are my brother as far as I'm concerned. Always have been since you joined our family. I feel that more strongly now than before this conversation. A lot more."

"Thank you."

Lee looked at him and smiled. "Shall we have an hour's fishing before we go back to our beautiful women? Janet is lovely, Daniel. So are her children. I am very happy for you both. So's Angel. And I just wish Mum and Dad had been here to meet her"

Daniel smiled back and fired up the engine. They both enjoyed the fast ride across the sea to a place Daniel knew was good fishing.

It was done. There was nothing more to say and they both knew they would never mention it to each other again. Brothers should be able to trust each other and, as different as they were, and for all the time they never saw each other, they did.

Chapter 34. More questions than answers.

Back in the UK at the forensic department, work was complete. Even prioritised it had taken hours and it was now early evening. There was some strange evidence coming to light. The two dead men's luggage was on the back seat. The trunk on the car wouldn't open, the mechanism was broken. It was safe to assume that was why.

Both men were unarmed. Both had died instantly from the shots fired expertly by the police, in the belief they were returning fire. Head shots. Both had British passports and air tickets to the Gambia. Both had criminal records. Both were linked to drug gang activity in the West London area. One was linked to Amir Ferez, a known drug baron, importer, and a prime target of the drugs squad. Of Turkish origin, resident in the UK. The other to Bogdan Gentian. Same status, but Albanian. Distributor, running a large network of street dealers in many areas. Supplied by Ferez. Also suspected of people trafficking and running prostitution rings. Both hard cases. Both utterly ruthless.

But the trunk, when opened, had been the most startling. There was a suitcase in it. Medium size. In there was a large amount of peroxide based explosive, known as TATP. Triacetone triperoxide. It was also known as "Mother of Satan" by ISIS. In addition, there were two pistols and two hand grenades. And on the suitcase they had found fingerprints. And got two matches.

One match was to a known villain, Darren "Ginger" Baker, known to have been in the pay of Amir Ferez, and found dead at a recent shooting between drug gangs in a disused freight yard in Surrey currently being investigated by Marshall Bland of the county's Serious Crimes squad. The other match was to none other than Amir Ferez himself. This was big. And it was multi-agency. Communications flew between the units involved in anti-terrorism and the ongoing criminal investigations.

Marshall Bland got a call at around six p.m. as he was thinking about going home. A multi-unit ops room was being set up at Scotland Yard. Marshall phoned his long-suffering wife and told her not to expect him home any time soon. Fleming got another call. His case linked in, however tenuously. Any investigation that interfaced in any way was brought into the loop.

This had to be dealt with quickly and efficiently. This could be a huge break into possible terrorist activity, drug dealing, trafficking and multiple homicide. Given the resources, the police were pretty good at this sort of stuff, and for this sort of operation they got the resources. They were expected to get results.

Marshall had left Scotland Yard a confused man. He had sat through the meeting. The various units had agreed their further investigation strategy but the strangest piece of evidence of all was the bullet that had hit Bewes. It was non-lethal, designed to shock, or at most cause minor bruising. And it had hit squarely on the Kevlar body armour the officer was wearing.

Marsh had cursed loudly on hearing this evidence and all had turned to look at him. He had explained the MO from his latest crime scene and the possible military connection they were investigating, saying, "I think these bastards just got us to do to those guys in that car, what they did at that drug meet. They fired that to get us to shoot those two suspects, damn it."

It was agreed that that was the most likely explanation and it sent a sombre mood through the assembled officers. It was also agreed, in the light of the discovery of TATP in the car, and the fact it was en route to a major airport, that the investigation would have to look at not just the ex-military possibility. This could now be terrorist linked.

Marshall was tasked to bring Amir in. He arranged a warrant for Amir's arrest and set it up. When he spoke to the arresting team his instructions were, "Go to his flash penthouse and arrest the fat bastard. At ten to nine in the morning. Make plenty of noise and fuck him up with the neighbours. Don't screw it up, don't lose sight of him. I want surveillance on him through the night."

He spoke to Fleming who had shown up alone. Mick had gone home by the time Fleming got the call and hadn't picked up when Fleming tried to call him.

When Fleming had told him that they had been unable to interview Tremayne again, because he was on holiday in the Gambia, Marsh had done a double take. "Those two in the car had tickets to the bloody Gambia!"

They looked at each other, both wondering what the hell was going on here. Tomorrow was going to be a very interesting day. Marsh planned to see that Amir had a very bad day. He'd waited too long for this break.

Chapter 35. The letter.

In the Gambia, Rosie had the sleeping children under her watchful eye. Daniel and Janet were in Daniel's villa. Angel and Lee had gone next door. They'd all had a very active, enjoyable day and all wanted a quiet evening and an early night. Janet went into the bedroom, returning with the letter Angel had given her and handed it to Daniel. She told him what it was. Daniel looked at it and turned it over in his hands a couple of times.

"Do you want to be alone when you read it darling?" she asked quietly. Daniel shook his head to indicate no. He had dreaded this moment but only since he'd met Janet. Because this letter might be the one thing that would cost him the one person he never wanted to lose. Her.

But it had to be faced. He carefully opened the thick envelope and unfolded the two sheets of paper inside and read it slowly and carefully, aware of Janet's eyes on him. She watched as he read the two pages of typed print that made up the last letter he would ever get from John Tremayne.

He finished it. And when he looked at her he was clearly on the verge of crying. He could hardly talk. But he managed to say, in a voice thick with emotion, "You have to read this Jan. After you have, if you want nothing more to do with me, go to Lee. He will get you and the children home and see you are okay." He handed her the letter.

"Daniel please. I don't have to read it. If it could lose you I don't want to."

"You have to Jan. If you don't you won't fully know me. I maybe should have told you before. I don't know. Just read it please. I'll be on the balcony. Either come up after you've read it. Or go to Lee and Angel next door."

Without another word he walked away and up the stairs to the bedroom and balcony. Janet sat alone holding the letter in trembling hands. She looked down at it and started to read. It was dated almost exactly two years ago.

My Dearest Daniel,

If you are reading this, then I am departed from this world. I wrote this on my seventieth birthday, after you left the house and it has been in my lawyers' safe ever since. So here it is. My goodbye. If Ann has survived me I know you and Lee will look after her. She has been the love of my life.

I cannot express the love I have for you Daniel. It's been hard never being able to tell Ann or Lee, or anybody, the news you send me or of your achievements. Or of the bond that we have to each other. Or the pride I have that I am the only one you ever seek help, guidance, or counsel from.

But I kept my promise to you when you were eleven. And I have kept it throughout the years. It just hurt that you were perceived as perhaps distant and aloof, perhaps a little uncaring or ungrateful even. Because I know so very well how very wrong that perception is. But then it always makes me smile when I know you care nothing for anyone else's perception of you. And it always makes me proud to know that the only perception of yourself you ever valued was mine.

That day you told me about your stepfather was the most pivotal day of my life. I had no idea how badly you had been abused. I had no idea of the dreadful secret you were carrying for one so young. And I have no idea to this day, why I, a businessman and pillar of the community, could hold such as you told me from the authorities. And not only do it but do it without question or hesitation.

What you did was utterly premeditated but I have never forgotten the serene expression on your face as you told me what you had done. As if you somehow knew that telling me was your salvation from the terrible place you were in. Your total trust in me overwhelmed me Daniel. I had no hesitation from the moment you told me to keep your secret and I vowed to keep you safe from further harm. And I have no regrets today, on my seventieth birthday, for doing it.

For one so young to have to do what you did out of fear that the next time he abused you, you would die - it was a terrible thing to hear. You took his wallet after he came home drunk. And took a beating for it. And you told him you had hidden it in bushes up on the cliff path. You were dragged there by him in a drunken rage. Him hitting you as he dragged you up that steep path in the howling wind. As he went to the bush near the cliff edge where you said the wallet was concealed, you ran at him. And sent him to his death on the rocks below. Where he was swept away by the sea and never found.
I write this only because I want Lee to see it in my own words. Not to hurt you Daniel.

From anyone else my reaction would have been sheer horror. From you, all I felt was a total trust in me to guide you through your trauma. It was a trust I was happy to be given because I knew you had been guided to me by the strange forces so few of us understand. And I am so very proud of how you have turned out Daniel.

Your service in the Foreign Legion. Your excellence in martial arts. Your spirituality, matching, and even surpassing my own. Your generosity in Turkey and the Gambia and other places. Your moral code, different to anybody else's and unique to you, has been a credit to you and of huge benefit to those who have been lucky enough to have received your help or intervention. Backed up by mine whenever you have asked for it. And of huge distress to those who definitely deserved whatever you inflicted upon them. You have dispensed justice where it would never have been dispensed, to the common good. And funded yourself through it, to my constant amusement. Turning bad money to good use always warmed my heart.

My only hope Daniel is that you find true peace one day. I hope you meet a lovely woman and enjoy your life and a family. As I did. You cannot lead a life of endless atonement for doing nothing wrong as a child bar preserve your very life, when others, who should have, failed so miserably to do so - as in countless cases we have both read and heard of since, in this absurd, politically correct world.

Your endless quest to right wrongs and make things better for victims of wicked people; your fight against the evils of this world - Daniel they have to stop one day. Or change in direction. I know you are one in a million. Your skills and abilities are rare and needed. But you must find the will to pass the baton of responsibility to others, as I have done with Lee in my world of business. Please do it before your skills and instincts are one day not enough to keep you alive. It is my only constant and dread fear, my son.

Yes. You are my son. And to that end listen to your now dead father's last request of you. Your constant refusal to take any of my fortune for yourself has been admirable, if annoying. I have been happy to fund anything you have asked me to, in a philanthropic way, to help others. And gladly. Because as you know, I was anyway. My fight against the evils of this world was fought with money. Unlike your own.

But now I am gone. And I have left a sum of two million pounds to you. And you alone. I want you to take it. And I want you to build a life for yourself, and hopefully, a family of your own.

Please don't let me down on this last request Daniel. You never have and I will rest peacefully knowing that you won't. And please keep close to Lee and Angel and my grandchildren, Daniel. It's an increasingly dangerous world. And I will also rest better knowing that you are there to call on if they need you.

Show Lee this letter and talk to him. He will be there for you as I have always been. And he will keep your secret and understand you as I have always done. He is his father's son Daniel. Trust him.

He loves you as a brother but he cannot work out how to get close to you. He stopped trying after I told him he never would - until the time was right. That time is now Daniel. Lee and

Angelica will guide you through your journey into a family life when you choose to have one. That is where their skills lie. Very different to yours. But equally important.

Angelica is as one with you and I. She also will be an anchor and support to you whenever you need it, in her remarkable and irreverent fashion. She is a joy as a daughter in law. And a wonderful wife to my son and mother to my grandchildren.

I would never ask, let alone tell you, to do anything. But if you do bond with Lee as you have with myself I have thought very hard about the future Daniel. And sought counsel and advice from good people with great wealth and intelligence who have real fears for the future as we are increasingly governed by the delusional and dishonest, placed in power by a system no longer fit for purpose.

Things need to change. Together you could, with Lee, make these changes. Or start to. Your deadly secret fight against evil would become open and overt. You could aim not to just target the drug gangs and paedophile rings and people traffickers in the dark world. But aim to eradicate them all - in the open, along with the huge tidal wave of tolerated crime, that engulfs and blights the lives of millions, with the weight of real, state-run law enforcement on your side. Or make that the goal. And bring social justice to everybody who so desperately needs it. I am rambling like the old man I am. Forgive me but it is dear to my heart as you know.

Talk to Lee. And Alan Shand, who you should, by the way, talk to. You know why. He deserves his answers now. After all this time.

He has a briefcase in his care. A blueprint if you will. For the future. At least give my ideals consideration. And. If you choose to take the risks involved, strive to make a real difference for our children's futures. In a new way. With you as the guardian to those who will take the fight to a new level.

I am so very proud of you both. Together you could make a tremendous difference to many people's lives.

My last wish is that you do just that. Together.

Take care of each other. All of you. And our next generations. For me.

Goodbye Daniel.

Your loving father,

Janet finished reading. And cried like she had never cried in her life. Daniel hadn't thrown bad thoughts in a box into the sea in his imagination, like he had got James to do. He'd pushed his abuser to his death, while only a child, and clearly spent his life doing good things, no matter how dangerous, because of the chance he'd been given. To give others that same salvation. She thought her heart was going to break. And she loved him so much more, which she thought was impossible.

John Tremayne sounded a wonderful man. She felt so sad as she realised he would never have dreamed that his letter would be read after he had died violently. And so had the love of his life. She hoped they were still together in whatever afterlife there might be.

She folded the tear-stained letter, put it back in the envelope, left it on the coffee table and dried her eyes and walked up to the balcony. He was looking out over the ocean. As still as a statue. He turned as he heard her. She went to him and held him so tightly he was shocked. She walked with him into the bedroom and they undressed and lay down naked on top of the bedclothes, locked together in an embrace that neither of them wanted to break.

They said nothing. There was nothing to say. Daniel still had Janet. And had won his last battle in a very long war. Abuse could cost him nothing else now. Janet now knew the man she loved fully. And loved him all the more for it. She understood, as they lay there with the doors open, listening to the ocean, everything Daniel had said about good finding good.

John Tremayne had been the only person he could trust and rely on all those years ago. And the spirits had guided him there. And now she was the only person he would love because she, like John, had made things right for him. He would look after her and the children and keep them safe. The spirits had brought them together. When good finally met good it was both wonderful and indestructible. It all made perfect sense while making no sense at all.

Except of course, to Daniel. She felt so very lucky to be that person. They both went to sleep peacefully in the same unchanged embrace. Two troubled pieces of a jigsaw, from thousands of miles apart, were finally where they belonged. Clicked perfectly together. And at peace with the world and each other.

Chapter 36. Humiliation and rage.

Back in the UK, Amir Ferez was anything other than at ease. He was raging with anger and seething with hatred as he sat in the back of the police car which had its blue lights and sirens going, just to piss him off a bit more.

He had been laying in bed caressing Irena when, with an almighty crash, his fucking penthouse door had flown in, courtesy of a police battering ram. Then police cars, with sirens blaring, had roared into the street. They'd dragged him out of bed, deliberately prolonging the time he was standing flabby and naked, trying to hide his dick with his hand. They had leered at Irena, who was terrified as they read him his rights and had arrested him on suspicion of a ridiculously long list of charges. Told Irena she was expected to make a statement but she could stay at the apartment although it was now under police guard as a crime scene until further notice. And they had a search warrant.

Then they'd dragged him out without him being able to say a word to Irena and made a public spectacle of him by frog-marching him handcuffed, under close arrest, down all the stairs instead of using the lift. Just to make quite sure all his nosy bastard, snobby neighbours saw him. He sat in silence as the car sped towards Croydon Police Station. What the hell had happened to warrant all this was all he could think of. And he was very concerned.

Irena had been equally shocked but it was offset by watching Amir made to look the flabby, fat fool he was. She had nothing to mock in the looks department, and she knew the cops knew it. She had watched out of the window as Amir was led to the waiting car, with everyone watching. She smiled inwardly, as his little Danny de Vito body exerted itself to keep up with the burly police officers.

She needed to act the shocked, loving woman. So she grabbed the phone and rang Amir's lawyer, babbling hysterically down the phone about what had happened. He assured her he was on his way to Croydon. Then she asked the police woman by the door if she could shower and dress. Got a nod yes. She needed time to think.

Why had they taken Amir? Oh yeah. The case. Of course! He'd handled it. Loaded the cash in it for the meet. That Daniel was one smart young man. She'd wondered why he'd made such a big deal about handling it so carefully, after the taking of it a short while ago. Now she understood. Amir was really in the shit now - just where she liked to see him. But she'd have to put on an Oscar-winning performance when he got bailed. He'd be suspecting everybody, including the milkman.

She put on her clothes, then the right look and went out and down into the kitchen for a coffee. She needed to send some emails from her phone. She'd go to the loo and do it in a while. Apart from that, all she could do was wait. She gave a tearful statement to the police while she did so. Confirmed Amir's recent whereabouts as best she could. Told them she hired the car in question. And why. And later called the building's management to get the damaged door fixed.

At the police station, Amir was frisked and had his possessions taken and got bunged into a cell. They told him his call girl had phoned his lawyer. To piss him off a bit more. Filthy bastards. He knew they were trying to fray his nerves with their insults. But he was glad Irena had got straight on the case. He needed his lawyer. And he needed to get out of here. He had a bad feeling that wasn't going to be any time soon. He paced the cell and waited.

Marsh was making some notes to refer to when the interview began. Fleming was there with Davidson, who was asking about what was going on. Looked like he'd been on the piss last night as well. Davidson was as worried as Amir. The fat bastard would be looking for anyone to blame. He felt worse when a constable stuck his head round the door and said Bogdan Gentian had been brought in as well. In fact he felt sick. Fleming told him he could go do some other stuff if he wanted to. All he was there for was to see if there was any link to the Wesley Mason murders. The rest of it wasn't their concern. Mick was glad to get away. Fleming was glad to see him go. The man was a bloody embarrassment.

They went in to the interview room. Marsh sat down, with Fleming next to him. Amir was sent for and came in with his lawyer and sat down. The two parties locked eyes. And it began, starting with the usual 'for the benefit of the tape' routine.

Then Amir's lawyer, Michael Symes, legal advice to the underworld, said, "I wish, first of all, to protest most strongly at the manner of my clients' arrest."

"Noted," replied Marshall, clearly indicating his indifference to Symes' protest.

"DI Bland. My client had his door smashed in. Was dragged from his bed naked. And marched down the stairwells to the street. It was deliberate humiliation and you know it."

"Mr Symes. My officers knocked politely and received no reply. Only then did they force an entry. And I would remind you, your client is here on matters relating to drug smuggling, money laundering, multiple homicides, gun-running, supplying explosives and terrorist activity. Not for lending his bus pass to his mate."

Amir burst out, "What the hell are you talking about? This is a set up." Symes cautioned him to silence. Amir piped down. These charges were huge.

"I am sure my client will be exonerated. So the quicker you ask your questions, of undoubtedly the wrong suspect, the quicker we can leave."

Marsh led into his questions by starting with the hire car. Not mentioning the two men killed in it.

"Amir. One of your bewildering array of companies, AF Associates, hired a car. For one Ali Kamaci to collect and leave at Gatwick airport. What was the reason for that?"

"I have no idea."

"Well that is a good start."

"I mean, I don't deal with every little thing in my business. Irena does all the administration."

"Yes she does. She told us she hired it when asked about it. On your instructions. And why."

"Well why ask me then?"

"Well it was at your instruction. And very kind of you. Thought you'd know."

"I don't recall."

"Irena told us that the two men worked at your club, and were going on holiday. And you'd kindly sorted a car out for them to get to Gatwick. Booked it to the firm."

Amir thought to himself how smart that had been of Irena. And replied, "Ah yes. I recall. So what's the problem then?"

"No problem from where I'm sitting. But you might just wish you'd just got them a taxi."

"What are you talking about Bland? Get on with it. I have a business to run."

"That car was flagged up as a possible part of a terrorist plot. To attack the airport."

"What? I hired it so they could get to Gatwick to go on holiday. You just fucking said so!"

"It was stopped on a road on its way to the airport. By the anti-terrorist squad."

"And they looked bloody stupid right?"

Marsh looked hard at Amir. "No, they did not. After the car was brought to a halt the armed police approached it. A shot was fired. An officer went down. Both men in the car were killed by the police."

Amir went white. Marsh could see this was all news to him.

Amir felt numb. Another two men dead. Young men. But trusted. This was madness.

"You killed them?"

"I didn't."

"But they were just going on holiday for fuck's sake. You just said so. Irena told you that"

"She did. But. When the trunk of the car was opened, we found a suitcase. Here's a list of the contents."

Marsh slid a copy across the desk to both Amir and Symes. They read it. Both looked shocked now.

Amir spluttered, "This is nothing to do with me Bland. Explosives? Pistols? Grenades? All I did was pay for the car rental and you fucking know it."

Marsh had been looking forward to this bit. "Then Amir. Perhaps you'd like to explain just why your fingerprints were on the suitcase with all those items in?" Amir really did go a funny colour then.

Bland studied him for a few seconds then said, "Mr Symes. Now that I am sure you appreciate the gravity of the situation, perhaps you'd like a little time with your client? We'll suspend the interview for a while. I fancy a bacon sarnie and a nice cup of coffee. Interview suspended. 11.43. DS Fleming and DI Bland are now leaving the room. If you need anything, please feel free to ask the nice officer by the door. Your client remains under arrest." And they left the room. Let the fat bastard stew for a while, then hit him again with another big stick. Marsh was smiling as he headed towards the cafeteria. None of this made any sense yet. But he'd got Amir Ferez crapping himself. Which was something.

Chapter 37. Confronting the truth.

In the Gambia, Janet and Daniel had drunk coffee and talked for a while. Daniel had seemed very reluctant to show Lee the letter but in the end he had agreed with Janet it was best got over with.

She said gently, "John Tremayne sounds like he was a wonderful man, Daniel."

"He was. He saved my life, Jan."

"And he knows his son, Daniel. He wouldn't have instigated this if he thought you could be harmed."

"You're right. It's just not easy telling people you committed murder at eleven years old."

Janet went to him and cupped his face in her hands and said, "Now you listen to me, Daniel Cade. You didn't. You did what you had to do. To survive. And help others survive. And it sounds like you always have since. And this is something else you have to do."

"You're right. Let's go do it."

They strolled hand in hand towards the villa next door, Daniel holding the envelope in his free hand.

Back at Croydon Police Station, the interview resumed. Symes had had time to compose himself and launched in with, "As I see it, all you have here are these facts. That in a car, which you know full well my client admits to hiring, as a kind gesture to two of his staff, you found a suitcase that has my client's fingerprints on. My client clearly may well have touched that case at some time in the past. But, as he hasn't seen the case recently and has no knowledge of his staff using it, has no knowledge of the alleged contents, at no time saw, yet alone touched, the hired vehicle, and has no idea what any of this is about, I suggest this interview is terminated and my client freed to leave."

"Thank you for telling me how you see it. Can we get on?" was Bland's reply.

"Be careful DI Bland. You have no grounds for this arrest."

"I most certainly have. And you know it. Or you wouldn't be here."

He resumed the interview. "Amir. The two men who worked for you. The happy holidaymakers. In what role where they employed?"

"Security. At one of my night clubs. They are legally employed and on my payroll."

"Ali Kamaci and Mohammed Eker?"

"Yes."

"Ali's cousin, who also worked for you, was recently found dead. At a multiple homicide shooting between two car loads of armed villains. At a drug and cash exchange at a disused warehouse. That property is known to be owned by you through yet another of your companies."

"I have an extensive property portfolio. I had no idea my long term investment property was being trespassed on. I was asked about the matter at the time."

"You were. I asked you about Ali's cousin, not your investment portfolio."

"I only heard he had been killed in a criminal incident. On my property. I have no knowledge of the incident itself."

"Killed along with seven other men? On your property."

"If that is the case. Yes. Or I assume so."

"Another man who worked for you, also killed there, was Darren Baker. His fingerprints are also on the suitcase. Along with yours."

"I heard he was involved in the same incident."

"Do you not think there is a rather high mortality rate among your bouncers?"

"They are security operatives. And I have no control over what they do in their spare time."

Marsh smiled and said, "I see. Perhaps you should suggest stamp collecting Amir. But. Moving on. We found a large amount of cocaine at the scene. But no money. We believe the suitcase found in the hire car was none other than the case that contained that money we never found. Due to the blood on it. A match to Darren Baker who had nothing better to do in his spare time than get killed."

"That would still have nothing to do with me."

"You didn't handle that case when you loaded it with cash?"

"I do not load cases with cash, Bland. I do not know what you are talking about."

"Our investigations lead us to believe that two people, as yet unknown, fired on your drug purchase meet. To galvanise the two parties into firing on each other. And they also cold bloodedly eliminated any who were not killed by that exchange of fire."

Symes chimed in. "You have no grounds to refer to that event as my client's drug purchase meet, DI Bland."

"I do apologise."

Amir said, "I have no idea what you are talking about."

Bland continued, "We now believe that the non-fatal shot fired at officer Bewes, causing him to fall, was also fired by a third party. To galvanise the police into firing on your two employees, rendering their buckets and spades unused, as they never got to go on holiday."

Amir glared at him. "I still have no idea what any of this has to do with me."

Bland turned to Fleming. "Colin, would you ask your questions now please."

Fleming looked at Amir. "Are you aware of the recent murders of John Tremayne, a wealthy businessman. And Ann Tremayne, his wife. And the fact that their killers, Mason and Wesley, evaded justice for it?"

"Well, I recall reading about it. It was big news. You lot fucked up." Symes shot Amir a warning look.

"A smart-arse, criminal-loving lawyer got them off on a technicality," said Bland, giving Symes a filthy look. Symes looked away. He had been involved in that acquittal, controlling and advising the very junior legal partner in the court, for a cash fee that had been given to him by a very powerful man with no explanation - or option to refuse.

"I'd like to continue." said Fleming. Bland gave him an apologetic look. He just detested the likes of Amir. And Symes come to that.

Fleming went on. "The two suspects were found dead, around three days before the violent shooting incident that's been mentioned. In which your security staff were dramatically culled. On a property owned by your company, during their spare time. Unbeknown, of course, to you. Investigation has shown that the deaths were not, as first thought, caused by mutually-inflicted wounds by Wesley and Mason, but by a third party who had obviously hoped it would be assumed to be a mutual killing."

"What has all this got to do with me?" said Amir.

Fleming ignored him and continued. "The dead victims' son, one Lee Tremayne, was interviewed in relation to the matter. A similarity in the method, and certain skills used in both these crimes, caused them to be linked together for cross investigation by DI Bland's team and mine."

"So what?" asked Amir.

Bland re-joined the fray. "I'll tell you so what Ferez. Shortly after that interview Lee Tremayne went on holiday. To the Gambia. Still there as far as we know. Which just happens to be where your two goons were going."

Symes said. "That is absurd. Thousands of people go to the Gambia. My client wasn't. His staff were. In a car that, by your own admission, my client never even saw. In their own time. Apparently using a suitcase my client hasn't seen in recent memory or can even recall handling at any time. I demand an end to this interview. And the release of my client."

There was nothing more to be done at that stage. They'd done what they set out to do. Rattle Amir. He was released on bail pending further enquiries. Bland excused himself. He waited until Symes had gone, then deliberately appeared on the station steps as Amir came out to await his car. He stood next to him and said, out of earshot of anybody else, "Listen fatso. I know you are in this up to your non-existent neck. But I want you released. Because whoever is targeting you and your outfit is shit hot. And I want you out there. Where they can get you."

He turned and went into the building before Amir could reply. Amir was thinking that the bastard might well have a point.

Something was very wrong. Somebody was setting him up. Targeting him. Another gang? Hardly likely. Turf was pretty much established these days. And besides, Bogdan did the street dealing, and it was in nobody's interest to reduce supply. And these killings. The cocaine abandoned at the scene. Madness. The drug world wasn't like the movies.

Heroin made its long tortuous journey mostly from Afghanistan. The profits were huge. A colossal mark up. Around twenty to twenty three tons made its way into the UK every year. A multi billion pound business. Amir's suppliers in Turkey were careful in their plans, preferring large loads in one go, rather than the dribble of supply, using mules. But it was fraught with danger and getting harder to do. And no other gang would commit mass murder and bring down the sort of attention Amir himself was now suffering.

Threats and a good beating maybe. A stabbing or shooting happened but was rare. And normally between street dealers. Never importers. In the four years since Amir had left Turkey to set up in the UK, he had never had a delivery seized or a man arrested. He had gained the utmost trust of his suppliers and made a fortune. And now this. Six of his own men dead. Two shot by the police after apparently being duped into doing so. Four from a supplier, who were demanding to know why his men had fired on theirs. And not very convinced at what Amir had told them so far.

Something other than drug turf was on the agenda here. Somebody was, for whatever reason, targeting him. He intended to find out who. And kill them. But who? Hassan pulled up in the car. He got in. He called Bogdan as they pulled away from the police station.

Chapter 38. Explanations and revelations.

Daniel and Janet were in the villa next door with Lee and Angel. They all had coffee or orange juice. Angel and Lee could see the young couple were in a very serious mood.

Daniel said, "There's no point in delaying this, Lee. This is a letter to me. From your father. He states in it he wants you to read it. And Angel. I'd like you to read it as well. I'm going outside." He looked really choked up as he handed Lee the opened envelope and went outside. Janet thought about joining him but decided not to. She wanted to see this couple's reaction.

Lee read it. She watched his face go from incredulous to almost grief-stricken, and saw his eyes fill with tears. He passed it to Angel who also read it. And she started to cry, more over John's lovely words about her than the revelations about Daniel, but didn't show it. After a minute she composed herself and looked at Janet. "Have you read it Jan?" she asked in a thick voice.

"Yes. He thought I might leave him over it. He thinks you two will be appalled at him."

Angel said, "Of course we won't. Lee, will you go bring him in?"

But Lee was already on his way. He got to the balcony where Daniel was sitting like a statue on a chair and said, "So now I can finally get to know my brother maybe?"

"I'm truly sorry Lee. All these years. I just couldn't talk to you about it."

"I do understand Daniel. You were probably right not to. I never had Dad's wisdom and maturity in my early years. I have now. And I support everything he says in that letter the same way he did. Without reservation."

Daniel stood. And they embraced. Angel and Janet watched from inside. And then hugged each other.

It was a new era. They all knew it. A terrified boy who had grown into a lonely man, who had walked a fearsome path in life, a path chosen by himself, was going to have to come in from the cold. To a new life. With family and a relationship. New challenges he wouldn't have a clue how to face. They were all going to have to be there for him. As he walked through the door and was embraced by Angel, Daniel knew they all would be, just as John Tremayne had known they would. They all sat down and they started talking.

The brothers had a lot of catching up to do. Daniel needed very much to talk to Lee about keeping in place the arrangements and support put in place by his father, which Lee was both surprised at by the scale of it and very happy to do. They all had a future to map out. Janet was just pinching herself to make sure it wasn't a dream. How on earth she'd got here from a flat in South London she'd never know. But she was very glad she had. These were good people.

Daniel was a wonderful man. She and her children were finally safe and secure. And happy. Daniel Cade wasn't the only one here starting a new journey. She smiled. Knowing him, he was probably not looking forward to it as much as she was. He'd actually have to start having more to do with other people, instead of just avoiding them. Or killing them.

Chapter 39. Pointing the finger.

Amir sat in silence as he was driven through the heavy traffic by Hassan. Bogdan had been released over an hour earlier. He'd only been wheeled in as a known accomplice of Amir's, just to turn the screws a bit, but he was seething over it. Amir picked him up as arranged. Bogdan, with two of his men in tow, shoved themselves aggressively into his car. Before Amir could say a word, Bogdan said, "I've got two men looking for that fucking copper Davidson. And you Amir, need to deal with that bitch of yours. I have brought these men to help do just that."

Amir looked at him. "Irena? You think Irena is behind this?"

Bogdan was raging with anger. "Wake up man. Woman like that? Screwing you without charging? She's the one booked the car. She's the one knew Ali would have it at home. She knows everything. Because you think with your fucking dick. All those men dead. Our money and supplies gone. We're struggling to fucking supply, Amir. And Davidson told us Tremayne was going to the Gambia. So who the hell told the filth that the car was a terrorist threat? Where the hell do you think that fucking suitcase appeared from? I'm going to get it out of her. With or without your fucking say so Amir."

Amir thought it over. He was inwardly fuming at Bogdan's arrogance but that would keep for now. Because it made sense. He didn't want it to. But it did. "Okay. We go to my place. The police are gone. They found nothing. The business computers and phones are very well concealed. But no roughing her up Bogdan. Until we are sure."

"I'm sure already. You will be. She'll crack. But you need to toughen up again Amir. We're taking big hits here. One more disaster and our partnership ends. You understand me well, yes?"

Amir nodded, and thought silently. "Albanian bastard. You will pay for that screwing you without charging remark." But he felt a cold rage building. He believed in Irena. He really loved her. Now this. The car drew up at Amir's building. The four men went inside and Hassan drove the car away.

Upstairs, Irena had seen them arrive. She was frightened but she'd point blank refused to run away. This wasn't over yet. The email from Daniel, detailing the audacious plan, had given her the basis to survive this. Told her what to say. How to act. That man was just incredible at seeing the next move, the next game play. She'd never known anybody like it. She just had to play it right. Exactly as he'd said. Her very life depended on it.

The door opened and Amir came in first, followed by Bogdan, who looked evil. Well. He was. And two surly-looking thugs. She moved towards Amir to embrace him but Bogdan stepped smartly forward and slapped her so hard she nearly fell. A ring on his finger had drawn blood from a cut on her cheek. She screamed in pain.

"Amir! Darling why are you letting him do this? In our home?"

Bogdan dragged her further into the room by her arm and threw her roughly onto a huge couch. His men pulled the curtains. The room became gloomy and sinister.

Amir said, "Bogdan, go easy. This is not a good place to do this. The police may be watching."

"Fuck the police. And if this bitch doesn't start talking, those two," he pointed at his two men, "are going to fuck her," pointing at Irena, "at the same time."

He directed his enraged stare at Irena. Leaned down over her. "Who have you been selling us out to, you arrogant bitch? Don't look at him. Look at me! Who is behind this attack on our organisation."

"What are you talking about? I am part of this organisation. You think I want all this? You think I want to go to prison maybe?"

"I'm warning you.................."

"And I am telling you. I am Amir's woman and true to this organisation."

"Amir's woman. Ha! You screw all you need to know out of him. And sell the information."

"And who would I sell it to Bogdan? Who? Amir pays me well. I love him. We are Turkish. We have honour. Not like you. You Albanian pig!"

Bogdan leant further down and slapped her again. She was ready this time, and it caught her on the side of her head but it still hurt like hell!

"Hit me all you want. I don't even know what you want to know."

"Who did you tell about the hire car? Who did you tell it would be at young Ali's address overnight?"

"Nobody. Ali collected it. That is all I know."

"How did that fucking case with Amir's fingerprints on it end up in that car? Full of explosives. That case that had Amir's cash in it?"

"How the hell would I know that? I never saw a case or any fucking cash!"

"You're lying. Perhaps you want these two to fuck you, yes? Who did you tell about the exchange?"

"I never knew where the exchange was. Or when. I tell Amir I never want to know. And I fucking don't know. Even now after the shooting I still don't know where it was. You're an idiot"

Bogdan moved again, but Amir said "No Bogdan. Enough. I need to talk to her."

Bogdan stepped back. "Very well. You fucking ask her what she has been doing. But my patience wears thin Amir."

Amir looked at Irena. "Tell me everything Irena. I cannot watch this. You will talk in the end woman. It doesn't have to be like this. In the name of Allah, speak." As he said it, Bogdan's phone rang. He answered it. "Good. Start to soften him up. Just a little to scare the shit out of him. I will be there in an hour." He looked at Amir. "My men have Davidson."

Irena heard him and thought, "Perfect." It was time to play the part.

She looked at Amir. "You said 'in the name of Allah'. At last the light goes on in your brain Amir."

He glared in rage at her, "What the hell do you mean by that?"

She got to her feet and hissed at Bogdan, "Get away from me you bastard."

He was so startled he took a step backwards. She continued, eyes blazing with anger, a trickle of blood on her cheek, as she looked slightly down at Amir.

"Amir, will you look at yourself. This madness. You let this thug….this beast….hit me. Threatens to have these thugs fuck me, yes? In front of you. In our home? A time was you would have killed anyone who insulted me. You were my man. But no more. Kill me if you will, I no longer care. I do not know who has caused you and that pig such losses. But I have never betrayed you. But I have an idea who might have done these things. You want to hear it Amir? Or you actually want to watch these beasts fuck me maybe?"

"Mind your tongue woman. Just talk."

"Daesh"

"Daesh?" from Bogdan. "Ridiculous. Amir. Give her to the boys to play with for a while. We'll go and deal with the lying bastard Davidson. Then come back. Maybe then she will be more helpful."

"Wait. Irena why do you say such things?"

"Oh Amir, think! Davidson. This policeman in your pay. He tells you of the man going to the Gambia. He tells you of everything he knows. He tells you of the military weapons used against you. He tells you no lies. He holds nothing back. He does nothing wrong. Yet that idiot," pointing at Bogdan, "now has the man in his grip and is having him beaten. He comes here to beat me. I who have also done nothing wrong. You are looking for answers in the wrong places Amir." He looked intently at her. "Go on."

Even Bogdan was listening now. Irena could tell by his expression.

"Who has access to military weapons and explosives Amir? Daesh. Who do we know from all the news, needs money as they cannot pay their fighters? Daesh. Who attacks Turkey? Daesh."

"But how? Why our operation? It makes no sense."

"Oh Amir. I had thought this over while you were away with the police. After all I hear and the police questions. I thought of the reason to tell the police why the car was hired. Would I do that if I wanted to harm you? No. Did I tell them where your laptop and phones are that are hidden in this very apartment? No. I wished to talk to you when you returned. About my thoughts. But you show up with that thug and hurt me."

"Tell me these thoughts Irena. I want to hear them. And Bogdan will listen." Bogdan nodded.

Irena launched into a savage, expletive-ridden, angry tirade at Amir, with a fearlessness she wasn't feeling inside. But this had to convince them that she was beyond caring about him if he wouldn't listen.

"Ali and Mohammed were young men. Muslims. Say they were radicalised like so many. Say they had been. Say they were supplying Daesh with information. It might explain your meeting getting attacked perhaps? By snipers as you say, yes? And it might explain how that fucking car I hired, at your instructions Amir, that I never even fucking saw, was full of explosives maybe? Of a type used by Daesh. Maybe they were going to attack the airport? Or get the explosives there for others to do it? And if they took your money Amir, they would also have had your fucking stupid case, yes? And if they have died. Well, maybe your problems have died with them? Unless there are others maybe? That is where you should be looking Amir. But according to that genius there - the great Bogdan - I had the case all along? Oh yes. Of course. Where? In my underwear drawer maybe? You live here with me Amir. Did you see the case perhaps? You need information very urgently Amir. But just to make things even better, that brutal fucking stupid oaf…..," she pointed at the clearly shocked Bogdan, "Is having the one man who could get you information from within the police beaten up as we speak. Brilliant, yes?" Both Amir and Bogdan were speechless. Daesh.

Then Irena said, "Well. Have your thugs rape me if you will get a thrill from it Bogdan. And get it over with. Then kill me. And you and I are finished Amir. Even if your idiotic Albanian friend doesn't have me raped and killed in front of your once loving eyes. You pair of heartless bastards."

She slumped back onto the sofa. Then she started to cry. It was no act. She was terrified. Either they bought in to the Daesh theory and she lived. Or they didn't.

They did. Bogdan made the call to his men, telling them to hold Davidson there but treat him well. There had been a mistake. They were on their way. Amir asked Bogdan to wait down by the car with his men, after calling Hassan to come and get them.

Then he spoke with Irena and told her he was sorry. Begged for forgiveness. He had to go, but he begged her to be there on his return. He would make it up to her. She was clever. And her theory on their problems was brilliant. He needed her. He loved her. Such a thing would never happen again. They were under pressure. They had got it wrong. It was Bogdan who accused her, not he, Amir. It had not crossed his mind. She wanted him to go so tearfully, and reluctantly, she promised to be there when he got home. Amir left. Irena smiled to herself. She'd get some lovely flowers and some very expensive gifts later. And she was still in there. Stronger than before.

She got her phone from her handbag and called Daniel. He picked up. He was very glad she was safe and they had fallen for it. He said he would wait to hear updates from her and he wanted her to call him as often as possible, to discuss the final stage of this operation in detail. But she thought he sounded a bit, well, emotional. That would be very unlike Daniel. She dabbed at the cut on her cheek with a tissue. Bastard. Might leave a small scar. To remind her of Bogdan. After he was jailed.

Chapter 40. More explanations.

Back in Gambia, the two couples were out for lunch together. The conversation was lighter now. It had been an emotional morning and there had been a lot of revelations throughout it. Particularly about Daniel. His quiet descriptions of some of the events in his life, and they were, they all knew, only a fraction of them, had been fascinating. And quite frightening. The dojos in Japan. The years in the Foreign Legion, then more time in Japan. The spiritualism and meditation and discipline. The mercenary years. Then close protection for people who would pay for it. Some of them very unsavoury people. Where the idea to hit both individual criminals and gangs had come into play, resulting in paedophile rings smashed, people trafficking gangs destroyed and the victims helped. The good things. The ex-legionnaires who had joined him at times.

Ray and his skills with computer hacking. The help given to abused children, trafficked people and victims of crime using money extorted, or taken from, those who had caused their suffering, backed up by John Tremayne where necessary.

An incredible story.

They all agreed that they would meet up again in the evening. Both Daniel and Lee had things to attend to. Lee said he had a conference call regarding business. Daniel, well he didn't say. Some things would take a while to change.

Alone a little while later, Daniel was sitting with Janet on the balcony of their own villa and said he needed to talk to her. She smiled and said he always could.

"I am so sorry all this has happened so quickly Jan. It worried me a lot. The letter was a shock. I wanted to get to know you a lot better before all my past had to come up."

"It's not a problem Daniel, really. Perhaps it's better to just get it all out of the way quickly."

"It truly doesn't bother you? My past, what I've done, what I do? It's not legal. And I will never lie to you, I have killed people, caused suicides. Not if it's avoidable. But it has happened."

"No Daniel, truly it doesn't. I understand your motivation to do these things. Changing other people's lives as John changed yours. I know you well enough to know you're not a psychopathic killer."

Daniel smiled at her. "I'm not a killer by nature. But some of these drug gang members and traffickers are totally ruthless. So sometimes it got violent and there was no other way. Some of the paedophiles were respectable people who we extorted money from in return for not turning them in. But we always did once we'd got the money which we used to hit more of them and help victims. Some ended their own lives, rather than face exposure and justice. But it will end now, I promise. John was right in his letter. Enough is enough doing it my way and I want to be with you. And my life has to change. And I want it to."

"I'm glad. Because I can't believe how much you've changed my life. Yes, it's been a whirlwind. One shock after another. But I believe you love me, and I know I love you. And how you helped James was wonderful. The kids are happy and relaxed around you. I couldn't ask for more, it's like a dream. I still think I'll wake up."

"It's not a dream. I want what we have very much. I love you more than you'll ever know."

"Good. But I have to ask you something. It was you that got rid of Barry, wasn't it?"

"Yes, I did arrange it. I know what the law is like in the UK, you would never have been rid of him. Even if, you know, if we hadn't worked out, I couldn't have let you go back to that. Or James."

"Can you tell me what happened to him?"

"Not exactly. I wasn't there. But he would have woken up gagged and taped with a pair of eyes looking at him out of a balaclava. And a voice offering to snip his toes off with a set of bolt croppers if he didn't agree do the right thing, kill him if he reappeared. More effective than a court order usually. Which is why UK justice doesn't work. Scum like him aren't scared of it."

"Oh my God he would have crapped himself!"

"I am informed he wet himself and suffered a broken nose."

Janet laughed. "He was always pretty brave threatening women and children. Thank you, I won't mention it again."

"Good, it's the past. But now there is something I need to say."

"Okay."

"We are a couple now Jan? You mean it and we're going to be together?"

"Oh Daniel please, I don't say things I don't mean. Don't doubt me. I still can't believe you want me!"

"Well I do, I have no doubts at all. So please take these Jan."

He handed her an envelope. "Solomon collected these from Banjul for me earlier. In here there is a cheque book and debit card for an account in your name. There is twenty five thousand pounds in it, and there is a credit card in your name with a limit of ten thousand. At the end of each month they will be topped back up to those limits by whatever is spent, by automated transfer."

"Daniel! You can't, I mean I can't take these."

"Janet, you have to have your own money. We are a couple now but I can't live with you asking me if you can have money. I will be away sometimes, you have to have money. The children will need things."

"But it's a fortune Daniel. I don't need all that."

"Maybe not, but you have to get used to a new life. Our life, together. We are not short of money Jan. I care little for it, actually. But I like to buy things when I want to. All I want is you to do the same, without asking me for it. Or if you can."

"Janet looked at him. "It just doesn't seem right."

"You remember when I said to you that if you were my girlfriend it would be our money? And you said you weren't so it was a bloody silly thing to say?"

"She smiled. "Yeah, just before I said if you just wanted a shag just bloody say so."

"Well you are my girlfriend now. So saying it doesn't seem right is a bloody silly thing to say."

She smiled. "I'm sorry, thank you Daniel. It's a lovely thing to do."

"Good. Then we can leave it at that then?"

"No not really."

"Why?"

She smiled at him and kissed him. "I want you to just bloody say so. Now."

Chapter 41. Wrongly accused.

Amir and Bogdan had got to the lock up where Davidson was being held. They looked around to check for prying eyes, then banged the door. A bolt slid and the door opened and they went in. The door was quickly closed. Amir cursed, as he saw Davidson, sitting there in the gloomy light with a swollen eye and nose. He was holding an ice pack he'd been given on them. He looked terrified at Amir and Bogdan.

"Why are you doing this to me? I have done nothing other than what we agreed."

Amir walked over to him. Davidson literally cowered. He was scared witless.

"Michael," Amir said softly. "We have made a terrible mistake and I apologise profoundly. Tempers ran high after Bogdan and myself were arrested. Bad decisions were made. You have done nothing wrong and you are free to leave. My car will take you wherever you wish to go."

Davidson visibly relaxed. "Okay. Thank you Amir."

"But before you leave I would ask you to listen to me, Michael. I wish to keep our arrangement and I wish to compensate you for today. I would very much like to discuss that with you."

Mick looked at him and said, "Let's get something straight Amir - I've crossed the line. I'm a bent copper now. There's no going back, that's a fact. But I never sold you out to anybody. I will not sell you out. I don't like what you do, dealing fucking drugs. I just don't care about it anymore. But I don't like being threatened. So if we keep our arrangement, this sort of shit never happens again."

"Agreed Michael."

"I mean it Amir. Use violence on me again and you will have to kill me -and the police hunt down cop killers. If I survive it, I will confess to it and take you and that bastard with me." Nodding towards Bogdan.

"I understand you Michael. We need to respect each other. Again, I apologise. It won't happen again." Amir also looked at Bogdan, who nodded curtly.

"So, what do you want to say?"

Amir ran the ISIS theory by him. Davidson looked shocked but as he thought it through he said, "You know it does fit. The weapons, the skills. Explosives, young Muslim lads. Not my department, but it's common knowledge that they can be turned by radicals."

"Have you heard of any line of investigation into this, Michael."

"No, all I have heard is the ex-military theory. But it's probably a line that would be taken now the anti-terrorist teams are on this investigation, because of the airport road incident."

"Could you perhaps enquire into it?"

"Of course, I can try if you wish. But I will have to be careful. It's not our team's line of work."

"That would be very helpful, Michael. It may well be that, with the deaths of the two in the car, the problem has gone. It may well be that there are others within our organisation. That is for us to check. But if these events are being orchestrated by some radical group from outside of our business…. well, any leads to whoever is responsible would be very useful, you understand?"

"I understand. I would like to leave now. I will enquire about this tomorrow and I will keep you informed, as always."

"Thank you, Michael. Again, my apologies for the misunderstanding." He gave Mick an envelope. It felt a lot thicker than usual. Mick nodded and walked to the door. Hassan was told to drive him where he needed to go and then return to collect Amir.

Lee Tremayne was sitting at Daniel's desk in Daniel's villa, looking at the huge computer monitor, slightly to one side so that Angel, Janet and Daniel, seated on a couch, could see it. Alan Shand was on the screen. The system was on loudspeaker.

They had talked for a while about business matters incomprehensible to the three onlookers. Then Lee had asked Alan, "Do you have any knowledge of some political idea or plan my father had?"

"Yes Lee. The documents are in a locked briefcase in my safe at the office."

"You never mentioned it?"

"I was told not to by John. Until you asked about it."

"Well I am asking now Alan."

"I will give them to you when you get back."

"Have you seen them?"

"No Lee, he kept them very private. The case was added to over time, now and again. He talked about his views, obviously. But he never showed anything to me."

"Right. Well I have another idea Alan."

"Which is?"

"Bring them here yourself. You could do with some sun."

"Lee, we have a lot on. This bloody EU referendum and other things. We have to be ready."

"We'll deal with it from here. Bring your wife, book it to the company. Business trip, use the jet."

Alan knew it was futile to argue. And yes, the sunshine would be nice. But the wife might not be. Things weren't good, but he'd ask her. Wouldn't care if she didn't want to go. He sighed and said,

"Okay. Give me twenty-four hours."

"Something else I want you to bring, Alan."

"Go on."

"My children."

"Well they're due back at school soon, Lee. What will I tell them?"

"Just say," Lee thought about it. Thought about the pompous head teacher and her arrogant manner. The liberal nonsense his kids came home with their heads filled with. The pathetic stifling health and safety. Non-competitive sports days for fuck's sake, "Just say I said to mind their own fucking business."

"Lee!" From Angel behind him.

"I'll think of an alternative Lee," said Alan, unable to hide a huge grin. "See you out there soon."

Chapter 42. Sowing the seed.

DC Mick Davidson was in the station early the next morning. Fleming was in his office. The door was open so he walked in. Fleming looked up and said "What the bloody hell happened to you?", as he saw the bruises on Mick's face.

"Ah nothing. Broke up a fight at my local, looks worse than it is. Guv, I did a bit on the sexual assault at East Croydon station and a bit of legwork on the recent burglaries. Didn't get far. But I was thinking about this other business, the Wesley Mason stuff. Well, the latest thing with the car really."

"Well we gave that Amir the third degree. But of course there was nothing to pin him to the car. The case was the big thing but as he could prove he'd not seen either the case or the vehicle, we couldn't actually charge him. Marshall was pissed off. But Amir was definitely rattled."

"Well my thinking is this guv, those explosives in the car. I read the report."
"So did I. What about them?"

"Well that's not Amir is it? I mean guns yeah, grenades, well at a push maybe. But a load of explosives, bomb making? What the fuck would a drug importer or dealer want to blow up? No way."

"And your point is Mick?"

"ISIS. They have military skills and weapons. And snipers. I was thinking maybe they might have hit these gangs for the money? Just a thought."

"That is quite a thought Mick. I'll call Marshall with it."

"Well it sort of made sense. With that car, even the drug meet hit. I just can't see where Wesley and Mason fit though. They are the odd ones out in all this."

"Bloody well would be, they're our problem," said Fleming. He dialled Marshall's number.

"My DC, Mick Davidson, had an idea. I'll put him on." Mick took the phone and ran the concept past Marshall Bland, pleasantly surprised that Fleming hadn't edged him out. Bland took it on board. It did fit. It was every bit as good a fit as the ex-military angle.

Mick said, "With money as the motive and maybe religion as the reason to not touch the drugs, it might be worth a look Sir?"

"It might well be Mick," replied Bland. "And the anti-terrorist and intelligence agencies are on this anyway eue to the airport proximity, the alert and the explosives. So we might well get something."

It was a good call and he thanked Mick for his input. Mick hung up, passed the phone back to Fleming. It still left them no nearer to finding who'd offed

Wesley and Mason. But to be honest, he didn't give a fuck about them. Good riddance if you asked him. But nobody would. All he had to do now was keep an eye on the updates from the linked cases and keep Amir posted. If it was terrorist-related and Amir wanted to take that lot on, well, good luck with that.

Chapter 43. The Turkish connection.

Amir had gone home to Irena, laden as predicted with flowers and a very expensive bit of jewellery as well as an equally expensive watch. Irena had given him a hard time, a very hard time, but then relented and agreed to try to make this work.

After that had all been resolved, the conversation turned to matters of the police. And the problems.

Amir told her that Davidson was still in the frame, just, but had agreed to investigate the Daesh possibility and thought it was a viable suggestion. Amir repeated that Irena was very clever to have come up with the possibility.

Irena said, "But what if it is, Amir? Surely you do not wish to take on Daesh? They are fanatical to their cause. Not another gang you can fight and win. They are many in number."

Amir pondered this. "You are, as always, wise. Perhaps it is time to move on, my sweet."

"Well, all you can do is wait, Amir. If Davidson turns up evidence that this is Daesh, then you must make the decision. If it is not? Then Amir, I do not know where you could look next to find who has done this to us."

"It can only be a rival gang."

"But this theory of the police. This sniper attack. Amir, I am frightened. We are all turning against each other. Many are dead. Young men. This has to end, Amir. You have the clubs, property, a fortune invested overseas. You don't need this. We don't need this. Please say you will give it some thought."

Amir replied, "I will, of course. But I will wait until we know more. Now I have to go round the clubs and check all is at least well there."

He gently touched the cut on her cheek. "I am truly sorry Irena. Damn that Bogdan. If I did not need him right now I swear he would die. But we have another big shipment soon. That must go well. We are struggling now, damn it."

Irena said, "Try not to worry Amir darling. With some luck, maybe those two foolish young men in that car were the problem. And, through their foolishness, they are now dead and gone. And if that is the case, so are our problems. Let us just hope so and at least have a little normal time for a while, yes?"

He kissed her. "You are, as always, right, my beautiful woman. I will see you later." He left.

Irena unlocked her desk and booted up her personal laptop notepad and started composing an email, thinking as she wrote, "My beautiful woman. Ha! Never. I don't want you to quit but I have to play the part. I will see you weak and penniless as you left us, Amir. Or dead, I don't care which."

Her slender fingers tapped away at the keyboard writing to the man who would make it happen. Daniel Cade. The strangest man she'd ever met, but the only man she could have met to do this. Because her sister Aisha, had decided to make cheap bangles, to sell in a small market, in a quiet place in Turkey. And met Daniel Cade. She smiled, recalling the strange story as she typed.

Her mother, crippled father and her sister Aisha, had, along with herself, after her father was injured badly, moved from Istanbul to a place called Mavashir in Didim, on the Aegean sea coast. A place famous for its sunsets. A fair sized evening market drew people in later in the day, many of them tourists, who walked the market and bought whatever they bought and then went down to the pretty waterfront to eat and drink. They were living with her aunt, her father's sister. There was little money. Irena had completed her degree and was working in the financial industry in Istanbul. Aisha was at university.

They had both left those things to make the move to be with their stricken father, a policeman. Shot by a cowardly thug in the back and left paralysed. The man was never brought to justice. But her father's fellow officers knew exactly who it was. And that the pig boasted about it. Became more of a player in the drug world as he rose through the ranks.

Money was tight, home life was crowded. Her father was a shadow of himself and had eventually ended his own life by a drug overdose. Irena had gone to pieces and swore to herself she would avenge her father. But she had found out that the man who had shot her father had gone to the UK where he was operating a drug empire, promoted by, and supplied by, his former masters in Istanbul.

Against her mother's and sister's wishes and pleas, she had left for England. She told them she had to get well-paid work. An investment bank had hired her, her visas were dealt with, and she had left. Not only to work. But to get close to the man who had ruined their lives.

She had done both and was at the point of moving in with Amir Ferez, when Daniel Cade had come into their lives. Aisha, ever creative, had decided to make cheap, hand-crafted jewellery and bangles to sell at the market and was there, on the edge of the market, with a small table, when an Englishman had approached her and offered to buy all of it! Aisha, like herself, was a bright girl and fluent in English. Aisha had said she wanted four hundred lira for the lot. The man had insisted on paying one thousand! And after handing her exactly that, told her she could keep the stuff. Aisha had got angry, and demanded to know just why he was doing this. And the reply had been that she could now shut the stall, and come and talk to him. Because she needed to. Aisha had, she knew she wanted to. But never to this day could explain why.

Irena recalled vividly the email from her sister in which she said she did not know what Irena was doing but she knew it was dangerous, and that Irena had to talk to Daniel Cade and tell him the truth. She had to listen, and let herself be guided. She had experienced such things from Aisha in the past and so she had done as Aisha had said, despite her terrible fears of her family finding out how she had whored herself to her father's killer. She just trusted her instincts and now knew full well her secret was safe with Daniel. She now also knew that without Daniel she would not have achieved her aim. Or maybe even survived trying to.

Daniel Cade was buying a place for himself in nearby Altinkum. A nice town, although rapidly becoming a concrete jungle, with lots of construction work. But Daniel liked the place and the local people very much as well as the easy access to deserted coastline, and wanted to spend time there. Property was cheap if you bought wisely. Daniel asked Aisha to assist him in the purchase, for which he would pay her. He met their mother and aunt over the next few days and talked to Aisha for hours, and got the whole story about their father. And about how worried Aisha was about Irena. Where she was and what she was doing. Alone in the UK and that she knew something was wrong. Daniel had understood and told Aisha that he and Irena had to meet. And soon.

What happened next was even stranger. Daniel was buying off-plan in an apartment block build. Twenty-two dwellings. Four were penthouses with roof gardens. The rest were two or one bedroom apartments. After negotiations with the developer, he bought the whole bloody thing! He wanted two penthouses himself and offered one of the others to Aisha and one to her mother, rent-free, on condition they managed the rest of the block for him. Cheap rents to people who needed homes. He wanted them to collect the rents and look after the building. Aisha was astounded, couldn't believe it. But the deal went through, and she had dealt with the project, on good pay, until it was completed, moving in with their mother when it was. They gradually rented out the rest of the place. Everybody who lived there loved it there.

Daniel had, once things were settled and the deal finalised and with the building in progress, flown to the UK and met Irena. He listened to all she had to say about Amir Ferez and her intention to destroy him despite the disgust she felt at her own behaviour to do it. He had understood. And simply said that sometimes intervention against evil came with a terrible price to good, and joined forces with her to do it. They were now working towards doing just that. She adored Daniel. Neither she nor Aisha ever understood quite why he had appeared in their lives. He only said some things were meant to happen and sometimes you just had to let yourself be guided, by way of explanation.

But they were both very glad he had. Amir was both powerful and ruthless. She knew now she couldn't have done this alone. The mysterious man helping her was, quite simply, the most efficient, confident, person to do it with. She would be glad when it was over but there was more to do. She continued to type the email to the man who would get it done.

Chapter 44. Doubts and fears.

It was early, Janet was still asleep. Daniel smiled as he thought of her. He liked his new life. He had his fears. But none of those were as bad as the fears that had been with him for so many years. Lee was all his father had said he would be. Daniel now had a woman in his life. And because of her, a physical relationship, that he sadly, at times, struggled with. He loved their physical relationship but suffered sometimes with dark thoughts from his past. He froze when touched, was ill at ease. He hoped in time they would pass. It was his problem, not hers. She was so lovely. He would deal with it.

And an instant family came with the beautiful girl who was now his life partner. All were things he never thought he would attain. All were things he had always wanted. At times, it had been doubtful he would live to see them, but he had. He knew there were changes to be made. He wanted to reduce the risks in his own existence, which wouldn't be easy, but it could be done. It had to be. He didn't want the violence of his past to catch up with him and hurt the woman and the children in his life, not now. It would be addressed. But, for now, there was still work to be done.

Daniel focused himself and read carefully the email from Irena. So brave. Isolated in London. Making terrible sacrifices to destroy the man who had destroyed her family. She wouldn't quit. So Daniel wouldn't fail her now. He would see this through to the end for her and her sister Aisha.

Amir Ferez would never have dreamt, all those years ago, that when he pulled the trigger that night in Istanbul, he would unleash such a vengeance on himself in the future. That the very last person he would want pitched against him, now was part of it, because of his own and Bogdan's evil brutality. Trafficked girls, some very young, forced into drug use and prostitution. Lives destroyed. They were both everything Daniel Cade despised. They just didn't know that yet. And wouldn't. Until it was far too late.

So. Amir was receptive to the idea of Islamic terror groups possibly funding themselves by hitting his deals. That was good. The bent officer, Davidson, was still in place as a conduit of information. That too was good. Amir could be weakened further without violence if this information was used wisely.

Daniel deleted the email and switched off the computer and went for his run and a swim. He thought better while doing that.

Chapter 45. Getting nowhere.

Bland was pissed off. He had read through the files again on Amir Ferez. Non-stick slime ball. Never able to pin anything solid on him. The recent drug seizure was the first major success against the fat bastard in nearly three years. So well hidden they struggled to find it, even knowing it was there, concealed behind a skilfully fashioned false bulkhead, in a refrigerated lorry trailer. Which wasn't as long inside as it was outside, by about seven inches. A lot of heroin, it would have to hurt him. And his cocaine purchase lost the same day as well as, it had to be assumed, a lot of his money. And four of his men, then two more in the hire car.

Word on the street was he was struggling to supply that scumbag Bogdan Gentian, who dealt it out through his dealers and pimps. He was taking big hits. But not from the police. Marshall wanted to find out who he was taking them from. This was murder. Involved guns. And now it involved provoking a police shooting, this had gone too bloody far! Things were fucking bad enough without some wise arse getting the old bill to do the shooting for them.

But he was getting nowhere. There was no intelligence to suggest any terror group's knowledge of, or involvement, regarding that bloody hire car. Not a chance of a trace on the shooter, who'd fired that bullet, setting off the police response.

He looked at his notes, yet again, with increasing frustration. The facts. The two men in the car were Amir's and Bogdan's thugs. The case had been handled at some point by Amir, probably when the fat git had stuffed it with cash to buy his poxy cocaine with, but no way of proving it. The car was hired by Amir through his bloody dodgy front company that owned his clubs and casino and other properties. Tremayne was in the Gambia, still was. Marsh had checked with his office. The shot fired that hit Bewes was deliberate. But deliberately non-lethal. So it was fired to hopefully make the armed police fire at the two men in the car. And they quite justifiably had. Same MO as the drug meet. Those were the facts. Which only left more questions.

The two men were going to the Gambia. Why? It had to be linked to Tremayne. If it was then how did that fat git Amir even know he was there? Marsh made a note as he thought about that, to call Fleming.

The only person who had remotely linked the deaths of Tremayne's parents to the drug meet shooting, was Fleming. And that remote link had been agreed as a possible lead by himself. So how did Amir know that? If he did, then had that maybe got to Amir from within the police? If it had, then just possibly Amir thought he could slap a connection to the attackers of his drug meet out of Tremayne? Okay, remotely possible.

But. Amir was a shitty drug baron, not a shitty terrorist. So where did the explosives fit? Why were they in the car at all and how did they get there? And why, on a well-maintained hire car, was the trunk mechanism broken? Marsh had a bad feeling about that. The two men had to get to the airport, they would be in a hurry. Tried the trunk, didn't work. Cursed, threw luggage on back seat, left for Gatwick airport. In a car that had been flagged up to the police as a terrorist threat.

Marsh knew the answer. Those two saps weren't meant to look in the boot, they were meant to do exactly what they did, and drive to a place where they very likely would be shot by armed police. Who were duped into doing it, by a bloody sniper who must have watched them setting up the intercept. Who had fired a shot knowing full well the most likely outcome of doing it. But for fuck's sake why plant the explosives in the car? All that could have happened without that case being in the boot. Amir Ferez was hardly likely to have stuck a fucking suitcase with his own bloody dabs on in the vehicle, yet alone stuffed with explosives. Marsh held his head in his hands. He had a poxy headache now. He rang Fleming and arranged a meet. Be nice to get out of the office if nothing else. This investigation was getting on his tits.

Chapter 46. Sex and money.

A couple of days had passed in the Gambia. Good days. The four adults were getting to know each other well and all liking what they were finding. Lee and Daniel had taken James and Katie out in the rib. Janet had gone for lunch with Angel. She'd talked to Angel throughout lunch and mentioned the money situation and what Daniel had put at her disposal.

"I suppose he could do it after, you know, John leaving him all that money?"

Angel replied with a smile, "He could do it comfortably without it."

"Really?"

"Yes hun. He asked Lee if he was okay about John's bequest, said he didn't need it. Stop worrying girl, Daniel was already wealthy, believe me."

"So you're all wealthy. Have you and Lee got like, titles or anything?"

Angel grinned at her. "We never use them these days darling, relax. And Lee isn't just wealthy, he's astronomically rich. Tremayne Holdings is worth a fortune, without the family's own wealth. Our bloody house is worth four million now. Ridiculous, John's was over three. Then poor John and Ann's inheritance and insurances. Daniel refused to tap into any of it but my guess is he was comfortably a millionaire before John's bequest."

"Oh my God, I guessed he was secure. The villa and all but never thought he was, well, you know, rich."

"Well he was, is. He never spent anything much for years apparently, lived out of suitcases. Bought just what he needed and that was that. Apparently, recently, some Turkish woman invests his personal money and handles his affairs. And makes a good job of it. John handled some of it in the UK, I believe. Then he decided to buy places in Gambia and Turkey. Because he loved both of them. He hates the UK."

"He has got a place there though?"

"I believe so, on the south coast. But Lee and I have never seen it."

"What's with Turkey, do you know?"

"Yeah, we went there for a look while it was being built. It seems Daniel bought a place there a while after he bought here. Drifts between the two. Leaves here before the humidity hits and goes there to live. In between whatever the hell he does wherever he does it."

"What does he have there, a villa like here?"

"No. It's totally different to here."

"Oh. What is it then?"

"Two penthouse apartments on top of a block."

"Oh wow, sounds lovely."

"It is. But Jan, he owns the entire block of twenty two apartments. The four top properties are three bed penthouses with huge roof balconies. Then a mix of one and two bedroom apartments, all rented out and managed by the family of the woman who does his finances. They live in two of the penthouses. Daniel has two, one is his, the other for visitors."

Janet stared at her. "The whole block? He never even mentioned it!"

"Well you know him. He never tells you anything."

"That bloody man!"

They both laughed. Then Angel said, "You have to remember though that property prices aren't the nonsense they are in the UK. I recall Lee saying that the whole block was around a quarter of a million, off-plan. You can't buy a sem det bung, as the estate agents call it back home, for that."

"What made him do it though?"

"Apparently the family who look after it were in trouble. He wanted a place in the area. By buying the block he gave them somewhere to live, an income, and knew his place was in safe hands. Same as he did here. He's very shrewd, and very kind. John was exactly the same, actually. All the rents are low and paid by local people who needed homes. All the rental income goes to the family who look after it after expenses, which aren't high. So they do well. And because of that he's well liked there, same as here. He's a bit of a Robin Hood character, your Daniel. Only you have to deserve his help. And he's not a good man to cross."

"He is strange, but in a nice way. I've felt safe since he walked into that reception area. Never doubted him at all." She smiled. "I did flip at him for being so vague once. Told him if all he wanted was a shag to just bloody say so. But I've never trusted anyone so much, yet alone instantly. Yet he seemed dangerous at the same time. And he freaks me out with money. It's like he doesn't care about it at all. Gets pissed off with me if I ask if it's okay to buy something."

Angel looked at Janet. She was such a lovely, undemanding girl, with no concept of the world she lived in now.

"Well for a start, he loves you Jan. He is dangerous, as in his skills are lethal. But he would only use them to keep you safe. And he isn't foolish with money. You need to realise that your days of budgeting are over. He is totally financially secure, anything he says you can spend he can afford. That money he's put at your disposal is just his way of telling you that. So don't feel you can't spend it, or accept it."

"I will try. I've never had money to just, well, spend Angel. It's hard to accept that I have."

"Enjoy him and the lifestyle Jan. You have changed his world. You have to let him change yours."

"I guess. It's just hard Angel. I have never had a man who looked after me before."

"Well you have now. Let him do it, because he wants to. If you don't, well he won't understand."

"I suppose you're right."

"I am. Let's finish lunch and go spend some of our men's money."

Janet laughed. "Okay Mrs Billionaire, show me how it's done."

"It will be a pleasure. To start with, you're paying for lunch"

"Barclaycard?"

"That's what it's for. You see your stiff friend earns you a flexible friend"

Janet laughed so hard she nearly choked.

"You can be very raunchy for a rich chick Angelica."

"I know. That's why I have several cards."

They both laughed then, causing people to look at them in amusement.

They settled down, finished lunch and went to spend some money. After shopping they stopped for a coffee. There was nobody else near their table. Janet, who had been deep in thought for a while, asked Angel if she could talk to her about something very private.

"Sure. Bedroom stuff right?"

"Yeah. How did you know?"

"The way you're blushing."

"Well I don't know you very well. And with you being, you know."

"A distant relative of the queen?"

"Well something like that."

"It's fine. Tell Angel everything."

"It's nothing serious."

"Wants to tie you up and torment you with a stick of celery, does he? I like a bit of that."

"Angelica! No. And I don't want him to do anything freaky. This is really important to me. I don't have anyone else here to talk to."

"I'm sorry." Angel saw she was really quite upset and reached across and gently squeezed her hand. "Tell me what's wrong."

"He just seems to struggle sometimes, I think it's the abuse. He's lovely and gentle and it's good, for me. But I think his mind gets bad thoughts while we do it. And it's like, well, something he's trying to get through. Rather than just relaxing and enjoying it. That make sense?"

Angel was serious for once, and replied, "Yeah, of course it does. That sort of horror must affect you, even him. He's a tough man. But he's obviously still got issues I guess."

"I love him so much. I want things right, is all. For us both."

"You only done it at night?"

"What the....,"

"I'm serious."

"Yeah. Of course. At night in bed. Where else?"

"Don't get me started on that," Angel smiled warmly, "Light on or off? I'm still serious," as she saw Janet's expression. "Tell me."

"Off. He's really a bit shy. You do know I'm his first?"

"Really?" Angel was truly surprised. "At his age. Cor! Did you have a total white-out?" She grinned lewdly at Janet.

"Angelica! Please. This is not a laughing matter."

"Sorry hun. But actually it needs to be lightened up."

"Meaning?" Janet was clearly getting a bit ticked at this apparently light-hearted attitude.

"Chill out beautiful. He must have been bothered by the thought of it all this time. Putting it off. Not wanting anyone touching him. Losing the control he risked everything to get back. Until he met you. That's really so sad. But nice in a way. For you."

"Yeah I guess it is. But he seems to almost freeze sometimes. You know, during anything intimate. It feels like he's struggling to get through it, fighting with his mind. Rather than just enjoying it."

Angel looked at her. "I think you need to give him some shock therapy."

"Shock therapy? How?"

"All this fumbling around in the dark. His mind can likely go to bad places. Away from you. You need to get it all out in the daylight girl."

"Daylight?"

"Yeah. Where he can see you, clearly all the time. Not in a dark bedroom where his mind can wander. Your hands might not be your hands if he can't see you. He's maybe drifting to another dark room in his mind? Seriously, you're bloody gorgeous, let him see you. Take him outside and shag him. In the sunshine. Make it fun. He needs to see sex is a fun thing to do. And enjoy it, not worry about it."

"Where the hell am I going to do that?"

"You know that boat, the big one with the two engines?"

"Yeah. What about it?"

"Well out at sea there's nobody around, is there?"

"Angelica! Are you being serious?"

"Sure I am. And it's got a foam rubber deck, comfy on the knees. And if you kneel across the seats, your arse is just at the right height for a good pounding."

"Stop it! I'm being serious here!"

"So am I. I might enjoy teasing you. But you guys need to get this squared off. Try it girl. You've got nothing to lose by it. And it will work. Plus," she grinned lewdly again, "It's great fun."

"Have you bloody done it then?"

"Oh yeah. I always get Lee to borrow it for a while when we're here. He's gagging for me to mention it this trip."

"Bloody hell! No wonder you've got several cards."

"I love sex. And my husband. We enjoy our love life. I like to shock him now and again, keep it fun. It's important Jan. He loves me all the more for it. We're good together."

"You are a lovely couple. So natural together. I just want us to be like that."

Angel got up from her chair and knelt next to Janet. Took her hand in her own and said quietly, "Seriously hun, lighten up. Get him out there, make it fun. He'll be fine. He just needs to see you, not darkness."

"Maybe you're right. I just want him to be happy Angel. And me. I saw him with the kids the other day. Throwing them around in the pool. And it flashed through my mind, you know, after Barry abused James. Watching him touch them. I felt awful. It's wrong."

Angel felt for her. "Child abuse doesn't only affect the victims Jan. It tarnishes a lot of things if you aren't careful."

"I fucking hate it. He's lovely with them. We should both be really happy." She looked tearful. Angel hugged her and said, "Really. You both will be, I promise you Jan. Give it time." They drank their coffee and strolled home, with Janet deep in thought. Again.

Chapter 47. Casting blame.

Bland met Fleming in the same place as before. Coffee was ordered. Bland brought Fleming up to speed on the lack of progress. It was a dead end. He told him all his thoughts, then focused on the Gambia Tremayne situation.

"Colin. If Amir was sending his heavies to Gambia to lean on Tremayne – well, he had to know that there was a link, however tenuous, between your case and mine. The link you made."

Fleming bristled inside. "You think that information got to Amir from my department?"

"Well don't get the arse Colin. I wasn't investigating the Wesley Mason case, you were. You made the possible connection, I appreciated your input. But it begs the question how Amir would know that there even was a connection surely?"

Fleming digested that slowly. "Well, yes it does I suppose. Marsh, do you think there is any chance at all that those two thugs were just going on holiday?"

"Do you? It's too much of a coincidence Colin, I'm sorry. This is not a pop at you or your department. But this link, however slim, it just might be all we have to go on right now. None of this makes sense."

"It is a bit of a puzzle," said Fleming, a bit pissed off he'd even called his case in now. A leak from his team wouldn't sit well with his promotion prospects.

"I will look into it Marsh. But apart from Mick Davidson who was with me on the Tremayne interview, there's only a couple of civvies doing the filing would know anything at all."

"Is Davidson straight?"

"He's lazy Marsh, he's battle-fatigued. His wife has left him, he's miserable. He's just over a year from his pension. He was a very good officer and wouldn't risk his pension now. No Marsh, he's freewheeling, just wants it over. And he was so uninterested in the Tremayne angle, thought it a waste of time. Never uttered a word at the interview, sat there sulking. So no, not Davidson."

"But you will check it out Colin?"

"Yes Marsh. I will. But it doesn't make sense. If Amir was wanking away money, sending heavies to Gambia, well he would be clutching at the same straws we were. It's most likely Tremayne knows bugger all."

"I agree Colin. But somebody, somewhere, for whatever reason, is orchestrating this. It's most likely an attack on Amir and his empire. But where those explosives and your two dead suspects fit the jigsaw, I'm damned if I know."

On that note they left and went their separate ways, both wanting to see a break in the fog of this investigation. Twelve dead if you added the drug meet, Wesley and Mason and the two killed near Gatwick together. And not a single glimmer of who'd caused it all. Or the reasons why.

Chapter 48. A plan and politics.

The man who'd caused it all had finished his thinking. He had a plan. A quick email to Irena with one query. How much could Amir pay out in one hit to save his empire? The demand had to be right. Not so much to make him refuse point blank, but enough to hurt him a lot. He made a couple of phone calls to trusted people who would help. For a fee. He would wait until Irena replied with her information.

Then he would put it together. No guns, no dead bodies. This would be a different type of attack. If it worked, Amir would be weakened financially. One more hit after that would make him cash in and run, hopefully. Then they could finish him. Irena wanted him left a broken man, in jail, and would settle for nothing less. Daniel was more than happy to see it happen. And take Bogdan down with him. Bogdan was evil through and through. Worse than Amir. Daniel wanted him finished for good as well. And he would be.

Alan Shand had arrived in Gambia, with Pat, his wife, and Angelica and Lee's children. More introductions. More getting to know people.

Alan was a charming man and Janet liked him straight away but his wife hadn't been very pleasant at all. She was dour and moody and said little. There seemed to be an atmosphere between her and Angelica. Janet ignored it. The woman might be in a bad place and it was none of her business.

Alan had handed Lee a large briefcase. It was quite heavy. His father's papers. His plans for the future. For his and Daniel's eyes only. Lee asked Daniel to lock it in his safe at his villa. They would deal with it later, at a convenient, quiet moment. Although both curious, there were things going on and they both knew it would be both raw and emotional when they did undo the case to read papers that were dear to the heart of a man they both loved dearly, a man taken from them horribly and without warning.

Janet was keeping an eye on Daniel. Didn't want him to get to freaked out over things. But he was fine, if a little distracted. The children soon got to know each other and were all under Rosie's watchful eye by the pool.

All the adults were on Daniel's balcony and the conversation was, after apologies from Alan, and a grumble about it from Pat, dwelling a bit on the business and political front. At Lee's polite request of them all. Janet found it quite interesting. These were wealthy, top flight, business people and she wanted to learn more about them and how they thought compared to the mind set she had always had back in South London. Alan was basically bringing Lee up to date on the domestic front.

"Cameron has rocked the boat hard. This Brexit referendum is causing a lot of uncertainty. And the problem will continue in or out of the EU after the vote."

"In what way?" asked Lee.

"Because the polls have it neck and neck, with a very slim chance of an out vote. Far closer than Cameron would like it. The idea, in my opinion, was to give the nation a referendum purely to try to strengthen his own negotiating position with the EU itself, but assuming the vote would comfortably be to remain in the EU. Stay in and then be able to tell the nation to stop moaning about the EU. You were asked. Shut up now. But it's going wrong."

"Why though?"

"Well a lot of things. When the decision to hold a referendum was made, as a vote-winning carrot, things were different. Now you've got immigration at the top of the agenda. Terrorism and fear, Greek debt. Spanish unemployment and property crash. Big problems that people blame the EU for. Often correctly."

"So where does it go from here Alan?"

Alan glanced at his large leather-bound notebook and continued,

"The population at large will be split. Our analysts are saying that if we stay in by a slim margin, the out brigade will say it was rigged. If we vote out the in brigade will clamour to stay in. Factor into that the ridiculous constitutional laws, that apparently a referendum isn't legally binding, will lead to a lot of straw clutching by the remain camp. And you've got a mess on your hands. Seriously, out might not ever mean out. It's a farce. Like everything fucking else we do in the UK and EU."

"Alan!" said Pat.

"Sorry," Alan seemed used to getting ticked off and continued,

"An out vote might spark a panic in the markets. So the haves, who own shares and property, and the pro Europe Guardianistas might well legally challenge the result. If it's out. Add to that the EU position after an out vote is very unclear. You've got some right wankers, sorry ladies," as Pat went to intervene, "in the high command there. Angela Merkel is on the descent. This vote will hinge on the immigration issue. And that problem, especially the Syrian refugee fiasco, is laid at her door. If they pitched a review of the current policies and offered real change in return for a rerun of the referendum, in, say, a year's time – well, that might settle things down. If, and it's our peoples view that they will, they come out hostile to the UK…well that will be another massive uncertainty."

Lee looked at him. "Balls up in the making then?"

"Very much so I'm afraid. A panic is the last thing the UK needs right now. It's broke as far as government money is concerned so anything that causes a downturn is very unwelcome. And finally, there is every chance that, in the event of an out vote, Cameron will probably step down. But there are no effective leaders in the wings - since Corbyn took over at Labour, they're busy squabbling among themselves. So no effective opposition. If we vote out, we need to trigger Article Fifty to start the leaving process which could take two years anyway. But if we have no real government with the will to do it, we're in limbo indefinitely."

"Where does that leave us as a business?" asked Lee.

"We'll be fine. We have a wide spread of international investment. We've moved a lot of investment to areas least likely to be affected by it in the short term. I can't think of very much more we can do Lee."

Lee pondered this for a moment, then said, "One more thing then we'll get off this boring stuff. What is the immediate effect of an out vote? On trade. Travel. Finance markets?"

Alan thought for a while. "I'll keep it short." He looked at his leather bound notebook. "Our crystal ball gazers, soothsayers and number crunchers are telling me this, Lee. In the immediate aftermath, things will look bad. Panic mode. Particularly if the EU takes a retaliatory, spit the dummy position. Which the chances are it will. There are no real pros up there in the top echelons to do a bit of joined up thinking and react sensibly or even pretend they are listening. And if the UK has the gall to vote out they will sulk. And sulk hard. Threats will be made regarding trade and borders. Trade tariffs, travel visas, expats situation etc. And the markets will react to that. In the short term. Our guys and gals think nobody will immediately see the elephant in the front room as per usual. Including the markets, most of the politicians and the electorate"

"Which is?"

"There will be an immediate huge whinge about the fear of an out vote triggering a recession. Especially by the combined Facebook and Twitter armies of armchair economic experts. Cheerfully ignoring the fact we've had two while we've been in the bloody EU. Tedious. But it adds enormously to hysteria and public perception of things."

Lee nodded and smiled, "Takes their mind off climate change I suppose."

Alan continued, "Yeah and Cecil the lion and stuff. And cheerfully ignoring the fact that it won't be the UK that has the real problems if they vote out. It will be the Eurozone. The UK pays 13 billion a year into the EU budget. Gets 4.5 billion spent on itself so gives a net contribution of around 8.5 billion. A hell of a lot of money that the EU stands to lose and the UK stands to gain. The UK has the city of London, trading capital of the world. We deal in Sterling. We don't have to reprint a currency. We have a huge economy for a country our size. Fifth, sometimes sixth, largest in the world. Massive secured collateral in property, both residential and commercial. Owned by investors and buyers from all over the world. We buy far more from the EU than we export which gives us real clout. We don't have the euro as currency. The EU does. And it is dealing with Greek debt. Italy is right in the shit. Sorry ladies. Spain is not in a good place."

He took a long draught of beer and continued after glancing at his notes again. "Other EU countries, bar Germany, are polling up pretty level about how they would vote in or out, given the chance. In other words, Merkel, Juncker, Tusk and co are not in a good place. Because around half of the massive combined population they preside over would rather they bloody didn't. The extreme right is on the rise because of that unpopularity. And gormless immigration policies are leading to a constant fear of terrorism, crime, pressure on public services like health and education, causing racial tensions. And a surge of popularity for far right parties. It could, in theory, lead to the collapse of the EU as we know it. That could get very messy. If they had any sense they would pre-empt it and compromise. Revert back to a trading bloc and damp it down. But not a lot of sense there as I say."

"Bloody hell," said Lee.

"It could be better my friend. But politicians know best."

"Let's all go and get changed and go to Scalas," said Lee. "I think we've heard enough Euro doom."

"What a great idea," replied Alan.

They all went off to do just that, each with their own thoughts on the uncertain future faced by the UK. Bar Daniel. He was skulling over extorting a million pounds or so out of a drug baron. But then he'd always been a bit different.

After they got back, they were having last drinks on Daniel's balcony. Lee asked to talk to Daniel alone. They excused themselves and went down to the lounge with their drinks.

"What's up?" asked Daniel.

"Nothing really," replied Lee. "I just wanted a word with you. About that case."

"Sure. What about it?"

"Well, I know I got Alan out here to bring it. The man needs a break anyway. But I actually don't want to open it now."

"Okay. Fine by me Lee."

"The thing is Daniel, I was in a bad place back home after they were killed. And that bloody court case farce. Treated Angel like shit, and the kids. And poor Alan, he was running the business solo. I just think that maybe it would be best to just enjoy this break. You've got Jan and the kids now, all new to you. Opening that case is going to be very emotional. And I think it will be a pretty big deal in there Daniel. Needing a lot of thought."

"You got any idea Lee? What is in there."

"At a guess, yeah. I think the old man wanted to change the system of politics in the UK. He was talking to some serious players about it, regarding funding. He was sick of the what it had become and the way it was going. And he was dead set on doing something about it."

"And that will involve us?"

"We've both read the letter he sent you, Daniel."

"Yeah, you're right. It will involve us. Big time, knowing him."

Lee smiled. "He was quite a guy Daniel, he really cared about people. Tremayne's was run ethically and honestly from the start, with the workforce being the most important thing to him. And still is. And he seethed over the way people are treated and ignored by politicians."

"Yeah, for sure. Everything I did was to help people who were in terrible trouble. He was the most decent, caring man I ever met and he did all he could to make people's lives better."

"Well that tells me that bloody case is going to be a big deal. So how about we leave it locked, brother? He won't begrudge us a bit of time out before we start. Open it when we're done here, yeah."

"Agreed. You say when and we'll do it."

"Cool. Come on, I need another beer." They grabbed one each and went back to join the others.

Both were curious. But both were happy to wait. There was enough going on for now. Lee needed to get over his grief. Daniel was locked in a battle to bring down a drug lord. And had a new relationship to deal with. That case could stay shut for now.

Chapter 49. Where's the leak?

Fleming rang Mick as he drove back to his station and asked him to meet him in his office. He was waiting when Fleming returned. Fleming didn't beat about the bush. He told Mick what Bland had said.

Mick reacted angrily. "What a bloody nerve! You, make that we, only tried to help him, guv."

"Yes, I know that Mick. But there's no getting away from the fact that those dead guys in the car were going to the Gambia. And the only thing that fits is that they were going to lean on Tremayne. For Amir. And the simple fact is, only you and I knew that's where he was going. Apart from maybe a couple of admin staff maybe."

"Amir could have rung bloody Tremayne's office and found out where he was."

"I know that, Mick. But why would he? How would the fat git know the two things were connected?"

Mick pondered that, his brain thinking like crazy, but keeping a calm expression. "I don't know guv. Maybe. Well just a thought like."

"What Mick. Anything could help. Throw it out there."

"Well, those two were users right? Did they buy through Amir? Or one of his mate Bogdan's dealers? Could somebody who knew them, another junkie maybe, have told Bogdan or Amir there was something iffy about how they were killed? We weren't keeping it a secret"

"I don't know Mick. It's possible. Remotely possible."

Mick continued, "Well that shitty block of flats where Mason lived, where they were both found. It's crawling with lowlifes and druggies. Our guys were talking. The SOC guys. Especially the second visit. We were both there. You'd floated the Tremayne revenge killing theory by then. Hence the second visit right? Did we talk about it there? Did Tremayne's name come up? Amir knew who those two had murdered. The whole bleeding country did after we screwed up and the press went to town."

Fleming thought about that. "We could well have, I suppose."

"Well if some dirt bag was ear wigging it could have got back through the grapevine to that fat bastard."

"Okay say it did. Why would Amir try to get at Tremayne?"

"Well why not? He's a billionaire. In Amir's world, you want somebody whacked, you pay for it. If he heard our theory he just might have come to the same theory we did. That maybe the same men that ambushed his deal were the possible killers. Which I still think is wrong anyway."

"That is bloody thin Mick. But okay. Remotely possible. I'll run it past Bland and tell him we're having a dig through admin here as well. Hopefully he'll forget about it. Amir's thugs never got to the Gambia. And I agree with you. I don't think it's Tremayne."

"There is one other thing, of course," Mick added. "Is it just remotely possible that Wesley and Mason had pissed off these sniper guys in some way? Don't ask me how or why. Or. Wait a minute. Yeah. Maybe more likely."

He paused gathering his thoughts. He'd been a good copper and at heart he still was. His methodical mind came up with a much needed plausible theory. He continued.

"Guv, I think we're missing something here big time. Your theory linking these cases is right in one way. But actually wrong. We're looking in the wrong places. Over Wesley and Mason."

Fleming looked at him dubiously. "In what way am I wrong Mick?"

"Well you're right in one respect. It could be they were murdered by a skilled killer. But. Who knew and liked the Tremaynes? Answer. Lots of people. Wealthy people. And military people. Going back years. Agreed?" Fleming nodded.

"Right. One of these many people is pissed at their friends' killers walking free. And pays out to have them whacked. Which gives the killings the military angle you called in to Bland, right?" Fleming nodded again.

"But that is where you're probably wrong guv. Because maybe these are not related killings at all. We should be looking at John Tremayne's circle of friends. Particularly military. Maybe from years back. Not Bland's snipers, not at his son. The two crimes, if both correct in theory, as in military trained, skilfully executed homicides, could be totally unrelated to each other. Carried out by totally different people. That means the guys that hit the drug meet know absolutely nothing at all about it. And neither does Lee Tremayne."

Fleming said, "Now that is good thinking Mick. Very. Similar but totally unrelated and coincidental. And maybe explains why none of it makes any sense. I am going to email that line of thought to Bland. Thank you."

Mick nodded and they both picked up folders to read. He'd hopefully muddied the waters of this situation a bit more, hopefully enough to make Fleming think it just wasn't worth the ball ache of trying to unravel it all. And Fleming would jump at getting it to Bland, to avoid the suspicion of a leak from his office.

And Mick was going to have a word with Amir. He hadn't liked that conversation one little bit. Amir was going to have to forget about Tremayne. And hopefully, so would bloody Fleming. And that pain in the arse Bland. Mick was blissfully unaware that both he and Amir were going to be forgetting Tremayne in the very near future. Because they were both going to have far bigger problems.

Chapter 50. Another revelation.

After the meal out, the three couples had returned and were all on Daniel's balcony when Alan Shand excused himself and left, saying he would be back in five minutes. They were having a drink and just making small talk when he returned. Holding a folder. His wife said, "Alan! Don't you dare start talking business!"

"This is not business Pat. This is personal."

He looked across at Daniel and said, "We have never met before, Daniel. I just want to say it's been a pleasure getting to do so at last. John spoke of you quite often."

"Been nice meeting you too, Alan," said Daniel.

"But you have been indirectly involved in my family's life in the past, Daniel. Are you aware of that?"

The balcony had gone rather quiet. All there were a bit puzzled to say the least.

Daniel was looking a bit uncomfortable at being the centre of attention. "I really don't know what you mean Alan. I'm sorry."

Alan opened the envelope style folder and took out its contents. "This folder was left to me by John after his death. I have no wish to embarrass you Daniel. But you are among friends here and I hope you will enlighten me about this matter. And give me the opportunity to say what I want to say in front of others."

"You will really have to explain Alan," replied Daniel, sounding a bit on edge now.

"Well. At a certain difficult time some years ago, you were known as Adrian Jones for a while, were you not?"

Daniel looked intently at Alan. Thinking. Shand. And it clicked. "Norman was what? To you?"

"My eldest brother, Daniel. You saved his life and went to jail for it. In Africa."

"Oh my God," from Pat. She looked at Alan. "All these years. You keeping on about it. Why the hell didn't John tell you? He damn well should have, in my opinion. He knew you wanted to know."

"He never would," replied Alan. He looked at Daniel, "would he young man?"

Daniel looked at him with his intense eyes. "No. He wouldn't. He wouldn't compromise me Alan. It's not like the movies doing a thing like that, where Chuck or Arnie wander around high profile after doing something illegal in another country."

Alan smiled at him. "I'm sure it's not. But surely you can understand people would have liked to show their appreciation?"

"I was a wanted man. I needed it to die and be forgotten. And it was. Apparently until now. Why are you doing this Alan?"

"Because Daniel, Dad died a couple of years ago, but my mother is still alive. In a nursing home now. But very sprightly with all her faculties. They always wanted to know who saved their son. Norman wanted to know too, and thank them. But John warned him off politely so he never got the chance. He was very ill when he got home. But he fully recovered. Recently retired. He told Mum and the rest of us he was rescued. He was feverish and very ill when it happened. He remembered the prison. Gunfire. Smoke and explosions. Being dragged along terrified. Running from the prison in a vehicle. A helicopter ride. And eventually, a private hospital in South Africa. Then home in a plane chartered by Tremayne Holdings."

He looked at Lee, who was clearly mystified. "Your father arranged this. And that young man there rescued my brother. You also know nothing I assume?"

"No. Nothing." replied Lee. Then thought about the letter. It had said, "You should talk to Alan Shand. You know why." He carried on listening to Alan along with the others.

"It made the newspapers in a small way. At separate times. Regarding my brother, diplomatic protest to the British government. It was damped down and the official line was that Norman Shand had absconded during a prison riot. A couple of trade deals and some ass-kissing and it was agreed that he'd served enough of his sentence for fraud and corruption. And the matter was quietly dropped. The other thing that made the papers in a smaller way was a trial, three months after the event, of one Adrian Jones. A UK national apparently, whose illegal incursion and actions in Burundu had resulted in the deaths of government employees. Accused of being a mercenary in the pay of rebel forces. Had attacked a prison to free rebel supporters and fighters. And caused the riot in which Norman Shand had absconded. It was covered by the press. Adrian Jones was disowned by the UK foreign office which in no way condoned such actions blah blah etc. He was subsequently tried for those actions and was looking at a long prison sentence, which in those conditions would likely be a death sentence. But

Adrian Jones escaped. From the dock. In the court. And was never heard of again. But Daniel is Adrian Jones. Aren't you?"

He looked at Daniel. "Please tell me about it now, Daniel. I really would like to know and be able to tell the old dear and Norman I met the man who saved him. And that you're okay. They thought you'd died. You did. As Adrian Jones." Daniel nodded. His eyes half-closed.

Alan passed round the papers. "And can you all look at these please?"
There were press clippings and a couple of enhanced photographs of Adrian Jones in the dock. It was without a doubt Daniel. Gaunt and bearded but definitely him. And a few more hastily taken shots, of fallen guards and a courtroom in a state of bedlam.
They all looked at Daniel, who sighed deeply and started to tell them in a quiet voice about the rescue of Norman Shand.

"John contacted me. Apparently, a good friend of his was worried about his son who was in jail on trumped up-charges in Burundu, a small banana republic with a Mugabe-style president. Corrupt to hell. A strong rebel movement against him. Civil war flickering on and off when anybody had enough money to buy arms. But big mineral finds. Tremayne's invested in the exploration and mining company. The guy whose son had been jailed was a long term friend. John employed his other son. You as it turns out. The friend had tipped John off on the investment opportunity." Daniel glanced at Alan, who smiled gently at him.

Daniel continued, "The son worked for the mining company. Executive. Went there to wrap it up, get the contracts signed. Probably hadn't paid the right bungs, or bunged the wrong people. Another company had made a higher bid, after his contracts had been signed. And they got torn up. The guy said the wrong things in the wrong places. Made allegations. Found himself in jail for attempting to corrupt officials. Insulting the president. Usual crap. Africa jails its problems and forgets them. African justice system dragged on. Foreign office as usual ineffective. The Brits were going to do business there. The place was volatile, no consulate. So they weren't going to rock the boat very hard. Formal procedures were getting nowhere. The guy was now ill and getting worse by the day. John asked me if I thought we could get him out. Illegally. I said no."
Alan said, "You didn't want to do it?"
Daniel replied. "That's not what I said. I said no, we couldn't. Like I said already, it's not the movies, Alan." Alan nodded.

Daniel continued, "But John was pretty insistent. Money was no object. I agreed to look at it and came up with a plan. The only way I could see to do it was to hit the jail. It was quite isolated. Cause mayhem, extract Norman in the chaos. Helicopter in and out. Hated the plan. Too many unknowns. Too many things that could go wrong. Unhappy at exposing the only people I could ask to help to that sort of high risk, of death or punishment. I knew if it went wrong we would be on our own. John said that anyone I needed would be very well rewarded. So I put it out there. And got five men who agreed to form a team. Good men, all ex Foreign Legion. We'd all served together. Ten grand per man. Plus a grand a day each during the set up and op. Helicopter wasn't a problem. Loads of them out there for big companies, plenty of ex-forces pilots. Arms and equipment are easy to get if you've got the cash. We had. Borders in Africa are often no more than lines on maps. So we were set to go. And we did. Eleven days after John asked. Was the quickest we could do it. Norman was apparently very sick by now."

They all sat there in rapt silence looking at him. He stopped talking. Took a drink of his beer.

Then continued again. "We took the helicopter from the Niger Delta. An oil company one. Big enough for the job. Extra endurance tanks fitted. Crossed the border at night. Low, in case of any radar, but it was unlikely. Not a sensitive area, no military bases or airfields. Landed four kilometres from the prison near a good enough road. A crew cab Toyota pick-up was there as planned, with two of the guys in it. They had got there posing as mineral surveyors. John set it up through his business contacts. We loaded our kit from the chopper into it. I got in with one other member of the team, leaving the pilot and co-pilot in the helicopter. And the last member set up a position to defend the chopper if required." He paused again, recalling the events.

"We got to the prison area. Killed the lights. Got as close as we could with the vehicle, about three hundred metres away. One stayed with it, ready to drive closer after it all kicked off. The other three of us got our kit and headed to the prison. It was pitch dark. All as shown on the plans. One tower with a searchlight, big timber gates. Guards were all inside. There were no perimeter guards outside. They were lazy. Complacent. Guarding half-starved, often sick prisoners. They weren't expecting trouble. We set explosives on the gates. Then went for it. As the gates blew in, we shot out the searchlight. Myself and one other ran into the prison. The last man watched the gates, firing on any guards that tried to come out. Launching smoke grenades into the prison yard. Not trying to kill them. We tried to keep deaths and injuries to a minimum. They were just prison guards. Didn't deserve to die over western big business and government corruption. Just causing chaos. We needed chaos. And time. Because the hard part would be finding Norman. We threw incendiary grenades as we went through the place. Set a couple of huts on fire. Prisoners were pouring out of them. We grabbed one. Slapped him around. Found out where the white man was. Norman was in what passed for the sick bay. We kicked the door in. Punched the only guard in there in the face, he was yelling blue murder, laid him out cold. Dragged Norman out of bed. Headed back to the gates, firing at anyone in a uniform just to keep them away. They were panicked and scared shitless. Made it to the gates and out. Prisoners were running out and away. Those that were fit enough. Norman was slowing us down big time. Weak and delirious. But we were out and heading to the pick-up truck." He paused again.

"Then it went wrong. An army lorry showed up. Somebody had got a call out for help. They must have been local. About twelve soldiers jumped out and fanned out heading towards us. We were in the shit, big time. They fired on us. I told the other two to get Norman to the vehicle while I covered them. I did. Kept them pinned down. And I shot the tyres out on their truck to stop them following our vehicle, which had driven in to get them. They made it. And they left for the helicopter. I was caught by the soldiers. Thought they would shoot me out of hand. They didn't. I ended up in the jail Norman got out of for three months. Awaiting trial. That's it really."

Janet was aghast. "The others just left you there?"

"I would have left them. But this was my call. I had dragged them into it, I was the one to take the drop. I told you. It's not the movies. They did their job. If they'd stopped we would all have been killed or captured. And Norman would have never got out. They got away clean. Norman got home."

Alan said, "But you only escaped from the courtroom?"

Daniel replied, "Only chance I had. I was locked up very securely. I wasn't restrained in court. I guess because the press were there. And I was acting weak and ill. Picked my moment. Hit the guard next to me. Vaulted out of the dock. Took down the guard on the door. Grabbed his gun and ran. Over in seconds. And got away with it. Because they weren't expecting it."

"Where did you go after you ran?"

"Went to ground. Stole some money from a big house. I had a gun, I had food. I was fine. Contacted John. And a helicopter got me out a couple of days later near the border."

"Weren't they looking for you?"

"Of course." Daniel smiled. "But I am very hard to find, Alan. I had the skills to evade capture. It's what I am trained in. It's not rocket science. And Africa is a very big place."

They all looked at him, astonished. Not just at the tale he'd told. But his calm attitude to extreme violence, capture and escape. Alan said, "And neither you nor John told anybody?"

"We couldn't. And I wouldn't hear of it, even if he'd wanted to tell you. Or anybody else. I was a wanted man Alan. The guard I hit in the throat, well he died. In a courtroom with the press there. There was uproar apparently at diplomatic levels. This had screwed up diplomatic relationships and business deals. The authorities wanted to know who Adrian Jones really was. They couldn't. He had to cease to exist. I wanted my anonymity back. John arranged for false information to get back to a few people. That Adrian Jones, or whoever he really was, had died in the Congo of malaria. A couple of journos. A couple of diplomats. A fake letter and death certificate from a coroner's office in the Congo. Sort of got circulated. Just skilled disinformation. The matter was closed. Until you brought it up tonight I never even made the connection between you and Norman."

Alan looked intently at him. "Well I want to say, in front of these people - my wife and friends and your lovely lady - just how very grateful I am to you. And I can finally tell my mother and brother what happened and who we have to thank. It won't go any further Daniel, I won't tell them your name even. Just that I talked to you. I understand the need for secrecy even now. But truly, thank you. I just wish to God I could have had the chance to thank John. All these years. I had no idea. Excuse me please. I need a little time..." His voice was breaking a little.

He got up and walked away into the villa and they heard him leave, then saw him on the path heading towards the beach. Alone with his thoughts.

Janet was also having thoughts. She looked at the man she had come to love. Looked at his hands. Those hands that caressed her, picked up her children, held her hand, had killed a man, with one lethal blow from a sitting position. She was very glad he loved her. He was not a man you wanted disliking you. She walked over and kissed him. There was little else to say.

They all left and turned in. Another day over. And a bit more told of the story of Daniel Cade.

Chapter 51. Setting up the mark.

The next morning Daniel arose and checked his emails. One from Irena. A maximum of one point two million pounds was what Amir could raise at short notice. It would almost clear Amir out of liquid available cash. Daniel decided to make it a straight million. More realistic as a demand.

And an email from a young Syrian man who Daniel had helped in the past. He would, of course, help Daniel. And he accepted it might be dangerous. But he very much wished to help. After Daniel had saved his and his sister's lives most likely, it would be a pleasure. Daniel sighed. He didn't want to go. He didn't want to leave Janet. It was strange to feel like that for the first time in his life.

But it had to be done. He couldn't leave it all to Quan this time. He'd done enough. He would go to the UK in a couple of days' time and be back in two days. If all went well. And it would.

Daniel sent an email to Irena detailing what she needed to do. The time to do it would follow. He sent an email to Quan asking him to get a list of things. The most important item was the listening device with bone conductive headset. A good one. The best you could get. Then an email to Ray with a request to make the strangest thing Daniel had ever asked him to make. To fit a young skinny Syrian lad.

Then he phoned the young Syrian, Ahmet. Now at university in the UK.
"Ahmet, how are you?"
"Fine Daniel. Very much fine, thank you. And you?"
"The same, thank you. You understand the email, Ahmet. And the great danger?"
"I understand fully Daniel. As you did when you came to my aid. This will be my pleasure."
"Okay. Are you bearded or clean shaven Ahmet?"
"Clean shaven."
"Then grow stubble until after this is done Ahmet. You have to look at least a little different after this is done. For your own future safety."
"I will do it."
"Good. I will see you in a few days' time Ahmet. You know who you have to portray. Practice what such a person would say. Remember everything in the email. Become that person. I will see to everything else. And I will be there near you the whole time."

"I will be ready Daniel."

"Thank you Ahmet. Goodbye."

It was Sunday night. He emailed Irena to start this on Wednesday morning. Then phoned Quan.

Mick had just had the shock of his life. He'd got out of bed in his dingy flat. Gone to make a coffee. And there, on his own bloody kitchen table, was a mobile phone. A good one. And a note that simply said. *There is one number stored in the contacts. Call it if you value your life.*

Mick looked at the phone. Who the hell had just walked into his home and left it? While he was in fucking bed! He could see no sign of a break in. He made a coffee and lit a fag. And called the number. It was answered on the second ring.

"Who is this?" demanded Mick.

"Be quiet," came the reply. "Hang up. And you will receive two picture messages. Look at them. Then call back." The line went dead. Then the phone beeped. Then again. Mick opened the first message. His blood ran cold. The second one made it worse. They were a picture of the drug meet as the two cars had driven in. And a picture of everything on fire. They had been taken by the bloody snipers. Mick felt sick. He called back.

"You accept my credentials, DC Davidson?"

"Yes. What do you want?"

"To give you a choice."

"A choice?"

"Yes. Between losing your job and your pension and going to jail. Or doing as I tell you. And possibly avoiding it."

"Losing my job? For what?"

"Don't fuck me around. Taking bungs from Amir Ferez. Bent coppers don't have a good time in jail"

"Okay, okay. What the hell do you want?"

"Not that much. But today, as a matter of urgency, you will meet Amir and tell him this. That it is a terrorist group that took his drug deal down. That he is being targeted by them. For money. That it is beyond doubt. From the intelligence services themselves. The spooks do not make mistakes"

"That's it?"

"That's it."

"Then what?"

"You tell him that for the security services this is not a priority. They are stretched for resources. And these communications imply no tangible or imminent threat of attack or atrocities. Just raising finance. Including from him.

It's being monitored but that is all"

"I see."

The voice continued talking calmly. "You'd better. He must believe that there is no chance of any further information from you that could assist him. You fully understand that, Michael?"

"Yes. Yes fully. Then what do I have to do. He'll go mad."

"Fuck him. The madder the better. Just tell him you can't give him any more than that. He will believe you. Why wouldn't he?"

"Okay. I get that. And that is all I need to do?"

"Yes. Then, you keep this phone hidden. If you do as you are told, and if Amir is convinced, you will get a text message telling you where to pick up an envelope. With far more in it than Amir has been giving you."

"Okay. But what if Amir doesn't buy it?"

"You're going to jail. Get this done. As early today as possible."

"Okay. But assuming he does. What then?"

"Nothing Mick. Absolutely nothing. Collect your money. We won't need you again." The line went dead. Mick smoked another fag held in trembling fingers and called Amir. After a short conversation, Amir called Hassan to pick him up immediately and left, telling Irena an urgent matter required his attention, which gave Irena time to do what needed doing. Irena let the printer finish its work, printing A4 photographs, and carefully deleted all relevant files on the computer while they dried. She sealed the A4 photographs in an envelope and hid it carefully in her wardrobe.

Amir looked at Mick aghast. "You are absolutely certain?"

"Yes Amir. One hundred per cent."

"Daesh?"

"Sorry?"

"ISIS damn you."

"I don't know Amir. There are a lot of terrorist groups. Different factions. I will try to find out more but it is certain. They are definite about it."

"This is a nightmare, Davidson."

"I'm sorry Amir. I just thought you should know as soon as I found out."

"And they aren't investigating further? Surely they must be?"

"Amir, London is in a state of high alert. These communication intercepts. They handle literally thousands."

"But surely if these bastards that hit me are terrorists they will pursue them?"

"All I heard was that they were monitoring them. The security services are at full stretch. This situation poses no imminent threat of actual terrorist activity.

No real urgency. And not worth collating evidence on yet. And let's face facts, Amir. They aren't going to give a shit about a drug gang getting its ass kicked. They'll wait until they actually pose a threat to decent people."

Amir gave Mick a savage glare but saw the point he was making. "You can't find out more? Fuck you Davidson. I am paying you well. I want to know who these people are"

"Amir. I only found this out by chance. I got it to you, I can't ask questions. I am not a spook. I don't investigate terrorist activity. So don't give me a hard time Amir. I didn't have to tell you at all. It's not actual police business as such. And even Bland can't get anything more. He wants whoever killed your men. For murder. But even he can't just demand the intelligence services pony up intel. They won't let local plod just go trampling around all over a delicate situation they are monitoring for information. They do their job and do it well. We do ours. End of."

"Okay okay. You didn't have to tell me this. And at least I know what I am actually dealing with here. I appreciate it, Michael."

"Be nice if you showed it, Amir."

"Yes yes okay. I will sort out some reward for you. Call me later, yes. Try to find out more if you can. Damn it, this really is a total nightmare, Michael"

Mick said he would try and got out of Amir's car. Bloody hell! The fat bastard was crapping himself! So he should be. If these guys could get into Mick's flat unnoticed and take down armed drug gangs, Amir was up shit creek in a barbed wire canoe.

Amir went home. He'd messaged Irena before he got there. Told her she had been right. But what to do? What did she think would happen? He got home, kissed her. He looked haggard. She was pleased about it. She poured them both drinks. He asked her,

"Have you had time to give this some thought Irena? Where is this going darling?"

"Amir, I truly do not know. Okay, the police have found this to be so. But these people have had money from the meet. Perhaps that is the end of it."

"But why the business with the car?"

"I don't know. Perhaps your two men were working for them? Carrying explosives to Gatwick? Maybe it went wrong and they were caught? Maybe that policeman was shot by others like them. Trying to help them escape perhaps?"

"It is possible. Damn it Irena, who are these people? Daesh?"

"Who can tell my lover. I have read up about it on the internet. There are many terror groups. Many independent, many linked together. Many allied with Daesh, some are not and have their own agenda."

Amir groaned. "But what can we do, where do we look?"

"Amir darling, it may be all over. All has been quiet since those men were killed. Perhaps the money they take is all they wanted?"

"Yes, it has. Perhaps it was all they want. You are hopefully right my darling."

"All we can do is wait Amir. With luck this is over."

"Yes. We must hope so. I must go. I need to see Bogdan urgently, I will be back later."

He saw Bogdan who was very angry, but they agreed there was nothing more to be done. They must hope that the money from the meet was all the bastards had been after and the seizure of the last shipment by the police and border control nothing more than a damaging coincidence. They discussed the next shipment. It had to go smoothly.

Men from their respective organisations were ready to be drafted in from all over the UK to handle it, from the big midland cities and the coast towns. Hand-picked and utterly reliable. No young hotheads, no newer recruits. There was hopefully not too long to go to the shipment. They were desperate for supply. They were struggling to supply their network of dealers. They had lost some ground. They both knew they couldn't afford another disaster.

Chapter 52. The set up.

Back in the Gambia, Daniel was preparing to leave. He had dinner alone with Janet and they went to bed early on Tuesday night. She went with him to the airport in the morning and cried a little after he said goodbye, as Solomon drove her back to the villa. Daniel boarded on a false passport, and flew to Gatwick, arriving as planned on the Wednesday morning.

In the UK, Irena crept quietly out of bed and carefully took the envelope containing the photographs from the wardrobe. She laid them by the main apartment door, one corner just under the door, looking as if they had been slid underneath it. She used the toilet and returned to bed, and lay there until Amir woke up. She felt him kiss her as she feigned sleep. Then he got up and went out of the bedroom. She waited until all of a sudden she heard, "Irena. You fucking need to see this. Get up woman!"

"Amir. What is it? Please calm down." She ran out and down to the lounge, doing up her skimpy silk dressing gown as she did so. Amir was holding an A4 envelope in one hand and a photograph in the other.

"Calm down? Look at these pictures woman. It's our vehicles at the meet. These are from those bastards who kill all our men. Steal our money."

"Oh Amir! What does this mean? Why have they sent these?"

"Sent! They were not sent, woman, they have been put under our door. I will go see those fools on the security desk. How could they get up here Irena?"

"I don't know Amir. I am frightened darling."

"I must get dressed. Go back and wait in the bedroom."

Amir got dressed in a hurry and went down to the main entrance where he was assured nobody had got past who should not have been in the building. Nothing on CCTV he was assured. Damn it! Was he being attacked by fucking ghosts? He went back upstairs and called Bogdan who made his way to Amir's straight away. Irena told Amir she would not sit in the apartment while that beast was there, making sure Bogdan heard her and went out to do some shopping. She called a number after she had left the building to say Amir and Bogdan were together.

Amir was sitting with Bogdan when his mobile phone rang. An unknown number. He answered.

"Amir Ferez?" The voice sounded young. A foreign accent.

"Speaking."

"Excellent. You got the photographs?"

Amir went pale. He looked at Bogdan, signalled him to be quiet. And put the phone on loud speaker.

"Yes I got them."

"Good."

"What do you want?"

"I want you to meet me. Bring Bogdan, as your driver. Just you and him."

"Meet you? Why?"

"My leader wishes me to address you face to face."

"Your leader?"

"Yes. He thinks it will demonstrate his sincerity if we meet face to face."

"Is that so?"

"Yes. It is so. Now are you coming?"

"Yes. Yes of course. When? Where?"

"Pull up by West Croydon station. This evening, ten p.m. Down the side of the station. The car park. I will find you. Bogdan driving, you in the back seat, in your Range Rover. If anybody else waits near there we will know. Do not try anything. You have been warned. Ten p.m." The phone went dead.

Amir looked at Bogdan and said, "What the hell do we do now?"

"We get some men down there early. Take this bastard when he arrives."

"Bogdan you are an idiot at times who never thinks before he acts. You blamed Irena, and Davidson. Without thinking or waiting before acting."

He looked intently at Bogdan, "You insulted me and you hurt the woman I love, which I have not forgotten Bogdan, I assure you. And now you wish to do the one thing that will result in not meeting these crazy bastards. We have to meet him. We have to find out what they want. Why they do this to us. We have to do a deal with them. We have no choice Bogdan. And these people know it."

Bogdan looked at Amir. He had insulted a dangerous man and he knew it. Partnership or not, Amir was ruthless and dangerous to cross.

"I am truly sorry Amir. I was angry and I was wrong. And I do not want these people to cause a rift between us. I can only ask your forgiveness about Irena. I have tried to apologise to her but she will not even listen to me Amir."

Amir nodded. "I forgive you, yes, because I understand your anger Bogdan. But I will not forget it. You will curb your actions and think in future. You agree?"

Bogdan nodded. "Yes Amir, I agree. You are right. And we must meet this arrogant fool. And see what this madness is about."

"I would be very careful who you consider a fool right now, Bogdan.

Whoever these people are, they have taken our money. Seen six of our own men killed and four from another organisation we need to deal with. Turned us all against each other. And are still in total control of the situation. It is us who are being made to look fools."

Bogdan nodded again. All they could do was wait. It was going to be a very long day.

Their nemesis had landed at Gatwick airport. He was picked up by a taxi, driven by a Vietnamese man. They left the airport behind them and drove to meet a young Syrian who had once been in the clutches of a people smuggling gang. Daniel had rescued him from his situation, along with the young man's sister and he was about to take a huge risk to repay his debt of gratitude. They spent the rest of the day going over the plan. Coaching Ahmet. Hitting him with different questions and scenarios, curbing him when he got frustrated. Making him learn to listen, without showing any facial expression, when instructions came through the bone conducting headset. Setting the volume so only he could hear it when he was next to somebody. Refining it until it could be no better. Finally, they dressed him carefully in the outfit he would wear. All the while, Amir and Bogdan waited as the day dragged slowly by.

Chapter 53. A quiet moment.

Back in the Gambia, Daniel was being discussed in his absence by Angel and Lee. Janet was having time with her children while Daniel was away and had taken theirs along, gone out with Solomon in the car to give them all a tour of the area. Angel and Lee were out walking by the sea. Angel was telling Lee about how Janet had met Daniel, as they strolled hand in hand, along the quiet beach.

She told him what a lovely girl she thought Janet was, giggling as she told him Janet seemed to firmly believe she was from a very upper class family like him and that they had titles they just didn't use. And she was letting her be rather deferential for now. But would tell her eventually.

"You can be very cruel," Lee said laughing.

"I know, it's part of my charm."

"So you're telling me he met his life partner while she was having a row with a hotel receptionist? And knew right then they would be together for life?"

"Yes darling. That is exactly what happened. Might have been her big boobs that helped, mind."

"I hadn't noticed." Lee grinned at her.

"You lying bastard. You can't exactly miss them."

"Big boobs or not it doesn't make sense to me, Angelica. I hope it doesn't go wrong for them."

"You are so unromantic, Tremayne."

"I am not! I just think you need to get to know each other."

"Well you are pretty slow I guess."

"And what is that supposed to mean?"

"What I say. I wanted you when I first saw you in your father's office."

Angel had been John Tremayne's PA since leaving college. Lee had shown up, after he left the army, to join the company.

"Well you got me, didn't you?"

"You were bloody hard work! I was half-naked some days, the clothes I was risking wearing to work. I know damn well your Dad had to give you a push towards me as well."

Lee smiled as he recalled the time. "Yeah he did. He told me you were beautiful. And asked me if I needed glasses or runway lights."

"A billionaire's son is a bit of a challenge. I just thought you were cute. I only wanted to use you for pleasure."

"Well you did."

"Yeah. But then you asked me to marry you. I had to cease my wanton existence."

"Sorry my love."

"No I'm glad you did. I do love you Lee. I'd have married you if you were our milkman. In fact, I fancied our milkman."

"Lucky I got in first then."

"Yeah it was. But my point is, my romantically challenged, rich husband, we met through my job and you leaving the army when you did. And a big kick up your arse from your Dad. And me being such an incredible shag you wanted to marry me. A right palaver. So don't knock your brother's far simpler methods. She is a lovely girl and they just fit together perfectly. Daniel decided that in ten seconds. You needed ten months of skilled blow jobs before you asked me to marry you. They will still be as good as us together, believe me."

Lee laughed. "I utterly adore you Angelica. Shall we go back to the villa?"

"I hope it's not just because I mentioned I'm an incredible shag, Tremayne!"

"Actually it is."

"At least you and Daniel have one thing in common."

"What's that."

"You're both totally honest. Come on then. You've talked me into it."

"Good." He grinned. "And don't forget we need to fit in a boat trip before we go home. Just the two of us."

"I won't. But we're in a queue for it."

"Sorry?"

"Shut up. Villa time." She put her arms around him and gave him that wicked smile.

They kissed on the beach and then walked back towards the villa, just a little faster than they'd been walking away from it. This break after the recent horrors was exactly what they had needed. Being around Daniel always made Lee relaxed. Life just got somehow simpler. And it was, thankfully, getting back to normal.

Chapter 54. The meeting.

Daniel patted Ahmet on the shoulder. Perfect. He checked yet again the comms equipment Ahmet was wearing. They went outside and Quan pulled up. They got in the taxi and headed towards West Croydon. The comms were checked again. Daniel looked in distaste at the busy streets and the people on them, as they sat in silence as they drew nearer to the meeting place. He hated it here.

They pulled into the car park at the side of the station and parked discreetly in the corner. Quan would stay in the front, seemingly a taxi driver having a break. Many did near the station. Daniel would operate comms from the rear of the vehicle, crouched down out of sight. Ahmet got ready to leave the car. Ahmet got out the phone he'd been given. Looked at Daniel. Daniel nodded. He pressed call.

Bogdan was driving, Amir sitting in the back. They pulled down into the short, dead end road, beside West Croydon station. Amir's phone rang. He answered. "Yes?"

"You will see two gates leading into a deserted work compound. Adjacent to the track."

"I see them."

"Pull up near them. Stay calm and have the car unlocked. I will get in the back." The call went dead.

Bogdan saw the gates and pulled up. The area was street lit. A good few people around. Late commuters. Young people. There were several takeaways and late shops on the main road. It was busy enough to remain unnoticed. Not so busy as to be unable to park up for a while.

The rear door opened on Amir's car and a young man got in. Arabic facial features. What you could see of them. Light fuzzy beard, a baseball cap pulled low. A hoodie, with the hood up, obscured a lot of his face.

"Good evening gentlemen. A very doubtful pleasure to meet you."

Amir fumed at this light-hearted arrogance.

"What do you fucking want, you young punk?"

In a taxi about fifty metres away in the dark corner of the same car park, Daniel and Quan grinned tersely at each other as they listened. They wanted Amir aggressive. To start with.

Ahmet replied, "There is no need for such unpleasantness gentlemen."

Bogdan snarled from the front of the car, "I will fucking show you unpleasantness in a minute. I'll kill you."

Ahmet replied in the same light tone, "Amir. My leader, may Allah bless his wisdom, insists I talk only with you. He considers your very good friend Bogdan here, something of a fool."

As Bogdan started to snarl another response Amir said, "Bogdan. Be silent. We must listen to this young man. Like it or not. Not another word, damn you." Bogdan lapsed into enraged silence.

Again, Daniel and Quan glanced at each other. The kid was playing a blinder. They kept listening.

"Amir, I am tasked to pass to you my leader's request. In person. And I am honoured to do so."

"Really? Well before you fucking do that, I have a question for you."

"Feel free to ask Amir. I have a little time to spare."

Amir glared at him again. At the sheer impudence of this, well, boy, damn it.

"Did you take my money and kill our men?"

"Oh Amir, I so wish I had. It would have been such a great honour to serve our cause in such a way. But sadly I am not a fighter for my leader. It is not, as I believe you say, my department."

"Not your fucking department!" The rage burst out of Amir. "You punk. Whose department is it then?"

Amir heard in the bone conducting headphones a quiet murmur. "Ease him back down Ahmet."

Ahmet said, "I apologise Amir. I was not trying to anger you. I meant I am very young. I know nothing of guns and bullets."

"But your organisation did it, yes?"

"Oh most definitely Amir."

"Why?"

"Well we take your filthy money. To fund the great campaign against the infidels."

"My filthy money?" Amir lost it. He pulled out a gun and pointed it at Ahmet.

"You want to go back to your fucking leader in a body bag?"

"The vest. Now Ahmet," came the murmur through the headset.

Ahmet replied, "Amir, I would not fire that if I were you."

"Give me one good reason why not."

"I show you."

Ahmet held his hand out. He had a gadget about the size of a pager in it, with a wire disappearing up his sleeve. His thumb was firmly placed on a button in the centre of it. He lifted the hoodie from the bottom. Amir gasped when he saw the bulky vest and the wires attached to his skinny body. "If I let go of this button, which I would gladly do for my leader, there will be very little left to put in a body bag Amir, of all three of us. So put the fucking gun away."

Amir thought he was going to faint. He was in his own car. In the back behind tinted glass. Where nobody could see him or help him. With a fucking human bomb! He put the gun away and waited for Ahmet to speak. Bogdan sat rigid with fear in the front seat.

Ahmet heard, "Let him have it now Ahmet. Slowly. Calmly. Just like we practised." from the headset.

And he did. "Now Amir, I have, I am sure, your undivided attention. And I can convey to you my leader's message. My leader wishes you to donate a sum to his worthy cause. Then Amir, you are free to carry on with your sordid business, with no further interruption."

"Donate? You mean your leader wants to extort money from ME? Amir Ferez!"

"An ugly word, Amir. I think donate is much better. As my leader requests."

"Well your leader already took a lot of money of mine."

"He desires more."

"How much more?"

"One million pounds."

Amir spluttered with rage. "A fucking million pounds! Are you mad?"

"No Amir. Quite sane. I need your answer. I do not wish to sit here too long. My thumb is aching."

Ahmet nodded towards his hand. Amir looked down and saw the thumb on the button."

"I haven't got it. It would ruin me, damn you."

"Amir you have got it. And you could free yourself from these problems if you pay it."

"Oh sure. Like you won't come back for more."

"I can only convey my leader's word that we will not. And his word is his bond."

"Well if he thinks he can get money from me with threats, why did he attack my exchange? Why did he set my men up to die in that hire car? Why was I arrested over that? His word? Sure."

"Oh Amir. I am but a new recruit to our beloved leader. But I know why. He told me so I can tell you. To show you he can do this. To show you that men in your employ were his to control. To show you he had the case that had contained your money which he desired for his cause. To show you he can destroy you and your infidel-funded empire should he so wish."

"And now he just wants me to hand over a million pounds?"

"Well, donate it. Yes Amir. He feels it is so much better than adding to the deaths already incurred. Easier for you and himself."

"Easier!"

"Of course. A simple bank transfer is so much easier than all that shooting surely?"

"A million pounds. And no guarantee you won't be back."

"Nothing will guarantee that we will."

Amir tried one last approach to what he knew was a hopeless situation.

"And you'll do what if I don't pay?"

"Well Amir. My leader anticipated that question, bless his wisdom. Your two night clubs and your casino will be the repeated targets of terrorist threats. And then one time there will be no threat. And one or two of our leader's loyal servants such as myself, they will visit your clubs. Wearing what I am wearing now. Many will die. You will lose trade and business. Confidence in you will evaporate. And we will target your drug activities again. We will target every aspect of your empire. And crush it."

Amir looked at him. "You swear that will be the end of it? If - and it is if - I pay?"

"My leader is a man of his word. And he wishes to leave here to take a place of power in the new caliphate. And we will be proud to journey with him. You, Amir, will be contributing to that noble cause. And then you can continue feeding your vile drugs to the infidels. In your own way destroying them as well."

Amir looked hard at the young man. "If you, or anybody else, threatens me again I will shoot them. Do you understand? Bomb or not I will suffer no more in this life. Is that clear?

"Very clear Amir. You will be troubled no more by us in this life. You will just suffer in the next one."

"I can't raise that sort of money instantly."

"I fully understand, as does my leader. I will convey your message, that you are donating to his cause. And you will receive instructions for payment within a week. No longer."

"Okay. Now fuck off out of my car."

"With pleasure Amir."

"And be careful with that fucking button!"

"Of course. Bogdan. Pass me the car keys."

Bogdan started to argue but Amir said, "Just give him the fucking keys, Bogdan."

Bogdan passed them over his shoulder.

"Thank you. I will leave now. The keys will be in that waste bin over there. You Bogdan, can pick through the garbage for them, like the mangy rabid dog you are."

And he was gone. He ran across the car park. Threw the keys in the waste bin as he passed it. And vanished into the street into the night.

Daniel and Quan picked Ahmet up and they drove to Quan's apartment, all coming down from the high of the operation.

"You did so well, Ahmet. Thank you."

"My pleasure Daniel. They seemed very bad men."

"They are."

"You should be in a drama academy, not doing accountancy," said Quan laughing. "Like the mangy rabid dog you are," he mimicked Ahmet. "That wasn't in the script."

"I know Mr Quan. But I was very much into the part by then."

They all laughed and they soon pulled up near Quan's home.

Daniel said, "Ahmet, before you go. Give me your bank details please."

"I do not require paying Daniel."

"You will be paid. Amir is paying you. Let's just say you and your sister won't have any student debt once you leave education."

"Very well Daniel. I will email them to you later. Thank you. For letting me repay your kindness. And for getting the very unpleasant Amir to fund us."

"You're very welcome Ahmet." Ahmet left and rode away on the motor scooter he'd arrived on.

He was a little shaken up inside. But it had been exciting. And far less terrifying than the war in Syria and the terrible journey with the people smugglers. As he weaved through the late London traffic he was thinking how boring accountancy was after all he had been through. But at least people didn't point guns at you.

Daniel and Quan were left sitting there. They talked about the situation. Where Irena was at. The concern for her safety now this situation was escalating. But they had done all they could. And this was both driven by and for her. They would have to wait now, for her updates on how Amir responded. He should pay. He could afford it. He was in uncharted waters here. He could fight another criminal gang, evade the police. But a jihadist gang. They were banking on him taking the easy way out. Pay up. And hope the terrorists kept their word. They turned in. Daniel had an early flight out in the morning and Quan was going to drive him.

The next morning, they left for the airport early. Daniel didn't mind a wait at the airport. He wanted to buy some stuff and read the papers, get some breakfast. And Quan would miss the worst of the traffic. They were quiet until they got near the airport.

Then, unusually, Daniel broke the silence, "I just wanted to say thanks for everything Quan."

Quan looked at him. "No problem. I get paid my friend."

"I know. But, you know, not for that bastard ex of Janet's, you didn't. And you had the car thing to deal with alone."

"Wasn't a problem, Daniel."

"I know. But truthfully, I didn't want to come over. You know, because of Janet."

"Well that's good isn't it?"

"I guess so Quan."

"Are you looking forward to getting back to Gambia? And Janet?"

"Yeah. I am. Very much."

"Have you missed her while you've been away? For just two days?"

"Yeah. Yeah I really have."

"Then welcome to the human race, mon ami."

"Meaning?"

"Have you ever actually missed anyone before, Daniel?"

"No. Actually I haven't Quan."

"Well then it's long overdue. Enjoy it. Take care of her."

"I will."

They pulled into the drop off at Gatwick.

"I'm pleased for you, Daniel. Truly. All this needs to stop after this one, you know that. For Janet. And my lady and me. Well, we want to start a family. You've got a ready-made one. We can't keep taking risks Daniel."

"It will stop after this. It's time. I know that Quan. We've done enough."

"Oh and something you maybe should know", said Quan as he got back in the car.

"What?"

"I missed you when you were in jail in Africa."

"Really?"

"Yeah. I couldn't wait for you to get out."

"Thanks."

"I couldn't wait to tell you what a wanker you were for getting caught."

"Fuck off. And be lucky."

"You too. Give her a kiss from me."

Quan drove away. He had a large envelope with cash in it to go and deliver later. To a rather unpleasant person apparently. He was looking forward to it. He didn't like unpleasant people. And this one wouldn't like Quan after the meeting, not one bit. And wouldn't want to see him again. Ever.

Daniel walked towards the tedious security and departures area. Missing someone. How strange did that feel? But he was. And it felt pretty good. And he was going to buy her a present. He'd never bought anyone a present before either. What was he going to get her? He sighed. This wasn't going to be all plain sailing. But he had missed her. And the children. This was the first flight he'd ever taken in his life that he was impatient to get off.

Chapter 55. Terrorist threat.

Amir, Bogdan and Irena were sitting in Amir's apartment, discussing the extortionate demand that had been made by whoever the hell they were. Bogdan was all for ignoring them. Deal with whatever they threw at them. Amir was not so sure and was considering ideas.

"We could ask for help, from our suppliers. They would lose out if we get hit hard enough to shut us down."

"You mean get them to pay them off?" asked Bogdan.

Wasn't his problem, Amir was the importer. Bogdan got it out there to the dealers on the streets, where he ruled with an iron fist. And knives and guns. His prostitutes were nearly all users. Most of them were trafficked women, lost in a world they had no way of escaping from. He was Amir's means of shifting large amounts of heroin and cocaine in every city and major town it was worth dealing in. Bogdan held his own ruthlessly against rivals, be they Asian, Afro-Caribbean, Russian. He never lost ground to anyone and few tried these days.

Which meant Amir was held in high regard at the very top of the supply chain. There was no love lost between them, but they worked well together. Bogdan paid Amir without fail. The money was cleaned by artificially high takings run through Amir's clubs and his casino. The profits from those were skilfully invested by Irena. Amir was at the top of his game and seemingly above the law. And all had gone well. Until recently.

"Well they can easily afford to," replied Amir.

"Well then, you should consider it."

Irena was sitting there saying nothing, reading a magazine, drinking a glass of wine.

"Irena," said Amir. "Should we approach the suppliers for assistance in these matters."

"I do not think you should ask me, Amir," was the abrupt reply.

"But I value your advice Irena. Please."

"Amir. I have to sit here in the presence of a man who threatened to have me raped, hit me and scarred my face. And believes me to be a liar. Even though I was the only one who really tried to help."

Bogdan said, "Irena, I was wrong. And you were proved right. And I am truly sorry I hurt you. Amir needs your help, we both do if we are to stay in business. If you wish me to leave I will go."

"No stay." Irena got up and moved gracefully to the well-stocked bar, poured another wine. She came and sat back down. "Thank you for at least apologising. If you truly want my input then I will gladly give it to you, Amir. This is my life too, with you. We all need resolution to these problems."

"Please speak, Irena," said Amir.

"Very well. But I want no cursing me if you do not like what I say."

"Amir said, "You have my word. Our word." He looked sharply at Bogdan, who nodded.

Irena continued. "I have not been involved in your business that long. I have more dealings with the clubs and casino and the investments in property and shares of your end gains that come through them, than I have with your drug dealings. Which I prefer to know nothing about. And I do not. Please note that Bogdan." She looked sharply at him. And he nodded.

She continued. "But I understand it is that which makes the clubs and casino so much more profitable, after you run your gains from these dealings through those businesses. So, it is important to you that you continue, Amir?"

"Yes darling. Of course. We must continue."

"Well you say that Amir. You could retire from this. You have plenty of money to do that. And leave these problems behind us."

She saw the look on Bogdan's face. He didn't want Amir to quit and she knew it. He didn't want his supply to his brutal empire cut. He didn't want Amir vanishing, with the haughty bitch she knew he thought she was, to live like a queen, for doing nothing, in his opinion, but shag Amir. She didn't want Amir to quit either. She wanted to destroy him. And anyway, like most in his disgusting line of business, it was power not money that was the incentive. They never quit after making enough. They were bullying nobodies outside of the criminal world. A world where so-called hard men confused fear with respect. And they usually died in that world, or prison. Or at the hands of another thug.

She quickly continued. "However, if you wish to continue, ask yourself this Amir. If you go to the very top of this business, to your suppliers, with this situation. How will it be perceived Amir?"

"Well I would hope they would help. After all this time. And millions in business."

"Possibly. Or would they think you have lost control?

"Explain." Very abruptly.

"Amir! I told you do not take an attitude with me. I am trying to help you, not insult you. I simply mean that surely there is a risk? That they could think you are losing your grip. You might appear no longer reliable to them. They may not think they owe you any obligation to help. Would they have doubts about supplying you? I talk from a business perspective, which is my world. Confidence, it means a great deal, Amir. In any business. If you sell, say, bicycles wholesale, would you supply a bicycle dealer with known problems? It is nothing more than my thoughts Amir."

Amir considered this. "You are right. I apologise, my nerves are frayed. Yes, perhaps it would be foolish to let them know we have problems. We need future deliveries, the next one most of all. To risk a delay by telling them we are having more problems here, after the last shipment is taken, maybe is not a good idea."

"Only you can make the decision darling. It is a bad situation I know. Pay and get rid of this nightmare. Or ask the suppliers to help. With every possibility they may not, or they will be alarmed by the news. With every possibility they then may not supply you. And it is not a decision either I, or Bogdan even, can help with. It is your money Amir darling." She enjoyed that twist of the knife. This was a far better way to screw with the fat evil bastard. She smiled lovingly at him as he moved in the direction she wanted him to go.

He said quietly, "But a million pounds. The thought of paying this to those madmen. It makes me feel sick."

"It is a great deal of money my love."

"Can we raise such a sum?"

"Well, in short, Amir. Yes. You would have to authorise the withdrawals and transfers to put it all in one place, ready to move. But it would leave you with little more than four hundred thousand in liquid cash. You are wealthy. But you cannot spend buildings and assets, Amir. It takes time to realise cash from such investments."

"Well there is at least enough to pay for the next shipment if I pay these bastards off. And that is what matters."

"Then you at least have a choice Amir. Settle it and keep your problems private. Or you can ask your suppliers for help. But they will surely have to know the problems that make you ask. Only you can decide my darling. That is not for me to say."

Amir pondered this. Then, "Thank you Irena. Bogdan. We will call it a night. I will sleep on this. I will call Davidson again tomorrow, and then, I will make my decision. Either to call Turkey, or to pay these madmen off and hope they then leave us alone." Bogdan left. Irena and Amir sat there for a while in silence, then Amir said he was going to bed. Irena said she would finish her wine and be in soon. She sat there thinking about the situation, idly fiddling with a strand of her long, jet black hair.

Amir was worried sick and struggling to deal with this. She was just enjoying watching him squirm. And glad all had gone well with Daniel's very clever deception, made up by him to suit the situation as it unfolded. He was so calm and clear headed and seemed to think so quickly as each challenge arose. And had the right people in place to do whatever he'd decided put into action.

Fancy him having a woman now, damn it. She would always hate her a little bit, however nice she was. She would hopefully meet her soon. All being well she would leave for Turkey in the near future, and Daniel would meet her there. To end this by placing Amir's money where it needed to be. It would be nice to relax again and for good, drop her guard. Never whore herself to Amir again. This life of hers was dangerous. And she hated the lying to her family about her life in the UK. But she would see this through, and destroy Amir. Then the rest of her life would be hers to live as she wished. All they needed now was the details of Amir's next big shipment.

She looked across at the broadband router, replaced one day when Amir was away. It had been supplied by Ray, delivered by a young man in Telecoms overalls, who had been half an hour setting it all up. Identical to the one supplied by BT but with a little extra gadgetry inside, its lights twinkling in the dim light. Electronically sending all Amir's emails and communications from this penthouse, to a server somewhere where Daniel's rather eccentric, wheelchair bound, geek friend Ray, sifted through the information. Relaying it forward to Daniel. And would hopefully guide them to the details of the next delivery.

A million gone in cash if he agreed to pay the demand, would weaken Amir badly. A seizure of the next big consignment and the loss of what would be the last of his available cash would finish him as a player in this ghastly business. Then he would decide to cash in his assets. Then the final stage. He would be left with nothing. Except arrest and jail. And no means of paying to avoid justice this time.

That bit was Irena's to do alone and she had it covered already. The huge sum of money would simply vanish into the ether. She smiled and rose gracefully from the couch and went to clean her teeth, then get into bed with Amir - something she hoped she wouldn't have to do for very much longer.

Chapter 56. Straightening out the bent.

Mick Davidson was looking at the phone that had appeared in his flat as if placed by a ghost. The single text message wasn't what he was expecting. It just said. *Call.* "Bastards!" Mick was angry. It should have been about a payment, an envelope. Might have known, whoever these cranks were, it was too much to hope they would keep their word. He sat looking at the phone for a minute.

He sighed, poured a glass of cheap scotch, lit a fag. And called. It was late but fuck them. They hadn't put a time to do their bidding. The call was answered same as last time. Second ring.

The same voice as before, English definitely, said, "One moment." About fifteen seconds later it said, "Michael."

"Yeah, what do you want? I thought we were done."

"We can be if you wish."

"What the fuck does that mean?"

"If you calm down, cut the hostility, and listen Michael, I will tell you. You did well by the way, Amir was very receptive to us."

"Okay, but you lied to me and I don't like that. You told me I would get a text and I would get money."

"I did Michael. Yes."

The voice was strangely calm and soothing.

"So, what happened?"

"Well we had you checked out, before we even approached you. Found out a lot about you Michael."

"Like what?"

"Like who the loan shark is you're paying the money from Amir to for openers. For your gambling debts."

Mick was a bit stunned to say the least. "And that is?"

"Frazer Williams."

"Okay. So what? It's none of your bloody business."

"Maybe not. But we have chosen to make it our business."

"Well I wish you hadn't. I just want paying if you are going to keep your word. And I want you to piss off and leave me alone, I don't deal with terrorists. I did what you asked because I had no choice."

"You can console yourself that you are not dealing with terrorists, Michael."

"Really? Well ten dead men tell me different. And you told me you were."

"Ten dead drug dealers and people traffickers, Michael. All well known to the police, all carrying on their trade despite that. All carrying guns or happy to. And

I didn't tell you we were terrorists. I told you to tell Amir we were."

Mick digested that for a moment. Then said, "Well who the hell are you then?"

"Just say we are people who don't like drug dealers and people traffickers. Particularly Amir and Bogdan."

"Okay, let's just say that, it doesn't change anything. You blackmailed me into talking to Amir. And you've lied to me about paying me."

"Michael. If you learn one thing from this conversation you will learn I never ever lie."

"Really? Well I haven't been paid."

"Frazer Williams has. Every penny you owe him. He won't bother you again, Michael."

Now Mick was stunned. "Are you shitting me? I owed that vicious bastard eleven grand. And that went up every fucking day."

"Call him Michael, later on. Don't be scared to. After you have, call me back."

And the call was terminated. Mick looked at the phone, it needed charging. He'd have to get one for it because he was going to have to talk to this person again. Because he had to know what the hell was going on here. He went to bed. It was two in the morning but he couldn't sleep. Was he really out from under with Williams? If he was, well maybe he would do something he hadn't done in a long while soon. Sleep properly.

Chapter 57. Can't stand the place.

In the Gambia, Daniel locked his phone in his desk and walked upstairs and back into the bedroom. It was one in the morning there. Janet looked at him sleepily. They had had a rather, well, physical reunion after a nice afternoon with the other two couples, after she had gone with Solomon to meet him at the airport. She was tired, in a good way, but still worried about him. How tense he was at times when they made love.

"You okay darling?" she asked.

"Yes fine. Sorry, call from another part of the world. Had to take it."

"No matter. Want a drink on the balcony before we go back to sleep?"

"Yes. That would be nice thank you."

"I'll get it. Orange juice?"

"Yes, fine."

Daniel was sat on the balcony when she got out there after getting the drinks. She sat next to him and he put his arm around her. They sat quietly for a while. Then he said, "You are quite happy now, Jan? You know, living here and in Turkey? I only ask because you have a say in things. And you are from the UK, had a life there. I would go wherever you were happiest to be"

She smiled at him. "I have thought about it a lot Daniel and I have talked a lot to the children. And I have talked to Angel and Lee. And I truly don't want to go back. Not just because you hate the place either. I know you wouldn't make me or the kids live abroad if we didn't want to."

"I can't say I'm not pleased Jan."

"Why do you dislike it so much Daniel? I know what happened to you as a child, of course I do. But you left at sixteen. And you've never really gone back. Even though you lived in a beautiful home with John and Ann."

Daniel thought about it before replying. "I don't say too much to people about it really. My views make them angry. So did John's."

"In what way?"

"Well in the UK they believe they have this great freedom. All these so-called rights. But in real terms it makes life frightening and miserable for thousands of people."

"I don't really understand that."

"Well what is the point of rights, if it gives dangerous criminals the right to repeatedly be released. To offend again and hurt more people. Paedophiles freed to roam. Having to lock everything up or lose it. If it gives certain people the right to get drunk and brawl in the street without being arrested and punished. Make town centres a no-go area. Unless you're hard, or think you are. Race souped-up cars through estates with children playing. Daub graffiti on everything with little or no punishment. ASBO's, cautions, suspended sentences. Foul language in the street. On beaches, in parks. Where families have to sit and say nothing. Or move away from it. Out of fear."

Janet thought about that, recalling the flat she still needed to empty. The loud music, the gangs of youths, the revving cars keeping the kids awake. Old people scared to go out after dark, nervous during the day. And yeah, she didn't call it in. Didn't want to be targeted, just tried to keep a low profile. And get through it a day at a time.

"I do get that Daniel. It is tough in places."

"And then there's the people. Can't have a good time without being pissed. Watch gormless television programmes. Complaining about austerity while watching a flat screen TV. And then post whinges about it on a bloody computer. They wouldn't know austerity if it bit them on the arse. They should visit the Sudan if they want to know about austerity. Always money around for fat middle aged men to come here and screw teenage Gambian girls. Abuse kids in Vietnam and Cambodia and Thailand. But tell you on Facebook their pets are actually people, if not actually far more important. And make more fuss about the Vietnamese eating dog flesh than the fact it's a paedophiles' paradise with hundreds of kids being abused by westerners. They make me sick."

"Well that's told me!"

"Sorry. I've just seen too many kids abused, or dying for want of a glass of clean water, to take some prat moaning about a dog's three grand vets bill, on a laptop in a centrally-heated house, very seriously."

"I know how much you care about people, Daniel. And how things make you feel."

Daniel smiled at her. "I just stay away from the place as much as I can. I don't feel safe or at ease there and it's just too crowded. Nothing but shit weather and traffic jams all day."

"Well yes, that is the case in a lot of places. But you, or we, could live anywhere we wanted. Somewhere nice. And safe"

"Like John and Ann?"

"Oh God, yes, I see what you mean. Even they weren't safe."

"And their killers walked free. Because of their rights."

"Really?"

"Yes. Because a rookie police officer made an error in handling physical evidence. The killers' defence team seized on it. Although the poor rookie officer swore she didn't and actually wept in court. And the case was dropped. That they did it was beyond doubt. But they evaded punishment. Nobody gives a shit about the victims."

"So they'll never face trial ever you mean?"

"No, they won't Janet. They're both dead."

"Oh Daniel. Did you? You know. Did you...,."

"No Janet, I didn't kill them. I don't lie, I didn't."

Janet looked at him. "I know you don't lie Daniel and I don't either. And I swear to you, I wouldn't care if you had. And I also know you would have been something to do with it. And that doesn't bother me either"

He turned and kissed her. "You are a very amazing lady Jan."

She smiled at him. "Let's have some time for just us, today. I'll show you how amazing."

She couldn't deny it. This man's strange combination of total honesty, amazing kindness and utter ruthlessness. Well, it really turned her on. She just needed to get him to feel the same without the hang-ups from his past. They were there, lurking in their life together. And they were her enemy. She would deal with them for him, like he'd dealt with Barry. She'd intervene this time, and make them go away for ever. Angel's way.

Chapter 58. I'll pay.

Amir awoke after a short sleep he'd finally managed to have. Irena was already up and dressed in the kitchen. He went in and sat down, poured a coffee. She was reading the newspapers. She smiled at him.

"You okay, my darling? You were so restless last night. I got up early after you finally got to sleep so I didn't wake you. You need to rest darling."

He looked at her. She was so lovely. He was tempted to cash it all in and quit, and live his days out with her, but he wouldn't. Damned if he was going to be forced out. And even that was a dangerous move. His suppliers would not appreciate a sudden end to their relationship. Quitting wouldn't mean these ruthless fanatics wouldn't still want paying. So he had made up his mind. To pay the huge demand. In or out of the business they had him marked. He was going to bite the bullet and pay. And hope they would keep their word. He knew for certain in his mind that if he didn't pay he would never live to see retirement with Irena. In or out of the business.

He looked at Irena and said, "Later on, once we are dressed. I want you to get that money together and prepare to pay these mad bastards. We have no choice. We pay and we continue. That is my decision."

Irena looked at him. "I think it is the right one, Amir. Truly. You are in a difficult place my love. But if they are paid, and this leader, whoever he is, truly leaves for the East. Well then perhaps it will be worth suffering the loss. And life will be good again I am sure"

"It had better be. How long will it take to prepare their thieving demand? For transfer"

"Two or three days at least."

"Then get started Irena. That insane little bastard said a week and I would hear from his exalted fucking leader."

"I will darling."

"I have to go. I will go and get dressed."

He went back upstairs. Irena smiled as she read the news. Fat pig. He was handing over the gains from the misery of a lot of addicts' suffering to a very good cause. And they weren't done with him yet. Not by a long way. She took her time with breakfast. Kissed Amir goodbye as he left.

She went to her small desk and started her day by sending an email bearing good news. And then she started shifting Amir's ill-gotten wealth around to where it could be transferred from when he got the instructions.

Chapter 59. A boat trip to remember.

Janet had asked Daniel to take her out in the big boat, just the two of them. Said she wanted some private time with him. He launched the big, twin-engined RIB, and they set off.

"Anywhere in particular?" he asked.

"Just well out of sight of land."

"Okay." He gunned the twin engines and the boat flew across the calm sea.

Janet said, "This will do. Cut the engines." The shore was hazy in the distance. She stood up and promptly stripped off her bikini. Daniel just stared at her, at her gorgeous naked body, with its clearly defined tan lines. Her shapely, full-bodied curves. She looked wonderful in the bright sunlight. He was speechless.

"Undress Daniel."

"But."

"No buts. Please. Just go with me on this okay. It's important."

He removed his shorts and sat there naked. He felt nervous, awkward and foolish.

She sat next to him on the seat at the steering position and kissed him. "Relax Daniel. This is nice isn't it?"

"I guess. I don't feel comfortable though."

"I know. That's why we're here. We need to talk."

"Naked?"

"Yeah naked. And when we've talked you are going to shag me."

"I am?"

"Yeah. Not just make love to me. Which you do wonderfully. Despite the fact that you sometimes make me feel like I'm an obstacle course you just need to get through."

"What do you mean by that?" He sounded stressed and angry.

"What I say Daniel Cade. I know what you went through. I know what's going through your mind at times when we make love. About being touched, not being in control. Flashbacks to a terrible time. We are going to work through it. Out here. In the sunshine, where you can see me clearly. Your woman. Not in bed in the dark, where I can be eclipsed by your memories. I'm not sharing a bed with them ever again Daniel. I mean it." She was stroking his hair as she spoke. He could feel her breath on his ear, as she ran her fingers over his chest. Tracing over the scars on his chest and stomach.

He said, "I'm fine. Really."

"You're not. I'm yours Daniel. I love you. And you're mine. But it's about your pleasure too. Making love to me is something you should look forward to. Not be apprehensive about. Because I'm yours. I want to feel like I am, Daniel."

"I'm sorry. I do get bad thoughts. I hate them." He looked sad and desolate as he spoke.

"So do I."

"I should be able to deal with it. As I can deal with other people's. But sometimes, you know, they're just there."

"I know. So am I."

"You really notice it do you?"

"Yes darling. I really do. Now notice me, Daniel. Come here."

She sat down in the well of the boat between the centre bench type seat and the forward steering seat they were on. Facing him. Her shapely legs wide apart. Made him sit facing her.

"Nearer." Her voice thick with lust. He moved nearer. Their bodies almost touching.

"Touch me." She grabbed his hands and placed them on her large boobs. He felt a different firmness in them. Her nipples were rock hard. "Do it Daniel." She pulled him to her and kissed him. He started to fondle her breasts and she grabbed one of his hands and pushed it down between her legs. "Just fucking do it Daniel I'm so bloody horny."

He did. She was. And she reached for him as he did it. His body shuddered as she did. He was very aroused now. She was kissing his face and neck, as her hand sent waves of sensation through him.

"You fucking own me, Cade. So act like you do, yeah."

He stood and started to push her gently back but she resisted him. "Not yet you don't."

She quickly knelt up then dropped forward. He gasped as her mouth engulfed him. Her lovely green eyes looked wantonly up at him, locked on to his. Her tongue flickered around him making him groan. He was so aroused it shocked him. She worked her hand up and down him as she rose to kiss him savagely, then turned and knelt down across the centre seat.

"Now shag me, Daniel. I'm not made of eggshells, tough guy. Do it."

He gently edged forward and slowly went to enter her.

"I said shag me Daniel." She shoved herself back hard onto him as he did. And groaned with pleasure. "Do it Daniel. Now."

He pulled back and drove into her hard again. "Oooooh yeah you bastard. Give it to me hard."

She wiggled and squealed as he did just that. He was so turned on. So into the moment. He felt her starting to orgasm. And instinctively stopped. Barely inside her. Tormenting her. She literally juddered with frustration and cursed him. Writhing madly as he easily held her tight with his strong hands. Not letting her make the movements he could feel she desperately wanted to make. And as that moment ebbed away he drove hard into her again. She rammed back against him in ecstasy.

"Oh yeah. That's it baby, keep going. Oh my god I'm coming!"

He held her hips and pulled her hard back onto him and kept her pinned there as she shook with the force of her orgasm. As soon as it stopped he drove hard into her again and kept pounding her. Hard and relentlessly, reaching under her and fondling her breasts and rock hard nipples. Kneading his strong fingers into her butt. She really was his right now. His strength was dictating events. He had the control this beautiful woman he loved so much had given him. The African sun he also loved leaving no dark places for his mind to drag him into.

She was swept away in the sensation of wanton, needed, helplessness. She was bucking and gasping and cursing with her hair flailing around. Lost in the pleasure engulfing her. He was desperately trying to prolong the moment. But it was hopeless, it just felt so good. And he came. He held her to him and groaned as he did, holding her shuddering body against him effortlessly until they were both spent. They both became still. And he moved back from her. She turned to him. Her lovely green eyes had a dark, lust filled shine he'd never seen before. She wrapped her arms around him, and kissed him long and slow, her wicked tongue flickering around his mouth.

She let go and lolled back into the well of the boat. Bronzed legs shamelessly wide apart. Her hair was messed up and her face was flushed. She was breathing heavily, as the perspiration shone on her body. She looked simply beautiful as he gazed at her in yet another new light.

"Enjoy that did you, Cade?"

"Yeah. I did. That was amazing. And you?"

"Oooh yeah. It was lovely. You better get my shattered body back to the beach I guess."

"Later." He moved towards her again. Even more aroused now if that was possible. She looked gorgeous and he wanted her like never before.

"Daniel no!" She feigned resistance as he lifted her legs and then went down on her. His tongue flickered and slid around her already over aroused crotch. She groaned and wriggled and came again and again. He watched her stomach and chest heaving as he looked up at her, ignoring her unmeant pleas to stop. He finally did stop. And moved slowly up her trembling body. Fondled her large breasts. Sucked hard on her engorged nipples, then kissed her gently on the lips. Then firmly lifted her legs higher and pushed her knees back towards her shoulders.

"Daniel no! I'm done in! Oooooh you fucking randy bastard!" As he drove deeply into her. And she found out what done in really meant.

Over forty minutes later, they lay quietly in the sunshine, just kissing and saying nothing. Nothing to say. It had been amazing for both of them. Then he put his shorts on as she did the same with her bikini and he fired up the engines. She sat next to him on the forward seat as he held the wheel.

"Daniel wait. There's one more thing you need to do."

"What's that?"

"See that big red button on the radio?"

He looked at her intently. "Yeah. I see it."

"I want you to press it. And believe that if you do you won't ever let your past share our bed. Ever again. Dark or not. It's me there. Nothing else. But you have to believe in it Daniel. You have to take control now. For good."

Their eyes were locked together for what seemed an age. He saw just love, not lust now, in her sparkling green eyes.

He reached out and pressed the button. And hugged her tight and whispered, "I'm so glad you're finally here. I love you so much. And thank you."

"I love you too. Don't thank me. We intervene. It's what sets us apart. Remember? Now take us home, Daniel."

She sat close next to him, her arm around his shoulders as he gunned the boat towards the shore. He skilfully beached the boat and got out, helped her down and embraced her warmly.

"I need to winch her up and run fresh water through the engines babe."

"You do that." She kissed him tenderly. "I'll go along the beach. Angel and Lee are there. I'll see you along there."

She walked away along the beach with a smile on her face as she realised her legs felt a bit wobbly even now. That bloody man was just too fit! And lasting that long? That was surely down to his years of martial arts induced self-control. That was bloody cheating!

Angel was sitting on the beach near the villa gates in the shade. Lee was down near the water line, about a hundred metres away, fishing.

"Hi Angel," said Janet as she got to her.

"Oh dear," said Angel with a big smile on her face.

"What?"

"Responding well to therapy is he girl?"

"Shows does it?"

"Just a bit. You're all flushed and walking bandy. And look like you've shagged a rugby team." Janet laughed and immediately held her tummy. Her muscles hurt. Angel of course, had to notice.

"Cum strains have we?"

"Will you pack it in."

"Looks like he did." Janet laughed and winced with pain again.

"Thanks a lot, rich bitch. That hurt," said Janet with a big grin. "Seriously Angel. You were right. It was so different. He was different. It was really lovely."

"My sexual counselling clinic is always open."

"Among other things," Janet laughed again, then, "Ow!"

"Serves you right. Want a beer?" asked Angel. "There's some in the ice box that Lee's got his arse on as a seat while he's busy not damaging fish stocks."

Janet laughed and winced again. "Yeah, love one thanks," as she stretched out on a sunbed. Angel wandered off towards the sea and Lee and fetched a beer.

When she got back Janet was fast asleep with a cute little snoring noise on the go. Angel smiled warmly at her. She really was such a lovely girl. She needed a word with Daniel about her. No time like the present. She gently draped a big beach towel over her and softly kissed her cheek and waited for the man responsible for her tiredness.

Chapter 60. Out from under.

Mick Davidson was nervous. He hated Frazer Williams. The man was a dangerous thug. But he had to find out if what the man on the phone had said was true. Or more bullshit. He needed to talk to Williams anyway if it wasn't, to make payment arrangements. Amir still owed him as well. He'd need to get that if the phone call was bullshit. He decided to go see Williams face to face. He made his excuses to Fleming, saying he was going to lunch, and went to the betting shop Williams owned, and where he had his office.

He walked in and nodded to the manager, then towards the door at the back that led to the stairs. The manager nodded back and walked over and unlocked it. Mick went up and knocked on Williams' door. It was opened by Williams' minder, a new one apparently. He went in. Williams looked up at him and looked shocked to see him.

He said, "Mick? Look. We're all settled, right?"

"Well I was just checking Frazer."

"Well if you want a fucking receipt I'll write you one."

"No need."

"You didn't need to do that Mick. Sutton is still in hospital. If you'd brought the money yourself I wouldn't have screwed you over."

"You mean you haven't been up to now?"

"Okay, I was shafting you Mick, it was wrong. But we're all done now. I don't want to see you again. Or that vicious little gook bastard who brought your money in. You won't hear from me again. Paid in full. And if you want to bet downstairs, well your account's open again. And you're okay with things now, yeah?"

"Yeah, I'm okay with things Frazer. Just checking you were. Close my account." Mick turned to leave. And was pretty shocked when the heavy actually opened the door for him.

He went to buy a Samsung charger. He had a call to make later. He was smiling as he went into the phone shop. Amir's money, he still had that to come. Well he might treat himself to a long overdue holiday. He laughed to himself as he thought, "And it won't be to the bloody Gambia."

The pretty girl behind the counter smiled at him. "You're in a good mood today."

"Yeah. Yeah I am thanks. I need a charger for a Galaxy S7 Edge sweetheart."

He left with his purchase and headed back to the station. He'd make the call later after work. He went back to work. Today even Fleming wouldn't seem quite so insufferable.

Chapter 61. I want a word with you.

Daniel appeared a short while later. Angel was drinking a beer on her sunbed. He looked towards the sea and saw Lee sat looking intently at the tip of his beach caster fishing rod and saw Janet on her sunbed. Fast asleep.

"Hi Angel."

"Hi. You okay?"

"Yeah. She's asleep then?"

"She is. Looks totally shagged out for a girl who only went for a relaxing boat trip." Angel grinned wickedly as Daniel blushed and said nothing.

She said, "I want you to come for a walk with me Daniel. I'll just go tell Lee we're going off for a while okay."

"Okay." He watched as Angel walked down to Lee, kissed Janet gently on the forehead, and they set off together along the beach when Angel returned. Leaving Janet dozing in the sun.

"Everything okay Angel?"

"Yeah. Just want a word Daniel. In private."

"Sure. What's up?"

"You mostly. In regard to that lovely girl of yours."

"Has she told you there's something wrong?"

"No, you silly sod. She adores you. But she won't in time if you don't face up to a few things."

"Like what Angel? I don't understand. I thought she was happy."

"She is. Never been happier. But it's all happened in your bubble so far hasn't it? What about hers?"

"I still don't understand."

"I know. That's why I want to talk to you Daniel."

"Okay. What do you want to tell me?"

"You ever heard the line from a song? Living in a powder keg and giving off sparks? Elkie Brooks."

"No. Can't say I have."

She looked sharply at him and said, "Well that's you Daniel. John said in his letter you were one in a million. And you are. You've lived in Japan and here and in Turkey. And travelled fuck knows where else in grand isolation. With your own set of rules and values. Travelling the world righting wrongs. With little or no contact with anyone. And those you do interact with are all like you. No normality."

"Yeah. I guess. Put bluntly, that's true."

"Daniel, I only do blunt. I was John's PA. I know more than you think. And more than Lee even thinks. John trusted me. And he couldn't do all he did with you unaided. Your funny money, air tickets and dodgy identifications got to you through me. And you have done a great deal of good. I know that. And you've achieved wonderful things for a lot of vulnerable people. Along with your like-minded confederates. But this is about you and Janet. To you the UK is a powder keg of daft rules and morons and you go there giving off sparks. And it could blow up in your face if you don't deal with it."

"That's a bit harsh Angel."

"Really? I've heard you talking. She's told me what you say to her. Thick bastards who can't enjoy themselves without getting pissed. Live in queues and traffic jams like mindless idiots. Post drivel on social media. Watch moronic soap operas. Obsessed with their pointless, noisy, destructive pets. She's worried about it. She's got friends. Your kids, yes Daniel, your kids now. They have got friends. And their new Dad won't like a single bloody thing about any of them if he doesn't get his act together."

"Bloody hell Angel. Am I really that bad?"

She continued, "Yes Daniel. You are. I know the UK can be, and is, a shithole in a lot of ways, with too much freedom to be a lazy twat or a total arsehole. And get paid to be one if you can't be arsed to work. But not everyone wants to train for hours a day at martial arts and read meaningful books and meditate. Fire guns and kick ass in the Foreign Legion and chase down bad people and help good ones after they left it. Because they wouldn't know how to. They've got their lives and it's all they know. Yes. In far too many cases they're ignorant and uncouth. Sadly lacking in standards. Lack any compassion or consideration for other people. And they do watch crap and post drivel. And put their noisy, irritating, shit-dispensing pets on pedestals. Way above the world's desperate, dying children you care about and can't understand why they don't. And get pissed before they can look like they're enjoying themselves. It's not ideal. And it worried John deeply, as you know. But it's not all bad. There are thousands of good people there. Your Jan was one of them."

Daniel said, "Yes. Exactly my point. She was. Living a bloody shit life."

Angel glared at him. "Yes. She was Daniel. But it was her life. And you need to stop making that lovely girl feel ashamed of her life up until now and being worried sick that not only she, but her friends too will meet your exacting standards. Because that world is where she came from. And she is just as entitled to her past as you are. They're both pretty grim. But she's learning to live with yours. And helping you with it. All you're doing is slagging hers off."

Daniel went quiet and thought over all Angel had said. And she was right. He was intolerant and unreasonable about the UK.

He said, "I'm sorry Angel. You're right. I'll go talk to her about it now."

"You so will not! What sort of man wakes up a woman he just boffed half to death?" Grinning again at how awkward he was looking.

"Come on. You can buy me a drink over there. Give the poor girl an hour, yeah."

"I guess. Some of this is a nightmare for me Angel. You do know that?"

"Yes Daniel. I do. That's why we'll all be here for you. And I hope you know that?"

"Yes I do. And I can't thank you enough."

"A beer will do, super stud. Come on."

She put her arm through his and walked him to the nearest beach bar. He felt the connection he always had when she was near him and wasn't surprised she was John's PA. And Lee's wife. John was a good man and had surrounded himself with good people who were guided to him because of that.

Daniel Cade had a lot to learn about his new life. Angel was a very good teacher. An hour or so later, as they walked back, Daniel was a lot wiser. And loved his brother's lusty, outrageous, beautiful wife, even more than he had before. He wasn't simply lucky enough to have the right people around him in everything he did. They were guided to him as he was to them. And he accepted not everyone would ever understand that. It didn't matter. What did matter was that they were.

Chapter 62. A spiritual experience.

Later Pat and Alan had returned and the three couples were all still on the beach near the villas, ice boxes and cold beers topped up. The children were with Rosie back at the pool. Conversation drifted from one subject to another. Janet was half listening. Daniel, well now he was asleep next to her.

He'd come back from a walk with Angel and told her she was amazing. It had been and it would be next time. She smiled, maybe just not for quite as long. She still ached a bit. That bloody man. She quietly got up leaving Daniel where he was and got a beer from the ice box and joined the others.

Pat was saying to her husband, "Well everything you're saying John said makes sense. But it would be a terrible risk for Lee to take, surely? Openly backing a radical new political party."

"It would. If it didn't gain popularity fast. Yes. Lee would be tainted for life in business. For rocking the boat. And an element of risk too. Some very powerful people like things just the way they are"

"Well, is it worth it? Everyone here has good lives. Why would you risk it all?" Janet saw Angel flick a contemptuous look towards Pat. She'd noticed a bit of static between those two.

Alan replied, "Well simply because John cared enough about all the people who have awful lives. And he felt that if social inequalities and law and order aren't addressed, and starting soon, none of us will have good lives or be safe. And sadly, that came true for him and Ann." They were all quiet as his words made them think of the tragic deaths.

Janet asked, "Do you mind me asking what the idea is?"

"Not at all. He felt that there should be certain basic issues that the nation should agree on. Once and for all. By referendum, like the one we are heading towards about the bloody EU. Such as, health, defence, security, immigration, transportation infrastructure. And above all, law enforcement. And retribution for breaking it, at all levels from petty crime upwards. With mandatory sentencing that is a deterrent to offending, not up for dubious interpretations by slick lawyers and dotty judges. Restore order and make everyone feel as safe as humanly possible."

"Put like that you'd think everybody would want that, surely?" said Janet.

He smiled at her. "There's a lot that don't, pretty lady. And we have a very divided society." He took a drink of beer and continued,

"John believed that these basic things should be agreed by everyone. Regardless of party issues, race issues, religious issues etc. To ensure a safe, fair, prosperous society. Set in stone. With adequate budgets enshrined in law to achieve it. Run to a good, proven business model. With real time updated accounts in the public domain. With no vast unexplained waste by an unaccountable bureaucracy. A new Magna Carta if you will. The basic foundation block for everything else. And the only way to achieve that is to roll into parliament with a new political party with a clean sweep of every seat in the place, or at least a colossal majority, to have the power to push the legislation through. Because the existing establishment will never agree to it. And yes, it would be a risky thing to do. You'd upset some powerful people who make a lot of money the way it is right now. And you would only get one chance at it. Because of that."

Janet asked, "Would you take the risk Lee?"

Lee smiled. "Probably. I've got a brother asleep over there who's taken a million risks for the old man."

"And a huge one for mine," said Alan.

"Yeah. I guess one wouldn't do me any harm," said Lee.

"I hate being discussed," came from a little way away. From Daniel.

"Can you hear while you're asleep?" asked Janet.

"Yeah I can. You're very noisy on the loo when you think nobody's listening."

"You cheeky sod!"

"Could you pass me a beer please?"

"Get it yourself."

They were all laughing as Daniel lazily got up and came over. They all looked at him. The several scars, prominent where he was tanned. The muscled, wiry frame. He probably could hear while he was asleep. Things he'd done and the situations he'd been in, he'd probably had to.

They carried on with the afternoon. The political discussion over with for now. They all needed to relax. The deaths of Lee's parents. Janet's ex-husband. Alan's workload and worries while Lee was in a bad place. Angel's concern over Lee. They were all resolved or at least behind them now. It was time to unwind before life took over again. So that's exactly what they did.

Then Angel said to Daniel, "Lee wants to borrow the rib tomorrow if that's okay. Take me for a good ride. If you know what I mean?"

Daniel looked at her. "Yeah. Sure. Of course." He was blushing again.

Angel gave her wicked grin and said, "Thanks. I'm going for a last paddle." Looked at Janet and said, "You coming? Or are you too tired to come?" Janet tuned into the blatantly deliberate innuendo, and replied, "I'll come. I'd like to come actually." she replied with a smile.

Angel giggled dirtily as Janet got up from her sun bed. Watched as Pat glared at Alan for looking at her shapely backside as she shimmied by, then deliberately wiggled her own right past his face, to aggravate her a bit more. Janet got alongside her and they walked together towards the sea which was well over a hundred metres away as the tide had ebbed. The beach was deserted.

Once they were out of earshot Angel said quietly, "I told you your arse is at just the right height in that boat, didn't I?"

"Yeah. I recall you did." Janet was blushing now. Angel was outrageous.

"Feeling better about things now?"

"Yeah. You were right. It was lovely. He was much happier with, well, you know."

"Shagging the arse off you. Making you have it till you squeal?"

"Angel stop it! You're terrible!"

"It's gonna really turn me on tomorrow. Knowing I'm getting shagged where you were pounded half to death."

"Angelica!"

"Those great big tits bouncing around."

"I swear I'll...."

"All squidgy and gooey. I hope you hosed it all off."

"Stop it!"

"Never."

Janet laughed again, "You've got to. You're dreadful."

"It's fun. Like getting banged in a boat. Can't wait."

"You're sex mad."

"I am right now. I'm gagging for a shag since you fell back into camp ruined. He's getting nothing tonight though. He performs better champing at the bit." They got to the surf.

Angel said, "You'd better get right in and give your pussy a rinse out and a cool down."

"Angelica Tremayne, you're disgusting!"

Janet shoved her into the surf, but Angel grabbed her hand and took her with her. A small wave broke right over them. As Janet surfaced she heard, "Was that the sea or did you just orgasm?"

Janet was helpless with laughter. "Are you always like this?"

"No darling. Sometimes I really misbehave."

The others couldn't hear a word they'd said. But clearly heard the dirtiest laughter, as they sat there looking at the two women splashing around, in the distant Atlantic surf line. Daniel looked at Lee who just grinned and rolled his eyes upwards. His lovely wife was utterly incorrigible and he wouldn't want her any other way.

Janet sat cross legged in the shallow water. "I'm ignoring you now. Unless you promise to behave."

Angel sat the same. Very close. Facing her. The shallow surf rolling to and fro around them. "Bet that feels nice on your battered fanny."

"You dirty cow!" She grinned sheepishly, "Actually it does."

"Seriously, I want a word with you."

"You? Serious?"

"Yeah. I am Jan."

Janet could see she meant it. "What's up?"

"I just wanted to say I've been around this turf a long time."

"I don't understand."

"The money, the lifestyle, Daniel, us. You'll find it hard at first Jan."

"I already do."

"I just want to say I'm glad you're here."

"Thank you."

"And that I've got you. You don't need to worry. We need each other Jan. Those two silly buggers will do what they have to do. The next big deal. Or try to save the bloody world. But you and me. We've got our kids. We hold the future. For them, and above all, for John. I love you Jan. And I will be there for you. That's all."

Jan looked into her smoky grey eyes. And felt a jolt in her tummy. Like electricity. Saw truth and trust. And love.

"You know I'll be there for you too Angel."

"I knew that when I met you. I'm just glad you got here. Daniel needed you. We all do."

"I don't understand."

"Well you will. Right now. The time's right. They're here. Don't move away from me Jan. Just trust me completely."

Angel leant forward and gently kissed her forehead. And placed her hands on the sides of her head, staring into her eyes. Jan looked at her. Angel's hands were getting warm. Janet felt suddenly strange as she heard Angel say, "Look in my eyes beautiful. Concentrate." Janet did. There was a sudden, vast depth in the beautiful eyes. Then she heard Angel utter a soft "Ahhhh," as her hands slightly increased the pressure on her head and got a little warmer. And suddenly Janet was lost in a void. A vast, ethereal space. And she whimpered as her eyes closed unbidden. And she saw all the horrors of the years. Whirling like a kaleidoscope in the weird vast space in front of her.

She heard, "I've got you baby. Don't be scared." Angel? But where? She sounded distant. Oh please. No! Her childhood. Her dad killed in a car accident when she was fourteen. Mum gone to cancer three years later. Grief. Misery. Married. To Trevor. The kids. Better times. For a little while. Then the violence. Jealous of his own children. The business failing. The drinking. She sobbed in fear as every single blow landed on her. Again and again. Heard Angel, "I'm here darling. Be brave. I'm with you."

The business gone, then the house. The escalating violence. Fled. A council house.

But a new start. Then Barry. And she moaned in sheer horror as the vile images of him and her son whirled into view. Images she'd created in her damaged mind in the absence of knowing what had actually happened. They shrieked around in front of her. In a monstrous, disgusting, slide show of misery. All the evil bad memories of all the years. Mocking her. Saying she would never be truly free of them.

Then they transformed themselves again. Into trees. Stunted, horrible black trees that looked like the aftermath of a nuclear disaster. They formed a forest in front of her. A bleak, dark and forbidding horror of a landscape. Daring her to challenge it, or to try to destroy it. "Walk towards them. I've got you. Walk forward beautiful." She whimpered in terror as she walked towards the last place she ever wanted to see. Then. In the distance. Light. Behind the trees. Oranges and yellows and reds. Hurtling towards her. She gasped in fear. Fire! A huge fireball was bearing down on her. Nowhere to escape it.

Angel's soft voice again, "Don't be scared. Walk towards it darling. I'm here." She moved forward again. Into the dark, fearsome, malevolently evil forest. And stared in wide-eyed fear as the now massive fireball surged into the trees which burst instantly into flames, exploding with deafening bangs in huge showers of sparks. And cracked and fell over, still blazing ferociously. The trees screamed in dying agony. Cursing her in their hatred of her. The fire didn't burn her at all. It swept around her but wasn't burning her. A cleansing fire. She heard herself murmur, "Fucking burn, you bastard things. Burn."

Then a massive blue wall of water appeared as the fireball passed. A huge tidal wave was bearing down on her. Towering high above her. She whimpered with fright but heard, "Stand still darling. I've got you. Be brave."

And the gigantic wave crashed through the burning landscape. Sweeping away everything in its path. It engulfed her and surged around her. But didn't sweep her away. The filthy, debris-carrying, powerful wave, was black with the foul remains of the trees. And then slowly got lighter in colour as it surged past. And the force of the wave diminished. Became a calm, shallow, beautiful blue. There was sunshine and palm trees. Her children waved to her as they paddled ashore. Smiling. Happy at last. Then it was quiet and warm. And she was sitting in the sea cross-legged.

And opened her eyes. To see her beautiful new friend Angelica. Who was rubbing her hands together. As if dispelling some sort of charge? Looking weary and a little drained.

"Angel? What has just happened to me? To us?"

"Another time beautiful. When we've time to talk. Come on. We need to get back to them."

They walked together back up the beach. But Janet had a much clearer understanding of everything Daniel had said to her after that first night. Without any explanation. She had felt it and seen it now. And she felt wonderful. It didn't make sense. But she realised, when good met good it was an unstoppable force. It actually didn't have to make sense in her world. Because it just did in theirs. And she was now part of their world. Had been welcomed in to it. And loved it there.

John. Daniel. Angelica. It was all a lot clearer now. They were joined by a rare bond. Had abilities she was only just starting to comprehend. Angel slipped her arm through hers as they walked. And she felt that little jolt again. And smiled. Of course! The letter.

It had said, "Angelica is as one with you and I. She also will be an anchor and support to you whenever you need it, in her remarkable and irreverent fashion." And she had been. Her smile got a bit wider. Twice in one day.

Chapter 63. Another chance.

Mick Davidson got home, made a coffee and put the mysteriously delivered phone on charge. He felt good. Better than he had done in ages. Williams had bled him dry after he'd got in too deep with his stupid gambling. It started after his wife had left him. So had the heavy drinking. He'd let the job rule him. Let her down one too many times. Anniversaries, birthdays, invitations. Even holidays. Their social life had vanished. She was a work widow. And it had led to her leaving him.

He wanted to progress. He hated villains. Wouldn't delegate or let up in an ongoing investigation. He had loved her. Still did. So much. He'd given her the house, made no claim on it. She had a good job and could afford the payments on a mortgage that had been paid for years. The three kids were grown up. He had grandchildren he never saw. He knew what he'd lost, after it was gone. The kids had nothing much to do with him now, the odd card at birthdays or Christmas, phone call once in a blue moon. He didn't blame them. He'd been as shit a father as he had a husband.

He lit a fag, picked up the charged phone and dialled the only number in it. It wasn't picked up. He cursed mildly. Then it rang. He snatched it back up and answered it.

"Davidson."

"Hi Michael."

"Hi."

"I assume you now know I wasn't lying?"

"Yes. Yes I do. Thank you. It was a lot of money."

"You earned it."

"Okay." Then. "Well thank you again. It's a real weight off my mind."

"Must be."

"I have to ask. Why? I would have been happy with five hundred quid. What that bastard Amir gives me."

"Would have just left you where you were Michael. In the shit."

"I guess. But you didn't have to get me out of it. But I'm glad you did."

"Well we felt we should. It was Williams that put you under Amir's control."

"What?"

"Amir wanted a copper he could lean on. Bogdan knew Williams. Williams put you in the frame. And ratcheted up the interest rates and the threats once you were locked in to it after the first payment. On Bogdan's say so. Amir and

Bogdan underwrote your debts. Which is why Williams let you rack them up so high."

"Those bastards!"

"Yeah. They are."

"But it still doesn't explain why you dealt with Williams."

"No. So I will. If you want me to?"

"Yeah. I do." Mick did. He was intrigued anyway. And this calm voice, was reassuring. And he felt there was more to this than using him as a just, well, what he was. A bent copper.

"You were a bloody good officer one time Mick."

"Yeah. A hundred years ago."

"Not so long ago."

"Well so what? Doesn't matter now."

"It does to me."

"Why?"

"Because I want you to be one again."

"Why? What's it to you?"

"I have reasons."

"I'd like to hear them."

"Okay. You screwed up after your wife left. You drank. You gambled. Got in debt. And that was the only reason you went rogue. And the only reason that fat little bastard Amir could get you to take bungs. You were just vulnerable Michael."

"Well yeah. That's true."

"Well we all do things we regret Mick. You deserved a break. Another chance. I'm giving it to you."

"Okay. But why? You don't even know me."

"Because one. I know you regret what you've done."

"Ahuh. Yeah. I really do."

"And two. You are because of it, in a position to help me do what I am going to do."

"Which is?"

"Destroy Amir and Bogdan."

"Jesus! Where would I fit into that?"

"Are you interested?"

"Of course."

"Mick, you could get your career and reputation back. If you want it?"

"By doing?"

"What you are doing now. Feed Amir information. That I give you."

"Keep taking his money?"

"Yes. Look on it as a bonus."

"And this is what you want for sorting out Williams?"

"No. That's done with. We had a deal. You can walk away now. But Amir will still have his claws in you. Or you work with us and get him out of your life. And off the street. You still interested?"

"Yes. Yes I bloody well am."

"Okay. There's five grand in an envelope at your local post office. Take ID. Collect it."

"Okay. Five grand. Bloody hell. Then what?"

"It's not a bung Mick. Amir is funding his own downfall. This is pay. Earned doing work for me that I need done. In your own time. Against a vicious criminal the police can't seem to get at."

"Okay. Yeah I get that. It feels far more right."

"Good. Buy new clothes. Get a haircut, get busy at work. Slowly. Don't attract too much attention. Cut out or right down on the booze and fags. Square your bills. And your family. Start to get your reputation and respect back."

"Okay. And then?"

"Keep this phone safe and hidden well. Check it every evening. About six."

"For what?"

"A message to call me."

"And then?"

"You feed Amir information Mick. Start tomorrow. Tell him the organisation targeting him is known as the A.R.R."

"Okay. Who the hell are they?"

"Nobody. They don't exist. But it will give the fat bastard something to focus on. Explain you got it from a friend in the intelligence services. That it's an unknown, newly formed group. Intel indicates that they have intentions to form up in the new caliphate. And the leaders seem to originate from Libya. Text me your email address. I will give you the details on what to say. Delete it totally."

Mick laughed. "Okay. I will. And I'll make it sound credible when I meet him tomorrow."

"I'll leave the pitch to you. You're on the ground there."

"What if he knows I'm clear of Williams?"

"If he mentions it just say you shifted your debt to a new lender who paid Williams off. You had to find a better deal. Williams was giving you hell and bleeding you dry. It's what Williams thinks anyway. Amir and Bogdan will just think they overplayed their hand. Made him put too much pressure on you."

"Okay. You certainly think of everything."

"I have to. So do you now Mick. You're not out of the woods yet. Be careful. Stay edgy and stressed about money around Amir. It's important he thinks you are still in dire need of him."

"I will."

"Good. And then eventually, you will lead the police to a couple of successes. Your intel. Your legwork. Your reputation."

"Amir will have me shot!"

"No he won't. By then you will be the least of Amir's worries. I won't put you in any avoidable danger Mick."

"Okay."

"You in?"

"I'm in."

"Good, send me your email. Collect the money and make a start Mick. Take care."

The call ended. Mick looked at the phone. Just who the hell was that on the other end? That calm assured voice that had all the bases covered. Then he grinned. Amir was really in the shit with whoever the hell it was. And he was going to help whoever the hell it was. Shove the fat evil little bastard right down in it. He thought to himself sombrely. If this was kosher, and it seemed to be, he'd been given another chance. He'd take it with both hands. He text messaged the email address to the single number in the contacts.

Back in the Gambia, Daniel put the phone on charge, locked in his desk. He smiled as he did so. People like Amir and Bogdan were good at being ruthless. But they always ruled by fear. They never remembered the old adage. One volunteer is worth ten pressed men. Mick Davidson had been foolish, but he wasn't a fool. He'd done bad things, but he wasn't bad. He'd just been vulnerable. To evil. He would be very useful. He needed a break. Daniel and Irena needed him. And if it got him out from under. Well, that was a bonus. It was just good strategy. Nothing more. But good strategy won battles. And this was one they had to win.

Chapter 64. I can't tell you much more.

Janet said she wanted to talk to him. It was important. So they went to the balcony. And Janet told him everything. About what she had experienced earlier. Tearful as she told him about her horrid fears about the children with him. And how sorry she was to have had such thoughts. How much better she felt now. But how confused she was. She asked him if he could just give her a little insight into what this was all about.

He looked at her and smiled. "First of all you don't have to apologise for what you were thinking. You didn't put those thoughts in your mind. Barry did. By abusing James. He wasn't the only victim of the abuse Jan. You're his mum. You lost trust. You told me you were done with relationships. You were badly damaged. Like I was. Damage that you have guided me through. In my own boat." He smiled at her as she blushed a little.

"It was wonderful Jan. Us. All of us. We do what's right to mend the damage evil causes. Help people. Every single time we can, we intervene. You included."

She smiled. "I am starting to see things differently now."

"Good."

He continued. "I had to get to John, I was guided there. You had to get to me, you got here."

She looked at him. "I'm glad I did. But how? Why me? There are surely hundreds, thousands, of damaged people."

"I don't know Jan. Truly. Were we chosen? I believe we are. And you both deserve it and are needed somewhere."

"That's a huge concept to take on board Daniel."

"Maybe. But how else did an eleven-year-old boy get through a huge bureaucracy to the only man who would save him and keep his secret? A man of vast wealth and vaster kindness. Who would see to it, that later, I was able to intervene to save victims of evil. In so many places, all over the world? At least able to save some?"

"I guess so. Put like that."

"Then there's you. What made you borrow money from an expensive source? The only place you could get one last bit of cash from. And why come to the Gambia, two days before I landed back here? Why were you in that reception area? Why did Solomon want to stop off there? We would never have met, Jan."

She looked at him and said quietly, "I don't know. There were cheaper deals and shorter flights. But I wanted that package holiday. To the Gambia. Even the girl in the travel agency said it wasn't the best choice for a woman alone."

"Well my belief is the spirits guide me. And they guided you."

"I'm starting to think maybe they did. But that experience with Angel? How did I see such things? How was she able to do that?"

"It's a huge subject Jan but I'll try. The good against evil part first. But I can only tell you my beliefs and my thoughts. If you get it from somebody else, you will get a different version or outlook. Okay?" She nodded as he collected his thoughts. "The battle between good and evil is centuries old. Put simply, imagine a big circle on a bit of paper. Size of a plate. In that big circle are the mass of, for want of a better word, ordinary people. Humankind. Going about their lives. Billions of people. They only want good lives. Without fear or pain or early death. Now imagine a thick black line around the perimeter of that circle, okay?" She nodded.

"That is evil people surrounding the mass. Trying to get to them. Often succeeding. Including absurd politicians and religions. As well as despots, criminals and perverts. That black line is populated by millions, believe me. Now imagine a thin white line between the two. Trying hard to protect the centre. Those are the true good. The risk takers. The sacrificers."

"And that's where you are Daniel?"

"Yes. But to an extreme and, I believe, wrongly, illegal level. It is also all the police and paramedics. Lifeboatmen and firemen. Military men and women. Who genuinely want to do good. Doctors, nurses and carers. But sadly they are often just clearing up the aftermath of evil getting through. I tend to try to prevent it. Rightly or wrongly, that was the path I chose, or rather was guided to, after John saved my life from becoming a living hell of detention centres and jails. Does that make sense so far? About me?"

"Yes darling. It makes it a bit clearer."

He continued. "Good. So briefly, I operated, with John's backing, against paedophile rings, drug gangs and human traffickers. And some individuals. From all over the, so-called, civilised world. Aided by Ray hacking the information. And by my Legion comrades when needed. Who were paid well. Every single gang and person was known to the justice systems of their nations. All were free to operate. Often released from jail. British wealthy perverts buying ten-year-olds in Cambodia."

He paused, then continued, "We were intercepting trafficked young girls and boys destined for the sex industry. Stealing money from the gangs to fund it. We smashed them. Ruined them. Why? Because we weren't constrained by laws and rights favouring nobody but the perverts. We did nothing a nation's law enforcement couldn't do unless it was being deliberately restrained. For a reason. But why? Barry won't re-offend Jan. He would have under the UK legal method. That is how, rightly or wrongly, we justified all we did. But why was it so hard for you to get the help you needed? And justice dispensed to him? Peace for James and your family?"

She looked at him sadly and said, "I don't know."

"Well John believed he did know and it worried him greatly. And he was working towards trying to deal with it. The plans Alan brought with him are the results of that work. " He smiled, "Talk to Alan about that. He knows a lot more. He spoke to John every day. You heard him on the beach."

"Okay. But the healing? It's wonderful. I couldn't believe what I saw. Or think I saw. Or how much better I feel."

He collected his thoughts again and continued. "Spiritual healing is using positive thought energy, in its simplest form. And really it releases the patient's own positive thought energy, via the healer. Where Angelica, John and myself are is on a higher plane. Guidance from the spirits is disputed by anybody who can't achieve it - and they are ignored by those of us that can. But. Are we? Or are we just using powers within ourselves we have unlocked? Indian yogis have been able to slow their heart rate dramatically to a point where death would occur in a normal person by deep meditation. Karate. You use your mind to make your hand break a rock. Along with training. Ninja can heal their own wounds in a ridiculously short time through power of the mind. The power of the brain and mind is hugely untapped by most human beings."

She nodded. "I have read and seen stuff on television about it."

"Yeah it's well written about Jan. The concept of pure good is just my faith and belief. It is also John and Angelica's. I believe I was guided to John. As was Angelica. To be with Lee. To guide him forward after John was gone. As you were guided to be with me. Is it real? Or only real to us? You are here now Jan. You've seen it work twice now, once on yourself. Good forces driving out the dark evil thoughts. Angelica couldn't, and didn't, know your past or the evil thoughts that haunted you. She released them, to where she could see them. And took you to confront them and you saw them destroyed by, I believe, powerful spiritual forces that she could harness and channel to do so. On a battlefield in your mind. But you have to decide. I would never force you to agree. I can't tell you much more darling."

She kissed him. "Thank you. It's the most real and beautiful thing I have ever known. Let's go to bed now."

Chapter 65. Spinning the web.

Mick got straight on the case and called Amir. Said he needed a word, had something for him. Needed paying for it, and for the last lot of information as well. Amir agreed to meet. Usual place.

Mick got a beer at the bar and went upstairs to the room. Knocked. Hassan opened the door.

Amir and Bogdan were there.

Amir said, "What have you got for us?"

"A bit of info on this terrorist group that's on your case."

"I thought you said you couldn't access such information."

"I can't. Not directly. I'm not cleared to access it."

"So how have you got this?"

"A friend from way back. He moved onto the anti-terrorist division. I called him, told him we were stonewalled on the Wesley Mason case. The possible connection to the attack on your meet. Needed a little input."

"I see. And this input? Did you find out who these people are?"

"The little there is, yeah."

"And?"

Mick took a notebook from his pocket and opened it.

"Right. Apparently it's a new splinter group. Islamic. Been named as the A.R.R by the spooks. What that stands for? Don't know. It's what they have called it. I can't ask, it's not relevant to my enquiry."

"Go on."

Mick did so. "Apparently it's newly formed. London based. Communications appear focused on financing themselves rather than any planned domestic, as in UK, activities. Some approaches have been made to wealthy people sympathetic to the cause with a view to forming up in some position of influence in the new caliphate. The leaders seem to be of Libyan origin. One in particular, as yet unidentified, is UK based but seems set on leaving for the Islamic-controlled regions to join the fray. Allegedly wants to take up a senior position when he does. And apparently money buys power. What you can bring to the table by way of money and men dictates where you can sit at it basically." He looked at Amir who nodded.

Mick looked at the notebook again and continued,

"Possible connections to, or has members that are, suspected jihadist fighters who have been in the caliphate war zones, who may well have returned to the

UK undetected. No established connections to any known extremist imams or mosques currently being monitored. No website or social media activity found as yet. Low priority rating. Being monitored."

"I see. Nothing else?"

"No. That's all they have. Like I told you before. It's rated low priority, with no actual threat of planned atrocities in the UK at this time. That hasn't changed. Just a bit more detail is all I got."

Amir pondered this. Then said, "It makes some sense. The young madman who we met was of Arabic descent I am sure. He talked of a leader who planned to travel to the caliphate. They want money. And if there are time-served jihadist fighters here, with them - even one or two - well, that would explain the sniper attacks perhaps?"

Mick nodded. "I guess so. It's all a bit vague. And doesn't fit at all with Wesley and Mason getting offed. I think that case will just get closed. Tremayne just doesn't fit either. Maybe they did kill each other by a fluke. And, as I told my boss, it could well be a different killer entirely if it was a double homicide. Maybe somebody who knew the Tremaynes and wanted them dealt with. Whacked those two, or paid for it. It doesn't have to be even connected with the take-down of your meeting. The police are at a dead end with it Amir."

"Yes. I think it was foolish of me to send those men to the Gambia. But you gave me that information Davidson."

"I did Amir. It was all we had at the time. It was a theory pitched by my superior after the attack on your meet. He made a vague connection and contacted Bland at Regional Serious Crimes who was investigating your meet. And I gave you that information. Nobody had a sniff of a terrorist gang involvement at that time, Amir. The police were looking at an ex-military line of enquiry in regard to Tremayne. Until your hire car got whacked." He saw Amir scowl at the mention of it. "That shifted the goalposts again."

"Yes. Yes, I agree. This is a fucking mess."

"It is for the police as well. Ten dead. Twelve if you count in Mason and Wesley. And nothing leading anywhere."

"I know. Well, thank you Michael. I appreciate you do give us what is there."

"Well if I could have my usual Amir, I'll be off."

"Yes." Amir pulled an envelope from his pocket and put it on the table.

As Mick went to take it Bogdan put his hand over it and said, "I understand you no longer have as much need of this, Davidson?"

"What the fuck do you mean?"

"I am informed you came into some money. Quite a lot?"

"By who?"

"The person you had your debts with is known to me."

"Williams, I guess? He's a total shit. You two should get along really well."

Bogdan said, "Are you looking to die Davidson?"

"No. I'm actually not. That's why I got a new lender. Williams was threatening to kill me. Ramping up the interest and payments. I couldn't even pay my rent. I got another source to pay him off, got a little more added to settle my bills. And a payment I can afford to make and still live. Just about. Without that vicious bastard giving me a hard time every five minutes. Not that it's any of your fucking business."

"Everything is my business, Davidson."

"My finances aren't. So fuck you. And remember what we agreed Bogdan, after last time you had me beaten. Never again. Or you kill me. Or I rat you out. Amir, can I take my money or not? I need it badly."

"Yes. Yes, just take it. Bogdan leave him. We need him. Give it up."

Bogdan released the envelope. Mick picked it up and left. That bastard Bogdan. He looked forward to the day he got what was coming to him. He headed home. And not via the pub.

Chapter 66. A new approach to things.

A lot of talking had been going on back in the Gambia. Daniel had talked at length to Janet after his time with Angel and had assured her that if she wanted to spend time in the UK, he truly was happy to do it. That they were a partnership of equals. And she wasn't to sever ties to her past and friends. And he truly wanted to buy a place in the UK. Things were different now. They had family there too in Lee and Angel and their kids and it all had to be embraced in their lives. He'd been really pleased at the effect that had had on her. Angel was a diamond.

Daniel and Janet had then sat and talked with the children. Daniel had let Janet do the talking, and it had been put to them that they would not have to return to the UK if they chose not to. They would be schooled by a private tutor at home most of the time, with time at English schools in both the Gambia and Turkey. Daniel was very pleased that they were just so receptive to it. He wouldn't make anybody do anything they didn't want to. And they were fine with some strict rules about social media. Thankfully, because of the business with Barry, it had been minimal anyway but they were told that, because of Daniel's work, they mustn't broadcast their lives on Facebook or anywhere. But there were no major issues. They were active kids. Not really into phones and screens. Daniel adored them.

The other two couples were going home and the children said they were fine with staying with Rosie and Solomon if Daniel and Janet flew back with them. Janet wanted to hand back the flat and withdraw benefit claims and square the schools. Settle her affairs, little as they were, and had no qualms about doing any of it. In fact, she just wanted it over and to get back. Could do it in three days hopefully. This was her life now and it was the better for it.

And like Daniel had said, they would have a place in the UK. They could go there when they wanted or needed to but she truly wasn't missing it at all. And she'd talked to Daniel. He had made her acutely aware she had to be sure that it wasn't just the "holiday syndrome" so many people got while away from home. Living abroad wasn't for everyone. But she was sure. The UK. Well. Her life and her place in it hadn't been kind. Part time crappy jobs. Benefits to top it up. A constant struggle. You wouldn't starve to death but it was like being in a rut you just couldn't get out of. Fucking silly rules about bloody everything. She felt lucky to be out of it.

She told Daniel she wanted to work with children voluntarily in the future, here, and if possible, in Turkey. He'd told her that would be no problem. It would be appreciated and there were plenty of organisations to do it through. He was just so pleased at her approach. She was a lovely girl and very intelligent. She knew you could, as she put it rather bluntly, "only shag and sunbathe for so long." She was so down to earth and always made him laugh. He was very thankful she'd finally made her way to him, with her rash decision to take out a loan and just go on holiday. He loved her very much and never questioned how good they were together. He knew it was meant to be and she was happy to be there now it was. Even after such a short time now neither one of them questioned it.

Then Janet had spoken to Alan for a while, said she needed to ask him a few things. She politely asked Pat if she minded and got a sour nod for a no. They went to a quiet bar and Alan said, "What's up lovely lady?"

"Well, I wondered if you would tell me a little more about John please. And these plans and his ideals. I am sure Daniel will be involved if they go ahead. In place of what he's been doing."

"Well I don't know what's in the case I brought, Jan. That will be the detail. But I spoke with John enough to know what his ideas were."

"A letter I saw to Daniel, from John, asked him if he would work with Lee."

Alan looked at her pretty, earnest face and smiled. "He will be if Lee decides to do it. Because there will be dangers. I'm not trying to frighten you Jan. But they will take on a dangerous task. Rocking a world with many powerful vested interests."

"Why? Don't people want good lives?"

"Of course they do. The argument is for how many. You can't have power without the powerless. If you try to empower far more people, it reduces the power and control of those who hold it now. And their wealth."

"I don't understand. Sorry, you must think I'm thick."

"Far from it. Because you were never meant to. Let me explain. Or try." He took a long drink from his beer and signalled the waiter over and ordered two more drinks for them.

He continued. "The UK and European governments exercise huge control over their people and take huge sums of money from them in various forms of taxation. Okay. You can argue that there has to be some element of control. In fact it's vital. You need an elected government, a structure and a system. And we have them. Plus a legal system. Laws. A justice system. And sentencing. To keep law-abiding citizens safe. Pretty simple, right?"

"Yes. And that's what we have, isn't it?"

"In essence and far better in the past. Our democracy was once the envy of and an example to the world. But now, John believed, and I agree with him, it's corrupted terribly. Controlled by the wrong people. And working against the best interests of a lot of the people. Deliberately."

"But why?"

"Power. Control. Greed. Trendy thinking. Weird ideology. And huge sums of money."

"So why do we put up with it?"

"Because you can't stop it. Not when you look at the once good systems they have slowly and carefully bastardised and changed so it can't possibly reflect the will of the people. Let me try to explain. You've seen the wonderful way the children here get to school. Been in the car when Solomon, like many others, pulls over and the kids all pile in. And pile out again at the school gates." Janet smiled. "Yes, it's wonderful."

"Would you let your two get in a stranger's car back in the UK to get to school?"

"Good heavens no!"

"Why?"

Janet was trying to form a reply when Alan said, "Because you're fearful. They're not here. They treasure children. And if any Gambian hurt one, it is doubtful he would get as far as a prison. And if he did, he wouldn't come out. But we're the civilised ones, right?"

She looked at him aghast. "That's awful."

"It is. But now ask why? What sane person would release a person with urges to hurt children. Or try to excuse them? Why do we have so many? Because there is no real deterrent. And the greatest threat to foreign children is western perverts as a result."

"But how did we, well.........," she let it tail off.

"Let it happen? Put simply. Rights. Or an excess of them. There has been an era from the sixties of people with absurd ideals. Well-meaning maybe? I don't know. Possibly in the rank and file it's well-meant, even if misguided. By others. John believed it is, deliberately. These people were created in the education system and rose to power within the once good systems of government. National and local. Mainly, because they were keen to do so where people who should have didn't bother, so John believed. So, away they went. Liberal ideas. Excuses. No bad people, just people doing bad things. There had to be a reason, find it and cure it. They deserved our understanding not punishment yada yada. Anybody who dared to disagree was silenced. Labelled. Old-fashioned, fascist, racist, intolerant."

Janet reflected on that, "There are some wacky things out there Alan. I get that"

He smiled and continued, "There are. With each new generation of reforming zealots, trying to out-reform their predecessors. They were the new vanguard, the enlightened ones. Freedoms. Leniency, soft sentencing, suspended sentences. Probation, community service, no capital punishment. Parole system sneaking criminals quietly back out. Who constantly re-offend. There are often huge outcries in the press over a crime committed by a long-term serial criminal. But nothing is done about it. And, more sinister, nobody is held to task over that release happening."

"Yeah I remember some of them. That Roy Whiting and Sarah's law?"

"Great example. Whiting had previous. Was released. Killed Sarah. Sarah's Law enables you to ask questions about a person to see if they are on a register of offenders. Nothing more. Megan's Law in the USA was what spawned it. Made the details public. Problem is, that with a register that's available in the public domain, the offenders on it leg it and go to ground. It happened."

"What a mess Alan."

"It is. But never once have the options regarding offenders been reviewed. Just the ways to placate the whinging public over another dead kid. Because these offenders have rights. And they aren't about to reduce them. And it's across the board. Freedom to scrawl graffiti, art darling yah. Freedom to produce and sell vile audio tracks and video games promoting violence. Drunken hordes in the streets. No drunk and disorderly arrests anymore. Releasing vile criminals back into the community. Result. For many, you're scared of every passing car and won't accept a lift, scared to go out, on edge. Everything locked or it's gone. Live in a state of fear. Hoping the next rape or assault victim won't be you. Try acting like that in Dubai. You wouldn't dare. And why? Because the law is harsh and it deters. Too harsh? Maybe. But it proves a point. We are too lenient. John wants to redress to the right balance. On everything."

"I have never even given it any thought. It's horrible."

"Believe me, you weren't meant to Jan."

He took another drink from his glass and smiled at her. "That was all John was saying. A great concept that worked and was appreciated by people, now corrupted and ruined. The, as we call them, left-wing, liberal zealots have slowly exerted more and more control over people's lives and choices and spoil millions of lives. Like the one you were trapped in. Survivable but tedious. People are compliant if you give them just enough to live, but never enough to have real choices. Until you are much further up the food chain. Which created the required rich poor divide. John wanted to go to the nation. Just once. And offer them an alternative. Where everybody was important enough to live safe and well and have choices, in return for their taxes, which would be openly accounted for. And complying with the law of the land. On all levels. But, like I say, it falls to Lee now. And it will offend some very powerful people if he does it. That's it, pretty lady."

He finished his beer and said, rather sadly, "I suppose we'd better go back."

Janet looked at him. He was such a nice man, but seemed so sad and said, "You're not happy, are you, Alan?" Then blurted out, "I am so sorry. That sort of slipped out."

"Don't apologise, Jan. I'm not."

"Pat?"

"Yeah. She's a bitch. Cruel, frigid, selfish and unkind. She's my second wife. My first was a darling. She died, heart problems since she was a kid sadly. I married Pat three years ago after being alone for three. Against good advice from friends who knew her. But she sold me a different face to the real one. I loved her. Until I married her. Then I found out who she really was. I was lonely. I screwed up. I can't afford a divorce. She isn't happy but doesn't seem to want the indignity of one anyway. If I do it she'll leave me too skint to retire in a couple of years for the lifestyle I've earned by working hard for sure. And I want to retire. I'm tired now of business. I hang in there for Lee. And John bless him. I'll see this grand plan launch if Lee goes ahead and Tremayne's is through the aftermath of this referendum. Then that's me. I'll retire and make the best of it."

"Have you told Lee, Alan? How bad you feel?"

"No. It's not his problem. And with poor John and Ann, last thing he needs is a middle-aged man who should be able to look after himself whinging to him."

Janet looked at him. "I was in a very bad place Alan. My ex abused my son. I was broke. I took a payday loan and came here. And I still don't know why. But my life is wonderful now. I hope you find your salvation, Alan. You're a lovely man." She stood up and he rose to his feet. She kissed him gently on the cheek. "I was lonely when I met Barry. It makes you vulnerable. You've got good people around you Alan. They'll guide you out of it. If you let yourself be guided. Come on."

She put her arm through his. As they got to the villas he tried to remove it but she wouldn't let him, returning Pat's hard stare when she saw them. "Thank you for your time, Alan. Remember, it's a valuable commodity. See ya later. Pat," she nodded at her and walked away to talk to Lee. She smiled. Intervention for good was a part of this world. And it was her world now. And she was going to intervene. And did. Lee listened to her intently.

Chapter 67. Heading back.

Travel plans were made and the plane was arranged for Monday. They enjoyed their last couple of days and then it was time to go. Lee and Alan were missing the business now. It had been an emotional trip for all of them. A lot of things had been revealed and dealt with, with no negatives, bar Alan's issues. And they had relaxed and unwound after that.

But now. Now it was time to get back. Run the company John Tremayne had built. Keep secure the jobs of their many employees, and the funds of their many investors. And guide it through the uncertain times they knew were coming, with the referendum creeping ever nearer. And, of course, the information regarding John's political ideals would have to be considered when time allowed and the decision made on whether to launch a new political movement. A huge undertaking that could not be entered into lightly. It would put literally everything at stake. The business, their reputations. Even, if it was perceived as a too big a threat by the wrong people, their very lives.

The morning came to leave. Big hugs with Janet's children and away in a hired car and the Land Cruiser. They got to the airport, which was when Janet realised there was something different. They were whisked through VIP then, out on the tarmac, she realised something else. She was going home in a private executive jet. She spoke very quietly to Angel as they walked up the boarding steps, well ahead of the others who were talking to the pilots on the tarmac along with Angel and Lee's children.

Janet whispered, "I don't believe this, Angel. A private jet."
Angel gave her a hug. "I know. It still freaks me out."
"You? I thought you had always, you know. Lived like this."
"Me?" She laughed and whispered, "I was his Dad's PA and secretary. My dad was a lorry driver, mum was a nurse. Just showed a bit more tit and leg when his son was around. They're all the same. Don't matter how much money they've got. I just fancied him something rotten. Was a real bonus when he asked me to marry him"
Janet glared at her and whispered, "You could have bloody said."
"Why?" came the whispered reply. "I was just pleased you thought I was a lady of breeding. To the manor born yah."
"You total cow. I was nearly curtseying when we first met."
"I know. It was hilarious."

"How was your boat trip by the way?"

"Great. Minor cum strains but then I train harder than you."

"Will you bloody stop it! Forget I asked."

They were both giggling like schoolgirls as they went through the aircraft door. The pretty flight attendant greeted them.

"Hi Angelica."

"Hi Kelly. This is Janet."

"Hi. Welcome aboard."

"Thank you."

Angel said, "Can you make sure the bedroom cabin is made up please, Kelly. Janet is a bit sex mad and won't last the journey without a good seeing to."

Janet blushed to her roots and spluttered out, "I'm just so sorry. I do not need a bedroom, Kelly." She glared at Angel her face bright red. "How could you?"

Kelly laughed, obviously well used to Mrs Tremayne. "Ignore her, Janet. If anyone creates extra work for me by using the bedroom cabin on a short daytime flight, I know who it will be."

"Bloody right as well." said Angel, then looked at Kelly. "And I know who uses it when the plane's flying with just crew as well. They don't call that bit up the front a cock pit for nothing, do they sweetie?"

"That's for aircrew to know and you to guess at Angelica Tremayne."

Now the young girl was blushing. Angel smiled wickedly at her. "I already guessed, didn't I pretty one. But in return for my silence, we'll have two large vodka and tonics with ice please, sweetheart."

Kelly laughed and went off to get the drinks.

They sat down in the luxurious seats and Angel said, "Don't fancy joining the mile high club then, gorgeous."

Janet gave up. "You know what. I just might."

"Well you've ticked a boat off your fuckit list. You might as well add a plane."

When the rest boarded the two women were laughing their heads off.

The men didn't bother asking why. A few minutes later they were taxiing towards the runway.

Chapter 68. A glimpse of the plan.

The flight passed uneventfully. Ian and Natalie were asleep in the bedroom Janet didn't want and Janet was talking to Alan again. Alan seemed rather interested in her life in the UK since they had spoken the day before, in relation to John's plans and ideals. He asked her if she'd mind talking to him a little more about her views and opinions. She said not at all.

So he said, "I need you to understand this is not a rich poor divide thing. I am not an elitist. John wasn't."

"I know that Alan, I have never thought you were. You're all nice. You've all been nice to me, well nearly all." With a glance at Pat, who just stared out of the window.

"Good. So, with that established, I would be very interested in your views based on your life experiences in the UK on a few subjects."

"What subjects?"

"Let's see. Right. The NHS. Transport. Pet-owning. And, let me think. Environment. As in recycling and conservation. You pick one. I will ask you questions about it."

Janet laughed. The others were listening. "Okay. Here goes. The NHS."

"Good. My favourite. Do you think it's underfunded?"

"Well yes."

"Why?"

"Well everybody says so."

"Who's everybody?"

"Well, the papers. Television. Social media. Always talking about cuts to funding."

"Okay. Numbers. When the NHS was founded in 1948 it had a budget of 437 million pounds. That equates to around 15 billion pounds today. What do you think the budget is today?"

"I don't honestly know, Alan."

"It's 116.4 billion pounds. 101 billion pounds of that is managed by England alone. Can you see the cuts? I see a six fold increase."

"It is a huge increase."

"Population in 1948 was around 50 million. Today it's around 65 million. Six times 1948 figure would be 300 million so it's not population numbers. So where's the shortfall?"

"I don't know."

"Combination of medical advances and poor management maybe?"

"I don't know that either. Is it?"

"Yes. It's not the doctors and nurses and our amazing surgeons and teams. And our paramedics. It's because it's run by the state, by bloody civil servants, implementing and funding policies they can't bloody well afford. They've sold everything the nation owned in the process. If they ran a private company it would fail. But because it's taxpayer's money, they just demand more every time they run out. There is plenty of money collected through national insurance to provide a health service. But they don't deliver and they never will. But big companies are fleecing the nation's funds with overpriced drugs and supplies under very dubious contracts. And with PFI's. Private funded initiatives. The nation's skint so they lease the new hospitals. Don't own a single brick. At a hugely inflated cost. As of April 2015 the UK owed two hundred and twenty two billion pounds. Three thousand four hundred pounds of debt for every man, woman and child in the UK. Bart's Health Trust in London was ninety three million in debt at that time. It has a forty-three year PFI contract. And that will cost over seven billion over that period, for works with a value of just over one billion. It's an abomination. And the one area the Corbynistas are correct in. Big business is fleecing the nation. But they are totally wrong in thinking the current state system could possibly run it efficiently enough."

"So what can be done about it?"

"What John wanted to do. Explain it to people simply. Keep it state-owned. That's how it should be. It belongs to the nation. But run it like a proper business. Cut out the huge waste. The piss-poor buying. Often corrupt. Take thousands of basic drugs off the prescription nonsense altogether. Cut out as much state meddling and interference as possible and put more money in people's banks and not the state's wasteful coffers by cutting the cost of it. Not keep increasing it."

"Could that be done?"

"Of course. If it isn't, the NHS will cease to exist anyway."

"Really?"

"Without a doubt. When the NHS was created it was a wonderful idea. And it worked. Everyone paid a bit. Those who were lucky enough to stay healthy, paid to care for those that didn't. Like your privately-run travel insurers are doing for you right now. But now. Medicine has advanced. And because of both uncontrolled immigration and long-term unemployment, literally thousands of people who have never paid into it are using it for free. Plus an ageing population. When the NHS was conceived there weren't hundreds of people off work with stress or people unhappy with their gender having tits and dicks added or removed at everybody else's expense."

"Alan!" said Pat.

"Pat. I'm not offended, thank you." said Janet.

"Probably not. I've heard you talking. But it offends me."

Alan continued, "And it will cease to exist. It has to. Or it has to change."

"Well I never thought of it like that. I really didn't."

"No. Because those sort of arguments aren't trotted out by the existing parties. Huge vote loser. So the fantasy that it's simply underfunded continues because politicians under the current party political system daren't tell the truth. John wanted to gamble on telling the truth. What you can have for what you pay in and no more. Like a BUPA policy does. And winning. And on everything, not just the NHS. Every single thing that affects our lives. A choice of budgets and costs for each of them. Let the nation choose one for each. Set the minimum required taxation to fund them. And then manage it properly and make the accounts public domain, like the private sector does."

"Well that was quite enlightening."

"It was. Thank you. I just wanted to see how you reacted Jan. Because one day and not so far in the future, everyone will have to face the truth about the whole shit cart."

"Alan please!" said Pat again.

"Sorry. But it is. From parliament down to town councils. Let's have a drink shall we. That made me quite thirsty.

Conversation was relaxed after that and they all agreed to really keep in touch with each other. Video link chats and get together again as soon and as often as possible. The airport security was problem-free VIP style.

And they were in the UK, with light rain and strong winds. Janet was bloody freezing. Cars had been arranged and were waiting. Janet and Daniel got into one of them after saying goodbye and having hugs and handshakes all round. Then they were off. It was eleven in the morning and Janet wanted to get to her flat and start there. Check the mail and arrange collection of her stuff to get it empty.

Chapter 69. Intervention from the top.

She looked at the vile weather and heavy traffic as they crawled towards Erith. She squeezed Daniel's hand and said, "Quick as we can, yeah. And get home." He put his arm around her.

"You think Gambia is home after sixteen days?"

"Yeah. Excuse my language darling but yeah. I so fucking do." She rested her head on his shoulder as the car continued its journey and started to doze off after the flight home.

Daniel had his own thoughts. One of them was Bogdan, not a pleasant thought. But all the pressure was on Amir. He was stressed and weakened, which was good. Bogdan wasn't, he was not greatly affected by the recent actions, apart from venting at Amir over lack of drugs to supply.

Which Amir was just, according to the communications they were intercepting, managing to keep on top of, by calling in favours and doing small deals to tide things over. Bogdan was in business as usual mode. That needed to change. They needed supply and distribution in a bad place at the same time. Bogdan shouldn't be left confident and arrogant, he should be encouraging Amir to pay up. He gently stroked Janet's hair as she slept and cleared his mind, focused on forming a plan to give Bogdan a personal problem. By the time the car got to Janet's block, he'd thought of one. They got out of the car and Daniel looked round, immediately very glad he didn't have to live here.

Lee was travelling in the back of his limousine with Alan. He had asked Angel if she would take the children and travel with Pat in the other car that would take Pat and Alan home, just for a while. They'd stop and swap over later. He had something urgent to discuss with Alan. Angel looked less than thrilled but did so.

Lee poured whiskies for them both. "Talk to me Alan. Jan did. You should have."

"Why? It's my business. My problem Lee. Personal."

"My parents getting murdered was my problem and personal. You ran my company single-handed while I behaved like a prat. You put me back on track Alan. We're friends as well as business colleagues."

"I guess so. Okay. All I blabbered out to Jan was I am so unhappy with Pat. And locked in financially. I can't face life without the money I'm used to Lee. It scares me. I've made promises to my three kids I want to keep. If that makes me a coward so be it."

Lee smiled at him. "You're no coward. Tell me the details Alan."

"Well, I'm well off by any standards. But I have invested heavily in my pension. She'd get half of it. And half my savings. Half the house. I'm putting my four grandchildren through private schooling and I've promised all their university fees, pissing her off, but I am. My three kids work but they don't earn huge money. If she took half of everything, which she would, I'd be fucked for retirement. And I'm not going to break my promises to my kids about their kids' educations and futures. So I'll get through it."

"How much is the hit Alan?" Lee asked. "If you leave her?"

"I don't know Lee."

Lee topped their glasses up. "You bloody liar Shand. You know every number you need to know. Now cough."

Alan smiled wryly. "Nine hundred and thirty four thousand plus change you nosy bastard."

"That all?" said Lee with a big grin.

"Fuck off! I'm not up there in the stratosphere where you are."

"I'm winding you up, I get the habit from Angel. She's driving Jan nuts, it's hilarious. Here's the deal. If you want a divorce from Pat, tell her. And you get her lawyer, not yours, to agree a one-off, all time settlement. Whatever that amount is you will get a cheque for, plus interest over the time it's been out of account for, either into your pension, or wherever you want it put, as soon it's legally out of reach of her. And this conversation has not taken place yet so it's not an asset of yours yet. And stop looking shocked and drink your scotch, you daft sod."

Alan looked at him in bewilderment. "But why? And how? You can't take shareholders' money to pay for my divorce settlement, Lee. It's, well, it's unethical." Lee gave him a stern look. "Alan. It is not unethical. A proposal to pay you a bonus of that amount would get past the board and shareholders without anyone even blinking, with your track record and all your years of service. And it's a drop in the ocean to Tremayne Holdings, and you know it. And that might still happen at a later date. That is business Alan, this conversation is not. Understood?" Alan nodded yes. This was Lee Tremayne the businessman talking.

Lee continued. "It's coming from the old man's money, in recognition of all you did for him over the years. Your father was instrumental in making his business a success in the early days. You know damn well he would help you in a personal matter and would have done something for you when you retired if he'd lived. And I owe you as well. He would want me to do it, I want to do it, so I am.

And that's an end to it Alan. Here's to John." He held up his glass. Alan did the same. "To John."

Lee held out his hand and Alan shook it warmly. "Thank you, Lee."

Lee smiled. "There's another reason for doing it as well."

"What's that?"

"Maybe next time you join us on holiday you'll be with somebody who doesn't get on my bloody wick being miserable all day."

Alan smiled. He might well be. And he knew who it would be. With a little luck. He sipped his whisky, opened his leather notebook and made a note to send a huge bunch of flowers to a very special young woman who was at that moment heading to a bleak council flat in south London.

Chapter 70. Bleak housing.

Daniel and Janet walked through the cold drizzle, down a concrete path flanked by scruffy lawn, then up the concrete steps to her first floor, two-storey flat. A small gang of youths lounged in the covered walkway, blocking it, smoking. Puffa jackets and hoodies and the usual baseball caps.

Daniel smiled as he recalled Quan saying, "If you ever need a wanker you'll find one on top of a skateboard or under a baseball cap. Or sandwiched between the two." The youths didn't seem inclined to move until one of them made arrogant eye contact with Daniel. Then looked quickly away and moved over. They walked through with Janet saying, "Hi Nathan." to one of them.

She put her key in the door and they went in. Pile of post, Janet picked it up and went through to the kitchen. She put the kettle on and they sat down. Daniel looked around. She'd made it as nice as possible. It was clean and warm and friendly. A bloody sight more than you could say for the place outside. She smiled at him. "I'll make some calls and we'll get this over with."

He nodded. "Can I have a look round?"

"Yes of course."

He went for a wander round while she got on the phone. Smiled at the cosy children's bedroom. It was all as nice as anyone could make it. But there were signs of damp and a couple of the windows were cracked. Then he sat in the tidy lounge and sent some messages and emails while he waited. He could hear Janet on the phone. She was getting on with it at a rate of knots. He was glad she felt like she did. He badly wanted to get out of this place too. And he didn't live here.

Janet came in to the lounge with another black coffee for him. "All okay?"

"Yeah fine."

She said, "I've got most of it done. A drone from the housing is coming here tomorrow at four, to check the place over and take the keys. Gas, electric and water done. Council tax done. Got a charity coming to take the furniture and stuff at eleven in the morning. Got a friend coming round from two doors down to pick through it and take what she wants. Be here in a minute. Need to buy a couple of suitcases to pack some of the kids' toys, clothes and bits to take back. And a couple of bits of mine. I can do that tomorrow if we get here about nine. So by tomorrow night we can go. Is there a night flight?"

Daniel laughed. "I know you want to get home to the children. But can I suggest we take at least a couple of days? Go see the place I have here maybe?

Check it over."

"Yes of course, sorry, it's not the kids at all, they're fine. I just want this over. As in this place."

The doorbell rang. Janet went to answer it. Daniel heard her talking for a minute, saying she was moving abroad which got a shrieked, "Oh my God hun," And then the visitor said, "Don't tell me you've met a tribal chieftain in Africa."

Janet came through the door and gestured towards Daniel. "No. I've met this man."

The young woman looked him up and down and said. "I'd go abroad as well for him." Then to Daniel. "Hi. I'm Tracey." She was a rather short, plump girl with a very pretty face and bobbed brown hair. And a very large bust, straining against the low cut, bright yellow T shirt she was wearing outside of a pair of jeans.

"Hi Daniel." Daniel got up and awkwardly shook her hand. "Hi Tracey. Nice to meet you."

"You too. If you're taking my best friend in this dump away you look after her, yeah."

Daniel smiled. "I will." Just then the house phone rang and Janet dashed into the kitchen to answer it. Tracey sat down and smiled at Daniel and said, "I'll miss her Daniel."

"How long have you been friends?"

"About a year. I got lumbered with this place about two months before she showed up. My fella left me and we were in private rented. I couldn't afford it and the council gave me a place here. All there was."

"You don't like it?"

"Hate it. But I've got two kids, same as Jan, boy and a girl. Getting older now and won't be able to share a room. Fingers crossed when I get enough points for a three bed we'll get somewhere nicer."

Daniel nodded. "I hope so."

"Yeah, well at least she's getting out. Living abroad too. She deserves it after everything. I guess you know about her ex?"

"Barry. Yeah. All of it."

"Bastard. I used to sit with her when she was scared he was around here." She grinned. "I chased him out of the walkways with a cricket bat one night"

Daniel smiled at her. "I'm glad she had you around Tracey. I hope things work out for you soon."

"Thanks, I hope so too."

Janet reappeared. "You ready? Or you want to keep chatting up my man?"

Janet ushered her friend away and the two of them set about the kitchen sorting out things Tracey would want to take. Daniel's phone beeped. Text message, from Ray. It said. *"19 Lenham Avenue. Woolwich. 8 vics. From near Dover."* Daniel replied with just *"Thanks."* And messaged Mick Davidson to call him. He put the phone away. Mick wouldn't ring until six or after. He looked at his watch. It was only one p.m. He had an idea to use up the time.

Daniel walked into the kitchen where the two women who were chattering as they sorted things out.

"Janet, you have things to do and your friend's here. If it's okay with you I have a friend a few miles from here, guy called Ray. Could do with seeing him really. If I get a cab I can be there in half an hour."

She gave him a hug. "Yeah sure. There's nothing you can do here. And if you clear off I can tell Tracey what a great shag you are."

Daniel replied awkwardly, "Well, whatever you ladies talk about."

"I'm kidding you."

"Oh right. Well I'll go flag a cab down and I'll book a good hotel for later. And buy two big cases if you want?"

"Great. Okay, no rush. If I get done here I'll wait at Tracey's. Two doors down back the way we came in."

"I'll phone you. Take care."

Janet kissed him and closed the door as he left and got back on with sorting the flat out while telling Tracey all about the Gambia and Daniel's home and Solomon and Rosie. A place in Turkey they'd go to later in the year. How much the kids loved it and their new education plans. And how much they liked Daniel. And what a great shag he was.

Chapter 71. A scruffy genius.

Daniel walked out through the bleak estate and equally bleak weather, glad of his leather jacket. It felt strange wearing heavy clothing and long jeans. Be very glad to be back in just shorts and sunshine. He got to Erith town centre and grabbed a taxi from the rank to Orpington, phoning ahead to Ray as he travelled. Ray would be in. For a very good reason. He never went out.

He arrived at Ray's home, a three bedroom semi-detached house with gardens front and rear. He paid the driver off and walked up the short path to the door and knocked. A short Afro-Caribbean woman with glasses opened it. "Daniel!" Gave him a hug and a kiss. "I never knew you were coming."

"I phoned ahead Kim."

"He's such a prick. Come in. You know where he is."

They got into Ray's domain. What should have been a dining room. Well it looked like air traffic control. After an earthquake. Long kitchen worktops had been fixed to three of the walls. They all had electronic equipment strewn over and under them, dozens of three pin sockets. Electrical tools, rolls of wire and tape. Compartmented boxes of connectors and fuses. Four computer monitors were on, driven by big powerful towers that sat on the floor under the work surfaces, as well as a laptop and an array of mobile phones and tablets. Ray was the guy everyone brought stuff to to fix. He was also the guy who'd made up and fitted the adapted router in Amir's. And the fake suicide vest Ahmet had worn. He'd wired the listening devices into it. He knew a young man's life might depend on it. But he knew it would work. He was a wizard with electronics but wouldn't go out to work for a company. He could. Any electronics or software company would snap him up. But he said working in computers would fuck up his hobby. And drove Kim to despair with his hobby. And out of her dining room.

Ray was staring intently at one of the screens from his wheelchair which he used to propel himself around the room to whatever bit of kit he was looking at or fiddling with.

"Daniel's here. Why didn't you tell me? Look at the state of the place."

"It's always a state, I like it like that. And I'm out of tea." Waving an empty mug around without taking his eyes off the screen he was looking at. Then a, "Hi Danno," as an afterthought.

Daniel said, "Hi Ray." As Kim snatched the cup from him and said, "You want a coffee Daniel?"

"Yes please." She knew how he took it and flounced out of the room muttering obscenities. Daniel vaguely caught wanker and Ironside among them before she was gone from view.

"How's things then Ray?" asked Daniel. Ray finished whatever he was doing and spun the wheelchair round so he was facing him. He had scruffy, curly, brown hair with a bit of beard. Glasses. Getting a bit fat. He was forty-four years old but looked ten years older. Daniel really liked him and they had been friends for a long time. Ray had been good to him in the last care home he'd been in and Ray appreciated the help he'd got once his illness had left him wheelchair-bound. A lot of it had come from John Tremayne at Daniel's request. The adaptations and stair lift.

The house was owned by a property offshoot of Tremayne's and the rent was low enough for Ray to get it paid through benefits. Even in London. And his for life. On a proper lease. Daniel paid him discreetly and well for his work for him. John had known about all Ray did to help Daniel in his endeavours.

He said, "All good mate. Thanks for, you know. What you pay me. It really helps."

"No problem. You really help me. Couldn't do a lot of what I do without you Ray."

"Well for me it's a paying hobby. Can't do much else with this shit, can I?" Nodding at the wheelchair.

"You could Ray." Daniel said gently, looking at his friend.

"Don't you start. Bad enough her keep trying to get me to go outside."

"Well you should once in a while maybe?"

"Fuck that. What's so great out there today Danno? Tell me."

Daniel smiled at him. "To be fair Ray. Today. Fuck all."

"Well there you go then. Ah, about time."

Kim reappeared with their drinks. "I'll give you about time you slob. Here you are Daniel. She handed him his coffee and banged Ray's tea down so a bit spilled.

"Thanks. Can't you go and trim your moustache or something. Danno and me have stuff to talk about."

"Really? Can't think what as you never see anything bar these four walls, you boring slob."

She went to leave but Daniel caught her arm. "Kim. I'll talk to Ray for a while. Won't take long. Then maybe we could go for a walk. Get a beer or something? I'm sure Ray won't mind."

"Mind? Take her to Africa with you if you want. Does my head in."

"Don't bloody tempt me, you fat git. And yes, thank you Daniel that would be nice. I'll go make myself look pretty."

"He's only here two days."

"Fuck you." And she was gone. Daniel smiled. They were always like this. Yet he knew they loved each other. The overt insults that flew between them and the apparent indifference to each other were covering a far deeper problem. One that Daniel felt very responsible for. And he intended to rectify it. Hopefully soon, but not yet. Ray was vital to this epic struggle to topple Amir Ferez. Daniel needed him focused on nothing else until it was over.

Chapter 72. People traffickers.

Daniel asked Ray to show him the intel about the address he'd sent. Ray brought it up on the screen and he read it. It was a Skype message Bogdan had sent, obviously through Amir's router to, he assumed, one of his goons, detailing the collection of eight trafficked women. Currently near Dover. At a farm apparently, looking at the address. Daniel guessed it would be a drop point for trafficked people. Remote and out of sight of prying eyes. Bastards. He continued reading.

To be taken to an address in Woolwich. Tomorrow night. He guessed they would be girls Bogdan was going to set to work as prostitutes. Conned into believing they had real jobs to go to after their families had struggled to pay the smugglers to get them safe to a new future. Away from whatever war-torn, or poverty-stricken hell hole they originated from. Daniel cursed the police silently. Nothing he found out was anything they couldn't. But hacking just wasn't cricket old boy. People have a right to privacy you know. Got to have a warrant. He knew if he gave the police this they wouldn't get a conviction, because the evidence was illegally obtained. Inadmissible, according to the bloody lawyers who acted for scum like these criminals. Even if they acted on it in the time available to set up an operation. They were terribly under resourced and underfunded now. Well fuck that. Bogdan had no rights in Daniel's eyes. But his victims did.

And Daniel knew, from all the intel they had gathered over time, exactly what happened next. Threatened, beaten, forced to have sex by Bogdan's men. Given drugs, broken into submission. Forced to send messages to families to say they were fine. Then banged by any bastard that paid for the privilege in whatever strange town or city they found themselves lost and alone in, with Bogdan and others like him taking the money. Well maybe these ones wouldn't, if the delivery went down as per the message. And another plus was, this situation could be used to further convince Amir and Bogdan of the reality of the threat facing them. Make the illusion Daniel was creating a lot more real. And hurt Bogdan a bit.

He phoned Quan and spoke to him. Quan wrote down the list of people, equipment and vehicles to get together in time for tomorrow night, ending the call saying it would be good to work together again as Daniel had been such a lazy bastard since he'd got a hot chick. Daniel hung up with a grin. He so had.

He chatted with Ray for a while and stressed the urgency of Amir's intel. Anything about the next delivery was urgent. Anything indicating Irena was compromised was more urgent.

He called up the stairs to Kim he was all done. She came down ready to go and despite Ray's comments she did look pretty. They left into the cold weather but at least it had stopped raining. Ray was peering intently at one of the screens before they were out of the door.

They found a local pub and ordered lunch and drinks. Daniel was hungry now as he hadn't been on the flight, whereas Janet had eaten well, amazed at the sheer luxury of the private plane. He smiled as he thought of her. It was good to see her wonderment at things. Things he'd taken pretty much for granted after John and Ann had fostered him. Money bought a very different kind of life. He felt a sudden sadness at the thought of them being gone. Then shrugged it off. Lee was onside. Any arrangements he had had with John were still ongoing. They had discussed it in the Gambia. Lee had been a bit shocked at just how much John had done to help Daniel and the awful plight of the people that Daniel said needed help, but he was utterly committed to carrying it on. If not more so.

Daniel put it from his mind and passed the time talking to Kim. She had met Ray while at the foster home when she too had worked there. Ray's disability had never bothered her. She was a very thoughtful and caring woman. Still worked in nursing and was very qualified. And Ray was a thoroughly nice guy. She did love Ray very much and he knew, under the overt hostility, they really were very close. She just wished he'd look after himself a bit better. So did Daniel. But they knew he was a stubborn bastard. He'd explained to Kim that what Ray was doing for him was very important, and very demanding and stressful. She knew that. She knew it wasn't strictly legal either. But it didn't bother her because she knew that the house and living well in spite of Ray's disability was a result of it. Daniel told her he couldn't be specific about when but he would see to it that Ray was in a better place and soon. And that things would be different in the future, for them both. Kim squeezed his arm and said she hoped so, because she couldn't take a lot more of Ray's increasingly slobbish behaviour and uncouth attitude. She was near the end of her tether with him. Love him or not. She had a life too.

They lightened up and agreed Kim would visit in Turkey or Gambia later in the year. She had before, with her sister. Daniel told her about Janet and the children and Kim was really pleased for him. Said it was about bloody time. She really was a nice girl. Daniel just wished Ray would make a bit more of an effort, same as she did. But they had both agreed now wasn't the time. And she promised Daniel she would be there for Ray until the time was right to face the issues in their relationship.

They enjoyed the lunch. Kim was glad to get out of the house and have a change of company. They finished up and went for a walk. Daniel bought two large suitcases, then got a cab and dropped Kim back home. He asked the driver to wait and went in to say goodbye to Ray, saying he'd pop back before they left for the Gambia. Kim insisted he brought Janet and the last words he heard as he left the house were Kim's. "Ring me Daniel about when you're coming. Because if you ring that dick head he won't bother to tell me."
"I heard that," boomed from the dining room.
He promised he would and retreated to the taxi.

After telling the driver where he wanted to go, he phoned Janet to say he was on his way and he googled up a hotel-booking website and booked the best suite available at the Bexleyheath Marriot for two nights. In the taxi he sombrely thought about the personal costs and risks to people he cared about in doing what he asked them to do in this twilight, dangerous world he led them into. He recalled the letter from John and the calm words about the future. He smiled as he remembered the kind and wise man who had transformed his life. This would be the end of it. There was another way to live. And another way forward. He was going to take that road. With his new family and friends.

He phoned Janet when he got to the estate. She was ready so he asked the cab to wait and went up with the two new empty suitcases. They came back down with their luggage and set off. They got checked in and ordered coffee, and were sitting talking about booking return flights when his phone rang. It was Mick Davidson. He took the call and asked Janet to excuse him so she said she would go shower.

Chapter 73. Applying pressure slowly.

He talked quietly into the phone.

"Hi Mick."

"Hi. Everything okay?"

"Yes fine. All good with you?"

"Yeah. All pretty quiet. The investigation into Wesley Mason is pretty much shelved."

"Good. Any news on the take-down of the meet?"

"Well it's not my department's investigation. But according to my boss who is in touch with Bland, they're getting nowhere. With that or the airport car."

"Good. Any word from Amir?"

"No. But I'm not expecting any. He swallowed the terrorist group story so I left it at that."

"Okay. Well call him anyway. Tell him there's no significant news. Investigation is stonewalled but you'll keep tabs on the terrorist faction that's targeting him as best you can. It's very important to keep that theory uppermost in his mind Mick. He has to believe they exist and pose a massive threat to him and his empire if their demands are not met."

"I'll go see him soon and pile it on a bit more."

"Thank you. It's vital we keep him where we have him right now."

"Okay. That it?"

Daniel said, "No. I'm giving you the heads up now Mick. To be prepared. Bogdan is going to take a hit in the next twenty-four hours."

"Right. What sort of hit?"

"Bogdan should lose some trafficked girls tomorrow night. If it goes to plan he will think it was the police. At first"

"The police?"

"Yeah. But it won't be. It will be us."

"Jesus."

"You nail it into him that you can find no trace at all of any police activity in regard to it. He's bound to ask."

Mick laughed. "I dare say he will."

"The next day Amir will get the instructions on where to pay a money demand to. Then Bogdan will find out it wasn't the police at all. It was the terror group. Personally teaching him a lesson. You will be proved correct again in what you said. On all counts. Then you'll be in a far better position for the last part. And they will both be far more convinced they have no choice but to comply"

"Okay. I think I've got it. You're playing these bastards like a violin, I'll give you that."

"They have to believe. If they don't then we are all in a very bad place, Mick. Do your bit and we'll be fine."

"I will."

"Just play it as it unfolds Mick. The next forty-eight hours are going to be a bit manic. I just want you to be prepared is all."

"I'll be fine."

"I'm sure you will. If anything changes I'll be in touch. If not. Sit back and watch the fireworks."

"Okay. Later."

"Later."

Daniel hung up. Janet came out of the bathroom so he went and got showered. While he was in there, room service knocked with a massive bouquet of flowers for Janet. From Alan Shand. All Janet got from Daniel when she asked how anybody knew where they were was an, "Oh yeah. Lee called, wanted to know where we were staying." She smiled. That bloody man! They went to dinner, afterwards, both tired from travelling they got an early night, but made each other a little more tired before they slept soundly.

They got up in the morning and had an early breakfast in the hotel. Daniel read emails. One from Lee saying all was fine and he was going in to the office and hoped they were getting everything sorted. One from Irena saying Amir was very tense awaiting the payment instructions, asking everywhere he could about terrorist factions but getting nowhere. But apart from that all was quiet.

He replied to both. Irena was told that the payment instruction would be arriving with Amir in the morning. They would go for payment on Friday. And he told Janet he had to go out that night for a while. About ten. But shouldn't be gone too long, which she was fine with. She knew enough about him to know there was a good reason to go. And enough to know that she'd probably rather not know what he was doing.

Chapter 74. A night in the country.

They were at Janet's place by nine in a cab and everything went pretty much to plan. It was arranged that Tracey, who helped them all day, and her two children, would come out on holiday soon. Janet had asked Daniel if it was okay to ask her and he was fine with it, telling her to pay for Tracey's flights. She had money. Use it. Janet asked him if he was sure. Got one of those looks. She hugged him and said thank you and rushed off to tell Tracey who turned up and hugged Daniel, crushing him into her ample chest and repeatedly thanking him. Which he found all rather alarming, clearly to the great amusement of Janet.

Daniel helped the guys from the charity take all the furniture down to their truck which was appreciated by them given the long walk and flights of steps and the congregated youths hanging around outside. The girls carted stuff the couple of doors down to Tracey's. Bagged rubbish and cleaned up.

Janet had started to ask Daniel if she could go and settle the payday loan she'd taken out but got the look halfway through asking so she nipped off and did it. But it was a good day although busy. The rain held off and everything was done by the end of it. The housing woman arrived, was very pleased at the condition of the place and took the keys. Hugs and tears from Tracey when it was time to say goodbye. They got a cab back to the hotel about six with the cases packed she wanted to take back containing all that was left of her home and her life here in the UK.

He talked quietly to her in the cab as they travelled.

"You are okay Janet? I mean it must be hitting home now. That you're leaving."

"Yeah it is." She loved how sensitive he was to her feelings. It was never all about him.

"Well I hope you are not having any regrets."

"Actually I am."

"Oh."

"I regret not going on holiday about five bloody years ago."

He laughed. "I wouldn't have been there. There's a time for everything. And ours is now."

"I'm truly happy. And you know I think it's the first time in my life." She snuggled up to him feeling rather emotional as she realised that that was the stark truth. Sad as it was to have to say, it was. And he'd made it happen. Well they both had.

Daniel had taken a couple of quick calls from Quan during the day. Everything was set. Quan would pick him up at ten that night. They showered and had dinner downstairs in the restaurant and later, about nine-thirty, Daniel got dressed to leave. Black chinos with a black crew neck sweatshirt. Black leather three quarter length coat. Zip-sided black short boots.

Janet looked at him. "All rather dark and sinister."

"Not sinister. Just discreet and practical."

"I truly don't want to know what you're doing tonight, Daniel."

"I'd rather you didn't ask. Because if you did I wouldn't lie to you."

She smiled at him. "I know. But tell me the truth about one thing, yeah."

"Of course."

"You will take care of you?"

"I always do. And I have a whole lot more reason to now. You."

"Well remember that. I'll see you later then."

"Yeah. I won't be too long. I'll text you when I'm on the way back."

"I'll be ready to welcome you then."

"With open arms?"

"I was thinking more legs, my dark, mysterious man."

"I'll be even quicker then."

"You do that. Just stay safe, okay?"

"Plan to. See you later."

He kissed her and walked out of the door.

Janet sat there looking at the door. She wouldn't sleep until he got back. They both knew it. Daniel had never left anyone waiting for him to return before in his life. Janet had never had anyone in her life she really wanted to come back in a hurry. If at all. But she knew he wouldn't go if he didn't have to. And that was how it was. For both of them.

Chapter 75. The raid.

Quan picked him up in a black Nissan Juke and they headed out of London on the A2 towards Dover. As they drove through the light traffic, Quan updated Daniel on the plan. Where they would meet, and the people they were using.

One minibus with the two women, Elaine Harvey and Tessa Lovejoy in it. Himself, Daniel, Dave Payne and Adabele Ojo in two cars. This one and an X-Trail. Adabele had put his beloved motorbike where it needed to be. All the equipment was in the minibus. RV was just under a mile from the farm in a quiet road. Mick Hay was watching the farm. Had been for the last three hours.

Two men, presumably Bogdan's, had arrived just under an hour ago in a minibus and had gone into the farmhouse, not come back out as yet. Daniel nodded. "Sounds good."

They didn't talk again until they got to the meeting place just over an hour later. Both had their own thoughts, both mentally preparing for the task ahead. They were the first there. It was cold and dark. The other two vehicles arrived and everyone got out and greeted each other. The two women got changed in the minibus. Got back out dressed as policewomen. The men each took wallets with fake warrant cards. All took a handgun. Clicking sounds were heard as magazines were clipped in and actions checked. They were good to go. So they waited.

Quan's mobile vibrated. He answered. He looked at the others. "The delivery is on its way there. In view. ETA five minutes."

They all went to their vehicles. Quan's phone vibrated again six minutes later. He looked at Daniel. "Delivery unloaded. Eight as expected. Delivery vehicle has left." It was time to go. They pulled out onto the lane and headed towards the farm. Daniel was driving. Quan was holding an open line to Mick Hay who was watching to see if the situation changed during their short journey time. It didn't.

They arrived at the farm. The minibus, the last in the line, stopped and turned out its lights, blocking the lane. Each car passenger door opened. Quan got out, as did Adabele Ojo, and they went quietly on foot to the rear of the shabby small farmhouse. Daniel's phone vibrated. It was Quan. "In place." Daniel replied, "Copied." He reached out of the window and clamped a magnetic blue light on the roof and switched it on. Dave Payne did the same.

They roared into the small farmyard making as much noise as possible and drove nearly up to the door and jumped out, leaving the blue lights flashing. Daniel kicked the door in and saw one of Bogdan's men right in front of him. Aimed the pistol at him. "Armed police. Down on the floor. Now." The man turned away and literally crashed into his partner who was running from the "police" who had burst in through the back door. They were on them in seconds and pinned them face down. Cuffed them. "You're under arrest. And don't expect to get read your rights you pair of scumbags." The two men said nothing, speechless with shock.

They knew they were bang to rights as the officers looked into what had once been the lounge and saw eight terrified young women huddled together, exhausted from their long dangerous travels and constant fear. Daniel walked slowly towards them, holding out the wallet with the fake card to hopefully give a little assurance to the frightened girls. "It's okay. You're okay now." They stared at him wide eyed.

Then two policewomen came in. One or two of the girls spoke English and one asked, "Will we get sent back now?"
"No darling you won't. Don't worry," said Tessa soothingly. "Come with us now. You'll be fine. I promise." And they would be. Daniel knew that. It was what Tessa did best. The girls were going to a large, very secluded, safe house with her. A one-time rural hotel. Officially a battered wives refuge, a formally registered charity.

Tessa would carefully sort their asylum or visas one way or another - legally or otherwise. These poor girls were the direct result of idiotic policies put in place by useless politicians, the same absurd policies that had created bootlegging. Only this wasn't fags and tobacco. They'd created a vile trade. In human beings. An estimated eight hundred thousand of them worldwide every year. By ruthless wealthy criminals. Ruined innocent, trusting lives. As far as she was concerned, if they'd got this far without the politically correct, self-restricted, official law enforcement agencies intervening and been treated like less than cattle, which were monitored far more diligently....well they'd been through enough. That was her job and she did it well, discreetly funded by John Tremayne and now, with him gone, Lee, through charitable donation. Tax deductible. Lee had loved the irony as had his father. Tessa and Elaine gently escorted the badly frightened girls out to the minibus. Once they were aboard she drove them away, to what would probably be the first place they would feel safe and welcome in a very long time.

The two men of Bogdan's were handcuffed and each one placed in the back of each of the two cars. They headed back towards London where the men would be held securely in a lock up until it was time to let them go. The two men said nothing. When they had, they had got a gun pointed in their face and told to shut it. So they had. They were clearly frightened. They both knew there was something very wrong about this arrest but had no way of finding out what. So they just sat and did as they were told. In silence.

Once they got to south London the cars drew up on a small industrial estate. A small unit was unlocked and the men ushered in. They were sat on hard high back steel chairs, back to back, cuffed by the ankles as well as their hands. Gagged and taped to the chairs, eyes wide with fear. The huge African "policeman" Adabele had the job of watching them until it was time to let them go. He shook hands with the others and closed the door as they drove away and sat patiently, glaring at the two terrified thugs, idly turning his gun over in his hands, waiting for the message telling him to let them go.

Daniel got in and Janet was awake, laying on top of the bedclothes. Naked, watching television. Or trying to. He took off his jacket and lay next to her and they kissed long and slow.

"How did it go?"

"Really well."

"Am I glad I don't know what it was?"

"You'd probably approve."

"Well tell me one day then."

"Sure. Remind me to."

"I will. Now get undressed. I haven't welcomed you home properly yet." And she kissed him again.

"I've had a busy night you know."

"Man up, Cade. Get showered. Now."

Daniel laughed as the tension drained from him. "I'll get a shower then." He kissed her and got undressed. As he showered he thought about just what a very special lady he had in his life. He went to bed for what would be the far nicer part of the night.

Chapter 76. Where the hell are they?

The next morning Bogdan phoned Amir, who was still in bed. Bogdan was in a massive rage, even by his standards. Amir told him to calm down and come round. Irena was sitting there looking at him.

"Bogdan," he said. "I'm sorry but he is coming round."

"That's okay. He apologised. There is nothing more to say. Everyone has been very angry. And he is a total aggressive fool when he is."

"Well he's angry now. Ranting about some problem his men had last night."

"I see. Does this concern you, Amir?"

"No. It is about some women or something. His men have problems. I couldn't make sense of it."

"Let's get up and dressed darling. We'll have a coffee. Sit with me until he arrives." Amir did and she kissed him warmly. "We'll be fine darling," she murmured. Amir hoped so. He was expecting that bloody demand any time soon. The very thought of it frayed his nerves. A fucking million pounds. Now Bogdan was on the way with his problems. Amir could actually do without it right now but he'd have to hear him out. They had business to deal with, whatever the seemingly endless problems were.

Bogdan arrived about half an hour later and came up to the penthouse, wild-eyed and furious. Irena smiled inwardly as she saw the state he was in. He accepted the offer of a coffee and Irena went out to the kitchen to make them all one, listening as she took her time over doing so.

"Amir, you will not fucking believe what is happening." He was pacing up and down their lounge, talking at the top of his voice.

"Bogdan please. Stop shouting. Sit down and calm yourself. And tell me quietly. I cannot understand you when you are like this."

Bogdan breathed deeply, taking a seat on the edge of a plush leather armchair, still in his heavy leather coat. Sweaty and unshaven, he had clearly been up all night.

"My men have vanished. Two of them."

"Vanished?"

"Yes. No call from them. No answer when I call. The phones rang at first. No answer. Now they are both switched off."

"They vanish from where exactly, Bogdan?"

"Dover. Well in the countryside near Dover."

"Why on earth were they in Dover Bogdan?"

"They go to collect some women."

"Women?" asked Irena, as she walked back in with a tray bearing their coffees. Bogdan accepted his without a thank you. "Pig." She thought to herself. "It is good to see you suffer."

"Yes, women. They come to work for me. My men go to collect them. Last night."

Amir looked at him. "You mean trafficked women, Bogdan, yes?"

"Yes. I pay for them. All was arranged. My men go to collect them and now they vanish."

"With the women, you mean?"

"Yes, damn it. I call my contact. He swears my men were there at the meeting place. And their vehicle was there. And the women were delivered to them"

"And since then, nothing?"

"Nothing. But my contact, as a favour to me, goes back to the meeting point. And my vehicle is still there. But not my men. No women. Nothing. I ask him to remove the vehicle and he has. And that is it. Nothing"

"Perhaps they were caught, Bogdan. Arrested?" asked Irena.

"It was my first thought. But no call? They are allowed a call. They would want a lawyer. Just silence."

"It is most strange," said Amir.

"Strange! Very. Amir, can you call Davidson? Please. Maybe he can find out something, yes?"

"Of course. Drink your coffee, Bogdan."

He picked up his phone and called Michael Davidson. Amir passed the phone to Bogdan, who repeated the story to Mick, asking him to help find out what had happened.

"So where exactly were they Bogdan? Where was the abandoned vehicle?"

Bogdan told him the name of the farm and the lane it was on.

"And your men were there when the women were dropped off? Definitely?"

"Yes. Fucking definitely."

"Okay calm down. And these men. Nationality?"

"One Albanian. One Romanian."

"Names?"

Bogdan gave them to him, spelt them out as Mick requested while Mick wrote them down at the other end. Or at least Bogdan believed he was. Mick actually had his feet up on the desk.

Mick asked, "Any chance your men might have legged it with the ladies? Sold them to somebody else? Started their own knocking shop?"

"Davidson. You are very fucking quick to always say we betray our own. I warn you about it before."

"You did. And I fucking warned you. Don't get heavy with me again, Bogdan. My arrangement is with Amir. All I am asking is if there was any chance they had had you over. That's all. It's you takes anyone trying to help as a bloody insult. Get over it." Mick was enjoying this at the other end. He hated Bogdan. It was good to hear him stressed to hell.

"Okay. I swear there was no chance of that at all. Something has happened to them. If it was the police arrest them I need to know. It is the only thing that makes sense. Except I don't hear from them."

"Okay. I'll enquire. Now. And I'll get back to you soonest. But I want paying. Same as Amir gives me. Whatever the answer is. Okay?"

"Okay. Agreed. Amir will give it to you as normal."

"Good. Later." Mick hung up.

He called the only contact in the phone. Mick updated him and heard a short laugh. "Good. Do nothing for two hours. Call them back with the result of doing nothing. To say there was nothing. And take the money for nothing."

"And the chicks are free, right," said Mick, laughing loudly at the corny one-liner.

"Sorry?"

"No matter. I'll keep you posted."

"Do. And please text me after you call Bogdan with the information. It's important Mick."

"Will do. About two hours. Cheers."

He hung up. Whoever was on the other end wasn't into Dire Straits. Shame, Mick thought that was bloody funny. Mick busied himself for a while. Let Bogdan sweat.

Chapter 77. Money for nothing.

Janet and Daniel left their luggage in the hotel. Daniel had asked if they could take a trip to the coast. He wanted to show her the property he had here, maybe make a day of it, and book a flight home the next day after one more night in the hotel. She'd agreed. They hired a luxury car and set off in heavy traffic. He was very quiet as he drove. She knew something was troubling him but kept quiet, except to ask where they were going. "Hastings, Jan. Well, a small village near it."

She nodded and sat back and relaxed. It was bitter cold and spitting with rain. She would be very glad to get back to the Gambia. She smiled. Get home. Daniel drove on in silence, wrapped in his own thoughts.

Mick called Amir back and asked to speak to Bogdan, who grabbed the phone.

"Hello. You have been a very long time, Davidson."

"Well it's not a five minute job, Bogdan. I got hold of a friend in the Kent police. Told him a couple of suspects in a case we were working on might have been on their patch last night."

"And?"

"Well I told him that they were linked to a gang with connections on our patch and were being watched in regard to an ongoing investigation. They'd gone to Dover for sure. But we'd lost track of them. They hadn't returned. And we thought they might have been nicked on the manor down there."

"And he said what?"

"Well nothing straight away. That's what takes the time, Bogdan. He had to trawl through the night shift's work. Several police stations in the area. See if there had been any arrests in regard to trafficking. Any arrests of Eastern Europeans. It takes time."

"Well, were there?"

"No. Nothing. There were no major ops last night. No major incidents. And no arrests of anyone of any note. Just a couple of burglars, a flasher and a few drunks. And no Eastern Europeans."

"Damn it. Then where the hell are my men? And those women?"

"Wherever they are Bogdan, it is nothing to do with the Kent police."

"Okay. Thank you, Davidson. For trying."

"No problem. Sorry it was a blank. Tell Amir I would like to collect payment tomorrow."

"I will. Goodbye." Bogdan ended the call. Nothing. And now he had to pay Davidson five hundred pounds for it. His face was like thunder as he handed the phone back to Amir, followed by five hundred pounds from his money clip.

Mick sent a text saying nothing had been passed on and got on with his day. He felt good about things now. He put his coat on. He was going out on the streets to aggravate some villains. He'd got the appetite back for it now. He walked past sergeant Brett on the desk with a cheery, "Morning mate." Brett looked at the back of the man striding purposefully out of the station doors. "Bloody hell. He must have got laid," he thought as he worked his way through the custody records.

Just then Amir's phone bleeped. He picked it up. Text message. "*The account details for our money will follow in one hour. Make payment by noon tomorrow. And tell Bogdan that if he threatens one of our men again, last night will not be the last time he hears from us.*"

Amir passed Bogdan the phone. "I think that will explain the matter, Bogdan."

Bogdan stared at the message. Irena struggled not to laugh. He looked like he was going to burst a blood vessel. Actually, they both did.

Daniel set an alarm on the phone for an hour's time and put the phone away in his pocket, waiting for Janet to come out of the filling station where she'd wanted to use the toilets. They were just south of Tonbridge, with about forty minutes to go to their destination. Somewhere he had avoided for a great many years. But it had to be faced. As did all things in life. She came out, got in. Kissed him, put her seat belt on. He pulled out, up to the roundabout and left on to the crappy single track A21. Never improved much in all these years. He soon caught up with a row of cars creeping south behind an articulated lorry.

In a lock-up in a small unit on the outskirts of Orpington, Adabele read his text. Good. He was bored. He walked across to the two thugs and undid the handcuffs on their hands. He put the keys to the cuffs around their ankles on the floor in front of them and strode out of the door, shutting it behind him. They would have to tip their chairs over, or one of them would, to get the keys. He hoped it hurt. He got on his big Kawasaki motorbike, put on the helmet and roared away. Nothing like a good fast ride to blow the cobwebs of boredom away.

Inside the lock-up, the two men freed themselves awkwardly and got to their feet, rubbing painful joints to restore circulation. Their mobile phones were both there, on the floor. One of them picked his up, turned it on, and phoned Bogdan, who answered immediately. He started to babble the story of what had happened. Dreading the wrath of Bogdan. But Bogdan seemed quite calm and asked him where they were. They went outside and looked around, got the name of the small industrial park from the signage. Bogdan he said a car was on its way so they settled down to wait. A few people around the small industrial estate gave them cursory glances as they went about their day but there were was no interest in them. And no police presence, no problem, nothing at all. They were totally mystified.

Both had thought, as the armed police had cuffed them, that they were heading to prison. And now this. Free and just abandoned here. The car turned up and they got in and were heading back towards home. And Bogdan. And all they could do was hope for the best when they got there.

Chapter 78. A bad place revisited.

Daniel and Janet had arrived in Hastings. Daniel seemed very tense now but Janet kept quiet. He took a road out of the town towards a place called Fairlight, a narrow road which he turned off up a lane, coming to a halt outside a small, rather remote cottage. Janet looked at it in the grey, bleak weather. At the small front garden. And beyond that she saw the hill going up to what was obviously..... "Oh my God! Daniel. Is this where? Oh darling why have you come here. Drive away."

"I can't. This has got to be dealt with."

"But why?"

"Because I still own the fucking place, Janet. It needs sorting out." She looked at him. For him to swear like that was unusual. He was rigid with tension and sounded very strange.

"Own it? How?"

He sighed. "I was an only child. My father was killed on active service in the army. We lived in London. St Mary's Cray." His voice was a flat, bleak monotone. She sat deathly quiet, instinctively letting him talk.

"Mum went to pieces, started drinking, got broke. The mortgage was paid off on Dad's death. Sold up. Moved down here and bought this. Banked a lot of money from the deal. Set about drinking it. Met him in a pub. Remarried. He was a horrible man, I hated him from day one and he knew it."

He was looking at the path up to the clifftop as he continued. "She died after a year or so. Liver failure. The abuse started. The rest you know. Well nearly all of it."

He looked at her and she gently squeezed his hand. "After, much later that night, I reported him missing. The police turned up with a social worker. I was classified as at risk anyway. I told the police he'd come in drunk and gone to sleep on the sofa. Got up and gone out again. No, I wasn't sure of what time that was. No, I hadn't spoken to him. He hit me when he was pissed. I was hiding in my bedroom. I only heard him go. No, he hadn't got a car. Not any more. He was banned from driving. No, I never heard a vehicle turn up to pick him up. They knew I was under social services classified as at risk. I was taken into care."

He sighed deeply. "Two months later I was fostered by John and Ann. Before that I was looked after a bit by Ray, the guy I went to see in London. He was an older kid in the home. Been there a long time. He was ill, hard to place in the foster care system. Had ended up living in and working there. He was good to me. But because of his illness, he knew he would end up in a wheelchair. I eventually asked John to help him and he did. He's a wizard with electronics and computers. He's helped me ever since with what I do. I'll take you to see him tomorrow before we leave." Janet nodded, still saying nothing.

"John became my legal guardian. This place was that bastard's under the law. But there was no will. And after a time, because he was never found, it came to me. John saw it all through. Got it rented out. That's it really. I need to get it moved on. It's empty now. I asked Lee to get notice served to the tenants before he came out. Bung them if they left in two weeks, help them find somewhere else. They're gone. I've got a plan for the place. That's it really."

"Okay." Janet was talking almost at a whisper. This was awful. "But why are we here? You could deal with this on the phone. Or Lee could do it surely? Get it sold. You don't have to be here."

"Yeah I do. I want to walk up that path again. With you. I want to walk back down it to my new life. With you and the children. I can't leave it like it is, Janet. I'm sorry but I just can't. I have to revisit it. And I have to make my last memory of this place one I can live with. It's the only dark part of my life and I want it gone. And I might need to be able to come here in the future. If it pans out that way."

"If that's what you need to do my darling then we will do it together. Right now."

She got out of the car and waited for him, doing her coat up against the wind. It started to spit with rain. The whole sky looked, well, evil. She had the strangest thought. That it was as if the spirits knew. She shuddered. And not just from the cold.

He got out without a jacket on, locked the car, and walked around to her and opened the gate. She took his hand firmly and they walked towards the rear of the cottage. And the path. The alarm sounded on Daniel's phone. He cursed. Mumbled, "Sorry." Took the phone from his pocket. And sent a text that was in drafts. Then he turned the phone off and jammed it back in his pocket. And they continued to the bottom of the path.

Amir and Bogdan, much to Irena's relief, left. Bogdan had heard from his missing men and they were going to see them. And Amir had now received the payment transfer instructions. He had until noon tomorrow to transfer the million pounds. They were both absolutely raging with frustration and anger. She smiled. Good. They were both scum. And she was another step closer to her goal. Of destroying Amir.

Chapter 79. The start of suspicion.

Amir and Bogdan were in the room above the pub. The two men who had been missing were brought there, clearly terrified as to their fate. They knew Bogdan. And they knew the price that was normally paid if you failed him. But they were pleasantly surprised. Bogdan had told them, after they said that the police had turned up and policewomen had taken the women away, that he knew it was not the police. And knew who was behind it. He asked them many questions. About who they were, what they looked like. Everything they could remember. Once he was done he told them to go home. Get some rest and he would call them when he needed them again.

He looked at Amir. "Well it all adds up Amir. The whole thing was a fucking sham police raid. Whisk my women away from under my very nose. Hold my men. And they vanish into thin air."

"And I now have to part with a million pounds, Bogdan. I believe we must suffer our great losses and pay these bastards. And hope that is the end of the matter."

"I agree with you, Amir. But if it is not the end of the matter then we either find them and deal with them. Or we are finished Amir. You realise that, yes?"

"Yes. Yes I do, Bogdan."

"But there is something not right here Amir. This terror group thing."

"I don't understand what you are saying, Bogdan."

Bogdan was deep in thought. He looked at the piece of paper he'd jotted things down on as his men had told their tale.

"An Islamic terror group we are told is damaging us, Amir."

"Not only told, Bogdan. We met one of the mad bastards. You were there, damn it."

"Well yes. Possibly."

"Possibly! He was wired up with explosives. And prepared to die and take us with him. Just a boy as well."

"Yes, yes. I know that."

"Well what more proof do you damn well need?"

Bogdan studied his notes and replied, "Maybe none. But why is it that now we have white Brits, an Asiatic, an African. Black and white so-called policewomen. Posing as police. Where do these people come from, Amir? They are not Islamists."

"How do you know that Bogdan? These terrorists come from all walks of life. Jihadi John was from London. Made videos of himself cutting off people's heads. They could hire people, they have my meet money they stole to do it with. They probably now sell your vanished women to make more money. And they calmly await for my fucking million pounds, do they not? They are very real and you would do well to remember that, Bogdan."

Bogdan murmured, "Oh yes, they are very real. And I hope they never trouble us again, Amir. But I still think it is a lot more complicated than it seems."

Amir looked at him. "It is very simple from where I sit, Bogdan. They have funded themselves with our money. Now let us forget them. Hope they keep their word. And get on with business. It is all we can do. Agreed?"

"Agreed?"

Amir nodded to Hassan and they left the room to go and get on with business. Amir went home and told Irena to make the payment and get it over with. After it was done he sat staring at the wall with a large whisky in his hand. Irena savoured his misery for a while then went out to get some air and do some shopping. And sent an email from her phone. Telling Daniel he'd done it. Amir Ferez had transferred a million pounds out of fear, of a terrorist group that didn't even exist.

Chapter 80. Up the hill to pain and back down.

Daniel wouldn't read that message for a while. His phone was, for a very rare few minutes, switched off. He was holding Janet's hand and walking up the steep path he'd last gone up when he was eleven years old. Being dragged and slapped in the darkness.

The wind had picked up, the drizzle was slightly heavier. His shirt was stuck to his lean body as they continued to climb. Janet was horrified at the stark expression on his face. She wanted to scream at him to stop this and go back down, but she didn't. She stuck with him, cold and frightened as they walked higher. A couple of rabbits darted off the path but it was otherwise deserted and they were the only people around. She could hear the sea now, ominously loud, roaring against the, as yet, unseen bottom of the cliffs.

They made it to the top. A path, well more just the well-worn route taken by dog walkers and ramblers, muddy now in the rain, went from left to right in front of them. Daniel looked around him, his eyes wide and haunted, and walked to the left. She held his hand tightly as he approached the edge of the cliff. And then he looked down. So did she. The waves pounding and eddying around, white froth being thrown up. He stared down at the sea for what seemed like ages. And then he wept. And sank down, sitting in the wet grass and sobbing, in the very place he had lost the last of his childhood and innocence.

The place that had set him on a lonely path of training, spiritualism and atonement. Intervention and violence. In a fight against evil he felt obliged to take on, in return for his own salvation. She sat with him, frightened at how close they were to the crumbling edge, but wouldn't leave his side. Then he went silent, looked at her, with a calm serenity in his eyes, and stood, pulling her up. He kissed her and held her tight. Then whispered, "Shall we go now. I'm cold. I'm sure you are." She hugged him briefly and held his hand.

And they walked back down. Slowly, but with confident steps, hand in hand. To his new life, and hers. It was done. The wind had dropped before they got to the car and the drizzle stopped. As they drove away, wet and cold, a tiny bit of blue sky appeared. And Janet knew, without a doubt, that the spirits approved. She'd never know why. She just knew.

They drove back to Hastings and parked up and went to Debenhams and bought all new clothes. They left wearing them, to the amusement of the staff that served them, their wet clothes in the bags they carried. They went to get lunch in the store restaurant. And Daniel turned his phone on. Janet was very pleased to see the biggest smile appear on Daniel's face. Obviously good news.

He put the phone back in his pocket and then discussed maybe going to see Ray this afternoon, rather than tomorrow. That bloody man! He had no intention of telling her what had made him smile and what was going on. She smiled at him and just said, "Sure." They settled the bill and headed for the car and London. Daniel had needed to walk up that path again. He had. And back down. To his new life. It was done.

Chapter 81. Let's get this straightened out.

Daniel got sick of driving in the relentless heavy traffic and took the car straight back to the hire company. They got a taxi to Ray's place. Daniel phoned ahead, to Kim, and she opened the door immediately when they got there. Daniel introduced Janet to her and they went through to see Ray. Janet was introduced again and looked aghast at the room Ray occupied. Kim said, "This is his bit. Come and have a look at the rest."

Janet followed her out of the room, did the tour and then Kim made tea and coffee for everyone. She and Janet went to have theirs in the lounge. "Away from his shithole," as Kim put it. Daniel found a chair and sat with Ray.

"Everything working okay, Ray? The stuff in Amir's?. Irena's phone and laptop? All secure?"

"Yeah mate. I know how important it is. There's no sign of any reduction in use. The router's a simple thing, wi-fi link. Amir never turns it off on his computer or phone. Does a lot of Skype calls to the top guns in Turkey and Afghanistan, all his emails. The next shipment is due very soon. He's pushing hard for it. But no date or times yet. We get a little bit from Bogdan as well. He must have his phone logged in to Amir's router on auto. If he used his own data from his phone we wouldn't get anything. Irena has been a good girl. I've never lost track of her phone. Drummed it into her it must be kept charged and never switched off. I made sure she knows her safety might depend on it?"

"Yeah she does Ray. Her life might. I hate her being there but it's her call. And it will put a dent in the drug and trafficking trade if we put Amir and Bogdan out of business."

"Yeah I guess. How did it go last night?"

"Good. Eight women safe and well. And Bogdan in a very bad mood."

"Cool. Well there's nothing to report here mate. When there is, you'll know about it."

"Yeah I know. Be glad when you get the intel. The police can have the details. If they intercept it, Amir's screwed. Then he will cut and run. Sell everything. And that's when he gets left with nothing. I just want it over with now."

"Yeah. I can see you've got better things to do. She's gorgeous."

"So's Kim."

"Yeah I know."

"Well try telling her once in a while."

"Nah. She'll think I'm ill."

"Ray. I'm serious. You'd be in a mess without her. After this is done you need to sort yourself out a bit."

"Okay, okay."

"I'm going in with the ladies. I'd really like it if you'd join me. For Janet. And Kim."

"I got stuff to do, man."

"Please Ray. For me as well. I have things to say. Want you both to hear them."

"Okay. Lead on."

Ray wheeled himself after Daniel, mumbling obscenities, and they went into the lounge. Kim looked very surprised to see her husband come in.

They made small talk for a while then Daniel said he wanted to put something to them.

He said, " Ray. You know a bit more about me than the ladies. From way back. When we first met."

"Yeah Daniel, I do. You were just eleven and in a very bad place."

"I was. Well I have just come from the place where it all happened."

"Right," said Ray. "Why did you even go there?"

"I had to. Erase the bad stuff, a bit of confronting the past."

Janet looked at Ray. "You know about what happened there?"

"Yeah, but only after Daniel was fostered, years later. He told me what John Tremayne had done for him. Mainly because I didn't believe him about what Tremayne was prepared to do for me. At his say so." Nodding towards Daniel.

Janet smiled. "Thought you'd know he never lies."

Ray smiled, "He doesn't. But he would to do you a good turn. I wasn't about to sponge off him after I got stuck in this thing. When he told me that I was going to get a nice house and all the shit in it to deal with this, I thought he was ponying up for it. And refused it."

"Oh right. Do you know about it, Kim?"

"Yeah hunny, well a little. Enough to understand. That slob and Daniel can trust me. Love them both. Only he gets on my tits big time these days." Nodding at Ray.

Daniel quickly interjected before Ray said anything. "It's all in the past. It's done with for good. As of today. Now the fact is that what Ray has done for me, and for John who has supported me in things these years, and now Lee has taken that over, has been vital. And done a lot of good. To hammer that home, eight trafficked women who were destined to be forced into prostitution are now safe and well, as of last night, because of his work. And that's the tip of the iceberg, believe me. His skills have saved a lot of lives and misery, because he's been a key part in what we've been doing."

The women looked at Ray, who seemed a bit puzzled by Daniel's unusually long speech.

"Where are you going with this, Danno? It's been my pleasure. It gives me and gobby there a nice home. And an income. And done a bit of good along the way. So why all the yakking?"

"Yeah, it has Ray. But where I'm going with this is simple. It's over."

They all looked at him. "Over?" said Kim. "But why?"

Daniel nodded towards Janet. "Because of Jan and the children for my part. This project we have going on now is the last one of its kind. Others who help me need an end to it as well. We've not been lucky, we're just all very good at what we do. But I don't want to get injured or killed now. Or arrested. Because it matters now, very much to me, that I don't. And I don't want anyone who is involved in this to be either. We all need to move on. It's been a long time, ever since I left the Legion. We all have lives to lead. We've literally got away with murder. It's time to quit. And it's time to face the future."

Janet thought about John's letter as she heard Daniel talking. He was going to take John's advice. She was really pleased. But she had never seen him like this. He seemed to change a bit daily since she'd met him.

"So where does that leave me?" asked Ray. "And Kim?" Janet could see he was really worried.

"Up to you Ray. And you alone."

"I don't get it."

"You will if you listen. You might not like it."

"Shoot."

"You have, over these last years, become a total slob Ray."

Ray looked at him totally shocked. "That's a bit strong man."

"No it isn't Ray. You're in a wheelchair, not a prison cell. Your condition is stabilised, you won't get any worse. You've got a mobility car outside but you never go out. You don't look after your health. You don't get a haircut, keep yourself clean even. You don't have a day out with Kim or a romantic night in. You are fully functional apart from your legs but you don't do that either, do you? You don't have friends round. In fact, if it doesn't plug in and light up you don't do a bloody thing."

"Man, that is just such a fucking bad thing to say."

Daniel looked at him intently. "I haven't finished Ray. You are dragging Kim down with you as well. She's been there for you all the way, through thick and thin. And you bloody know it."

"You want me to keep working for you or what man?" Ray was furious.

"You want a woman's death on your conscience, Ray? You quit now and you might have."

"Oh right. Blackmail me, why don't you?"

The two women looked on in shocked silence as the two men locked horns.

"Fuck off," said Daniel. "I know you, you are a good man. You won't bail on this job, let people down. Endanger them. This isn't about this job, it's about the future, Ray. And you know it so don't act dumb. I am going back home tomorrow, to the Gambia. Where she's been," pointing at Kim, "with her sister, but not her husband. Because you are too selfish to go with her. Too rude and up your own arse to visit me. And we need to talk now, before I go home. And we are going to sort it out, Ray. Right now"

"Oh are we. And just how are we going to do that. I can't exactly fight you, can I?"

"Don't be ridiculous. I mean we are going to sort out the way forward and the future, for you and Kim. And there is a deal going on the table right now. And you are going to say yes or no to it. If you don't take it you sort yourself out, as in find yourself a job and go your own way. Or you do take it. The choice is yours Ray."

"And what is the deal? This great tomorrow, Danno?"

"You move out of here, out of London. You take that cottage near Hastings, fully adapted to your needs. You will own it, outright, pay-off for services rendered. You work in I.T for Lee Tremayne for a good salary. He wants you, it's not a favour, Ray. You go to his offices two days a week, you work from home two days a week, you earn a good salary. And you have a long weekend every week during which you forget screens and things that bleep and have a social life and get outside. You tidy yourself up, treat your wife and friends properly, and above all treat yourself properly."

Ray looked at him. He was clearly upset. But Janet could see he was deep in thought.

"Can you give me a few minutes, Daniel?"

"Take all the time you want Ray." Daniel's voice was quiet and gentle now. "I had a similar lecture from you a long time ago, my friend. I didn't like it, or even

listen to you. But I had an excuse, I was eleven. You don't have that excuse Ray."
Ray just nodded and wheeled himself out of the lounge without another word. The women looked at Daniel. He was calmly scrolling through something on his phone.

Kim asked if they wanted more coffee. They nodded. She went to make it, walked through the chaos of her dining room to do so. It was deserted. When she returned she said, "He's out in the back garden."

Daniel nodded without looking up from his phone. "Give him a while. He'll be back when he's ready."

They drank their coffee in silence. And waited.

Chapter 82. All paths led nowhere.

There was a meeting in progress at the operations room for the combined departments formed after the car interception at Gatwick. Fleming was there. So was Bland. And officers from anti-terrorism, border control, drug squad, the lot.

And they weren't happy policemen. The task force was being wound down. All avenues of enquiry had been exhausted. Every possible lead generated by forensic had been pursued. Each officer gave his report to the assembled team.

Fleming addressed them with his dead end on the Wesley Mason case and said they had got nowhere. He told them that DC Davidson had pointed out the possibility that, even if it were a double murder in retribution for the Tremaynes' deaths, that it could easily be an unconnected, possibly ex-forces killer that had done it for the Tremaynes, totally unbeknown to their son. And totally unconnected to the multiple homicide Bland was investigating. Or even, at a stretch, that it really was a fluke mutual killing during a fight between the two men. He wanted to shut it down and leave it on file.

Bland was equally frustrated. The tenuous links to Amir were without doubt. But his men at the drug meet all had one thing in common - they were all dead, either killed by other criminals or two snipers known to have been at the scene who had clearly provoked a shooting incident between the two groups. Ditto the two men in the hire car, both dead, killed in a subsequently investigated and justified shooting by the police after an officer was struck and downed by a bullet, subsequently found to be non-lethal. Again fired by a sniper known to have been at the scene. Again clearly to provoke a shooting by the police. No forensic evidence had led to even the smallest clue as to who these snipers were. No organisation had claimed any responsibility for an attempted attack on Gatwick.

No links between the dead men in the hire car and any extremist organisations or imams. No evidence of any contact with known jihadists. No way of proving they were going to the Gambia in pursuit of Lee Tremayne. No way of proving Amir Ferez had placed the case in the car, in fact they knew he hadn't. It was a dead end and he too wanted to leave it on file as an unsolved. The meeting continued for a while with input from the other agencies and it was agreed that no further resources would be committed unless new evidence came to light.

Fleming walked out with Marsh to the car park. They shook hands and Marsh said, "Whoever did those shootings are bloody good at what they do, Colin. Not a trace. I can only hope that they are after Amir and get the fat little bastard. Because I can't get them or him. I know it's wrong. But hey. I've never been politically correct."

Fleming replied. "Well. If by a remote chance they were involved with offing Wesley and Mason then, also being totally politically incorrect - good. But don't ever tell Davidson I said that. I bollocked him for saying it."

They both laughed and headed for their cars. There were always other crimes to investigate. These ones were done with. Fleming got back to the station to the news that Mick Davidson had arrested and brought in a known fence, and two young men responsible for a spate of local burglaries. Fleming thought how Mick had really changed up a gear these last few days. "Perhaps he's getting laid," he thought as he headed to his desk.

Chapter 83. It's a deal.

Ray wheeled himself back into the lounge, all eyes turned towards him. He looked at Daniel squarely.

"I'll take it. The cottage and the job. And thank you. It's a wonderful offer."

"I'm pleased Ray."

"Not because I don't have a choice Daniel."

"I know. You're good at what you do. You do have a choice."

"Yeah, I am good. But you're right, I've been a prat, I know that. I just lost interest after, you know, I couldn't walk anymore. Concentrated on what I knew I was good at. And ignored everything else that I knew I would struggle to do." He looked at Kim. "Including being a man in your eyes. I'm sorry."

She smiled at him. "I know who you are under all the anger and frustration, Ray. I just had to wait until you found yourself again. I know disability drives you crazy."

"Yeah, but being crazy and getting lazy and not even trying to deal with it, just makes it worse. And the worse it got the worse I got. It like feeds on itself Kim, I see that now. Thanks to that rude abrupt bastard over there."

He smiled at Daniel. "I'm sorry mate. I deserved it. I had it coming."

"You did."

"So what happens now?"

"We finish this job Ray. In the meantime you two need to go to your new place, maybe once a week. It's going to be gutted and rebuilt inside. New everything. You two choose it all together and oversee it. I'll get Lee to contact you about the job. And you move away from here and start your new career once we are all done with this last one."

"Okay." Ray wheeled himself across to Daniel and they shook hands. Daniel said, "There's just one more thing Ray."

"And that is?"

"The next time we see you two, will be when you visit us. At our place."

"Yeah. Agreed. Soon as we're done here with this, yeah?"

"As soon as Ray. Keep an eye on things now, big time and we'll get it over with. We have to go."

"Yeah okay Daniel. And as the sergeant in Hill Street Blues says. Be careful out there, yeah."

"Always am. See you soon mate."

They went to the door after their cab turned up and Kim hugged them both. "Thank you Daniel."

"It had to be done, Kim. I felt very responsible for the mess he was in."

"Why?"

"Another time."

"Okay. See you both soon. Take care." The cab pulled away in heavy traffic towards their hotel. Janet had a warm feeling. Daniel had said, "When you visit us. At our place." It just felt nice.

She sat tight to him as his arm went round her. He'd just given a house away as if it was an old phone he didn't need. Angel was right. The lifestyle, the money, Daniel, would take some getting used to. This was one crazy life she'd got into. And she loved every minute of it.

Back at the hotel, they just sat and relaxed for a while, having ordered coffee from room service. Daniel was writing something down on a sheet of hotel stationery.

Janet said to Daniel, "What did you mean when you said you felt responsible? You know. For Ray being in a mess?"

Daniel looked at her and replied quietly. "I was so wrapped up in what I was doing, Jan. That guy was hacking computers, chasing down information I asked him for. I put him under a lot of pressure. Everything seemed urgent. I never thought about him. Or Kim. I was never here in the UK. Never saw the effect it had on him until he was too far in to get him out of it. Hour after hour on computers, hardly daring to take his eyes off them because he knew somebody's life might end up awful, or even over, if he missed something. In the end, he was just lost in it. I had to drag him back out, for both of them. She never complained, or blamed me. But I knew I had been selfish, even for all the right reasons. And the cottage. Well it's not an evil place just because bad things happened there. It will just sit better with me if it's used for something worthwhile. My Dad paid for it with his life in a roundabout way. And I came up with the idea. Spoke to Lee. That's it really."

She smiled at him. "You really are a nice guy for somebody who can kill a man with one hand, Daniel Cade."

"Well that's not a thing I like to do. Helping Ray get straight is."

"I know that Daniel. What's this?" As he handed her the sheet of paper he'd been writing on.

"Somebody else this situation can get straight. Your friend Tracey."

"Tracey? How?"

"That's the address of Ray's house. And Kim's number. Get her to go there and look at it. If she wants it, Lee's cool with signing the lease over to her from Ray. Long-term rental at the same price." He grinned. "Tell her the place will be de-Ray'd and redecorated."

"Are you serious?" Janet was almost speechless.

"No. I'm winding you up like Angel does," he replied smiling at her.

"But you hardly know her."

"That's true. But you do. And she was there for you when you were going through hell with Barry, Jan."

"Yeah she really was. I don't know what I would have done without her, Daniel. She kept me company, had the kids at hers when I had to go to the bloody police or solicitors or court. Picked them up from school. Told Barry to piss off if she saw him hanging around. She was a rock."

"Then she's earned a break, Jan. That house has been owned for six years and gone up in value ridiculously like everything else in London. It owes Tremayne's nothing. She gets a nice place to live until she doesn't want it any more with no crappy short term lease or thieving deposit. The place will be looked after. And it's three bedroom in a nice area, with a garden. And it gets her and her kids out of that rat trap you got out of. It's just logical to me."

She looked at him and her eyes were shining as she was a bit tearful. "That is just so very kind. Of you and Lee, Daniel."

"You're either good or you're not. You intervene or you don't. It's not complicated."

"No it's not darling. I'm starting to see that now."

"Thought you might. Shall we get changed and go to dinner. And get a flight home booked."

"Can I call Tracey now?"

He smiled. "Of course, I'll send a couple of emails while you do it. Then we'll get changed and go to dinner shall we?"

She smiled at him as she got her phone from her bag. "Yeah. Maybe." And dialled Tracey's number.

Chapter 84. Lust and control.

Phone call made to a screamingly amazed and delighted best friend, Janet got undressed and saw Daniel was watching her intently, seated by the desk where he'd been using his phone.

"Like what you're gawking at, do ya Cade?"

"Yeah. I do. You're gorgeous."

She was naked now and brazenly, slowly, walking towards him. She leaned down, pressing her large boobs into his face, kissing him and fondling him through his jeans. "I am, aren't I?"

He groaned as her hand kept up the torment. "Yeah, you are."

"You feel like you want what you've been rudely staring at pretty bad." Her voice was a low, husky whisper in his ear.

"I do. Real bad. And it's getting worse." She darted her tongue around his mouth, quickening her hand movement as she did it, making him gasp with pleasure. He went to undo his belt.

"Oh no you don't," she whispered, pulling him to his feet and his hands up to her breasts, still massaging him through his jeans. He groaned at the combination of pleasure. And acute discomfort.

"It's torture." he gasped.

"I guess it must be my poor darling." She pushed harder against him and increased the torture. His body shuddered as she did it.

"Jan please," he groaned again.

"Ah. So now it's me that has the solution to your problems is it?"

"Yeah. Oh yeah, darling, you do."

"You want to hear the solution darling?" She squeezed harder through his jeans making him gasp loudly.

"Yes Jan. I really, oh shit, need to." His knees buckled a little. She kissed him slowly and sensuously, still massaging the front of his jeans and whispered,

"I suggest you ruin me, boat-style. Right now, slowly, for ages. Then we call room service later. And stay here all night. Unless you'd rather go out anywhere?"

He silently eased her back towards the luxurious king size bed. He didn't want to go anywhere other than there.

He realised as he undressed she'd just had total control over him. And shown him that it could be wonderful. No doubts or dark thoughts. He just loved her all the more for taking him a little bit further on a journey he'd waited so long to make. And would continue to make as she guided him gently along the route.

They had a lovely last night at the hotel and booked a taxi to the airport for the morning. All went smoothly apart from a short flight delay and they were back in the Gambia. Things to sort out. The children's education and their bedrooms in the villa itself. Daniel was happy to get on with it. There was nothing to be done until the intel came through on Amir's next delivery. He would be glad when it did. He very much wanted this over and the constant fears for Irena gone from his mind.

Chapter 85. The lull before the storm.

Irena was actually enjoying the lull before the next storm. Amir had come to terms with his huge financial loss. Bogdan had quit ranting over his missing women, they had never been found. No word of a rival stealing them. Nothing. Infuriating. But, he'd had no further problems. Business was steady. They were still covering their supply needs. Just. And still impatiently awaiting the next shipment. But the suppliers were careful and methodical. They sent huge amounts in one go, it had to get through, especially after the last one getting seized. If it didn't. Well there were huge losses instead of huge gains. Amir couldn't rush them. He didn't want them aware he was in trouble. He'd paid the extortionate demand rather than do that.

Life went on as usual. It seemed the madness was over. They were alert to any threat, from the law or otherwise. But it seemed as if the group that had targeted them had kept their word. Maybe they had left for wherever they were going. Amir didn't care. Neither did Bogdan as long as they left them alone. And it seemed they were.

Mick Davidson got a message now and again from his mysterious benefactor, just saying to wait until something happened. He fed a few bits to Amir, couple of places to stay away from. Told him that the Wesley Mason homicides, the drug meet hit and the hire car incident, were all on the back burner with no active investigations ongoing. All avenues of enquiry exhausted. Collected an envelope or two for his troubles. Pulled his arrest rate up. He looked better and felt better.

Fleming had congratulated him on his performance. He was pulling a bit more overtime and, after a bit of grovelling, he was seeing a bit more of his kids. He had taken the chance he'd been given and he wasn't going back to the mess he'd got in, ever again. Another year left of policing. He was going to make it a good one. After that, who knew? He was trying to get his wife to talk to him but getting nowhere. He couldn't blame her. But he wouldn't give up. All the while she was still single and alone there was a chance. He loved her too much to give up trying.

Daniel and Janet were enjoying a quiet time in the Gambia for just over a week, getting to know each other more as the days went by. The children were happy, Daniel was enjoying the respite, and his new family. Life was good and Janet looked at pictures of the place in Turkey and heard nearly all about the family who Daniel had befriended that had led to the apartment block purchase. And she looked forward to the adventure of living in yet another country. She was fascinated by the history and culture of both the Gambia and Turkey and rarely thought of her old life in the UK, except for Skyping with Tracey, who was excitedly awaiting her move and her holiday which was planned for the next school break.

A couple of days earlier, Ray had contacted Daniel. Still no date and time for Amir's next big shipment but the communications were indicating it was imminent. But Bogdan had obviously been in Amir's place and used his phone. There were six women being brought to London tomorrow night. Ray emailed the details. Daniel contacted Mick Davidson. Told him of the intel.

"Can you get this to the right place Mick? We can't intervene again."

"Yeah sure. I will pass it along. I'll say I got it from a reliable snout I'd asked for info on East European villains back when we were fishing around for Bland or something. I'll get Fleming to do it. He's got more clout than me to get it actioned fast. And he likes taking credit for things. It'll get him up the career ladder and out of my hair quicker." Daniel laughed and text him the details and left it with him.

Mick went to Fleming with it. Said he had picked up a sniff on some traffickers from one of his regular informers. Apparently there was a bunch of women being brought up from the coast that night. It looked kosher. So if Fleming could influence a prompt intervention, it might be worth the effort. Fleming did just that and asked to be kept informed on the outcome by the unit involved.

The next day came the big one, Amir's next big delivery. It was on a lorry, loaded with fresh vegetables, coming in through Harwich docks from Holland on a late night cargo ferry. Tomorrow night. Daniel was relieved. This was the second to last thing before this was over. Once Amir lost this shipment he would have to cut and run. He would instruct Irena to sell his assets. And they would sell. And he wouldn't get a penny of it, it would simply evaporate. Then a huge file of evidence collated by Ray would drop into the lap of the police. Via Mick Davidson.

Any babbling by Amir about Mick being bent would be dismissed as a desperate part of his defence. Mick had loved that idea. And Amir and Bogdan would go to jail, for hopefully a very long time. No money. No power. And no way to intimidate and threaten their way out of it. But it wouldn't turn out like that.

Daniel had made one wrong move with all the best intentions - giving Mick Davidson the information to arrest the men delivering those girls. And it was going to have fearful consequences.

Chapter 86. Being there, just in case.

Daniel told Janet he had to go to the UK again. Urgently. She was fine, she wanted to come with him. The kids were happy. Rosie and Solomon would look after them. It wasn't a problem. They would stay at Lee and Angel's which she was looking forward to very much as it happened. She adored them both, especially Angel.

Daniel wanted to be there to get Irena safely away. Amir was going to go mental when the shipment got intercepted. The information to seize the drugs had been given to the Dutch police and it would be done in the port area of the Hook of Holland. Daniel figured that a seizure in Europe would be far better to prevent Irena being suspected.

All Amir's problems, bar the Harwich seizure, had now been firmly established in Amir's mind to be the illegal activities of a vague Islamist group, who only wanted money. So much so, he'd paid a huge sum of money to be rid of them. A legitimate seizure by the police in Europe would, hopefully, be looked upon as simply the result of investigation, yet again, by the police, and as the occupational hazard it was to drug distributors.

It would be a catastrophe for Amir. Which made it more important than ever he believed it to be unrelated, sheer bad luck. If he pointed the finger at Irena, or anything went wrong, Daniel wanted to be on hand. But it went wrong earlier than that, terribly wrong. On the very morning of the shipment day. The day after Bogdan had lost six more trafficked girls. That loss, the decision to cause that loss, was the catalyst that caused the entire, carefully planned, long game, to turn into a nightmare.

They flew into the UK and the cold weather the next morning and went to the beautiful house in Surrey to enjoy the day with Lee and Angel. Conversation flowed between them. About the new political party idea. Janet and Daniel's plans. They had dinner in the beautiful dining room. The visitors were tired and went to bed early in the room where Daniel had a few things of his own. It had been a good day. Daniel waited for news via his phone. The shipment should get intercepted between midnight and two in the morning. He didn't know then that it wouldn't. It wouldn't even get to the port.

Chapter 87. Rumbled.

Bogdan got the news about the girls late the same morning. Two more of his men arrested, caught red-handed with the girls in the bus. He tried to talk to Amir, but Amir gave him short shrift and very little sympathy. "Bogdan I am leaving for the new warehouse. I wish to check thoroughly, in daylight, there is no unusual activity in the area. The delivery is coming tonight. I am taking just two trusted men to see it in, unload it and guard it. And then we will sort it out. I am sorry for the loss of your women, but it is surely to be expected?"

"Yes of course but even you have to..."

"Bogdan!" Amir cut right across what he was saying. "Border control and the police are very active in these matters. Too many people are involved in this trafficking. Some they smuggle, escape. And go to the authorities. They are watched for by many agencies across Europe. I discuss this with you but you never listen to me, or anybody else for that matter. I tell you to stay out of such things. That we have our business, you do not need to do this. But you do it anyway. So you have to accept there may be problems. But I cannot afford any problems this time. Not with this shipment, Bogdan. I call you later. I am leaving now." And hung up on Bogdan.

Bogdan was furious. Fucking Amir and his attitude. Bogdan liked running the women. They made good money. And he liked the power over them, the sex on demand, they became users. Good for business. Time was when Amir never complained about it, with his free samples he was so quick to ask for. Before he met that bitch Irena. Bogdan hated her. Her haughty disdain for him. Her influence over Amir.

He didn't trust her at all. He was sure he had been right the first time when he accused her, but she squirmed out of it. Daesh. Bogdan had not believed it, he still was unsure. Even after that maniac in the car. All that Davidson had confirmed. He was quite sure there was more to this, because nobody else had known about those girls, bar the supplier on the coast and himself. There was a leak from somewhere. There had to be. Amir wasn't listening. So Bogdan resolved to find out. He knew a man to talk to to make a start. Security flaws were his speciality.

And, very late in the afternoon, he finally tracked down, and spoke with the man, Anton, a Russian. He discussed the matter with him and asked him if there was any way that his phone was being tapped.

"There is very little chance really Bogdan, phones are very secure. And it is not easy for the police to get permission here in the UK."

"But there is something wrong Anton. Two lots of my activities have been compromised recently. An associate of mine too, many problems. I have always used my phone for business. But never had problems. Until recently."

"Do you use SMS."

"SMS?"

"Yes. Standard text messages from your number."

"Yes of course. Quite a lot."

"Anything else? WhatsApp, Viber, Skype?"

"I no hear of the others. But Skype yes. Calls, video calls and messages. Is free to use to other countries."

"Yes, but the weakness is maybe the wi-fi. Do you use it much? Or just your phone data?"

"Wi-fi?" Bogdan was getting a bit lost with this but tried not to show it too much.

"Yes. As in use your broadband router at home, for internet access. Rather than your phone data? Routers and wireless signals are not so hard to hack into, if you know how to."

"No. I no bother with internet at home." Then it hit him. Amir's wi-fi. He had used fucking Amir's wi-fi. He remembered the palaver with putting in a password for it. That had to be it. If it was anything at all, that would be it.

"Anton. Do you want to earn a hundred pounds for an hour's work? Like now. Is most urgent."

"Yes. Sure."

"Come with me. Bring some electrical tools," Bogdan checked his gun in the inside pocket of his long leather coat.

Then he phoned Amir, who at least answered. "What is it now, Bogdan? I said I would call you."

"Amir, you have two choices my friend. You listen. Or you do not. There is no time to explain until later."

"Speak."

"Divert that shipment. Now, do not let it even leave Europe. Do not let it anywhere near the port over there. If you can, do it. If not, do not go near it."

"But Bogdan…."

"There is no time Amir, I would not tell you this if I did not have good reason. Divert it. If I am wrong, make new arrangements. Do not call me. I will call you again in less than an hour." He hung up and smiled grimly. See how fucking Amir liked it. Being spoken to like a dog. And he was gone, beckoning

Anton as he went. Anton followed him to the car and Bogdan's driver headed towards Amir's penthouse. The traffic was heavy and Bogdan fumed at the progress but eventually they arrived and headed to the main doors and security desk.

When he got there, he smiled at the oaf on the security desk who had seen him many times. Explained politely that he was here to show this man up to his good friend, Mr Ferez' penthouse, as he was having trouble with his computer but was away on business. His good lady was expecting them. The man nodded lethargically and waved them through towards the lifts. Bogdan strode towards them, Anton struggling to keep up. They got in and the lift went up to the penthouse floor.

Irena was upstairs, reading a magazine. The evening was dragging. She was more than a little nervous. Amir was going to be very volatile later. She would have to be very alert. There was a knock on the door. She put the magazine down and opened it, not expecting anyone and the building was secure. She assumed it was a neighbour. But Bogdan burst in. With a gun in his hand. And told her that if she made one sound, she died. She stayed silent. Another man was there, looking very uncomfortable.

"Bogdan. What is this? I want no part of any shooting."

"Be quiet, Anton."

"You," to Irena. "Where is your router?"

Anton said "I see it." And crossed the room towards it. Irena's world collapsed inside her. Bogdan knew, somehow. And she knew she was going to die.

Anton got to the router. He looked at it, and knew straight away from the lights flickering on it that there was something wrong. He unplugged it and took out a small electrical screwdriver and carefully undid it. "This has been tampered with." He showed it to Bogdan, who understood nothing that he could see inside it. "Explain."

He did. "Been very well done. Put simply, there is a device in there forwarding all the information that passes through this router to a third party server. If your phone logs on to this every time it's in range… give me your phone please." Bogdan handed it over. Anton swiped his finger on the screen a couple of times. Looked at the serial number on the router. And showed Bogdan. "See. It's logged on since you've got in here. You must have been given the password at some time yes?

"Yes. Yes, I fucking was Anton."

"Well smartphones have a setting, used by most people, to auto switch to wi-fi, from the device's own contract data allowance. To save the contract data. Yours is set to that. So whenever it is in range, it logs on automatically."

Bogdan nodded, although Anton might just as well have said it in Russian. Bogdan knew enough though. Both he and Amir had been betrayed. And he was looking at who had done it. Amir's wonderful Irena. Just like he'd said all along.

Bogdan pointed the gun at Irena and motioned her to sit. He fished in his pocket with his free hand and pulled out a bulging money clip, which he tossed on to the coffee table. "Take two hundred pounds, Anton. You have done well. One hundred for your troubles, one hundred for your loss of memory. Take an extra twenty for a cab. And leave. Forget all you have seen. And don't worry about her. She will not be a problem for much longer." Irena cast an imploring look at the man called Anton. But he strode away without a glance. She knew he would not intervene, he wouldn't dare. And, if he knew and was trusted by Bogdan, wouldn't care.

The one person who might have flagged this up promptly was away from his computers for once. With his wife, in Hastings. Things were pretty much done anyway. The last vital pieces of information discovered and passed on. It was time to wind it all down, retrieve the router and put the proper one back. After Amir's arrest. Leave no traces of what had been happening, to safeguard Irena for the future. They were sorting out the cottage that was going to be their home. And they weren't leaving until late, after a dinner out somewhere, to miss the traffic going home. Amir was away, there would be no communications from his penthouse. And the shipment wouldn't get seized until the early hours of the morning anyway.

Chapter 88. Without a mark on her.

Bogdan left the router unplugged and called Amir on his mobile, put him on loudspeaker. Told him he was in his penthouse, with a gun on Irena. And about Anton. And the bugged router. Amir listened incredulously.

"And you think Irena knows of this?"

"Get real Amir, she must have put it there. Switched it for the real one, who the hell else could? She is sitting here looking at her expensive pretty shoes she buys with your money. Shitting herself and saying nothing."

"I see."

"Where are you? What about the shipment?"

"Not coming. I manage to get the driver, he turned round. And drove back away from the port in Holland. New arrangements will have to be made."

"Good. We have to deal with this bitch. What shall I do. Dispose of her?"

"No! You fool. If this is true, she has taken a million pounds of mine. You bring her to me, tonight. Unharmed Bogdan. You hear me well, yes?"

"I hear you. Where?"

"The new warehouse. It is safe. The driver of the lorry had not been given the final address. So even if he is caught, he can't disclose it."

"Very well. It is a good place to interrogate her. What time?"

"Between eleven and midnight, Bogdan. I want nobody seeing us. Make sure you are not followed."

"Of course. And that gives me time to pay another visit."

"To who?"

"Davidson. Another liar you told me I should trust Amir"

"Davidson? Why?"

"Amir. If this is all lies….if this is all this bitch - then all Davidson has told you is to back it up."

"But surely………"

Bogdan exploded with frustration at Amir. "There is no, but surely, Amir, we have been conned. Scammed! You have handed over a million pounds to somebody, but it is not Daesh. I fucking told you Amir. That punk in the car was part of it. And Davidson, your wonderful Irena, those snipers. The fake police. All working together. We will get it from your wonderful Irena later. But I am going to get Davidson, who you have also been paying to lie to you. About terrorist groups and intelligence services. And so have I. After Dover. That bastard made no enquiries at all to the Kent police. He already knew where those girls had gone. And charged me five hundred pounds to sit there taking the piss."

Bogdan was seething with anger.

Amir said. "Okay, I will assume you are right. But Bogdan. You will not murder a policeman tonight, in a rage and with no clear plan to do it. You will bring the wrath of the police down on us, you fool. It will not take them long to connect him to us, they are not total idiots. I want that shipment to arrive safely. And I do not need a full-scale police officer murder hunt going on. As for Irena, you bring her to me, Bogdan. Without a mark on her. I will get the truth. But it is for me to do, not you. Davidson will keep until we can deal with him properly. Is that very clear Bogdan?"

Bogdan knew that tone. Amir could be utterly ruthless. It was how he'd got where he was. "I hear you Amir. Without a mark on her. You have my word on that." He ended the call.

Bogdan looked at the terrified Irena. "We have a little wait ahead of us, bitch. But you heard your lover. Thank your stars Amir wants you delivered intact. I should fuck you now to soften you up for later. But as Amir insists you are unharmed, I wait until later. But I warn you. If he can't get what I want to hear out of you. I will. Now go make me a coffee, you whore."

He snatched up his money clip, and followed the trembling young woman into the kitchen. Saw her eyes go to her mobile phone on the kitchen table. "Don't even think about it bitch." He glanced at it. Turned it off and dropped it in his pocket. Might be useful later. See who the treacherous whore had been talking to. Another job for Anton.

Irena barely stifled a sob. That action had just sealed her fate. She remembered Ray telling her that it must be on at all times or they could not know where she was in an emergency. And now it was switched off and in the pocket of a man who hated her and was going to kill her. If Amir Ferez did not.

And Bogdan had no intention of letting Davidson get away with it either. He made a call. Irena listened in horror as he told one of his henchmen to go to Davidson's flat very late tonight.

"Collect a gun from the usual place. With a silencer on it. Take Henk to pick the door lock and do the driving. Let Henk drive away. Then go in there and kill him. Conceal the body in the flat well. Just to buy a couple of days." He grinned insanely at Irena as he ended the call.

"And you will die tonight as well, you bitch. Two bits of rubbish removed tonight."

"Maybe you will now you defy Amir. If he doesn't kill you, my death will not go unavenged, Bogdan. I will die knowing that."

"You will tell us where to find your clever friends, Irena. You will tell us everything. By the time we finish with you, woman, you will beg to die."

Irena wept. He was right. He was a brutal sadist who loved hurting women. She was terrified of him.

After an hour of silence, Bogdan made a call, summoning his car and driver to come to Amir's block door and wait. He motioned to Irena to get up. He put the gun in her back through the pocket of his long leather coat and told her to walk normally to the lift. They went down to the ground floor. She felt the gun hard in the small of her back as Bogdan walked closely with her to the large automatic doors.

She looked towards the security desk as they passed it but the man just glanced up and nodded and went back to his evening paper. She felt the cold air hit her as she was marched to the car and shoved into the back. Bogdan got in next to her and told the driver where to go. The man obviously knew where it was. And she was driven away. Towards wherever she was going to die.

Chapter 89. Panic and intervention.

Ray phoned Daniel. They were in bed in Lee's house. It was about ten at night and Daniel grabbed the phone quickly.

"Ray?" In no more than a loud whisper. Janet was sleeping next to him.

"Yeah. Daniel. Irena's in big trouble man."

Daniel sat bolt upright. No attempt at being quiet now. "Trouble. How? Why?"

Janet sat up as well, looking at Daniel. Seeing he was worried.

"Right listen. You need to get moving quickly, man."

Daniel got out of bed. Janet got up too.

"Tell me. I'm listening."

Daniel started getting dressed, awkwardly, the phone wedged in his neck. Then cursed and put it on loudspeaker on the bed.

"The feed from the router went off earlier this evening. Around seven."

"Okay. You think we've got a problem?"

"I know we have. Bogdan's found the router. The penthouse is bugged. I heard it all."

"Bugged? You never said!"

"Well I did it off my own bat on the quiet. Got young Nigel to fit them when he delivered the router. I didn't want Irena to know I could hear everything. Her shagging Amir and stuff. But collecting intel and her safety was the job you gave me Daniel. I always do my job."

"Shit!"

He was getting into a pair of black jeans, zipped on his black leather bomber jacket. Not bothering with a shirt. Janet started getting dressed as well, slipping on jeans and a sweatshirt, pulling on trainers. Daniel got into socks and put on soft high top black boots, lacing them up. He pulled a small case from the bottom of the wardrobe onto the bed, all as Ray's voice kept talking.

"The shipment has been diverted away, it ain't coming to the docks over there. I heard Bogdan talking to Amir. I also heard Bogdan put a hit out on Davidson, Amir told him not to but he did it anyway. Late tonight the goon was told."

"Fucking hell, leave that to me. Irena. Her phone. Have we got her whereabouts?"

"Bogdan turned her phone off."

"So she's fucking doomed then."

"Not if you stop flapping. It's with them."

"How are you sure of that if it's off, Ray? You told her it had to be on and charged. Oh shit, she's done for. I should have got her out of there earlier."

"Daniel, calm down and focus. Listen. But get ready to move. Okay."

Janet realised she was hearing the real Ray that Daniel admired so much. As much a master at his arts as Daniel was at his own. And he was taking control, shepherding a frightened Daniel back into line."

"I built a little bit of extra security into Irena's phone."

"Extra?"

"Yeah. Shut up and listen, only ask if you don't understand."

"Okay."

"She was told never to turn her phone off. Because all the time it's on it transmits and we know where she is. If she keeps the phone with her at all times, charged up and switched on. Drummed it into her time over. Right?"

"Right."

"Well I figured that maybe if she was ever caught and in the shit that whoever caught her might just take her phone off her. And if they did, they might well turn it off, right?"

"Yeah. They well might, and ?"

"Well I put a bit of extra tech in it, on a just in case scenario. That if it got switched off it would alert my system. And I would still know where it was, I could still track it, because it ain't really off. You follow man?"

"Yeah. Switched off you know where it is."

"Right. Good, well it got switched off, Daniel. By Bogdan, thirteen minutes after the router feed died. I just got here, been in Hastings. Played back the recordings from the bugs."

"Well where is it now?"

"That phone is travelling. It's in a vehicle that's been on the M25, been in quite heavy traffic. But thankfully been heading your way. Heading west towards outer Surrey. It's turned off the motorway at Reigate and is now out in the bondooks. Way out in the country near a place called Leigh. Still on the move."

"Oh no." said Daniel. "This time of night. This is it Ray, she's been caught. They're taking her somewhere to kill her. Or they've already killed her, just her body in the car. Oh fuck that phone might just be in the killer's pocket."

Janet was staring at the phone, her eyes wide with shock at what she was hearing. It was just unreal.

Ray said, "Daniel. Calm down. If she's dead, you'll want to deal with whoever killed her. But I think she is alive. Bogdan was told to deliver her unmarked by

Amir, to him. To deal with her. At some warehouse, I heard it. Think Daniel. They will want to know stuff from her, you've done a lot of damage, took a lot of money. Amir is out of town and you know why. He'll want answers, his money. There would be no reason to leave Croydon if they'd killed her. No reason to leave Croydon if Amir was going back there to deal with it. So assume she is alive, right. And being taken to Amir somewhere, by Bogdan. So focus on a course of action. Do what you're good at Daniel. They ain't got where they're going yet, you've got a bit of time. But you need to get moving if you're going to get her back. But if that phone battery dies." He didn't finish. He didn't have to.

"I know. She will die too."

Daniel was ready to go. "I'm on the way, I'll make some calls as I go. Keep me posted on the whereabouts Ray." He turned to Janet who was getting hurriedly dressed. "I have to go."

"I'm coming with you."

"You're fucking not!"

She glared at him. "Oh yes I fucking am Daniel Cade! You're not James bloody Bond. You need somebody to work the phone while you drive fast. I won't go near any trouble. Now shut up and move." She was right. He needed all the help he could get.

She looked horrified as he opened his suitcase and tipped it out. Under his clothing was a slim, flat leather, zip up briefcase. He quickly opened it and took out a flat, slim, skeletal, automatic pistol and a couple of other things that he stuffed into his pockets. He then added what she guessed were spare clips of bullets. He was stuffing them in his jacket as they raced down the stairs, the gun in the waistband of his jeans.

Lee was in the kitchen as they got down to the ground floor, in a dressing gown. He'd heard the commotion. "What's wrong?"

"Irena, Lee. In great danger. I have to go."

"Irena?"

"Later Lee. She's going to be killed and soon, I have to go. I need a car."

"Take the Lexus, Daniel, it's fast. No key ignition, just get in and press the start button. Now go." Lee handed him the fob. They headed outside and got in the car. Daniel fumbled a bit with the modern car's controls, cursing quietly as he started the Lexus, then tore out onto the quiet country roads. Daniel grabbed his phone and gave it to Jan. "Find Q in the contacts and call it."

She did and as it rang he told her to put it on speaker. He was concentrating on the road, getting the feel of the incredibly powerful Lexus. It was answered promptly. "Quan. We have a big problem. Irena. Ring Ray he'll fill you in. And if you can, get mobile. Towards the M25. Westbound. Now. See if you can get anyone else as well, Quan. One other. We've got big shit here mon ami. I'm on the way now." He hung up. Then to Janet.

"Find R in the contacts. Wait five minutes then try him. Quan will have spoken to him by then.

Daniel was driving at a terrifying speed in the darkness. She just hoped the police didn't stop them. But there was no choice, time was of the essence. And she held on tight as they flew through the dark night on the near empty roads. Called R as instructed. Ray answered, his tense voice filling the hurtling car. "Daniel. You're mobile. I have you tracked."

"Yes Ray. What's the situation?"

"Quan's mobile. He's got Adabele mobile. On his Kawasaki. I've got you tracked on here as of now. And Quan. But not Adabele. You are about thirty miles away from Irena's phone, travelling much faster. They are not in any particular rush by the look of it. They won't want to get pulled over. The signal is clear. Head on to the A24. And keep the hammer down, I'll call you in five. Quan's trying to get through." He hung up.

Daniel gripped the wheel and focused. He was on a good straight bit of road. The speed crept up to over a hundred, he overtook a lorry on a slight bend and got away with it, the lorry driver blasting the horn at the maniac who'd passed him. Kept going.

"Find MD on the phone quickly. Call it." Janet did so with trembling hands. A voice answered. "Hi Daniel."

"Mick. Don't interrupt. I need this line clear in seconds. We're blown. Bogdan has instructed one of his goons to kill you, late tonight. Don't look out of any windows. Just do as I say. It's all the help I can give you."

Janet looked in awe at Daniel as he rattled off instructions to the man at the other end. Finished with, "Text this phone later, don't call it under any circumstances. Good luck Mick." He ended the call and hurtled on through the night.

Janet was frightened, but stayed calm and just looked down and focused on the phone. It rang. She answered, Ray's voice came through the speaker. "Right, they've stopped. You are around twenty-seven miles away. Quan is nearer thirty-six. Adabele, don't know. He's in touch with Quan. And ease up, Daniel. You're no good to the girl wrapped around a bloody tree." Daniel eased off a bit to

Janet's relief.

Ray continued talking calmly, "Right. On Google Earth this place is a warehouse. Looks like a small industrial unit. In the sticks, one second. Getting a postcode and some details. Right. Put this postcode in the sat nav." He spelled it out slowly. Janet fumbled around as the car hurtled along but managed to enter it, the map flared into life, giving them a direction at least.

"Right. Fruit wholesalers. Importers. Merricks it's called. Stay on the A24. About another twenty, maybe twenty-two miles. Then left onto Mole Valley Lane, signed to Leigh, L.E.I.G.H, probably. About three miles down there is a railway bridge. Turn left just before it. Follow that down and this unit will be on your right. Isolated. The only unit there, a mile after you go over a small bridge of some sort. Farming area, drive carefully. It will be a big postcode area out there. Don't rely on the sat nav. I will guide you in. Later. I'll call Quan." The call ended.

Daniel was thinking feverishly. Twenty-seven miles when Ray called, say twenty four now. If he could average even sixty he could be there in under thirty minutes. He drove like a man possessed. "Not Irena. Please, not now," was rolling through his mind, over and over again, like an incantation.

Chapter 90. Sheer terror.

Irena was dragged by her hair from the car. Gagged, she couldn't scream. She looked wildly around in the dark. Some warehouse-type building, remote and isolated. Surrounded by fields and trees. She heard Bogdan tell his driver to wait there and not move. She sobbed as she realised that there was nobody around to help her, not even a slim chance of being saved. She was shoved through a pedestrian door into a lit, but gloomy, large warehouse. And there, with Hassan and another of his men, was Amir Ferez.

Bogdan dragged her across to him. "You wouldn't listen would you, Amir? I told you it was her. I fucking told you."

"Bring her here." Amir's voice was cold and harsh. She was thrown to the ground in front of him. Gasped in pain as her knees cracked into the cold concrete floor, her black tights tore open at both knees. And gasped again as the tape was crudely ripped from across her mouth.

"You will die here tonight Irena. I am sure you know that."

"So be it." she hissed at him. "I die knowing I damaged you badly."

He stood and kicked her savagely in the ribs. She howled with pain and writhed on the concrete.

"First you will tell me why. Then you will tell me anything else I wish to know."

She looked at him with such an expression it shocked him. Pure hatred in her eyes as she spoke through the pain in her ribs. And her fear. "You pulled a gun in Istanbul some time ago, Amir Ferez. And you fired at a policeman who was trying to arrest you. He was looking for you and your thug friends in those dark alleyways. He had his back to you, but you shot him anyway. He had no chance Amir. But you, you boasted of it. Tough hard man Amir, who shoots a policeman."

She took a gasping deep breath as the pain in her ribs made her wince.

"That policeman was my father. He was paralysed. And became a shell of a man who wished he was dead. The pain was relentless. And in the end, after two years of morphine and misery and having his arse wiped like a child, he took his own life. With the same shit you sell Amir. But given to him by doctors to mask his pain. My family lost everything. So I came to find you Amir, and destroy you. I did my best. But I have failed. So kill me. Like you destroy everything else your fat little hands touch."

"You have done all this? Over your father? All this time, you sleep with me to destroy me? So you can betray me to others?"

Amir was visibly shaken. It was beyond his imagination that this beautiful young woman could risk so much over such a thing. And now die over it. He seemed confused. Bogdan lost patience. "Kill her Amir. Get it done."

Amir raised almost dead eyes to Bogdan. He was coming to terms with this revelation. A rage such as he had never known was slowly building within him.

This woman, his Irena, had conspired with others to have his men killed, his money taken from their dead bodies. His supplies taken to cripple him. Extorted him of well over a million pounds in total. Would have seen the diverted shipment taken, finished him for good. Screwed with him in bed. All the while knowing exactly what was wrong, sweetly talking to him, with soft consoling words. With helpful wise advice, pointing him always in the wrong direction. Controlling him like a puppet. And now he looked a total fool in Bogdan's eyes. Bogdan, who now knew he had been right all along. He looked at her with such utter hatred she turned her head away. She knew then she would not die easily, here in this horrible place, where nobody would hear her screams. She was terrified and trembling with fear.

Amir looked at her. She would die. But first there was more he had to know. He snapped out of it and nodded to his men. "Strip her naked and tie her up. Over there." He pointed to a metal framework. Empty racking, designed to hold pallets of goods. The men roughly ripped her clothes from her and dragged her across the warehouse, Bogdan deliberately ramming his hand between her legs as he ripped away the tiny panties she was wearing. His face manic in the dim lighting, leering at her nakedness. They found rope. They tied her hands to the racking above her head with the coarse blue rope and forced her legs far apart, tying each ankle to the lower part of the framework, facing the grey wall behind the racking. Amir took off his belt and walked towards her. Bogdan licked his lips and murmured, "Flay the skin from the bitch, Amir." Amir raised the heavy belt as he got close to her.

Chapter 91. A race against time.

Daniel was now turning left as per Ray's instructions, onto the river bridge road. Making the best time possible. The phone rang. Ray. "Her phone's still transmitting, no movement. You are six miles away, Quan is about seventeen. Adabele is going to RV with him soon and abandon the motorbike. You all need to be in touch. Be careful, call me if you can't find it. You're close, don't get noticed." The call ended. Daniel peered into the night, driving fast still. Five minutes later the phone rang again. Janet answered it, as they lurched over a small bridge, nearly getting airborne. Ray again. "You're one mile, as of, now Daniel. One mile. Call me later. I won't call you again."

And he was gone. Daniel dropped to just sidelights and slowed right down. Looked at the tenths of a mile rolling down on the sat nav. With half a mile to go he killed the lights, drove slowly another five hundred yards or so and pulled over onto the grass. He turned to Janet. "Wait here. Stop Quan here. Tell him on foot from here, right? I'll see you later." And he was gone out of the car. Janet saw him taking the pistol from his waistband as he ran into the night. She had never been so scared in her life but she got out and peered up the road and waited in the cold, frightened and alone. Wondering who the hell Quan was.

Back in Croydon, Mick Davidson had done as he was instructed and crouched uncomfortably behind the bedroom door, also waiting. He'd never been so scared in nearly thirty years of policing.

Chapter 92. Torture, pain and death.

The belt cracked savagely across Irena's buttocks. She howled with pain, then gasped and writhed against the rough ropes that bound her. She felt Amir's breath on the back of her neck.

"Where is my money, you fucking bitch? Where is it?" He stepped back and cracked the belt across her backside again, generating another scream. "I do not have it." she gasped.

"Who has got it?"

"A friend. With an offshore bank account." She was buying time, she didn't know why. She was lost and she knew it. But survival was instinctive.

"Then you need to arrange its return, you whore. Give me a name."

"And then what, Amir? You kill me here in the dark? Let me live and I will give you your money. A million pounds, Amir. For a whore."

"Let you live? You fucking bitch. You will get one deal from me and one only. You tell me where my money is and die easy, a bullet in the head. Or you do not and you die badly."

The hatred she had for him surged through her like an electric current. "Go to hell Amir. Just kill me. That money will look after my family."

The belt cracked again, across her back this time and she gasped at the intense agony of it, her body shook as if feverish. The pain was unbearable. She urinated involuntarily, from fear and agony. "You think you will have any family left alive, Irena? I will kill them all. Every last one of them. Unless my money is returned. In which case your death will suffice."

"You think so," she hissed through the pain and humiliation.

"You think those who help me will let you live after you kill me, Amir? Would let you get near my family? I go to my death knowing you will follow soon."

His reply was low and menacing. "Really? I have the contacts to do this in Turkey. Tonight. You will die knowing they will follow you soon. Maybe you will follow them. That will depend on how long you take to die. Which depends on you giving me my money. I will let Bogdan do to you right now what you have done to me. Screw you and humiliate you. While he does it I will watch. Then you can decide if you alone die tonight. Or I make some calls and you die with your family. That is the last choice you need to make in this life, you treacherous bitch."

He had a grim look of satisfaction on his face as that hit home. He did have thugs on tap in Turkey. And she knew it. Her family couldn't be warned and her bastard murderous friends weren't there. She had killed her mother and sister by even mentioning them, and knew that. And the young woman finally broke mentally and sobbed pitifully. But it wasn't enough, nowhere near enough. He would put her through the hell he'd been through before she died.

He looked at Bogdan. "You made a comment about her screwing me for nothing, Bogdan. Now maybe you want to screw her for nothing, yes? Be my guest. We will watch you. Then maybe she will be more talkative." Amir walked away as Bogdan removed his long leather coat and walked to the stricken woman. He ran his hands over her painful buttocks and reached round and roughly squeezed her breasts. "I've always rather fancied shagging you, Irena," he snarled, with his mouth against her ear.

She writhed and struggled and screamed as she felt him mauling her. His hand was between her legs. Then gone. Then there was a loud popping noise and she felt something splatter into her hair and down her back. And then there was smoke and more noise. Shouting, cursing and chaos. And she hung there helpless with no idea what was going on behind her, absolutely terrified.

Chapter 93. Armed and deadly intervention.

Daniel had found the twin, farm-type steel gates on the right. Not locked. And saw the Merricks sign. Thanked the spirits for Ray. He quietly climbed over them rather than risk the noise of opening one. There was light in the large building a hundred metres away across the expanse of cracked concrete and occasional weeds. Two cars parked near huge steel shutter doors that were next to a pedestrian door. Nobody seemed to be guarding them.

Then he saw a glow, a man in one of the cars, smoking, looking at his phone, his face slightly illuminated by the screen. The car window was slightly open. Daniel crept quickly towards the cars, gun in hand as he screwed the silencer on to it. He got to the car. The man took a drag on the cigarette. It was the last thing he did, as the pistol a foot from his head made a soft pop. Daniel moved on. To the unit.

A window with light showing. He peered carefully in, an office with a desk lamp on. Nobody in it. The next window was in darkness, he ignored it. The next window was lit. He looked in and his heart nearly stopped. Irena, naked and tied. Amir hit her with a belt. She screamed.

He ducked down and focused his mind. He had to find a way in, he had to get in there and get close. Firing from out here was no use. Too far, even with a good rifle, yet alone a handgun. And they would kill her easily before he could stop them. Even if he could hit one of them they would take cover. Irena couldn't.

He moved swiftly along the building and turned right along the rear wall. Another piercing scream that made him shudder; he blocked it from his mind. A door, he tried it, unlocked. He opened it, into a corridor. Went off left and right, he guessed to the offices he'd just seen to the right. Left had a sign to toilets. And fire exit. In front of him, another door, into the warehouse. Wired glass in the top, he knew that was it.

He peered through the dirty glass and there, directly across the other side, was Irena and her captors, with their backs to him. He eased it open, and looked carefully. Amir was just sitting down, next to two other men, on some pallets. There was talking, but he couldn't make out the words. Irena sobbing and gasping for breath as she did so. Bogdan was taking off his full length leather coat. Then walking towards Irena. Daniel slid silently through the door and away to his right. Moved slowly and silently down the right hand wall, taking cover behind a fork lift truck. Then some empty pallets that were stacked high. Then a steel cage with gas bottles in it.

He heard Irena sobbing as Bogdan mauled her. The three men, including Amir, were riveted on the naked woman and her tormentor. He kept moving, getting closer and closer, the soft Magnum boots not making a sound. The distance was closing now. Irena was screaming and struggling wildly, the noise made by her resonating around the warehouse, masking any slight sound that Daniel might make. Bogdan was roughly groping her. Then he stopped, laughing at the girl's terror. Stimulated by it. Irena's loud gasping sobs, Bogdan's hands going to his crotch to undo his trousers.

Daniel was very close now, less than thirty feet away, still silently sliding along the wall. A little further and he would be sure of not hitting Irena. Seconds dragged by. He was well to their right hand side now, in the peripheral vision of any one of them if they just slightly turned towards him. But he was ready, they weren't. The angle finally came right. To fire. But just miss Irena. Bogdan was very close to her. And they hadn't seen him. But he had no cover, he had to get this right. Or they both died. It was time, he focused, pictured what was going to happen in his mind. Before he did it.

And with that came the clarity he needed. He fired. A loud pop resonated in the huge space of the warehouse. Bogdan's head literally burst. He launched a smoke grenade already in his left hand away to his left and the pistol popped again twice. Quickly, one shot into each of the men with Amir as they rose and turned towards the noise and smoke. Reaching into jackets, far too late. One fell, a huge red stain spreading across his chest. The other stayed upright but swaying drunkenly, same bloodstain as it pumped out of his heart. Still facing Daniel. Another pop and a hole appeared near his temple, and he fell.

Amir had dropped to the ground, crawling away desperately, trying to find cover as his men fell beside him. Amir was crouched behind the pallets they had been seated on, scrabbling in his jacket for his gun, when a powerful foot crashed into his ribs knocking him sprawling. A tall figure appeared over him, like a wrathful spirit in the smoke, silent and calm and looked at him square in the eyes as he aimed the pistol at him. Greenish grey eyes with not a hint of emotion.
Amir gasped out, "Please. Don't shoot."
There was no reply, just two pops from the gun. He only heard the first one. And it was the last thing he ever heard.

Chapter 94. The aftermath.

Daniel untied Irena, wiping the grey matter from her hair and back as best he could, with her torn blouse he had picked up, and helped her towards the pallets the men had been sitting on. She was sobbing with pain and fear. He wrapped her in Bogdan's leather coat, holding her tight and whispering soothingly that she was safe now, she would be okay. And gently sat her down. The door opened.

He spun around with the gun and dropped down behind the pallets. But there were Quan and Adabele, guns in hand. "Go and get Janet please, one of you. Bring the car here with her in it." Adabele quickly went back out. Quan walked across the warehouse, and then around each of the dead men, unemotional and detached as always. Janet appeared, way across the other side in the doorway, wide-eyed with fear. Adabele was just behind her. "Daniel, you're okay?" she called across, starting to come towards him.

"I'm fine. Don't come any nearer, Jan. Please. Wait there." He didn't want her exposed to the carnage. The shattered skulls, the pooled blood and the deaths he'd caused. He eased Irena to her feet and with Quan's help, they got her to walk shakily across the cold warehouse. A smell of cordite, the wisps of smoke still in the air.

He said, "There's an office down there, Jan. Take Irena there. See if there's any tea or anything. She's in shock. Keep her warm and calm. We'll be along in a minute." Janet put her arm around the trembling woman and led her gently away. Daniel, Quan and Adabele walked back into the warehouse. "We better dispose of the rubbish I guess," said Quan.

"Yeah I guess", said Daniel. "Want to go get the cars in here?"

Adabele pressed the switch on the big shutter doors and they clattered up slowly to the top of the loading entrance door, stopping automatically. They searched the bodies and found the keys to Amir's vehicle and Quan and Adabele went outside and then drove them in. Adabele had shoved the corpse in his across to the passenger side. They silently manhandled the four bodies into the back seats of the cars, two in each. Adabele saw the steel cage Daniel had crouched behind earlier, grinned. Grabbed a couple of gas canisters, full ones. Fuel for the fork lift parked in the far corner. He carried two across, one in each of his huge hands. He put one near each car, opened all the windows in the cars and closed the doors, and they went to find Janet and Irena.

Chapter 95. Sound advice heeded.

Mick Davidson heard the door to his flat open. Quiet footsteps, two sets of them. One set was going back down the communal stairs. He heard the front main door gently close. A minute passed. Somebody came into the flat, through the lounge. Into the bedroom that had the door wide open.

A figure, gun in hand, strode to the bed, obviously seeing the sleeping man's shape. Then a loud thwap, thwap, thwap filled the small room as he fired the silenced pistol held in his right hand into what he believed to be the inert, sleeping form, of a police officer. Mick silently rose from behind him.

He smashed the baseball bat down on to the man's right hand collar bone, as hard as he possibly could, doing terrible damage. The man screamed in agony as he fell, the pistol flying from his grasp. As he rolled on to his back Mick kicked him savagely in the balls, generating another intense scream of pain and a gasping, babbled, "Please no more please I beg you." An East European accent.

"Fucking beg me, you piece of shit. You came here to kill me. You thought you just fucking had."

"I am told to so I do it. Please I need an ambulance." He was groaning in agony, unable to decide which injury hurt the most.

"You can bloody well wait, I've got shit to do. If you so much as move I'll give you another kick in the nuts and shoot you with your own gun. And keep the noise down. Understand?" The man nodded through the waves of pain he was suffering.

Mick poured a large whisky and lit a fag, sat on his bed shivering as the adrenalin ebbed. Bugger the clean living for an hour. He took a slug of scotch and a long drag, glaring at the writhing, quietly moaning thug on his bedroom floor. He finished the cigarette and stubbed it out.

Then he removed the bullet-holed bedding and spare pillows and remade the bed with new stuff. Hid the gun in his wardrobe. The intruder watched through pain-filled eyes. Mystified and in agony. Mick looked down at him, having picked up the baseball bat again. The man cowered in fear.

"Listen to me, you piece of shit. I'm calling the police and an ambulance. You were burgling me. No gun. No charge of attempted murder of a police officer. I disturbed you and whacked you one, right?"

The man looked at him. Groaned out "Yes, yes. But why? I no understand."

"It's none of your fucking business, you bastard. Or do you want to go on an attempted murder and firearms rap?"

"No. No please. Of course not."

"Then shut the fuck up and do as you're told and stop pissing me off. Attempted burglary. And keep your stupid mouth shut about your scumbag boss Bogdan sending you here to kill me. Right?"

"Right. Yes. Please. The ambulance. I'm dying of pain."

"Good. You ever cross my path again, rat face, you'll really regret it."

Mick made the call and a few minutes later the police and paramedics removed the groaning hit-man from his flat. Mick said he was fine and would make a statement in the morning. He sat down with another scotch and switched the Samsung phone on and, with trembling fingers, sent a text.

Chapter 96. Time to leave.

The two women were sitting in the office. Irena was sipping a tea, trembling violently. "Daniel. You saved my life."

"I didn't. I was just given the chance to rescue you. Ray saved your life, Irena. But the main thing is you're alive. But we have to go now. You good to move?" She nodded and shakily got to her feet, unsteady but determined as ever, engulfed by the huge, full-length leather coat she was cocooned in.

He said, "Take her to our car please, Jan. And give Lee a call. Tell him we're on our way back and have a guest. And we need a discreet doctor. The number's stored in the phone. Under Doc. Give the number to Lee to get him to his house. He knows him anyway." The women left and walked slowly outside and got in the car that Adabele had driven in to the yard and parked right outside the door to the offices.

They talked briefly. Adabele agreed to be the last to leave. Said it would be best as he had the motorbike. He would set the cars on fire and go after they were well away. Daniel stood with them both and said, "Shall we make this the very last mess we leave for the emergency services guys?"

They both smiled and nodded. They all shook hands and Daniel walked to the car.

Quan looked at him before he got in his own with Adabele, who needed to collect his motorbike from a way back up the road where he had jumped in with Quan.

Quan said, "Good shooting in there, mon ami."

"It had to be. That was very, very close Quan. Too close."

"I know Daniel. But she'll be fine. See you when I see you man."

They hugged and Quan and Adabele drove away. Daniel got in. Janet was in the back holding the softly-sobbing Irena to her, whispering soothingly and stroking her lush black hair. He picked up the phone Jan had left on the front passenger seat. Read a text, and smiled and then he drove away. A motorbike passed them going the other way a couple of minutes later.

A few minutes later, in the rear view mirror, he saw a reddish light, glimmering against the sky. It was over. Bogdan and Amir were dead. It wasn't how it was meant to end. But that was how it had. He drove steadily and carefully back to Lee and Angel's house.

Chapter 97. What the hell have we got here?

Bland had got a call at four in the morning and got to the crime scene in under an hour. He was let through the police cordon. Nigel Carash was there. It was a food importing warehouse apparently, or what was bloody left of it. The fire brigade were clearing up and preparing to leave. Marsh stared aghast at the scene in front of him. "What the hell have we got here, Nigel? An air strike? Cruise missile? Atomic bleeding bomb? Earthquake? Just look at it!"

"Unfortunately I have to."

"Yeah I know Nigel. And I wouldn't be here if it was just a gas explosion. So what have we got?"

"You've got two cars inside the warehouse containing the incinerated remains of five men, who were barbecued to a crisp after being shot dead. In the head or chest or, in the case of one, both. 9mm pistol. And bad as it is to say, the most expert shooting I ever saw. They were loaded after being shot, into the two cars, making good use of the petrol in them, with an open canister of Calor gas that was on site anyway, forklift fuel, put next to each car for good measure. That's what blew off part of the roof and blew the doors out. The other canisters in there didn't explode. Been made safe by Trumpton. The windows in the cars had been left down so a fireball roared through them. You can imagine the scene we were faced with."

"For pity's sake, Nigel. Why?"

"Erase all traces of the killers DNA. All the victims' mobile phones were incinerated. Wallets, any ID. Everything. It leaves us nothing to work on, Marsh. No immediate identifications."

"Can we get any ID on the dead at all?"

"Later Marsh, yeah. Dental, DNA, if there's a match in records. There's not much left of them."

"There's not much for me to do here either is there?"

"Not a thing Marsh. Not a thing."

Marsh watched him wearily walk back towards the carnage. He went back to his car. All he could do was wait.

Chapter 98. Medical attention.

At Lee's house the doctor was still there. Nick Taylor. Lee knew him. A young surgeon who lived locally. Nick had explained he'd done a couple of discreet, out of hours jobs over time, for his father, John. Lee was surprised but not shocked. He was getting used to surprises about his father since meeting up with Daniel again after his death.

Nick had examined Irena after getting the details of exactly what had happened from her. And she left nothing out. Daniel told her the doctor had to know everything to check her out properly. And she'd nodded. He'd left them to it. The doctor had done it all with Janet and Angelica in the room, who were horrified at hearing what she'd been through. Janet had realised that Daniel had intervened just seconds before Irena was raped. And she would have been tortured and killed afterwards. It was just surreal and horrifying.

They had all come out together a while later, Irena wearing a pink, Pineapple tracksuit of Angel's which she had put on after a long shower. And they all came downstairs to the large kitchen.

The young doctor sat down and accepted a coffee. "How is she, Nick?" asked Daniel. Nick had patched him up once before on the quiet, on John's behalf. He was a nice guy. Totally trustworthy.

He spoke to them all quietly. "Well, as this is a very unofficial medical report you can have it in a very unofficial style." He smiled warmly at Irena, who returned it weakly, but looking better than she had. "A couple of nasty raised weals across the delightfully formed butt and upper back. Bruising to the perfectly-formed boobs." Daniel watched as the doctor's light-hearted humour brought a slightly bigger smile to Irena's gaunt face. "Badly-bruised, possibly cracked ribs to the left side of the chest. Sore raw wounds to wrists and ankles where restrained by, I guess, coarse rope. And intense indignation at being manhandled very roughly." He smiled at Irena again. "And seriously, severe trauma and shock. Nothing that won't mend with Savlon, Ibuprofen, a bit of time and complete rest."

"Thank you for turning out, Nick," said Lee.

"Not a problem Lee. I won't ask and I don't want to know." He turned to Irena. "But you pretty lady, need to rest and mend. And try to never get wherever you've been, ever again. It could have been a whole lot worse."

She smiled weakly at him. "I won't ever. And thank you." She looked around at them all. "Thank you all so much."

And then the tears came in floods. She sobbed as all the fear and adrenalin flowed out of her in a rush. Janet held her tight and the others left them there in the kitchen and went through to the lounge. Daniel and Lee showed Nick out. "Just let her get it out of her system." said Nick. "She's a very beautiful girl, guys. I hope she gets over this okay. Let me know how she gets on, yeah. Night. Well morning." And he left for his car.

Chapter 99. Nice times and mysteries.

After a couple of days where they all relaxed and Irena had recovered, at least a bit, from her ordeal, Daniel, Janet and Irena went to see Ray in London. They took a train in. Janet went off with Kim and they met Tracey, who was just so happy about her new home it made them both a bit tearful. As Janet said to her, "You can't believe it. Try where I'm at."

Kim had smiled and said, "Hang around with Daniel for a while and things change big time girls. Ask Ray and me." They all laughed, it was just so true.

"That bloody man," said Janet. "He does change things, always for the better. And he can't understand why other people don't."

"Well," said Kim. "Not everybody is good." And that just summed it up perfectly. They went off lunching and shopping. They were all in a better place now to enjoy life.

They had gone out to give Daniel and Irena time with Ray. Janet knew that they both had a real big thank you they wanted to say. She knew that Irena would have been raped and murdered, without his technological skills. And Daniel would never have forgiven himself.

They went to dinner together early evening and they had a great time. The two men had clearly said all there was to say. Ray was looking better. And there was a new warmth between him and Kim which was good to see. Janet was glad that Daniel had called time on the activities of recent years. For Kim as well as herself. She could see, by even her brief, terrifying exposure to it, what a terrible strain it must be on anyone involved. Irena still looked gaunt but was getting better by the day.

Marshall Bland got the final forensic report on the warehouse case and was shocked when he read it. Amir Ferez, Bogdan Gentian, the only two matched to recorded DNA, dead. Despatched with the utmost efficiency. Along with a mixed bag of their, as yet, unidentified henchmen. No evidence at all as to the perpetrators of the carnage. Just one pistol used. No bullet match. And, just to aggravate him a bit more, what had miraculously managed to survive the fireball, were some cut lengths of rope with skin tissue on, and traces of urine. Which, of bloody course, matched nobody on the DNA database.

Nigel felt that the most obvious and likely explanation of the ropes and urine was a hostage situation. Obviously somebody had been tied up. And, terrified or tortured, had urinated where they were restrained. And that, as always from Nigel, made sense. Just to add to the mystery of what had taken place. And there wasn't likely to be any evidence as to what had taken place. Assuming the whole ghastly scene was about releasing a hostage…well, whoever had done it presumably couldn't be arsed with negotiating before using extreme force to resolve the situation.

The poxy place was in the middle of nowhere. There was nobody to ask about vehicles or unusual activity. The warehouse was just a front company. Freehold site, owned by an offshore company registered in the Cayman Islands. No doubt something to do with Ferez, like the other place where men had died violently. Filed proper accounts but was without doubt a place where drugs and, whatever the hell else illegal, were, or were going to be, shipped into, concealed in legitimate loads of produce.

Nobody had come forward as responsible for the damned place or seemed concerned about it. There was no record even for an insurer for the building. A big fat nothing, another dead end, yet again. No CCTV out there in the wilds to look at. A warrant to search Amir Ferez' penthouse had yielded nothing. There was no sign of his girlfriend. No phones or computers to check, no paperwork, nothing. Amir Ferez had ceased to exist in that warehouse. And now it was like he never had existed. He felt another headache coming on.

Marsh phoned Fleming and brought him up to speed. "I am not going to waste my time with it, Colin. I know as sure as I've got a hole in my arse it's the same outfit involved in Amir's drug meet. And that fucking hire car fiasco. They must have decided to finish Amir once and for all."

"I agree Marsh. Hopefully with Amir and Bogdan dead that will be the end of it."

"I really hope so Colin. The boys and girls don't need this. Job's tough enough without dealing with bloody war zones."

"It is. Thanks for the call Marsh. Keep in touch."

"I will Colin. Might be in touch if you feel a move to serious regional would be good?"

"I would really appreciate the opportunity, Marshall. Thanks."

"Email me, leave it with me. I could use you Colin. Cheers."

Fleming hung up. A move to regional. And Marsh was no spring chicken. He was glad he'd chanced his arm a while back and made the call.

Fleming told Mick Davidson later when he came in that Amir and Bogdan were dead, glaring at him when he said, "Good!" But he didn't pull him up. Mick was working hard and pulling his weight. And it wasn't hard to agree with him in all honesty.

Ferez and Gentian had operated with impunity for years with the police never getting the hard evidence to nail them. Witnesses were terrified to come forward. They knew the police couldn't protect them. It was wrong and frustrating. But that was how it was. Fleming sighed. And he carried on with his work. That was all any copper could do.

He liked the sound of the new political party that was hitting the news. Their proposed reforms to law and order were staggering and made sense to every copper trying to fight crime with one hand tied behind his back and the other one with a pen in it. It wouldn't get off the ground with the civ libs, the bleeding hearts and the wets up in arms about it already. But it would be nice to operate under their proposed system. If only for one day. Fleming sighed again. No chance.

Chapter 100. A meeting followed by another one.

Mick told Fleming he had some stuff to do and left. He'd had a text asking him to name a quiet pub or cafe to meet in. He'd replied and been given a time. He went in the quiet pub and looked around. A young, slim, athletic-looking guy, with short black hair, was sitting near a window at a table for two. He beckoned Mick over. Mick sat down.

Daniel said, "Hi Mick. Daniel." It was the voice on the phone.

They shook hands and Mick looked at the face of the young man who had taken out two of the most powerful criminals on his manor.

"Hi. You don't think it's a problem meeting me, then?"

"Any reason I can't trust you, Michael?"

Mick smiled. "No. Not one."

"That's why I'm here. I wanted to say sorry and thank you. Face to face."

"Sorry? You cleared my debts and saved my life."

"I endangered it, Mick. Those last few girls I gave you the intel for to pass on. That was what screwed it up. Exposed Irena. I shouldn't have risked it."

"It was done for the right reasons, Daniel. Who's Irena?"

"A young Turkish woman. Amir shot her father, a Turkish police officer, a good while back. Paralysed. Two years on, he committed suicide. She wanted revenge. Was already on the inside as Amir's girlfriend."

"That lovely looking girl who lived with Amir?"

"Yeah."

"The guys who raided his penthouse were jabbering on about her. Said she was too good for him."

"She was. And never was his. She had seduced him and was moving in with him when I got involved. I met her sister in Turkey who was worried about her. Planning to rip him off solo and turn him in with evidence. Would never have survived trying. We were working with her. She was nearly raped and murdered, Mick."

"At that warehouse, right?"

"Yeah, I got there just in time. We had her tracked, via her phone. Well the cleverest guy I ever met did. Bogdan was kind enough to keep it in his pocket. She was trussed up naked and been beaten and was about to be raped by Bogdan when I got there. And then she'd have been killed."

"You killed all five?"

"Yeah. I was alone. Couldn't wait for help. There was no option, Mick."

"Bloody hell! I was worried about one thug. They had it coming. Raping a tied-up woman. Watching a woman being raped. All carrying guns. Fuck 'em. I'm glad you got the lass safe. We could never get them, Daniel. They knew the game. If it wasn't you it would have been another thug like them one day. It's how they roll. The bastards."

"Well I'm glad you're okay too, Mick. The old simple tricks are often the best."

Mick laughed. Recalled how he'd arranged an old quilt and pillows in the bed and hidden behind the door. "I had to buy new bedding. Bullet holes in mine."

"Better than buying a coffin, Mick. I'm glad you made it unhurt."

"Just glad he didn't look. Pull the sheet back. And turned around ready for trouble."

"I was banking on him not to. These men are just thugs Mick, not professional killers. He did it because he was told to by Bogdan. Scared shitless of Bogdan, scared of doing it and the consequences if he got caught. In and out the easiest, quickest way possible. They aren't very bright. And getting the idiot nicked as just a burglar lost the connection to Bogdan and Amir and any awkward questions."

"You cover the bases for sure. Are you going to be needing me any more, Daniel?"

"No Mick. I just wanted to explain everything."

And he did. How they had bugged and monitored the penthouse after Irena had moved in with Amir. The take-down and the first seizure. The choice to actually do that.

"The thing was, Mick, that Irena was already in there. I agreed to help. But Amir was wealthy and powerful. We had to weaken him. Scare him. Killing those two drivers was not something I was comfortable with, but we had to hit him hard. Both his delivery and the cocaine deal. Same with the airport car. They had to be stopped. And I wanted to use stopping it as a way to convince Amir we were terrorists. It really was the only way, so we did it. I just don't want you to think I am some cold-blooded killer for the sake of it, Michael."

"Daniel. Not one man who died at that drug meet was unarmed. The two in the car might well have killed Lee Tremayne. All of them were vicious, long-time criminals. They would have killed each other. And some of them actually did. They are violent criminals, it's what they do. You have nothing to justify."

Then Daniel explained the fake jihadist group to extort money. How that had just evolved with the changing situation, to give Amir an explanation he would accept. And swing the pointed finger of suspicion back away from Irena. How

Mick agreeing to substantiate that scenario, had done just that. And finally, how it should have ended. With Amir broke and powerless. And the information to put him away for life lodged with the police. Until the discovery of the router by Bogdan and the taking of Irena. They actually hadn't planned to kill Amir and Bogdan. They wanted them jailed and ruined. Irena wanted Ferez to suffer as her father had. As Daniel said finally, "If I had known I'd end up shooting those two bastards, I'd have done it weeks ago. From a mile away."

Mick had listened in amazement.

"Incredible. Just incredible. One question. You might not answer it. Wesley and Mason. Did they actually fit in to this anywhere at all?"

"Simply another coincidence, Mick. They murdered my foster parents. John and Ann Tremayne."

"Your foster parents! We never knew they had a fostered son. Only about Lee, their only child. And high profile in the business world. Funny enough, I said that suspecting him was wrong from the start. But Fleming wouldn't listen."

"You were right. But then if he had listened, you'd still be in deep shit. We wouldn't have got to you with our deal. We wouldn't have had your help. Some things are meant to happen, Mick."

"I guess." Mick looked at him. It was a strange thing to say but this guy seemed to sincerely believe that. "So you killed them?"

"No. But after they walked free and crowed about it I arranged it. Because I loved my foster parents dearly. And they deserved justice. A close friend who's been working with me for years did it. We were in the Foreign Legion together. He has far less qualms than me about such things and I'd saved his life twice in the past. Problem was, you connected it to the take-down."

"I didn't. Fleming did. Funny to think the bastard was sort of right and will never know. But it was truly nothing to do with Lee Tremayne?"

"No. Lee is my brother as far as we're both concerned. But he would never countenance a thing like that. He's a good man like our father. But, when you flipped that info to Amir and he decided to send heavies to the Gambia, to get at Lee - that spawned the airport car and the jihadists idea. It's big news these days and I thought Amir would buy into it. I had to stop them going one way or another. Lee has no idea how close he was to getting far worse than a grilling from the police. It worked. So I used it to further the cause against Amir. Made him think he was being hit by extremists. With your help it worked out well. Things do if you just let them. And let yourself be guided Michael, believe me. They do."

Mick looked at the softly spoken young man in a new light. He killed. But he was clearly no indiscriminate paid killer. He was clearly utterly ruthless when required. But he obviously cared deeply about anyone who worked with him to achieve a goal. Even himself, a bent, lonely, drunken copper. He hadn't had to. A couple of envelopes would have done, a grand max. He hadn't had to pull Mick out of the terrible mess he was in. Kick Frazer Williams' butt, pay him off. But he just had. And used it to his advantage over Amir. And it had worked. He said, "I guess it all makes sense in the end."

"Yeah it does." Daniel handed him an envelope. "In here are a couple of things. A bank account with a hundred thousand pounds in. Overseas. In your name."

"A hundred grand!" The couple of people in earshot turned at the raised voice.

"Easy Mick, keep it down. Yes. Same share as everyone who helped is getting. Out of Amir's money. And a name and number. If you call this man when you are all done with the force Mick, there'll be a good job there. If you want it. Available from whenever you want out of the police. Up to you. Keep the phone. Just reset it to factory settings please." He smiled at Mick. "And sort of do the same to yourself, Mick. Forget all this and look to the future like the rest of us. I'm leaving now. I don't live in the UK. I hope we meet again sometime. I'll email you in a few weeks if you want?"

Mick stood, still bewildered. They shook hands. "Yeah. I'd like that. I really would."

"Good. Because there is one more small thing you could do for me, Mick."

"Name it."

"A copy of everything in the police files on Wesley and Mason. My foster parents' killers."

"Consider it done."

"Thank you." Daniel handed him a card. "Have it dropped to this address please. Take care of yourself until we meet again."

"You take care too, Daniel. And thank you. Really. Thank you."

"Thank you Mick. But don't leave. There's somebody else here to see you. Be guided and good luck. You've earned it." Daniel strode towards the door. And was gone.

Mick ordered another coffee, looked at the phone he took from his pocket and went through the reset to erase everything. All he had to remind him of the strangest thing that ever happened to him. And, in reality, one of the best things. He was just going to let life happen now. See if it worked for him. Somebody else to see him? He looked towards the door. And saw his wife walk in. His heart literally skipped a beat. Had that man really taken the time to..................?

"Angie?"

"Mick."

"What are you doing here?"

"I'm more curious than actually wanting to see you, Mick."

"Sorry? Why?"

"I've been told, by a very strange, rather handsome young man that we should talk. Here. Today. After he told me you'd really earned another chance. And it was all you wanted. The message he asked me to give you if we met was that it was the last bloody time he was intervening in anything for at least six months. But we should maybe sort our shit out now. Do you want to explain exactly why I am being accosted by strange, earnest young man, knocking at my bloody front door? Or why I should even try to sort things out with you, Mick?"

He smiled at her. "Yeah. I would Angie. I really would."

If this panned out he knew he would look forward to seeing Daniel again one day. But could never repay him in a million years.

"Come and sit down. I'll get you a coffee. I just ordered one."

"Not drinking, Mick?"

"No Angie. If I get you back or not. Not drinking."

"It won't be easy."

"Things are different now Angie. Truly."

"Really? I know you've mended fences with the kids lately."

"Yeah. They've been great, considering."

"You treated me like shit, Mick. You're still a copper. What's going to be different now?"

"Me Angie. I'm different now and I'm sorry. For everything."

"And you think that will be enough?"

"Things work out if you just let them Angie. At least let me tell you everything before you blow me out, yeah?" She nodded.

He pulled a chair out for her and she sat down. And he went to get the coffees.

He got them and sat back down and smiled broadly at her.

She glared at him, "This isn't funny, Mick!"

"Sorry Angie. I'm just so pleased to see you."

"Well you might not be if you give me any more of your bullshit Mick Davidson."

"No bull Angie. I don't know how to say this but I'll try. I have got a hundred grand in the bank as of today. Earned legit. From that guy you met. For some private work in my own time."

"I told you not to............"

"It's the truth! And I have a new job outside the police to go to. I am going to discuss the earliest date I can leave later today."

You're serious aren't you?" She looked stunned.

"Very. But Angie. All I want the most is you to share it all with. Make up for being such a twat in the past. We could go on holiday soon maybe? Work things out?"

He looked so earnest she started to smile. And to his amazement leaned over and kissed him.

"Bloody hell," he said.

She smiled at him. "Don't you dare think it's the money, Mick. Because it isn't. And it sure as hell isn't your good looks."

"Well what is it then?"

"It's because you didn't have to tell me about it. You could have gone on the piss and lived the life of Riley if you'd wanted to."

"I guess so."

"Well now I know you want me. For real."

"Yeah I do."

"Then we'd better start working it out. But if you go on the piss....."

"I'm teetotal, Angie."

"I didn't ask you to become boring either, Mick Davidson. Just drink at the right time. With me. Not all the bloody time and never coming home. Come on. Talk to me on the way to the travel agents. You owe me a bloody good holiday, you prat."

They left and got outside and she linked her arm through his as they walked, while jabbering on about the grandchildren. He smiled. He would just let himself be guided now. Because it actually seemed to work!

Chapter 101. Father's legacy.

Back at Lee and Angel's, Lee had suggested to Daniel that it was maybe time to open the briefcase. Get it all out of the way before Daniel and Janet left. They had gone to Lee's office and done just that. In it were two large sealed folders. One addressed to Daniel. One for Lee. And a DVD with a note in it saying they both should watch it before they opened the folders. Lee put it in the computer drive and the screen flickered into life. It was John, being recorded talking to them. It was both eerie and emotional.

He was talking and they listened, staring raptly at the screen.

"My sons. And I assume you are both listening to me and are both well. I will not dwell here on my sadness at being gone from you. Or your sadness at my passing. It is done. Daniel will have read my letter to himself. And passed it to his brother. So we all understand the situation. We can only miss each other and move on in our separate worlds. In your world, there is much to be done. Or nothing. Only you two can make that choice. My plans and visions for the future of the UK were my own, and in setting up the funding and support to enact those plans I spoke to many. And not all were supportive. And it may well be that if I am gone and the cause was not natural that I spoke to at least one person I should not have."

Daniel and Lee looked at each other. Were Mason and Wesley something other than a random burglary?

The gentle voice continued. "One of the most successful although awful alliances in recent political history was that of the IRA and Sinn Fein. Do not be alarmed my sons. It is a concept of an approach. Nothing more. To that end, if you decide to proceed, Lee, you should read that which I have left for you. The contacts and the supporters you can rely on are in there. And you will launch and fund a new party. Unique in its approach. The man to lead it, in the fullness of time, is named in there. The approach must be slow and gradual. It is all fully explained.

Daniel. In your envelope there are my ideas to operate on the ground, in the UK, with the aim of taking the consequences of certain people's actions right to their own doorsteps and not to other people's while they escape those consequences. Using a task force combining boots on the ground with technical investigation and the exposure of other, certain people, who evade the responsibility of their actions. This is to be done in tandem with the launch of the new party. Strengthening its appeal and affirming the truths it will be telling, showing there is another way to do things, a different way to live that is fair and just for all. The choice is now up to you both. If you decide that you have lives to lead, and this is not an undertaking you wish to embark on, you would have my blessing. It is with great reservation that I even suggest this. But I must. In the name of the spiritual truth and goodness that I have always promoted and lived by.

Good luck in whatever you decide my sons. I love you both along with all my family." And he was gone.

Without a word they both opened the folders addressed to themselves and read the contents. And they both smiled after reading them. It was brilliantly conceived and radical. And they were going to do it. Dangers or not, John Tremayne's ideals were going into action. And Daniel was going to take a very close look at why Wesley and Mason had chosen their father's remote home to burgle that night.

Chapter 102. Moving the money.

Daniel and Janet flew to Turkey with Irena about a week later. She was much better and improving daily. They took her home. Daniel and Janet stayed for four days. Janet adored her family, her mother was lovely and Aisha was just delightful. As lovely as Irena but softer in her nature. Janet sensed the special bond between Daniel and Aisha, the same as with Angelica, and understood more about how Daniel had become involved in the revenge Irena was so determined to achieve.

The first day, after they had all been introduced and had a drink, Irena went off with Daniel onto the balcony. They had laptops out there and were gone rather a long time. When they came back in, Daniel said he had a few calls to make and vanished again. Janet was a bit puzzled and, yeah, a bit put out. And it must have shown.

Because Irena asked Janet if they could go for a walk together. They strolled up to the ruins of the Temple of Apollo at the very top of Ataturk Boulevarde. Janet loved the place at first sight. Daniel seemed to have a knack of spending time in places with, well, good vibes. As they walked up the hill in the mild March weather, Irena told her a little about the history of the place. They got a drink from one of the bars that was open out of season and sat down next to each other.

Irena said, "So you are the lady I hear so much about from Daniel? While all this was going on?"

"Well I hope so," replied Janet.

Irena laughed. "He is very much in love with you Janet. To my eternal regret. I like him very much. He has been so good to my family. And so brave in regard to me. I think during those horrible times I spend with Amir I have a little fantasy. That Daniel will be with me when I am done. But now I know that was not to be. I never want you to think badly of me Janet."

"I never would. He's an attractive man. You're a beautiful girl."

"He has chosen his beautiful girl. He told me a good while ago Janet. And it makes me happy to see him happy. And you."

"Thank you. You will find your man in time Irena. I never thought I would. But I did."

"I am sure you are right. But truly Janet. I just wanted to say thank you. For being there that terrible night. It must have been terrifying for you. And to say I am very glad he has such a lovely girl in his life now. And I am sorry. For dragging you into such a situation."

Janet smiled at her, "There is nothing to apologise for Irena. I insisted on going with him. He needed someone there to work the phone. And he wouldn't put me anywhere near danger. I am just so very glad you, well, you know, weren't hurt any more than you were. Or even killed. It must have been terrifying."

She said, "It was. That Bogdan was an animal. Far worse than Amir. The world is best rid of them both. My father is avenged now and perhaps a few more innocent girls will be spared the terrible lives they had under Bogdan. He was truly evil Janet. He hated me from the day we met. He didn't like Amir having me in his life. And he never trusted me from the start. I was very lucky to get as far as I did. Daniel was very clever in turning the policeman in Amir's pay to back up all Amir was hearing. Bogdan was going to kill him as well, that same night. Amir ordered him not to but Bogdan ordered it anyway. The attempt failed thanks to Daniel and Ray. Thankfully, Bogdan didn't live to carry it out later."

"It sounds to me that you were all very lucky to survive. But I am very glad you did. And it's over now."

"Well almost over Janet. I am sorry to take Daniel's time without including you. But Amir's money has to be moved. I had it all set up to do it. But it has to be done carefully. Without trace. It is a lot of money. Over eight million pounds. Lee is helping. And a man called Alan. They are who Daniel is talking to. That is all I needed to talk to him about. I hope you understand. Mama and Aisha know very little about this matter. And they must never find out. I have to bear the shame of sleeping with Amir, my father's killer. But I could not with them knowing."

Janet reached out and squeezed her hand gently. "You have nothing to be ashamed of Irena. I have to live with the fact that I slept with a man who abused my own son. But I am not ashamed of it. And you shouldn't be. What you did was for your father. And your family's future that Amir took away with a gun. Be proud of yourself Irena. Daniel is. And so am I."

"Thank you. I just wanted to talk to you alone. I will never forget how you held me that night in the car. I was so frightened and in so much pain. You made such a difference."

"You're welcome. I'm really looking forward to coming here in May."

"I'm looking forward to you both getting here too. Shall we go back now? I have to talk to Daniel again now. I just wanted you to understand why."

They strolled back together, arms linked. Janet knew they would become good friends, even if Irena would always hate her just a little bit over Daniel. That was just a girl thing that they both understood.

Things were sorted. Amir's money was moved to where it could eventually be put to good use. Then they left, saying they would be back in May and stay until October. The delightful Aisha and Irena were setting up a jewellery store in Altinkum with an accountancy office for Irena on the floor above it. They were happy. Their mother was delighted Irena was home for good and carried on keeping the apartment block that made life so much easier for those who lived there in immaculate condition. It was Daniel's and Janet's home too. And she looked forward to their return.

Chapter 103. A movement is born.

They then went back to the UK and stayed with Angelica and Lee for another few days. Alan Shand, looking very much happier, appeared now and again with updates on the progress of the new party slowly and carefully being formed. Big money was available from business contacts and friends of John Tremayne, but some of it was given on the condition it was done discreetly.

Out of fear. They didn't want to be tarnished. If this went wrong, they still had to operate under the regime they were going to challenge. Alan understood that. Behind the perceived political freedoms the UK crowed about, were powerful people with vested interests in maintaining the chaotic, highly unaccountable systems of government, both national and local. The sums of money involved were huge. The motive to keep unaccountable confusion and control over it was also huge.

It was hard going. Getting the right candidates with no skeletons in the cupboard. Correcting the lies already spewing towards them from the media artillery. Refuting the accusations that ranged from Nazi to nationalist to extremist. Monitoring social media and news. But finding there was a real groundswell of enthusiasm, at least in principle, to their proposals, at this early stage. It would be a long haul before the decision was made to actually contest an election. And a very costly haul. But they were rocking the boat. Alan's view was that even if it didn't get off the ground, if it shoved the others into making reforms, they would have achieved something for John. For now, all eyes were on the forthcoming in or out of Europe referendum. They would see if there was a vacuum to fill after that maybe.

They all had dinner and one last evening together. Alan brought his delightful old mother and elder brother with him. She, and Norman himself, were at least able to share a table with the man who had brought Norman home, even if they weren't aware of it. Alan thanked Janet again for talking to Lee. He was getting divorced. Lee had helped him. Life was better. Much better.

Alan asked them if they would watch a clip of an interview with one of their two prospective candidates on the television. Said they might find it entertaining. The interview was with the BBC's Katie Summerfield. Alan explained she was a very intense Corbynista socialist. The candidate was Anthony Graves, one of the men who had worked closely with John on the conception of a new political movement and had cheerfully put himself in the firing line as the first candidate to announce he would contest a seat. Alan said, as he put the DVD in the machine. "This guy's great. He loves a fucking argument."

And they settled down.

Alan flicked through it then stopped and pressed play. And they listened to the exchange.

Katie said, "Well. For instance. Your proposals for restoring capital punishment. Do you not think they are barbaric?"

Graves replied, "No Katie. Because we are not proposing any such thing."

"You most certainly are."

"We are proposing asking the nation if they would like it reinstated for certain specific crimes."

"It's unthinkable."

"Then don't vote for it."

"What sort of an answer is that?"

"The one to your question."

"Well how can you even justify proposing it?"

"Quite easily. Because nobody else does. We want to correct that, and let the nation decide. And we believe innocent people being murdered is barbaric. We believe they might well agree."

"But that is not a matter to just throw out to the public to choose."

"Did they choose to have convicted murderers and serial rapists released, who often kill or rape again? Or was it just easier not to ask them?"

"The most serious offenders are never released, Anthony."

"So more than thirty people who have been killed by released offenders between 2001 and 2011 were killed by non-serious killers? And we're struggling to get accurate recent information. Wonder why Katie?"

"It's still not a public vote issue Anthony. It's too complex an issue."

"Why? David Cameron is letting the nation choose on the EU. A more complex beast never existed. Or are you worried that the citizens of this nation might just say they would rather see their money go on something more beneficial, like health, education or policing, if they were given the chance which they have been denied all these years?"

"Yes. He is going to the nation about the EU membership. But that's very different to the subject of capital punishment where people could be executed while innocent."

"It is clearly explained. And you well know it Katie. It is only proposed for certain convicted offenders where guilt is established beyond all doubt. For utterly pre-meditated killing. For nothing other than the urge to do it."

"Assuming that is so. That makes the state's right to take a human life how?"

"Well. Their victims are dead. Life and right to life extinguished. The perpetrators remain a constant danger. And it costs the country a fortune. Ian Brady alone has cost more than fourteen million pounds to keep locked up."

"So it's about money?"

"Of course it is. The people's money. And just retribution for the crime committed."

"So what value do you put on a human life?"

"Enormous value Katie. That's why we want to make people as safe as possible."

"I mean the life of a person you would see fit to execute. And you know it Anthony."

"Oh. A serial killer or child murderer. Sorry. You should have asked the question properly, Katie. We propose the nation puts the same value on a killer's life as the killer did on the victims' lives. Nothing."

"But we did away with the death penalty years ago. Mistakes were made. Innocent people hanged."

"That was then. This is now. New science. There will be no mistakes. The criteria is clear Katie. Beyond all doubt. Not just reasonable doubt."

"And this is to save money?"

"Not at all, Katie. It's to avoid taking it from the citizens of the UK. And, of course, to keep them as safe as possible."

"Are you being deliberately obtuse, Anthony?"

"No Katie. I'm leaving that to you."

"Well perhaps you would care to explain the difference between the terms, saving money, and, avoiding taking it."

"By all means if you can't grasp the concept. We don't want to save any money at all. We want to spend it. Every penny the tax payers entrust us with. But. We want to ask the nation where they would like it spent. Across the board. On each major spending area. We simply want to arrive at the bottom line figure required to carry out the nation's wishes. And collect only the budget figure the nation have agreed on. For instance. If they want to spend millions on keeping dangerous serial killers alive, then we will do as they ask. And be clear about the cost to them, through taxation, of doing it, before they decide the matter. If they would rather not - we won't, and capital punishment on the basis we have proposed will be restored. It's their money, not ours. And the same applies to everything else the nation has to budget for."

"With the Brexit vote coming ever nearer you do realise that no country with the death penalty can be a member of the EU?"

"Of course."

"You don't consider that an issue?"

"Not really. We don't feel our legal system is any of their business for one thing. We will offer not to poke our noses into theirs by way of a returned courtesy, to secure a mutually acceptable deal. Like the USA does. Despite having the death penalty."

"Very droll Anthony. But can you answer the question please?"

"Of course. We rather hope the nation votes to leaves the EU in its current form anyway. If it doesn't we will propose leaving. Or demand the necessary reforms to accommodate our nation's internal policies that our people have decided they want."

"But the EU provides trade and stability, Anthony."

"Really? We had trade with Europe long before the EU. And I believe we have had two recessions already during our membership. And lost control of Europe's borders resulting in the ascent of the extreme right and a constant threat of terrorism. I will check that again now though. Thank you, Katie."

"There is no need to be flippant, Anthony. These are very serious matters."

"They are. That's why we need control over them with a clear mandate. The EU should be nothing more than a free trade zone. All member states should retain control of their own laws and border controls."

"Your proposal to end the right to silence after being arrested - are you trying to take us back to the dark ages?"

"No. We're trying to bring justice blinking into the light."

"It's a fundamental right of every citizen."

"No, it isn't. It's a fundamental right of every criminal. And a huge waste of police time."

"People have a right to protect themselves against state interrogation."

"And they have one. The state, quite rightly, ensures that any individual has legal representation present at a police interview and that there is a sound reason for that interview. The state has then carried out its obligations. The individual does not have a right to be deliberately uncooperative in return."

"But people could incriminate themselves."

"Only if they've done anything wrong."

"What if they haven't?"

"If they haven't, Katie, perhaps you would like to tell me, and your viewers, how repeating "no comment" like a retarded parrot assists in establishing that fact? The only people this gormless right assists is somebody who has done something wrong or has information the police require. Why else would you not wish to talk and resolve the matter?"

"Again, it is a complex issue."

"Really? We disagree. It is a very simple matter. The individual has a right to representation supplied by the nation. In return the nation has a right to answers to the questions put to them by the nation. A police officer is nothing more than the person asking the nation's questions in a controlled environment. If you refuse, under our proposals you will go in front of a judge. The validity of the questions confirmed. Be offered again the chance to answer the questions in front of the judge. And into custody for withholding those answers if you don't. Again. The proposal is for the nation to decide. We are simply pointing out we don't feel law and order is served by the current absurd legislation. And we want to change it."

"I see. You seem to be proposing quite draconian sentencing. And ending the parole system. Is that true?"

"To a degree yes. We would prefer to see the sentence handed down the sentence served. No time off for good behaviour. Time added on if you don't."

"But that's outrageous."

"Why? Our data is telling us that many people think that criminals being discreetly released early is outrageous. You see Katie it's not all about your opinion. Or mine. It's up to the nation by majority vote."

"So you think that it is right to ask the people about everything?"

"I think it's called democracy Katie. We simply wish to carry out the will of the people. Policy should come up to government from the people, not be forced down on them from a small elite with often absurd ideals."

"You have proposed sweeping changes to healthcare, infrastructure, taxation, employment laws. Just about everything. Even the number of constituencies. It's a staggering amount of change."

"Well it is all a bit of a mess. We don't believe you need four hundred and thirty-nine thousand civil servants to run this island. We don't believe you need six hundred and fifty MP's. The USA is one hundred times the land mass and ten times our population but manages with 535 congressman and 100 senators. Roughly the same amount of people. Except we have a house of lords as well. We believe you need around half that number in regional representation in the UK. But top people. Paid properly."

"Do you seriously believe you can win an election, Anthony?"

"We are not trying to win anything, Katie. We don't agree with the current system. We have to use it of course, just once, to get our people in place to do their jobs. We are simply asking the nation if it would like us to run the nation's affairs for them. And if they do. We will change that system. We are not interested in being in opposition. Or having any opposition."

"Really. What exactly are you then?"

"We're the new board of directors. We don't want another board sat over the other side of the room arguing for the sake of it. We want the chance to run the nation how the people want it run after consulting the people. Our shareholders. For top salaries. Matching the private sector. For the best people for the job. If we do a good job we keep our jobs. If we don't. Well we didn't do a good enough job. We're not politicians Katie. Left-wing, right-wing, green. They've had their chance. And, we believe, failed miserably. If people are happy with that, then they can keep it like it is. All we want to do is ask the question - just once - if they'd like to change things."

"And you think that enough people will vote you in on that basis. A total clean sweep?"

"Well it's early days. We can't implement the changes we want to make without a huge majority. And if they don't give us that, well, we think we will force the current system to at least work harder for the people by trying to stop us."

"I see. And you think people will be comfortable with a party in power with little or no opposition?"

"Why would you want an opposition?"

"Are you just trying to be awkward Anthony? It's called democracy."

"So your idea of democracy is two large groups of people in one room arguing with each other? Along with a mixed bag of other oddballs?"

"It is the system we have always had. And it works."

"For who? The balance of power was held by the Lib Dems in the recent Coalition who hardly got any votes. How does that represent people's wishes? It's not remotely democratic."

"But you claim to want to run the nation with no opposition?"

"Yes. But only if we win enough votes to do it Katie. If we don't, we don't want to be involved at all."

"You mean you will just forget about it?"

"Yes. Things stay the same. We get back to work. We don't care if we win Katie. We care that the nation gets the choices the established parties seem very reluctant to offer. That is all."

"You'll still be up against the two main parties that the nation is familiar and comfortable with."

"Good. Because their track record speaks for itself. And we're not a party. We are a group of individuals with a proposal to run the nation. Nothing more. The nation itself is our opposition. Any or all of us can be voted back out and replaced."

"And you believe you can do a far better job of it?"

"We know we can. Because we will have a clear mandate to do it. From the nation. If, and only if, they give it to us."

"Say you only win a few seats at the next general election? Surely that's possible?"

"Then they will have to be contested again. We aren't putting one person up for election who would be happy to work in that bickering, time-wasting, bedlam that we call parliament in its current form. Myself included. You see, we're all good at what we do. We don't need to be politicians to earn a living. We are governed by people who are who couldn't do our jobs in the private sector. And we're going to try to change it. And clear up the mess they've made. Just once."

Alan switched it off.

Janet said, "That was quite interesting. I liked a lot of what he said. People choose. Not have things forced on them"

Alan replied, "Well it's just testing the waters. We've got huge websites up and running now, collecting data on an unprecedented scale."

He looked at Daniel. "That's your friend Ray's baby. He's doing really well. And we are getting the inside track, from workers. On corruption, malpractice, fraud etc, through an anonymous whistle blower site he's set up. If it checks out, your guy Mick Davidson heads that up, we're adding it to our campaign data website. If it doesn't, as in it's lies or just malicious, it's dumped. And we're getting a lot of it. On everything. Railway, construction, healthcare, civil service supply, the lot. Budgets for disabled adaptations are in some places three times higher than needed through a tendering system we'd sack a manager for in the private sector. The price submitted to build is changing hands twice from the actual cost submitted by the contractor doing the work. And tripling the price. Ghost labour on county council highway projects. And the railway. Don't go there. Local councils. Ditto. The wastage and the skimming come to billions. If we could actually get a grip on it we could run everything better and cut taxes. It would transform lives and incomes."

He looked at Lee. "Your father was onto something here, Lee. If we could tap into the population and get their full mandate we could change everything. But we will make some enemies along the way."

"Well we've got him over there to deal with that," said Lee, pointing at Daniel.

Daniel looked at him. "I need a break from it all first brother. Don't upset anyone for at least a year."

They all laughed and then the conversation drifted to other things. Janet was deep in thought, wondering if anybody really could make such huge changes. Be interesting to watch them try. The new political force that was very dear to John

Tremayne's heart was germinating into a real entity. The decision to actually campaign would be a long way off. And all interest was now on the in/out EU referendum. Or Brexit.

Chapter 104. The mile high club and home.

They all had a last, early breakfast together, then Daniel and Janet left for the airport and the Gambia, home, and the children. As a special treat, Tremayne's had laid on the leased jet for them to go home in style.

They had their future mapped out. The UK political scene wasn't really their concern. But Janet did care about it, more than Daniel did probably, because she had friends there who were still living the life she'd left behind. Would the new party get off the ground in 2017 or 18? She didn't know. Would she and Daniel go back to help with it? Would Daniel use his skills to help keep whoever led the party safe and secure, if they made real enemies by doing such a thing? Maybe he would. But for now they were going home.

If it happened. and if Lee asked for Daniel to work with him, that was in the future. For now, it didn't matter to Janet one bit. The spirits would guide them both to wherever they had to be.

She rested her head on Daniel's shoulder as the beautiful plane thundered down the runway and took off. She smiled. Her life had changed so much. Never in a million years would she have thought she would see the things she had since she had left the UK for a holiday she couldn't afford. Never believed you could love a man who had killed people illegally. And the last time, while you waited just up the bloody road! And that such a man could be, and was, the kindest, gentlest person you could ever meet. Unless you were evil. And foolish enough to cross his path.

She smiled and kissed his cheek and nuzzled into his neck as he quietly read some papers taken from a folder. She looked at it, saw the police logos and the names Wesley and Mason. What the hell was he reading about that for? That bloody man! He never told you anything!

The flight attendant, a young girl called Melissa, came up to her. "The bedroom suite is all ready as ordered if you'd like to come through." Janet looked at her.
"Oh right. Thank you."
She took Daniel's hand and said, "Come on, let's go get some rest."

He looked mystified but followed her behind the attendant, who held the door open to the small, but luxurious bedroom and closed it firmly behind them. Janet locked the door. A huge bunch of flowers with a card in an envelope addressed to Jan. Champagne on ice. Realisation was already creeping in as she opened the card, which said, "Welcome to the mile high club gorgeous. Have one for me. See ya soon xx" That bloody woman!

Janet smiled and looked at Daniel. He saw the lust back in her eyes as she said, "Come here Cade." He got undressed. She was very pleased to see he seemed to be in quite a hurry to do so, as she did the same. It was a lovely flight home.

Chapter 105. A party in Turkey and a shock result.

Three months later.

June 24th 2016. Altinkum Turkey.

The long awaited result of the UK Brexit vote had been announced. And the UK had voted to leave the EU. Leave won by 52% to 48%. The referendum turnout was 71.8%, with more than 30 million people voting.

It was a warm Friday night and a party was in full swing in a beautiful beach side restaurant with large grounds. It was around three months after the dramatic events that had ended the activities and life of Amir Ferez.

And nearly everybody involved was there. And others who were not. Jan looked around and smiled. Everybody was enjoying themselves. A band was alternating with a disco and the dance floor was packed. It had been a big event to organise and host and had meant a lot to them both. She was glad it was going well, and Tracey and a few other friends from home were there as well which was really nice.

She had met Quan and Adabele again with their partners, young Ahmet and his sister. Other men of different nationalities. Ex-Legion. Mick Davidson and his wife Angie, a nice man who had spoken so warmly in private to her about what Daniel had done for him. Angie was fun and nearly as outrageous as Angel. Elaine Harvey and Tessa Lovejoy who did so much for the victims of traffickers. All of them were just nice, ordinary people. Good people. Who had fought evil in a dark world with her man with far more success than the pathetically constrained forces of law and order could do despite, as Mick had said, some great people trying their best. Treated as the enemy rather than the friend of the people they tried to serve.

As Daniel had said, "Pelted with rocks by morons claiming state oppression. With the freedom of the state to do it." She had to agree. It was a pathetic state of affairs. To quote Alan Shand, "A shit cart." She was glad they were all done now. And safe. They had done enough. And also there, was Alan Shand, with a delightful new lady. Sarah. She was an earthy, funny lady and very attractive. Alan looked relaxed and happy and it was good to see.

She sat down at a temporarily deserted table with a glass of wine, enjoying the atmosphere, when Angel appeared.

"How's it all going gorgeous?"

"Great. I think everybody is having a good time."

"He's hoping for one," replied Angel, nodding towards the young doctor who had examined Irena that awful night, who was earnestly chatting to Irena herself. She looked stunning, very different to the gaunt terrified girl of a few weeks ago.

"Why is he here Angel? I mean, yeah, he turned up for a while but?"

"Well you saw him that night. I know she was in a bad way. But all that perfectly formed boobs stuff. He had a hard on and was licking his eyebrows."

"Angelica! Please. Not tonight!"

"He asked me about her after it had all died down. Really! Repeatedly. Who she was. If she was single. So I bunged him on the guest list. He'll either tap her or he won't."

"Well I hope they get along. She deserves a nice guy. After, you know. That disgusting beast."

"Yeah. Me too. But you remember that night? When we were there while she was examined. Then got her showered and dressed."

"I won't forget it as long as I live."

"Yeah it was a bad night. But seriously. Did you notice how hairy her...."

"Daniel!" Jan caught him as he was passing.

"Hi babe you okay?"

"Yeah it's going well isn't it?"

"Yeah it's great."

"You know you said you'd do anything for me?"

"Yes. Of course I will."

"Then take her away somewhere. And shoot her."

Angel looked hurt. "Why would he shoot me? If it wasn't for me he wouldn't have had your chubby cute ass upended out in...."

"Stop it!" Daniel laughed and continued on his way to talk to Mick and Angie. It was good to see them together after Mick's fall from grace.

Angel looked over at the young doctor and Irena. "He's talking too much, she's getting pissed off. I'm going to sort it out. Get me a wine babe please. I'll be back in a sec."

"Angelica, don't you dare show him...." But she was gone, moving gracefully and looking simply stunning, in her short, figure-hugging, black dress. She went to the stage and spoke to the DJ first. Then she walked up to the pair and said, "Hi Nick. Irena."

"Hi Angelica," from the young doctor, clearly a bit ticked off at the interruption, Irena clearly glad of it.

"Nick. If you want to bore the delightfully formed butt off her, there's a better way than bending her ear."

Nick looked horrified and embarrassed. Irena was smiling wickedly at his discomfort. Nick said, "Angelica! Please."

"Slow track coming on. Ask her to dance. Press yourself against the perfectly formed boobs. And tell her you've been clanging on about her ever since you saw her in the buff. Can't get her out of your mind. You remember Nick. All the stuff you told me. Then shut up and let her talk, yeah." She winked at Irena. "Later hun." And she walked back to Janet and sat down. Took a sip of wine.

Jan said, "What did you just do?"

"Nothing." She smiled as the couple walked to the dance floor, Irena leading Nick. "Just gave them a nudge. As I was saying earlier. Did you notice how hairy her......"

"Angel! I am not discussing anybody's pubic hair!"

And then blushed as she'd said it a bit loud. And hissed, "You're a bloody nuisance!"

Angel looked across at the couple. Irena was letting herself be held pretty tight. And said, "I was thinking that...." But Janet cut across her, "Nothing vulgar Angel. I mean it!"

"I was just going to say they look pretty tight out there. And that if they really got it on and maybe got married, we could go halves on some B&Q vouchers as a gift maybe?"

"B&Q vouchers? Why?"

"Well he'll need a strimmer."

Janet had just taken a mouthful of wine and had snorted some of it out laughing. People were looking at her, which would piss her off. Angel decided to go mingle for a while. Just until she calmed down a bit.

Chapter 106. We'll ask the nation once.

Alan Shand was talking to Lee. "This is unbelievable Lee. An out vote."
Lee nodded. "It is a shock result. We'll talk tomorrow. Tonight there's only this party. And Alan....she's lovely."
"She is." Alan went back to Sarah and took her to the dance floor.

A vacuum had been created. The British Social Justice party had started in the planned small way John Tremayne had advised. It was the talk of the media and gaining attention. A party that clearly stated it wasn't a party. And didn't care if it won or not! With a mind-blowing approach of asking the nation about everything, with the real truth about the costs, before it wrote it's manifesto. It was letting the nation write it and pledging to carry it out to the letter if voted in at some time in the future. Using David Cameron's much criticised referendum on the EU as a precedent to do it. And if it was voted in, they were going to change everything. And if it wasn't....they weren't going to ask again.

It was drawing a lot of hostile flak from certain quarters already. The decision had been made. To contest the next general election. In the meantime, quietly fielding a candidate for any by-elections and getting their proposals out to the nation by doing it. A contentious and divided nation with ever increasing debts and issues. A dread fear of terrorism creating racial tensions. A busy social media and free press. A good thing in the right climate. But currently, with a million conflicting ideas, an overdose of freedoms, creating no freedom at all for so many people, causing the chaos they believed a ruling elite had created.

If they wanted to keep the chaos they lived in now, so be it. Everyone involved had the wealth and knowledge to escape it. But they were going to carry out the kindly John Tremayne's last wish. To give the nation one chance to change things. The nation would have to let itself be guided. By some very powerful forces.

A lot of those forces were dark ones. Resisting change. Driven by evil intent and strange ideals. And money. And the quest for control and power. It would be a dangerous path to walk for those who challenged it. Which way would the nation let itself be guided? It had just rocked the boat by voting itself out of the EU. Would it tip the boat right over and let a whole new crew run it?

Daniel would have to start the plans tasked to him by John Tremayne as the

UKSJ political impetus built, covertly taking on powerful people doing things that were not in the interests of the population at large, either for money and power, or the advancement of their own ideals; turning all they were doing back on to themselves, in a clear demonstration of what the new party could achieve, given the chance. That would be another challenge. And another story.

THE END

Printed in Great Britain
by Amazon